PRAISE FOR

The Company Car

"*The Company Car* is a wonderful novel. I lost track of the number of times I laughed out loud. C. J. Hribal writes with grace and unerring wit in this celebration of the American family."

—ROBERT BOSWELL,
author of *Century's Son*

"As with Larry Woiwode's *Beyond the Bedroom Wall, The Company Car* illuminates through one microscopically detailed family portrait the history of a whole era in the heartland. This is a strong, whole-hearted, and often very funny novel."

—ANDREA BARRETT,
author of *Ship Fever*

"This heartbreakingly funny and nostalgic story of a sprawling baby boom family, helmed ineptly by an overdrinking traveling salesman dad, vividly captures that era back before anyone understood the term dysfunctional or the fact that we all are."

—STEVE AMICK, author of
The Lake, The River and the Other Lake

"Comic and heartfelt, epic in reach, *The Company Car* tells the story of the American family with the kind of courage and insight we need most

THE COMPANY CAR

The
COMPANY CAR

A Novel

C. J. Hribal

RANDOM HOUSE TRADE PAPERBACKS / NEW YORK

2006 Random House Trade Paperback Edition

Copyright © 2005 by C. J. Hribal
Reading group guide copyright © 2006 by Random House, Inc.

Published in the United States by Random House Trade Paperbacks,
an imprint of The Random House Publishing Group, a division of
Random House, Inc., New York.

RANDOM HOUSE TRADE PAPERBACKS and colophon are trademarks of
Random House, Inc.
READER'S CIRCLE and colophon are trademarks of Random House, Inc.

Originally published in hardcover in the United States by
Random House, an imprint of The Random House Publishing Group,
a division of Random House, Inc., in 2005.

Grateful acknowledgment is made to HarperCollins Publishers,
Inc., for permission to reprint the first four lines of "Maturity"
from Selected Poems of Zbigniew Herbert, edited and translated
by Czeslaw Milosz and Peter Dale Scott. English translation
copyright © 1968 by Czeslaw Milosz and Peter Scott.
Introduction copyright © 1968 by A. Alvarez. Reprinted by
permission of HarperCollins Publishers, Inc.

Grateful acknowledgment is made to Charles Baxter for
permission to reprint lines from "At the Center of the Highway."
Copyright © Charles Baxter, courtesy of Darhansoff, Verrill,
Feldman Literary Agents.

Library of Congress Cataloging-in-Publication Data
Hribal, C. J.
The company car : a novel / C. J. Hribal.
p.   cm.
ISBN 0-345-47135-0
1. Traveling sales personnel—Fiction.   2. Parent and adult
child—Fiction.   3. Wedding anniversaries—Fiction.   4. Family
reunions—Fiction.   5. Rural families—Fiction.   6. Chicago (Ill.)—
Fiction.   7. Catholics—Fiction.   8. Wisconsin—Fiction.   I. Title.
PS3558.R52C66 2005
813'.54—dc22   2004058377

Printed in the United States of America

www.thereaderscircle.com

9 8 7 6 5 4 3 2 1

Book design by Victoria Wong

To Claude and Mary,
to Tosh and Roman and Hania,
and to the Seven C's

Part I

OBSERVATIONS FROM THE WAYBACK

It's good what happened
it's good what's going to happen
even what's happening right now
it's okay.

—ZBIGNIEW HERBERT, "Maturity"

1. A Day Late and a Dollar Short

There are times on this drive when I have been tempted to turn to Dorie and shout, "Our parents have been dead for years! Our father died while piloting a La-Z-Boy into oblivion, the remote still warm in his fingers! Our mother died in her bedroom; her last whispered words being 'More! More!' That's what happened to our parents! Not this! Not this!"

But it's Dorie's parents who have been dead for years. Mine are about to celebrate their fiftieth wedding anniversary, hence the drive up from Milwaukee with our kids. (I say "ours" although Dorie had already had Woolie and was pregnant with Henry when we met—a complicated story I needn't go into here.)

I don't shout out my denials, though, because (a) Dorie would point out my pronoun error, as well as the insensitivity of my having made it; and (b) Dorie, in her infinite wisdom, would simply shake her head and say, "Get a grip, Ace. What's the real issue here?"

In defense of the pronoun thing: because our parents beat it into our heads when we were younger, I have always thought of my siblings and myself as one unit, however scattered we've become. And it's not as though Dorie doesn't appreciate my referring to our three kids as "our three kids." But she's right about the other. The real issue here is that it has become increasingly evident to my siblings and myself that our parents may no longer be able to care for themselves. Besides celebrating our parents' fifty years together, my six sibs and I are going to be talking about the disposition of our parents' future. "The disposition of our parents' future"—I don't need Dorie calling me Ace again to know how ridiculous that sounds. The debate comes down to this: Should our parents, for their own good, be installed in the Heartland Home for the Elders? If I had a nickel for every flip-flop I've had over that I'd be a wealthy man. But it's not often we're all together in one place for a powwow, as our brother Ike would say, and this is not a question you answer by phone or e-mail. So along with the champagne and celebration, we have business to discuss. Messy business. Cloudy business. But then, when in our family have things been other than messy and cloudy?

As our father would say, "We shall see what we shall see." He could say a lot of other things, too: "Dollars to donuts," "Par for the course," "That'll put hair between your toes," and "You know what they do with horses, don't you?" Though given the situation, I don't know that he'd utter that last one.

"Relax, Em," Dorie says. "Don't get your undies in a bundle. It's not you deciding all on your lonesome. Let the Round Table do its work. No use feeling guilty over something you haven't done yet."

"What about the things I have done?"

She brings my hand to her lips and bites my knuckle. "I'll be the judge of that, sweetie."

Sophie, our youngest, pipes up from the wayback, "Are we there yet?" She'll ask this question at roughly three-minute intervals for the rest of the trip. My answer should be "No, not by a long shot," but right at that moment I'm thinking about how I called where Sophie is sitting "the wayback." Only, Mercury Villagers do not have waybacks. They have third seats, rear seats, or cargo areas, but not waybacks. Only station wagons—a species of family travel now largely extinct—have waybacks.

"What's up, Ace?" Dorie asks. "You've got one of your thousand-mile stares going."

I tell her about the wayback—those rear-facing seats where my siblings and I spent so much time on long family trips, though we had to fight each other for the right to sit there. We called it that because "Peabody's Improbable History" (the show about a dog and his boy housed inside *Rocky and His Friends,* aka the Rocky and Bullwinkle show), featured a time machine called the "Wayback." Looking out at every place we'd just been, we thought it worked like that for us, too. Which is how it's working for me on this drive back up to our parents'.

Dorie twists the cap off a water bottle. A modern woman, she likes to stay hydrated. "Tell me a story," she says, grinning. "Tell me a story from way back."

I know what she wants. Something from our childhood, something light, like the time Wally Jr. got his head stuck in the porch railing and we had to call the fire department to get him out, or the time Wally Jr. and Ike went windshield-surfing buck naked over the Lake Butte des Morts Bridge, or Cinderella mooning over our mother's bras, the fancy ones we found in our mom's underwear drawer, bras Cinderella was destined never to fill, or how Ike managed to become a Native American, or why Wally Jr. is our lightbulb in a hailstorm.

What she doesn't want is the only story I want to tell. It's our parents' favorite story, though I've never heard them tell it. Not all at one time, anyway. Dorie has heard it in bits and pieces over the years—straight from the horse's mouth, in all its convoluted permutations—and she's tired of it. Tired of the bits and pieces themselves, tired of the way the story runs up cul-de-sacs and dead ends because one of the tellers ain't so hot a storyteller anymore and the other cuts the first one off just as he's revving his engines to take us all down another memory cul-de-sac.

But then I'm not telling the story just for her. With our own marriage foundering, I know this is the story that someday I want our children to hear—a coherent story about things lasting, goddammit. Ours is not one of those "and they lived happily ever after" tales you'd like to tell your children. Our parents' wedding and marriage, though—that's a different story entirely.

Our parents were married on television in March 1952 on a show called *It's Your Wedding, With Your Hosts Alan Pickett and Billy Ray King.*

It's Your Wedding ran on station WILT in Chicago from 1948 to 1953, and for the first three-plus years of its existence the show was called *Billy Ray King's "It's Your Wedding."* Billy Ray King was the show's producer as well as its star. But like most people in television, Billy Ray King had his eyes on a larger prize. He thought the show could go national—like *The Colgate Comedy Hour* or *This Is Your Life.*

For a while it did, but there was a problem. Billy Ray King, born Miles Otis Oblansky, was fat. Or beefy, if you prefer. This was in the days before game show hosts were stamped like cookie cutters from the men's underwear section of the Sears catalog. In 1948 they could still look like real people, but by 1952 that was changing. Billy Ray King had three chins and looked as if he'd been stuffed into his suit like some pork-fed southern politician. His pants and sleeves were too short. He was frequently out of breath. He sweated under the studio lights. He looked like somebody's fat, red-faced uncle making the wedding speech. This made our father, who was skinny then but destined not to remain so, trust him, which was a mistake, as anyone who's worked with television people should know.

But then Billy Ray King should have known better, too. In his desire to take his show national, he sold it to the network, giving up his role as producer so that he could concentrate on being the show's star. The new producers brought in a pretty boy plucked from page 153 of the Sears Christmas catalog—Alan Pickett—and Billy's days as host of the show were numbered. Television executives were already discovering that they didn't want hosts who looked like they might drink too much at Aunt May's funeral. It might have been different if Billy Ray King was funny. You could look like a regular schmo on television if you were funny. But Billy Ray King was dead earnest, breathing too hard, always looking as though he feared the bride might call the whole thing off right at the last minute and then where would he be?

They made a strange pair, Pickett and Oblansky, that fourth spring season of *It's Your Wedding*. You could tell Billy Ray King was not comfortable with the arrangement. He kept trying to step in, excitedly and impatiently, while Alan Pickett was announcing how the game was played and what the couple could win that day and asking them where they were from and who their attendants were and what they had for future plans. "Kids! They're going to have lots of kids, whocka whocka," Billy Ray would say, nudging with his elbow whoever was closer, the bride or the groom. Brides tended to give Billy Ray a wide berth, positioning themselves whenever possible on the outside of their soon-to-be spouses. Pickett would nod assent and smile benignly, almost condescendingly, on Billy Ray's latest faux pas and then go on with whatever it was he was supposed to say next, oblivious to Billy Ray's futile and frantic antics to keep the show from being wrested from him. Alan Pickett was cool. He ended up hosting any number of short-lived game shows and in his later years was a regular on *The Guiding Light,* becoming famous as one of the few doctors on daytime television who didn't try to get into anybody's pants.

As television shows went, *It's Your Wedding* was pretty dumb. How it worked was, first, a couple agreed to get married on television. Then they'd fill out forms, provide family photos, get dressed in their wedding finery, and come down to the studio with their attendants and families. There they'd answer questions from the host that were gleaned from the forms while stiff wedding photographs of their parents and grandparents were shown on-screen. This being Chicago in midcentury, people knew their ethnic origins and were proud of them. There were Poles and Slavs and Croats and Germans and Irish and Italians and Lithuanians and even some Cubans. Then came the family snapshots—the bride and groom as children, as teenagers, the requisite photos of the groom as a soldier, the bride's high school graduation picture, maybe a picture of the two of them all dolled up for a fraternity dance or a night on the town. In between photos they cut back to the bride and groom looking nervous and a little silly as they answered Alan Pickett's questions or fended off Billy Ray King's clowning.

If you were to see such a show today, you'd be struck by how serious these couples seemed, but also how comfortable they were with each other. They knew each other's families, came from the same neighborhoods, had grown up together. Contrast that with the next generation of game shows that used as fodder people's willingness to celebrate their coupleness with an audience of several million strangers: *The Dating Game,* in which Jim Lange hooked up total strangers, and *The Newlywed Game,* in which couples showed the world how little they actually knew each other. Given what came later—*Blind Date, ElimiDATE, Temptation Island* (has there been a devolution in this country or what?)—*It's Your Wedding* was quaint and almost sincere. Billy Ray King was right. What lay in the future for these couples? Infants, offspring, foundlings, nudniks, bambinos, rug rats, little buggers, brats, sucklings, newborns, blimps, radishes, dumplings, cabbages, lumpkins, tax deductions—children. In the later shows nooky was naughty and occurred without reference to progeny, but on *It's Your Wedding* Billy Ray King believed it was all about results. "How many ya gonna have? Who do ya think they'll look like more, you or you?" The grooms all smiled politely. The wives looked pensive. They knew the whole deal was going to rest pretty much on their slim shoulders. And bellies. And backs.

So that was the *This Is Your Life* portion of the show, only without the surprise guests. The next thing was the couple got married, sometimes with a bit of subterfuge. At that time no priest or minister would think of appearing on television for the purpose of marrying somebody in a television studio. And the logistics and expense of doing remote broadcasts every week would have been impossible given the technology at the time. This wasn't, after all, the World Series. So the couples had two choices: Either they could really get married on the show by a justice of the peace, or they could get "married" by an actor sporting a collar and robes and after the show have the JP thing or a church wedding. "It makes no nevermind to me," Billy Ray King would say, "but then, it's not my family watching me get married on TV in front of a fusty old judge," gently coercing them to get married by the Bing Crosby look-alike he'd hired to lend the proper air of beneficence to the occasion. After that the couple would kiss, shake hands with their attendants, and then either engage in a contest or perform some talent to receive their prizes. The talents displayed were usually the kinds of time-filling acts Ed Sullivan was fond of using in his shows: singing, dancing, plate spinning, playing the musical saw.

The prizes were arranged in groupings of various-size boxes. Monty Hall would later borrow this idea, only he used doors. You might find anything in the boxes you chose: a pot with two rubber chickens in it, a color TV, a hi-fi radio, new tires, a set of cookware, a vacuum cleaner, cash, or a check. Billy Ray King took great delight in sometimes putting the smallest things in the largest boxes. The box that looked sure to hold an upright freezer held instead an egg. There was enough good stuff that it was worth going on the show regardless, but unless you got extremely lucky with your choices, Billy Ray King the producer was rarely nicked for more than a cheapo set of golf clubs, a lamp, and maybe a pair of his and her Timex watches.

By the show's fourth year on the air, Billy Ray King had the routine down cold, but when he got national syndication, he also lost control of the show. The national producers, in addition to bringing in Alan Pickett, wanted the show to move faster. Two weddings a show. Get rid of that hokey "my mama, she come from Albania" crap. Focus on the couple. Make it fun. More silly stuff. If you're going to show pictures, embarrass them. Skip the talent showcase. Marry them at the top of the hour, side by side or sequentially, then pair them off in contests. Heck, why don't we take them outside and have the brides and grooms and their attendants engage in a tug-of-war over a mud pit while still in their wedding regalia? Billy Ray King fought every change, but he had miscalculated his power and he was destined to lose the show the following season, when the fad for people getting married on TV had pretty much run its course. The show was canceled in February 1953, and Billy Ray King ended up selling appliances in downtown Chicago, Hoover and GE being kinder to him than the producers to whom he'd sold his show.

"How do you know all this, Dad?" Henry asks from the backseat. Henry is at the age when he wants to know how the world works. I'd explain it to him except I don't know myself.

"Because Grandma and Grandpa Cza-Cza have told him about a million and umpteen times," says Dorie, leaning her head back and closing her eyes.

"And what he doesn't know he's making up," says Woolie from behind his Game Boy. So he *is* listening, despite his attempts to hermetically seal himself inside his electronic media. I'm almost touched.

Dorie's right. They love to tell this story about themselves. Big and boxlike as they are now, it is sometimes hard for us to imagine them young and willowy, as they were then. But we have seen the pictures. Photographs taken before we were born, the pictures they used on the show when our parents were married: our father in an alleyway in Cicero with his foot on the front bumper of a Chevy Deluxe. He is wearing a two-toned Western-style shirt with the yoke a contrasting color, his hat flying away down the alley behind him, his grin as wide as any man's could be if he owned a car like that. And our mother, in a black velvet dress with a mock turtleneck collar and sun-ray cutouts from her neck to her bosom, the curvature of which is shown to best advantage by the dress's snugness. She is sitting backward on a tricycle in front of a row house stoop and looking up into the photographer's gaze, smiling. She shows us that photo and we ask her, Why are you sitting on that trike? And we don't hear her answer because we're too busy thinking: My God, our mom was sexy!

Which is why our mother loved to tell the story of how they got married. It had "sexy" written all over it.

But before our mother can tell us how Billy Ray King oohed and aahed and drooled and slobbered over that picture of her, like a generation of boys had done over those famous photos of Betty Grable, Lauren Bacall, and Rita Hayworth, our father always jumps in to tell us about the photo taken of him.

It was taken in 1950. He is posing with his foot on the front bumper of a brand-new Chevy Deluxe. The driver's side door is open. The art nouveau Winged Victory with its feet tethered to the hood looks like it's going to take flight any minute now. His hat already has. There's a big grin on his face—the car's his for the day—and he's posing in the narrow alley behind his folks' house in Cicero. There's a brick garage right behind him, then open space to the street beyond, where an open wood-frame garage yawns in the background. The arresting thing about this photograph is the fedora that's blowing in the space between the garages.

What amazes me is that grin, a grin he maintained even while his hat was flying off his head. I'd like to think that wide crooked grin reveals something elemental about him. Our father is grinning, he seems ecstatic even, that this miraculous event—a car loaned to him by a friend, his hat dancing away behind him—is happening to him.

When our parents talk about their earlier selves, it does seem like it was a miraculous time—each and every minute of it. But I know that's not the case, and I wish I had more to go on than the couple of pictures that were used on *It's Your Wedding* and another dozen or two that our parents pulled out from time to time. I have them with me now, a tiny pile between me and Dorie, and I would hand them one after another into the backseat, Daddy's show-and-tell, only Cinderella and Peg Leg Meg have made copies of these and other family photos, and scanned them all for a slide show, which will be shown at tomorrow's dinner. My kids are more likely to pay attention to that than to me, but I plunge ahead anyway, certain I can't do justice to what the pictures reveal, and—yes, Woolie—making up what I don't know but certainly feel.

It's an act of will as much as it is an act of imagination. Desperate, sure of their boredom, I want them nonetheless to feel the magic of those stories. As disjointed and piecemeal as they were often delivered, those stories still let me believe that, somehow, the world made sense, and if Dorie and I are indeed heading toward Splitsville, then I want our kids to have at least that—a belief that even in dark times the world still makes sense.

Besides telling us over and over again about their wedding, our parents loved to tell us how they had grown up in Chicago. For our father it was Cicero, land of bungalows and savings and loans, and home to Mr. Al Capone. Mr. Al Capone figured largely in our father's childhood, or at least in his mental landscape of it.

The way our father talked about it, Cicero possessed a certain *je ne sais quoi.* In the early years of the Depression it was Poles and Czechs—Twenty-second Street was called Dwa-Dwa Avenue—and a smattering of Italians. Our father's neighborhood boasted a Sokol, some bungalows, rows of two-flats, and not much else. An empty cookie company warehouse lined one end of his alley, with a brick garage behind it. Next door was an empty lot where a house had burned down. Across the street were more empty lots, where our father and his friends went skating. Enter Capone. He gets Cicero's city hall built. He rehabs buildings. He buys the cookie warehouse and the garage behind it. He buys lots of other buildings. Clubs open—the Paddock Club, where Capone gambled, and the 4811 Club, a no-alcohol social club that always seemed to be jumping. Cicero—still in Cook County but outside the Chicago police department's jurisdiction—was a wonderful place for Capone. He owned the town. And as long as he was hiring and spending and taxes stayed down, what was the problem?

Another photograph, this one taken at the Divisek School of Music in 1934. Our father, seven years old, is in the lower right hand corner of five rows of stacked students, every one of them swaybacked from an accordion. Eighty-nine of them, plus the teacher, on a stage with a wide gilt proscenium arch behind them. The people on the ends are blurry, as if the rows, with fifteen, nineteen, twenty, twenty-one, fourteen people each, were so long the curvature of the earth had to be figured in as well, and the photographer had failed to consider that. You can tell our father from the sad, serious look on his hawklike face, the disbelieving eyes, and because his name is done in inlaid mother-of-pearl up the front of the accordion: Walter Czabek.

His mother wanted him to be a doctor. She was disappointed when he didn't become one. She was disappointed when he married our mother. She was disappointed about a great many things, and this must have started early, judging from the look on our father's face. Whether it was in addition to being a doctor or in preparation for it, she also wanted him to be an entertainer. Hence the lessons at the Divisek School of Music. And once she discovered he had some talent, that his fingers could fly over those keys, his mother shifted into high gear as a stage mother. In addition to the accordion lessons with the personalized accordion, he was given a costume, a stage name, publicity photos. More pictures tell the story: the silver cape, the cadet hat, the military-striped wool pants, and the corded and heavily buttoned tunic with the square-cut collar and braided piping at the cuffs. Our father is smiling shyly, his fingers frozen in place on the accordion's keys and buttons, and white cursive script across the photograph's bottom, almost as though the words alone are supporting his feet, proclaims that this is "The Little Bohemian Prince."

If he escaped his own father's fate—henpecked, cowed, constantly given his marching orders by his imperious wife—it came down to this: he could sing. He opened his throat and the most marvelous, mellifluous tones escaped from it, first a boyish alto, then a rich, mature tenor. His voice gave him a freedom he would not otherwise have; it took him places—clubs, weddings, bar mitzvahs, band shells, auditoriums—where his mother did not want to go.

But that came later. Let us put him back at the time of the photo from the Divisek School of Music. He is seven. It is February 1934. The Twenty-first Amendment to the Constitution has just repealed the Eighteenth, but that hasn't changed much the way things are run. Liquor licenses have yet to be granted, liquor is still tightly controlled, and Capone, though in jail, is still running hooch in from Canada and northern Wisconsin. Given that nobody was all that crazy about Prohibition in the first place, and given all that Capone had done for Cicero, it is easy to see how the romance and myth of Capone grew, especially if all the shooting was happening someplace else. Even as I'm telling my kids this, I'm lapsing into silence. What do Woolie, Henry, and Sophie know of Al Capone? Their figures of evil are Osama bin Laden and swarthy guys flying into buildings. There's no romance there, and there never will be. And what do I know of Capone and everything else I'm telling them that I'm piecing together from all those shards given us by our father and mother? I know only what our father told me: in his mind there is a seven-year-old Wally Czabek, with the narrow serious face and haunted eyes, standing in his own backyard. A car comes roaring up his alley and drives full steam ahead into the abandoned cookie warehouse rumored to be owned by Al Capone. A few minutes later the same car, only with different plates, peels out. Seven-year-olds notice things like that. And the drivers of those cars notice seven-year-olds watching them as they speed by. The driver slows down, throws the serious-faced boy a dime. "You didn't see nuthin', kid," the driver says and roars off. Sometimes they exit the other side of the warehouse, and our father runs around front to watch the cars roar by. And they always, always toss him the dime.

"You didn't see nuthin', kid, you didn't see nuthin'."

Our father played by the rules, but he was fascinated by those who didn't. His admiration was purchased a dime at a time, and he came to believe that the rules were indeed suspended for those who acted as though the rules didn't apply. Later, for example, when he was in college, he had a friend in "the syndicate." Eddie Santucci. Our father double-dated with him at the Spring Formal. They were going to the Top Hat, where Eddie "knew some people." There was a bouncer out front and valet parking. No cover and a show. Eddie and our father arrived with their dates. The best seats were taken. Eddie whispered to the bouncer. The bouncer went front, whispered something to a couple sitting at one of the front tables. The couple moved. Our father never got over that kind of magic. Maybe that's why he became a company man. He thought things would happen for you if you just aligned yourself with the right people, people who got things done, and you agreed to look the other way.

No question, our father had a romance about Capone. When we were little he'd drive us all across north-central Wisconsin, and as we watched the countryside—fields, woodlands, marsh—roll across our bleary eyes, he would point out all the places where Capone allegedly had stills or hideaways or camps.

"They used the rivers and the lakes for transportation. That's why all those communities along the Fox and the Wolf River prospered," our father told us, his voice warming to the task. "They put the coils for the stills inside of silos, and did the cooking at night so the smoke couldn't be traced." And we would dutifully stare at the silos and barns and wonder if *that* was the one, if that was where it all happened. A lot of old money in New London, our father said, was Capone and Baby Face Nelson moonshine money, but nobody wanted to talk about it. "I suppose you can't blame them," our father said, "but if it was me, and enough years had passed, I'd say, Heck, sure we ran moonshine for Al Capone. It was a pleasure and an honor."

I think he felt the same way about the dimes. It was a pleasure and an honor.

What our father liked about Capone was that he was a man who lived large, who remade the world as he saw fit. Our father wanted to do that. He wanted to be one of those people but knew he couldn't, so instead he moved us to a place near where Capone did business, and regularly took us fishing where Capone fished. *"C'est la vie,"* our father would say, as though that explained everything, which maybe it did.

Our father believed in clichés. He had scads of them, which he trotted out with great regularity whether they were appropriate to the situation or not. If you hurt yourself: "Well, you know what they do with horses, don't you?" On asking you to consume whatever noxious food was put in front of you, be it Brussels sprouts or broccoli or, later, beer mixed with tomato juice: "That'll put hair between your toes." At the beginning of all family projects, particularly the ill-fated ones: "We shall see what we shall see." Or "I see, said the blind man, as he picked up his hammer and saw." If we protested the lunacy of his latest plan to make us rich, he'd say, "Another county heard from" or "No guts, no glory." On allowance day, which in the fifties and early sixties meant a dime accompanied by a nickel: "Don't spend it all in one place."

Our father's favorite cliché was "A day late and a dollar short." He said it often, and we came to understand that, although he was frequently both, he was determined to be neither.

That was certainly the case on the day he married. And while he was determined not to be a day late and a dollar short, in some ways he was always that seven-year-old standing in the alley, waiting for his dimes with both hope and awe. And envy.

The danger is, has always been, what hope steeped in envy sours into. Bitterness? Despair? What? "You're getting ahead of yourself, Em. We all know what he's like now. Go back to the story of little Wally Czabek, round-eyed in an alley, waiting for his dime. It's a cuter story."

But I skip ahead nearly a decade to pick up the story. With Prohibition off, Cicero is booming. The Sokol gets itself a restaurant with a three-tier bar, and its horseshoe auditorium, complete with balcony, mezzanine, and a parquet floor, is used less for cultural events—folk dancing and such—and more for bands. Big bands upstairs, jazz combos in the basement. The Bohemian Prince (he dropped the "little" once he turned fourteen) plays the Sokol and clubs like it three and four nights a week. Everybody winks at his age because there's a war on. All the men are enlisting, and somebody has to play the damn accordion and sing. Two years later he lies about his age and enlists himself.

Like many seventeen-year-olds in the spring and summer of 1944, our father fought the Battle of Lake Michigan in a Coast Guard cutter. In the spring of 1945 they attack the state of Michigan, landing on the dunes near Holland, Michigan, and charging up the beach—preparation, our father later found out, for an amphibious assault on Japan. The trainers toss equipment up and down the beach, and after the landing craft hit the beach everyone charges out, picking up equipment as they run. It takes a while to figure out why they might be doing this. "It's like we're stripping stuff from dead guys," somebody tells our father. The antlike spots of families picnicking further up the beach make the idea that they could die unlikely. This is America, how could that happen? "They always use the new guys for these landings," somebody else says. "They figure we ain't smart enough to know how suicidal the whole damn thing is." The drill sergeant's whistle pierces the air. "Again!" he screams. "Hustle, hustle, hustle!" and again they run up the beach, grabbing what they can.

Then peace comes, and our father, like a lot of people, is out of work. It's hard to believe that six months after the war there might be a depression again, but there is. Littler this time, but still. Our father tries making a go of the band, but it's pocket money now, not a regular thing, so he goes back to school, courtesy of the government, and meets our mother.

Dorie says, "I've always wondered about your mother." She taps the photo of that woman on the tricycle, the woman in the black fitted velvet dress with the broad shoulders and the arresting cleavage. "How'd she come to be sitting there?" Dorie's interest is usually tepid at best. She's heard bits of our mother's story before: How she was a sickly child, the oldest of what would have been eleven (a brace of miscarriages and eight stillbirths, the final two being twin boys). How she missed a grade and a half from scarlet and rheumatic fever and pneumonia, yet when she finally got to school she skipped another grade and a half. There are only a few surviving photos of our mother from those years, and in them she looks preternaturally old and tiny, like Shirley Temple. What Dorie wants, I think, are the insides of that life, something that only imagination can provide. I could tell her about our grandfather, how Arthur owned a restaurant, which he lost in the Depression, and then owned a shoe store and a candy store, both of which he lost as well, and how he ended up an elevator operator, and how all through this his wife, Naomi, was getting pregnant and losing children, and how, when he'd finally, through Christmas tips and careful investing, reacquired a nest egg, he was approached by the milk shake machine salesman Ray Kroc, an old friend, and was offered to be one of the initial investors in a fast-food enterprise, which he turned down because, after three businesses had gone belly-up on him, he was wary of ever doing that again to his family, especially since he'd have to borrow money for his share of the investment, and how that fast-food business eventually became McDonald's, but that's Arthur's and Naomi's story, not our mother's.

But our mother herself? I glance again at that picture of her sitting on a trike in a velvet evening dress. It is 1949, and our mother is working as a secretary for seventy-five dollars a week, taking night courses at DePaul, then scattered throughout the Loop in rented brick office buildings. It is just after the war. A lot of G.I.s have come back from wherever, and they're getting themselves educated on the G.I. Bill. They've learned to talk dirty and to get what they want by speaking plainly. Our mother, seventeen, sometimes dates these twenty-five-year-old ex-servicemen, which frightens the bejesus out of Naomi and Arthur. Their baby!

They need not have worried. Our mother expects to be treated like a lady no matter the age or needs of her prospective dates. Tired of the wolf whistles and the excited sniggering, she takes action against all of them one evening by coming to class armed with a book bag full of Hershey's chocolate bars and nylons and Kools and Lucky cigarettes. She throws open the door and rains these items down on the servicemen's heads. Then she announces, "There! You might have been able to buy a woman with that over in Italy or France or England or wherever you were, but it won't work on me here. I already have plenty, thank you." Then she storms off, cutting class, and forever after, she loved to report, they were courtly and polite and correct, and damn near protective of her coming and going. They gallantly open doors for her, offer to carry her books. They have become boys again, and handsome young men eager to please.

This is the woman I see perched on a tricycle in a form-fitting evening dress and a look in her eyes that would melt ice.

Our father, of course, was one of those boys, though, not having seen action, he was never so forward, and so never rebuked. The picture was taken on their first date. She is wearing black stockings and heels and black gloves, the kind you have to pull off with your teeth. Her dress is clinging to her thighs, she's sitting on a tricycle, and the curve of her chest is amazing. That's what always gets me—this sexy young woman posing on a child's toy with a starred ball at her feet and some Buster Brown shoes running off the photo's edge behind her. The incongruity of it all. She is young, curvaceous, sexy, beautiful. She seems destined for better things.

Better, maybe, than ending up with the man in the other photo, the man with the hat blowing away behind him, the man who took this picture of our mother. That's probably what Dorie is thinking; I've thought it, too. Yet they married each other. I suppose that's not so amazing, yet it seems so to me. I've known them only in their later incarnations. They no longer grin like idiots at their new albeit borrowed cars, and they wouldn't think of hitching up a dress and posing on a tricycle. So how did they get that way? And when did they start leaving themselves behind? Did it happen when the photographs changed from black and white to color?

At the time of these pictures our father has been through one war and he's about to be sent off to another, though he doesn't know that yet. He is not quite twenty-three. He's been through the Depression and a postwar recession. He wasn't cut out for medical school, but then school was an afterthought; four nights a week he was singing and playing in a band. He had his buddies, his bandmates, and a bevy of young women he was dating, one of them our mother. Our mother, not yet twenty when she marries our father, spends the three years between that photo's being taken and her engagement keeping sometimes as many as seven or eight dates a weekend with five or six different boys. To the Melrose Park harness track with one, to church with another, to the museum with a third, meeting a fourth at the zoo or Navy Pier, a movie or theater date later, coffee with somebody else later still, when she should have been studying (or perhaps it was a study date that became something else). She had an Italian boyfriend who was constantly telling her, "I will present you with many babies," as though they would be gifts he'd go out and get her.

She thought she could love that guy but knew he wouldn't respect her, and she didn't like the idea of being barefoot and pregnant while he was off screwing other women. Our father said nothing about babies, he didn't think he could be that lucky. He only promised he would love her. The babies would come later, fast and furiously, and every one of them, at the time anyway, seemed like a gift.

And then, of course, came all the rest of it, what they couldn't see, what they couldn't possibly know was coming.

Not that it mattered. Not that it mattered to anybody back then. Like most people at that time, our parents were young and scared and hopeful. They knew there were things out there that could touch them, could devastate them, but they also felt that they were the exception.

It turned out they were the rule.

But our parents didn't know that. For some dates, especially after they got engaged—our father did the romantic thing, getting down on one knee in Grant Park while our mother sat on a bench, quivering with excitement—our parents took the bus out to Oak Park and walked around gawking at the stately old homes set back under the trees. They tried to imagine themselves inside these homes, but it was a stretch, a change in circumstance too large to contemplate. Mostly they took the trolley out to the intersection of Butterfield and York Road. The trolley shook something fierce, and our parents held hands, both for the touch and for the steadying influence of one hand linked with another. The trolley had a coal stove in the center of it to heat it in winter and it was a single line out and back and you had to wait in the cold for the next trip, which could take a while. But they would go out there, to York and Butterfield, and they would hold hands and dream. It was where they dreamed they'd live. It was mostly empty field and prairie, but in the stubble of cornfields powdered with snow they were putting up new houses. Skeletal wood-frame ranches and scaled-down foursquares with brick veneers. It looked lovely. It looked like obtainable possibility. It looked like the future.

You see photographs like the ones I've described, and you ask yourself, What happened to these people? Did it work out okay for them? You wonder, coming back to yourself, sitting across from a wife to whom you may not be married for much longer, driving up to see the subjects of those photos, How did they start there and wind up here? And where, exactly, is here? And then you think, And what in God's name are we going to do with them now? Do *to* them now?

It is, as is often the case, the children who save you. Henry pipes up from the backseat, "So did Grandma and Grandpa get married or what?"

He's right. Let us get them married, let us let them begin.

"To begin this properly," I say in my best once-upon-a-time voice, "you must know what a 1934 Hudson Terraplane looks like. Grandpa and Grandma fell in love in the back of one."

The Terraplane was a big black clunky behemoth of a car that was old already when our father came to co-own it with his bandmates in 1948. It had dark green leather jump seats and a hood that tended to flap up like a huge bird's wing in any kind of wind and then fold over and fall off the car into traffic, as though the bird had been shot and was cartwheeling into the water. It was a car they pushed more than drove, and it was a good thing it was co-owned, since the hood frequently did its popping off act while they were careening down Cermak Road on their way to the Loop for a gig. Whenever the hood did this (and it did so frequently, the hinges holding it in place being rusted through), they had to pile out, four of the six band members, and run into traffic behind the car, lift the heavy and humongous dead bird, run it back to the car, and set the tin casing back into place, the driver or extra band member directing traffic around them. All this performed while they were three sheets to the wind themselves. The car was, however, indestructible. It once went through a solid oak garage door and survived. (This when our father tried to teach our mother to drive. Our mother, indomitable with eager servicemen, was helpless behind the wheel of a car. She never did learn how to drive.) Like most first cars, it used more oil than gas, a typical service stop consisting of twenty-five cent's worth of gas, a quart of oil, and a refill for the radiator. The Terraplane finally died in 1953, when one of the few bandmates who hadn't gone to Korea used only water during a winter refill and cracked the block.

It was the second to last car our father owned, and he owned only a sixth of it. It seated five guys plus their equipment, which was why they bought it. Our parents courted in it, smooched in it, fell in love in it. For his wedding, there could be no other vehicle, no other chariot to deliver him to his chosen maiden than that 1934 Hudson Terraplane, the hood of which kept flapping off in the brisk wind off Lake Michigan as he and his bandmates—Louie Hwasko (piano), Bernie Zanoni (clarinet), Benny Wilkerson (bass), Ernie Klapatek (trumpet), and Charlie Podgazem (drums)—howled up Cermak Road toward WILT's television studio and our father's date with destiny.

Our mother arrived by bus with her girlfriend, Helen Federstam, who was also her maid of honor. Both were sophomores at DePaul. Helen, nervously chain-smoking Lucky Strikes, asked her, "So, why are you doing this? What, did you fall in love with the accordion?"

A fair enough question. Of the other men our mother had been dating, Helen considered at least two of them superior—at least as musicians— to the accordion-wielding flyweight who was to become our father: a twenty-eight-year-old violinist with the Chicago Symphony and an Irish tenor who also sold insurance. Helen also thought the dark-eyed, jet-haired Italian (the one who wanted to "present" our mother "with many babies") was "dreamy." She did not think the hollow-eyed, skinny-limbed young man with receding hair cropped in a military crew cut a suitable match for Susan Marie. But Susan Marie did. Maybe it *was* the accordion.

She tried to explain this to Helen as they waited for our father and his buddies to show up. She thought it, well, very brave that a five-foot-eight man weighing one hundred and forty-seven pounds would even con-template strapping that huge box onto his chest, and that he could sing, too, while laboring beneath that device, sing with a full, rich, resonating tenor—that in itself was something. But it was more than that, too. She thought their temperaments suited each other. They wanted the same things, she said, thinking of those trolley rides, those held hands, that prairie giving way to wood-frame houses. "And he isn't stuck on him-self," she added, thinking of the Italian, the violinist, the tenor–insurance salesman, and others besides, all of whom, she thought, were filled with vanity, who wanted a beautiful young woman solely because her beauty complemented theirs. "He loves me for me," our mother added, feeling a little defiant and pulling her woolen coat closer to her chest as a stiff March breeze rushed up East Wacker Drive.

Helen rubbed out her cigarette beneath her heel as the Terraplane roared up to the curb. "Suit yourself," she said, putting on her best meeting-the-guys smile as she added, sotto voce, "Me, I wouldn't have that surname if you killed me. It sounds like a rock on a garbage can lid, you know what I'm saying?"

The guys had their own story to tell, involving the Terraplane's hood flying off ten feet in front of a cop directing traffic at the corner of State and Jackson. "It looked like we were performing a Chinese fire drill," said our father. "He was going to write us up, obstructing traffic, I guess, only he was laughing too hard. The sight of these guys in uniforms and tuxes—"

"And Wally shouting, 'Please, Officer, I'm getting married!' " Louie

Hwasko, his best man, added. "That saved us. That Wally, always quick on his feet."

"I'm sure," Helen said. "Meanwhile, I'm freezing."

"Allow me to fix that, little lady," said Louie, offering his bent elbow and tilting his head to indicate somebody else should get the door. Ernie Klapatek, happy to oblige, stepped into the revolving door and set it in motion. The others followed one at a time except for Louie, who stepped in right behind Helen, and our parents, who tried to glue themselves to each other in the best tradition of the wackily in love but couldn't because our father was carrying his accordion.

Inside, waiting, was Billy Ray King. Alan Pickett was still in his dressing room. He did not come out until just before the show started, when he would quickly introduce himself to the couple, shake hands, and smile distantly, conserving the wattage of his smile for the moment when the red On Air sign started flashing. Billy Ray King, however, was a worker. He worked the studio audience, he worked the staff, he worked himself, he worked his marrying couples. And Billy Ray King, already dumped to second lead on his own goddamn show, worried that he would be edged out completely by this upstart pretty boy, was in a lather.

"Good, good, you're in uniform," he said upon seeing our father in his dress whites. "We got problems."

"Problems?" asked our mother. She didn't want to hear about problems. This wedding wasn't her idea in the first place. She was going along with one of our father's crazy ideas—a pattern that would continue throughout their marriage, with decidedly mixed results.

"A couple canceled, it was a last-minute thing." Already Helen and the groomsmen were being taken up an elevator by assistants. Billy Ray King needed to speak to this couple alone.

He leaned in confidentially. "They chose not to get married."

"Not married on the show?" our mother asked.

"Not married at all," said Billy Ray King, which caused our mother to gasp audibly. How could you back out once you'd decided? It was something altogether understandable if you'd been asked and you simply said no. Our mother had done that several times already—the Italian was persistent and greedy. But to say yes and then change your mind—unthinkable!

"We need you to be the first couple on today's show."

"But we just got here."

"I know, I know, it's a headache. My assistants even as we speak are scouring the list of upcoming couples seeing if somebody wants to make a move up. It's not easy. People have plans, it's a Thursday evening, who's going to come downtown at a moment's notice?" Billy Ray King, when the pressure was on, was at his unctuous best. He eyed our father's accordion case. One of the program assistants had attended one of the Cicero Velvetones' concerts to ascertain that the singing/accordion-playing groom was on the level when he listed himself as a professional musician and lieutenant JG. "Listen," said Billy Ray King. "There's even the possibility that your hubby-to-be here is going to dazzle us all with his singing for half the show if we can't locate another couple. What do you say?"

Our mother turned to our father. "Wally?"

"Wally, I love that, Wally," said Billy Ray King. "You kids are gonna do great. The audience is gonna eat you up. I could eat you up." He kissed our mother's forehead, then started pumping our father's hand.

The next thing our parents knew, the elevator doors had opened and they were being led away in opposite directions, somebody was slapping makeup on them, their attendants were ushered away from them again—only Louie and Helen would stand up for this wedding, the rest were seated in the audience, not needed till the next day's ceremony, though Billy Ray King promised a camera would show them to the home audience at some point—"So be ready to wave, dammit, and look happy"—and told our father "there might be a possibility" that his band could sit in with the studio band when he played during the talent segment.

I'm not sure when during the production of this broadcast our parents realized they were being had, or when they realized that Billy Ray King, a proud fat man about to lose his empire to the sleek and brainless, was truly desperate. Our father knew any number of club owners who could be shysters, so perhaps he wasn't surprised. Then again, it was his wedding, his call to have it on TV, he'd been the one to deal with Billy Ray King in setting this up, and he wanted to trust the man. No, more than that. He wanted to *believe* in the man and what he stood for—marrying couples and sending them on their way, off into the world (with a little cash) to reproduce and make the world safe for democracy.

That our parents ended up being married first on the show that day is important. It shouldn't have mattered—it was the show's seventy-third episode—but it did. For a season and a half *It's Your Wedding* ran one wedding a show. Then they switched to two. Our parents were to be that second couple, but they got bumped up a spot on account of the couple that supposedly decided against getting married. But this seems unlikely. America in 1952 was in a marrying mood, and the idea of a couple backing out of a TV marriage at the last second seems downright churlish. Our parents were not churlish, our parents were good soldiers, which was something on which Billy Ray King counted. In fact there were only two things about which our mother, who didn't much care whether she was married on TV or not, put her foot down. The first was her insistence that our father become a Catholic. Years later, when her children were marrying, this was less of an issue for our mother, but not then. Technically, our father was an agnostic, which to our mother's way of thinking was both the worst thing you could be and the easiest to correct. He'd been raised in a godless household by people who simply didn't think much about religion. He was a clean slate, ready to be written on with the finger of our mother's faith. On the morning of his wedding he was baptized, by noon he'd had his First Communion, and by late afternoon he was confirmed in his new faith. He was willing to accommodate her on all this if she was willing to accommodate him on the TV wedding. From agnostic to Catholic, what did it mean? asked his friends. "It means," said our father, "I'll eat perch on Fridays."

Our parents were also in a bit of a hurry. Our father was scheduled to report to the San Diego Naval Air Station in a week, it being the Korean War and all, and he had his orders to ship out just a few days after that. Plus there was the matter of the honeymoon. Our parents wanted one. They were planning on a couple of days in Madison, Wisconsin, which at the time qualified as bucolic wilderness, and they'd then stop at various wayside motels on the drive from Chicago to San Diego, being of modest means and a semipractical bent. Practical because it was Lent, and the only way they could have a honeymoon and a party afterward was if they got married on a Friday, and getting married on a Friday in Lent in the Catholic Church required not only a special dispensation but also a quiet and somber ceremony. The church wedding would be small, the reception—featuring tea cakes, coffee, and a few delicately iced cookies—would be held in the church basement. A wedding more like a penance than a celebration. Compared to that, a TV wedding with a party afterward was like having their cake and eating it, too.

Practical but only semipractical. How else do you explain them being on *It's Your Wedding* at all if there weren't something of the romantic in-fused in them, too?

Practical and romantic, our parents were almost always guided by these antithetical impulses, and it was invariably to the wrong pole that they gravitated when decisions had to be made. This did not make them in any way unique, and it was probably their desire to get married on TV that confirmed how much a part of the great wave of America they were, young and hopeful and not even conscious that if they were part of the wave, they were also subject to its undertow.

The second thing our mother insisted on was that church wedding. They were going to have it the very next day, but according to our mother, unless a priest officiated for the TV ceremony, it wasn't official. And if it wasn't an official wedding—a JP marrying them didn't count—then our mother would not be participating in Thursday night's honey-moon, for which our father had booked a room at the Sheridan Hotel.

Billy Ray King knew that, too, our father having pressed the point upon him. It had to be a priest, it had to be a priest, goddammit! But of course it couldn't be a priest. Billy Ray King had already been over all that with our father. And no JP was going to agree to impersonate a priest just to salve this one couple's conscience. So Billy Ray King did what he thought was the right, honorable, and expedient thing, knowing, as he did, that the couple was getting married for real the next day any-way. He told our father he'd located a priest willing to do the ceremony. This was what Billy Ray King called a necessary fabrication or, as Alan Pickett would have it, "utilitarian make-believe." A lapsed Catholic him-self, Pickett concurred with Billy Ray—Catholicism made good theater. On one set cellophane "stained-glass" windows and a plywood altar decorated with candles and daylilies served as a backdrop to the couple's earnestness.

Earnest, accommodating, practical, romantic. Our father terrified of being a day late and a dollar short. If our parents ever knew they were being snookered right at the moment of their snookering, their own character would have prevented them from saying anything. Still, they had to suspect something when, just before airtime, Alan Pickett and Billy Ray King engaged in a furious, sotto voce argument. It was about the couple Billy Ray King had "found" at the last minute to get married on TV. It was glaringly obvious that the other bride to be was pregnant. Alan Pickett, who usually didn't care what went on during the show as long as he looked good doing it, was beside himself. "Knocked up! I know for a fact she's knocked up!"

Billy Ray King was strangely calm, as though he knew this was an argument he was going to win. "How can you know 'for a fact' she's knocked up?"

"What, you can't see? Take a look at her front porch. How can you not tell? I can tell, the audience can tell. The sponsors and the folks at home can tell. They can simply *tell,* okay? She's pregnant, Billy Ray. She's got a bun in the oven. The little tax deduction has declared itself. Billy, can't you see? She's as big as a fucking house!"

"So?" said Billy Ray King, in the perplexed voice of a student who just doesn't get what his teacher is saying.

"So?" said Alan Pickett. "So we can't have that. Hey, it happens, I understand that. But we can't have that on the show. You know that, Billy. It's your goddamn show." Alan Pickett's anger had subsided. He was speaking now in the exasperated voice of that teacher whose pupil refuses to acknowledge the truth of some simple fact like that rivers, in the Northern Hemisphere, flow south. And pregnant women are not married on TV.

They were now arguing loud enough for the studio audience to hear them. Our parents had already been led to their respective toe marks on opposite sides of the stage when Louie got up from his chair and offered to cut the apparent Gordian knot. "I'll marry Helen," said the bespectacled and eager Louie, an announcement that was met with a roll of the eyes and a low groan from Helen, who found his chipperness irritating. Truth be told, Louie at that moment would have married Helen, or Agnes Guranski, another of our mother's friends who came down to watch the wedding in person, or any other woman in the studio audience, up to and including the pregnant woman over whom Alan Pickett and Billy Ray King were arguing.

Billy Ray King waved Louie back to his seat. "We'll just show them from the waist up," he said, as though he had solved everything.

"She's pregnant, Billy Ray. She's all waist, don't you get it? Her chest is surfing her belly. We can't have that, okay? Okay?" Alan Pickett, who towered over Billy Ray King, was hiss-shouting into Billy Ray's ear.

Billy Ray King tilted his head away. With his face all scrunched up and his hand waving at his ear, it looked like he was trying to shoo away a particularly annoying insect. Then he leaned forward on his tiptoes and hissed into Alan Pickett's face, "Yeah, okay, she's pregnant. So what? She's my daughter and she's getting married on this television show. On TV, okay? On her daddy's program. You got a problem with that?"

Alan Pickett stared up at the ceiling, which you could hardly see for all the cable and lighting girders. He sighed, shuffled through several sheets of paper he gripped in his fist. "Suit yourself," he said. "But you broadcast this and it won't be a wedding anymore. It'll be your funeral." Then Alan Pickett went to his place by our father and waited to be introduced. The stage manager yelled, "Fifteen seconds!" and flashed his open hand three times.

"Idiot," said Alan Pickett.

"Excuse me?" said our father.

"That man is an idiot. And because of him you're—" Pickett stopped. "You ready?"

Our father said he was, but he was a little nervous.

"We all are. But that's okay. Make it work for you. Just be yourself. You sing, right?"

Our father said he did.

On the opposite side of the stage, our mother stood next to Billy Ray King. A believer in other people's privacy, our mother had tried not to listen to King and Pickett's argument. She had not heard what the argument was about, only that it had been intense and short-lived. She could not help smelling the man standing next to her, however. She had thought back in the lobby that there might be an odor of alcohol about him, but she wasn't certain. Now she was. You don't spend that long in a restaurant with drunken customers without recognizing the scent of gin on someone's breath. Billy Ray King, in his cups, his mind reeling with everything he had wrought and the thought of its fragility—a daughter, pregnant, a show about to be taken away from him—misinterpreted our mother's sniffing.

"Aqua Velva," said Billy Ray King. "It drives women wild." His hand settled on the small of our mother's back. It could have been taken as a friendly gesture if you were inclined to take it as such. Our mother chose to ignore it. But she couldn't ignore the sight of the obviously pregnant woman dressed like a bride who was being seated right at the end of the row sporting our mother's and father's attendants.

"That woman is pregnant," said our mother.

"So what," said Billy Ray King. His hand slipped lower, coming to rest on our mother's bottom. Our mother chose to ignore that, too. "You aren't, are you? You wanna be? Ha-ha." He gave our mother's behind a squeeze. Our mother belted him with her flowers, which she'd already been cautioned by the show's censor needed to be held in front of her voluminous chest.

"Idiot," said Alan Pickett. "You wait for your cue. Good luck, and have a good show." Our father couldn't tell if Alan Pickett was saying all that to Billy Ray King or to him, or if it was meant to be divided equally.

"I will," said our father, but Pickett couldn't hear him. He was already strolling into the spotlights as the roll of drums and the brass fanfare swelled. Ready to do what evil needed to be done. Alan Pickett, waving at the home and studio audiences, his smile fixed and mammoth.

And so our parents, scheduled to get married during the second half hour of *It's Your Wedding, With Your Hosts Alan Pickett and Billy Ray King,* were instead married during the first. They answered Billy Ray King's embarrassing questions, they nodded, they smiled, they were a perfect couple. There are no still photographs of them that day, no pictures of them standing stiffly with the TV cameras looming behind them like alien beasts threatening this union. But our parents assure us they wore the same clothes the next day for their church wedding, so we'll have to go with that: our father in his Navy whites and a crooked grin, our mother in a short pearl-colored jacket over a tea-length pearl dress with a plunging neckline, a triangle of lace covering her cleavage. She is holding her carnations and lilies of the valley as if offering them to the folks at home. The nuptials were witnessed by their attendants and friends in the studio audience; other friends cheered in furniture stores or in frat and sorority houses.

Their parents watched at home. Arthur, Naomi, Bea, and Charlie had chosen not to acknowledge this wedding, which was just as well since the Catholic Church and the state of Illinois did not acknowledge it, either. The priest was not a priest, or a JP, and nothing was going to be legal and official until the next day, though our parents did not know this at the time.

After they chastely kissed, Alan Pickett said to the camera, his manner officious and pleased, "May I present to you our ninety-ninth happily married couple on *It's Your Wedding,* Mr. and Mrs. Walter C. Czabek." There was polite applause, punctuated by Louie Hwasko's and Helen

Federstam's wolf whistles, and then Alan Pickett said, "I understand that before our next couple comes out, Walt here is going to play us a song."

"That's right, Alan," said Billy Ray King, "and then we're going to present our lucky *one hundredth* bride and groom!"

By then our parents must have known they'd been had, snookered out of the good stuff by a desperate man who wanted his pregnant daughter to be the "lucky" one hundredth bride married on *It's Your Wedding*, but to their credit they refused to cry foul or even let on they knew. A certain tightness showed in their faces as they dutifully chose their boxes, their smiles the fixed and nervous smiles of losers abashed at their own defeat, but still game and grinning, and you had to be pretty adept to notice even that. With flourishes inappropriate to the paucity of their haul, Alan Pickett and Billy Ray King presented them with their winnings: a hundred-dollar savings bond, a Hoover vacuum cleaner, fishing tackle, a GE blender, and a gift certificate good for dinner at the Sheridan Hotel, where our parents were going to start their honeymoon.

And then our father was allowed to play. Billy Ray King, anxious to get his daughter off and married (she wasn't getting any less pregnant while she waited in the wings), wanted our father to perform sans his polka and swing band. "Not enough time," he said during the break, but Alan Pickett overrode him, saying simply, commandingly, "Let them," and so Benny, Bernie, Louie, Ernie, and Charlie took seats with the studio orchestra, and our father strapped on his accordion, and when they came back from commercial Alan Pickett, this time with a flourish appropriate to the moment, said, "Take it away, Wally Czabek and the Cicero Velvetones!"

And take it away they did. It must have been something to see. Our father skinny, sweating under the klieg lights, singing his lungs out. The accordion a huge black-and-pearl box strapped to his chest. He looked like he was stepping backward under its load. He was not yet the behemoth he would become, a three-hundred-and-fifteen-pound sagging walrus with a great belly hanging over his boxer shorts like a blunt-faced dead fish as he comes into the kitchen in the morning in a ratty mustard-colored robe, scratching himself in the groin, his fingers working through the not quite closed fly of those boxers while he waits for our mother to thrust a cup of coffee under his nose, which will cause him to open up the slits of his eyes and to stop, briefly, his tugging and scratching and rearranging of body parts while the smile of a coffee addict lights up his face.

But I'm getting ahead of myself. Let us remember him as he was in those early photos, a gaunt young man with a hawklike face and an ungainly instrument strapped to his chest. There he was, all one hundred and forty-seven pounds of him, the klieg lights beating down, sweat beading across his already receding hairline and trickling down his forehead. It is our father's one shining moment of fame, and he is not about to let them take that from him.

Let the other couple, the producer's pregnant daughter and her beau, be the "lucky" hundredth couple. Let them be showered with balloons, confetti, and toasted with champagne. Let our parents be the good sports, humiliating themselves good-naturedly on TV for a pittance, saluted as the ninty-ninth couple to get married on the program and then forced to watch this other couple, Billy Ray King's knocked-up daughter and her beau, get proclaimed the "Lucky Hundredth" and get showered with a thousand dollars cash, a Poconos honeymoon, a dozen place settings of Wedgwood china, a new TV, a Zenith hi-fi, and a brand-new, hot-off-the-presses-from-Detroit, Michigan, Chrysler Imperial. For right now our father, patronized, condescended to, smirked at, the soldier boy with the accordion who'll "entertain" the audience, is playing and singing his heart out.

And he is great. The band plays "In the Mood" and "The Boogie Woogie Bugle Boy," and our father sings "Night and Day" and "As Time Goes By" and follows that with "Ghost Riders in the Sky" in this powerful, haunting, vibrating tenor that brings down the house. Every time Billy Ray King tries to step in and stop our father, Alan Pickett thrusts a forearm across his chest and stops him. "Let him go," Pickett says. "It's the least you can do, you sorry son of a bitch." And let him go they did.

Frankly, I'm not sure they could have gotten him off the stage if they wanted to. He was already in the service, about to be shipped off to Korea. He could die before impregnating his bride, for chrissakes, and he was going to sing his goddamn songs if it killed him.

And the whole while he was performing our mother was beside herself with joy. By the time he and the Cicero Velvetones closed with "I've Been Working on the Railroad"—performed as a sing-along with the audience—Wally was a hit. A bona fide, ears-ringing-with-applause, standing-ovation-from-the-audience hit.

Alan Pickett did one more nice thing for our parents when Wally and his band were through. He took our parents aside, thrust a hundred dollars at Wally, and said, "Beat it. Get started on your honeymoon. You don't need to stick around for the rest of this travesty."

"But we're supposed to be there at the end." Our mother had seen the show to make sure she knew what was expected. "We're supposed to be presented again, at the end of the show."

"Do you really want to be around when this particular show ends?" asked Pickett.

"But Billy Ray King—"

"Billy Ray King is history," said Alan Pickett. "Fuck Billy Ray King."

Our mother blushed, but she shook Pickett's hand when he offered it, and then he kissed her on the cheek, and shook our father's hand, and got our parents and their friends out a side door while Billy Ray King was still fussing over his daughter. Our father started to say thanks to Alan Pickett, but Pickett waved him off. "You were great," said Alan Pickett. "You were probably the greatest guest this sorry-ass show has ever seen, and you got screwed. I'm sorry. I can't make that up to you, but don't worry about His Highness. I can handle Billy Ray King."

And then our parents were outside, in the cold March evening, in downtown Chicago. A brisk breeze was blowing off the lake, and there were flurries twinkling in the streetlights.

"Where are we going?" asked Benny Wilkerson.

Our father waved his gift certificate and the five twenties given him by Alan Pickett. "To the Sheridan Hotel," said our father. "For one hell of a dinner."

Walter Charles Xavier Czabek (Xavier was his confirmation name, given him the afternoon of his faux wedding to our mother) and Susan Marie Caroline Hluberstead were joined in holy and legal matrimony on the second to last Friday in Lent at Holy Redeemer of Angels Church on Chicago's Near North Side. They got married before God, before a priest, before their parents and friends, a day after they had honeymooned at the Sheridan Hotel, unaware of the sham that had been committed against them by Billy Ray King and an actor named Joseph Clintsworth, who later played a judge on both *Gunsmoke* and *Bonanza* (which once caused our mother to yell out, "There's the bastard who married us!" when he stepped off a carriage that had pulled up outside the Ponderosa). The bride on this particular Friday was giddier than a bride in Lent ought to be, but then how many brides show up for their church weddings just hours removed from a tumultuous and satisfying wedding night and wedding morning (this was 1952, remember), already initiated into the rites of connubial bliss, already a man's consummated bride, already, most likely, pregnant for eight hours or so?

Perhaps it was not so unusual. Perhaps it was a Korean War thing, just as a decade previous it had been a Second World War thing. Lots of couples were having quickie weddings prior to the husband's shipping out, the friends in attendance with their university books stacked on the pews next to them—a wedding, then Chem 101. It's just our parents got married on TV first, and exuberantly consummated their marriage a day early. As Billy Ray King might observe, So what? (It is testimony to our mother's discretion and sense of propriety that she would not tell us the complete story of their false wedding until most of us were grown and had children of our own.) After their own quickie church wedding, after what our mother came to call their "real" marriage, the bride and groom had finger sandwiches and coffee in the church basement with their parents and friends, and then they left in a borrowed car for a weekend-long honeymoon in Madison, Wisconsin, the Terraplane being too unreliable for such an important mission.

Back then Madison, Wisconsin, was not much. There were the lakes, Mendota and Monona, a few supper clubs, a few lodges, some craftspeople scattered about in cottages. The university was just beginning to be packed with soldiers in Quonset huts. Having saved the world and made it safe for democracy, they were pretty eager themselves for the white-collar union card that a diploma represented. Our father, squiring our mother about the lakes, looking at the bare trees and the lake homes and the ducks huddled in the reeds, kept driving by those Quonset huts as though they were a magnet. "I don't know what it's going to be like," our father said. "We could be living in one of those. You think you're ready for that?"

Said our mother, still giddy, "Wally-Bear, I'm ready for anything."

Of course it wasn't going to last. Nothing does. A weekend is not a life, after all, and squeezing from a weekend every possible moment for romance, mystery, and happiness only confirms its exquisite finiteness. They returned to Chicago, returned the borrowed car, and headed out for San Diego in a new Buick Roadmaster, a drive-away vehicle that our father had contracted to deliver to a doctor in L.A.

It is perhaps fitting that our father didn't even own the car he and our mother drove out to San Diego. He sold his interest in the Terraplane to Ernie Klapatek, and the next car he owned outright was the one he got after he retired.

The plan was for them to continue their honeymoon on the drive out, then our father would drop our mother off in San Diego and he'd motor up to L.A. alone and take the bus back, reporting for active duty just hours before he was due. They took Route 66 most of the way, following the song's route except for when they dipped into Mexico for twenty-four hours of international nooky.

While it's widely believed in our family that Sarah, the oldest, was a consolation baby, the product of our mother and father administering solace to each other for not scoring the TV dowry, Sarah herself maintains she was conceived a day or so later, fully within wedlock, either in the woods ringing the shores of Lake Mendota or during one of those festive rest stops, perhaps even—she'll waggle her eyebrows at the romance of this—in another country entirely. We don't believe her because our mother already knew she was pregnant while they were driving across the Southwest. Fast-acting hormones, according to our mother. She says she must have thrown up on every cactus from New Mexico to Arizona.

Some of the rest stops were more festive than others. At the Arizona-California border, the guards took one look at our father—a geeky-looking guy with lampblack eyes and scoops of hair already missing from his forehead—and another at our mother—a curvaceous brunette with the lips of Betty Grable and the eyes of Lauren Bacall—and they knew what they had were a couple of newlyweds. They recognized the look of a newly married woman when they saw one. A woman dazed with sex, which wasn't quite the case—she was dazed with pregnancy, but you couldn't expect these border guards to know that. They ordered our parents out of the car, asked them to please open their suitcases. When our father protested, he was told they were looking for contraband fruit from either Texas or Mexico. They had to search everything. And though they said they were sorry, they certainly didn't appear to be. Our father's suitcases received a cursory glance. Our mother's ended up all over the highway. Her entire trousseau was scattered across the car's hood and over the roof and trunk, her unmentionables toyed with, then dropped. Our mother went scarlet as the guard in charge held each item up for his compatriots, one after another, then passed it on. Each guard pinched each new item between his fingers like he was holding up a skunk, only his grin showed he knew better. "And what have we here?" and "What's this?" the head guard kept saying as he examined slips, half-slips, teddies, tap pants, stockings, garters, nightgowns, negligees, bras, panties, silk stockings, camisoles. You name it, they held it up to the stark Arizona sun, then let it trail away from their fingers in the hot Arizona breeze. "What are you doing?" our mother screamed.

"Checking for fruit," they replied. "You can't take fruit across state lines."

Four years later, driving back with two squalling kids in the backseat, our mother got even. Besides Sarah, she'd had Robert Aaron, another leave baby, and I was clearly on the way. I was a welcome-back-to-the-States baby, conceived on their fourth wedding anniversary. Besides the two squalling kids, who were turning a high pink no matter how much flesh our mother tried to keep covered—she had put diapers on their arms, pinned to the sleeves of their blouses, and tied bonnets onto their heads—our mother had a load of fruit with her. Three pineapples, a sack of oranges, and bunches and bunches of bananas—big stalks of them—were piled in the front seat and between her legs. Just to see, our mother said. Just to see.

She got the same border guard, puffier now, but unmistakably him. He took one look at Sarah and Robert, sunburnt and screaming in the backseat, another at our mother, still pretty but obviously far gone into motherhood, and waved us through.

2. Par for the Course

Dorie looks up from the *Bicycling* magazine she's been paging through. "Good story, Em, but still I wonder, What was it like for your mom? I mean, when they were first married. It wasn't like now, where you have options. I mean, she was just along for the ride, wasn't she?"

I don't answer. Dorie's planning her big bike trip for the summer, twelve hundred miles, Milwaukee to Connecticut. She has a tune-up trip before—a lap around Lake Michigan—but that's with her cycling club, the Acoustic Cyclers of Greater Milwaukee. Her Darien trek, though, is her first solo. Just her, her panniers stuffed with gear, and a Visa card. "It's all about testing limits," she tells me when I ask. "Besides," she says, touching my chest in a rare display of affection, "who's going to hold down the fort?"

Fort holding is my job. I knew this even before we married. When we were first dating, it was clear that her appetite for doing, getting, and going was far greater than mine. Perhaps my most exotic desire was wanting Dorie in the first place. A complicated story, but the short version is that, after a very tumultuous period in her life, Dorie wanted to settle down. And strangely enough, she wanted to settle down with me.

She was a single mom when we met, but comfortably well-off. Had her own business buying and selling farms in the town where we both grew up, then gave it up soon after the boom hit and moved to Milwaukee. Bought a funky old house in a funky old neighborhood—Victorians mostly—and got interested in rehab. A lot of the houses had been carved up into rooming houses, there were prostitutes on the corners and drugs in the alleys—the old urban decay story—and Dorie, God bless her, saw the possibilities of turning Veedon Park into a neighborhood again. Some gay couples and other single moms started buying properties from the slumlords and turning them into places people actually wanted to live in. We met when she came by my apartment on the third floor of a Queen Anne that had seen better days to inform me that she was now my landlord, and if I had any problems, to please come see her, she was living in the Arts and Crafts home down the street—the one with the porch roof propped up with I-beams while the porch itself was being re-bricked.

I was managing a used bookstore then. An English lit Ph.D. in a glutted market, I went with Plan B, which was not so much a plan as it was a series of lucky accidents, the culmination of which was having Dorie Keillor as my landlord. Over beers and brats at a neighborhood potluck, we got to talking. Catching up, actually. I had known her since I was ten, had a crush on her for years, then lost track of her when she was seventeen and she dropped out of school.

"I remember you were pretty wild in high school," I said. "At least for Augsbury."

"Yeah, and you were a straight arrow and boring. At least for Augsbury."

"Well," I said, "I'm glad we got that out of the way."

She had her son with her, a three-year-old kid with a mass of curly black hair (I could see that was where he got his name, Woolie). He was trying to get his mouth around a bratwurst. Ketchup was dribbling onto his lap.

"Cute kid," I said. "And so serious. A boy after my own heart."

"Yeah, he's sensitive," she said. "I'm hoping he grows out of it, but I think you pretty much have to take them as they come."

"My mother once told me, 'Emmie, you're the most sensitive, highest-strung of all my children. You're going to feel higher highs and lower lows than any of them. You're just going to have to get used to it."

"Did you?"

"He will, if that's what you mean."

Dorie had a slug of beer. "It's not. I was asking you."

"Not really."

She smiled. "I didn't think so."

We both turned to look at Woolie. "His father's in Greece," she said, as though that explained everything.

"On business?"

"I wouldn't know. I haven't seen him since the conception."

"He run out on you?"

She laughed. "Nobody runs out on me. I left when my mom died."

I didn't know what to say except "Sorry." She waved that away. Everybody in town had known what her mom was like. Dorie had been raised mostly by her grandmother. After a minute's silence Dorie raised her beer. "So, what do you do?"

"Work at a bookstore for an old guy with a bad hip who wants to move to Florida. I run the place, and he putters around."

"What's keeping him here?"

"Books."

"What, he can't bear to part with them?"

"He can't unload them."

"What's the name of this place?" she asked and I told her: "Rare and Used Books. We Buy, Sell, Trade."

"Catchy title. No wonder he's packing them in."

A week later she came to the shop, poked around for a bit, then asked, "You free for lunch?"

We ate at a Vietnamese restaurant on Water Street. "So, Czabek, why don't you buy that musty old store from that musty old guy and go into business for yourself?"

I stood and dog-eared my pockets. Then I sat down again.

"Money," she said, "is not a problem. The question is, can you make a go of a bookstore like that?"

"I don't think I'd want to own a bookstore like that."

"What kind would you want to own?"

I told her. One that sold CDs as well as books, because the two places I liked to linger in were bookstores and record stores. And new stuff, because the margin was better. And there should be stationery, and coffee and pastries, and a decent kids' section. A place where people could just hang out. "More of an intellectual houseboat," I said, "less like a mausoleum."

"And you think you can make a go of this?"

"With the right people, sure. I'd want people who feel about books as I do—that opening a box of books from a publisher or a distributor is like

Christmas morning. You never know what you're going to get, but you know it's going to be special. You don't even look at the invoice until you hold them in your hands, turn them over, sniff them, feel the tangible charge of *yes!* by God, *yes!* This is a *book!* With a staff like that, you'll get all the customers you want."

"Well, I'll tell you what, Czabek. I've got about eight or ten houses I own that are in need of some serious rehabbing, not to mention my own. You help me with the subcontracting—working with all the independent contractors, making sure stuff is actually happening when it's supposed to, and pitching in with some grunt labor when it's not—and I help you with financing your little bookstore. What do you say?"

"I say, Why would you be doing this for me given that I don't know squat about houses?"

"I like you, Czabek. You're the first person who noticed I had a kid who didn't get that Christ-she-has-a-kid look in his eye." She poked around her vegetables and rice with her chopsticks. "Plus I'm pregnant, and in about six months I'm not going to be feeling like doing a whole hell of a lot."

"Oh."

"Don't 'oh' me, Ace. You interested or not?"

We became partners, then lovers, then parents. I would rather not go into what I felt making love to a woman with another man's child already in her belly, and there was an unspoken rule between us that I was not to ask questions re: the fathers of her—our—first two children. She had taken me on as a partner, and my silence was part of the deal. We fixed houses, had Henry, opened the bookstore (Feed Your Head, my choice, was nixed in favor of Van Loon's, the name of her cat), got married, had Sophie. To keep pace with the competition, we eventually opened two more stores and a website. In hindsight, I can see that was a mistake. The website does great with textbook sales, but two of the three stores are floundering and threatening to take down the third; like my father, I'm a victim of my own exuberance.

I also made the mistake of hiring people who were too much like me. If my staff had their druthers, they'd stay in the back indefinitely, opening boxes, marveling at their contents, taking their 10 percent on their greatest treasures, and scooting for home. I have to urge them to wait on people, to take their turns at the cash register. "You're customer service representatives," I tell them. "*Customer service!* Doesn't that mean anything to you?" And my best employee, Jillian Kowalska, a single mom with two kids, early thirties, somebody who really needs this job, tells me, "This place would run a whole lot smoother if we didn't have any customers." "Well," I tell her, "you just may get your wish."

Dorie was busy, too. Tireless. Her days were spent working with tenants, finding buyers for her homes, meeting with folks from neighborhood associations. She had Veedon Park on its way to being "an urban success story," the kind featured in city magazines about neighborhoods on the rebound.

Then, a few years ago, everything changed. Her businesses were fine, but nothing else was. She turned thirty-nine, her father died, and she'd about reached the end of what she hoped to accomplish in the neighborhood. All of this coincided with Sophie turning four and going to halfday kindergarten. We had done the domesticated bliss thing since before Henry, but now Dorie was restless. She mulled a run for city council but decided not to. She spent a lot of time staring out the window. Sighing. She'd look at me, and there was something in her eyes I didn't want to acknowledge was disappointment.

Her thirty-ninth birthday was one of those watershed events better spouses than I know to roll with. She bought a road bike and a mountain bike on consecutive weekends. She started hanging out at REI and the various cycle shops around town. Bookmarked all the online gear and touring sites. Pored over catalogs and magazines and cycling books. Found new friends. Did not seem particularly interested in introducing them to me. Our front hall became a staging area. For training runs she'd bike eighty miles to Madison, stay overnight, then bike back the next day. This anniversary trip for my parents is the first time in months that we've been in the car together for more than twenty minutes.

Dorie marks her place in her magazine with her finger, stares out the window. She asks again, "What was it like for your mom, I wonder?" Then she answers her own question. "If it'd been me, I'd have gone crazy."

We were prosperity babies, but even prosperity has a price. Our mother recognized that when, just moments removed from her victory over the lascivious border guard, she burst into tears and our father had to pull off the road to console her. "It's over," our mother kept repeating as she wept. "It's over, it's all over."

What did this mean? Our father didn't have a clue. How could he? The most he'd had to deal with our mother during the last four years was a week or two on his leaves, and most of that time was spent in bed making little Czabeks. Billy Ray King would have been pleased.

"What?" our father asked our mother. "What's all over? What?"

Between bouts of weeping our mother sobbed, *"E-e-e-e-e-ver-ry-y-y-y-thing!"*

When confronted with female weeping, men generally are at a loss. The most they can do is offer perplexed comfort, stroking hair and shoulders, kissing foreheads, whispering, "There, there" and "It's all right," as though they know what the matter is when frequently it is their not knowing, their absolute ignorance, and/or their inability to intuit or ferret out what's wrong that is the problem's root. Our father was a prince in the principality of not knowing.

Another truism: Men like facts; women prefer feelings. Men like facts so much they are comforted by them even when the facts are against them. "Just give me the facts," men say. "Give it to me straight, I can handle it." Men like facts so much that what most people would consider opinion men turn into facts: "These are the cold hard facts," a man will say, when what he's just voiced is his own dubious view of a situation open to any number of interpretations. Women do the same thing, but there's no alchemy involved: "That's just how I *feel,*" a woman says, and the wall she puts up with her feelings is as solid and unscalable as anything a man puts together with his Erector set of facts. What women do that men don't is allow their feelings to change. Facts, being hard, impenetrable objects, do not change. A man will not allow that to happen. A wall of feeling, on the other hand, can be disassembled. Our father, therefore, wanted to know what the facts were, at least as they pertained to him. He stayed away from what he couldn't know, couldn't intuit, and for him the facts were these:

For most of the past four years he had been serving his country. For the second time, the second war. The first one he had lied his way into. Well, not exactly lied. He'd joined the Coast Guard at seventeen; his mother had signed for him. She thought he'd guard the Chicago River or something. Early in the war she'd seen Coast Guard boats slip upriver. She'd thought he'd do that. Pilot a patrol boat upriver and be home each evening for dinner. She wasn't far off. But when the war ended his ship was designated a troop transport—all over the globe troops were waiting to come home. So off he went through the Suez Canal to Egypt, to the Philippines, to India, to Japan, and back home by way of Hawaii. He made several of these trips before he was mustered out and met our mother. He stayed in the reserves, though, and when Korea heated up he received his commission. But spent only part of his hitch in Korea. He was called up while the French were losing their taste for colonialism, and as they were pulling out of French Indochina (now emerging as the politically schizophrenic Vietnam), his ship was assigned the task of evacuating citizens from North to South, and vice versa. Years later, as our own country became mired in that debacle, and sentiment for and against the war was waged in the streets and in newspapers and on television sets, our father always nailed shut his end of the argument by saying, "Look, bucko, I was there. In 'fifty-four and 'fifty-five, when the French were pulling out."

He also suffered a double ulcer and got shipped stateside for treatment. Like many of the boats in the "mothball fleet"—ships used in World War II that were put back in service first for Korea and later for Vietnam—his was understaffed, and the junior grade officers picked up the slack. Our father was in charge of a landing boat, a gunnery crew, served as the ship's decoder, the morale officer, and a medic, his time usually spent giving penicillin shots to men returning from leave— the men having found their own means of raising their morale. One of his men had had his morale raised so high he went AWOL and got court-martialed. Fallen in love, the man said. Love, said our father. Right. To make sure the man remembered his indiscretion, our father dropped the syringe needle point first on the table—plonk! plonk! plonk!—before giving him his shot. Then our father got him off on a technicality. That kept the man from being dishonorably discharged, but afterward our father was continually passed over for promotion. The Navy, like an elephant, never forgets. The accumulated stress, coupled with the ingestion of quarts and quarts of black coffee, ate not one but two holes in his stomach, and since his being shipped stateside coincided with the end of his four-year hitch, he decided it was time to become a civilian again, start being a daddy to his two kids, and start being a husband to his wife.

His wife, who had done what exactly during these past four years while he was serving his country? He didn't know. He had ensconced her before he shipped out in a one-bedroom ranch linked by a shaded walkway to the larger Mission-style ranch in front of it. The owner, an elderly woman named Mrs. Mapole, had lost a son early in the Second World War. She and her husband, a machinist from Chicago, had moved out here after the war and had hoped her son's wife would move into the guesthouse, but the daughter-in-law had stayed among her own people. Mr. Mapole had suffered a stroke and was rarely seen. Our parents' rent helped cover expenses. Our father thought Mrs. Mapole could help with the babies and provide company for our mother, and vice versa.

It was a fine philosophy when prescribed for other people. For our mother it was a death sentence. She liked the house with its sweeping lawn and its views (it was set on a hill above San Diego Bay, and the street, gracious and old, was lined with palms)—she could see the ships enter and leave the harbor, and watch the planes take off from the Naval Air Station at Coronado across the bay—but she would have been happier being right on base with the other wives.

That's about all we know of our mother's story from that time. Our father talks of his war years constantly, and we have his ship's yearbooks, which chronicle his travels, but we know next to nothing from our mother's perspective. I'm thinking of this as I hand another little stack of photos over to Dorie: our mother sitting on the big expanse of lawn with first one child and then two, our mother and Nomi, our mother's mother, holding Sarah, who's trying to walk while clutching Nomi's and our mother's index fingers in her chubby little fists.

Dorie flips through them, saying, "You know what these remind me of? The aftermath of that famous photograph by Elliott Erwitt. You know the one I'm talking about? It's called *California Kiss* or something, and it's like from the mid-fifties and it's in black and white and what you see is just part of the flank of one of those rounded fifties-bodied cars, the kind with the round rearview mirror, you know, that perfect circle, and there's a couple kissing with the woman's head thrown back, and her mouth's open and her eyes are on the sky, and her husband or whoever she's with is mooching her neck, and in the background is the sun setting over the ocean and all you see in that moment are possibility and romance. It's like they're so into the moment they don't have a clue what's coming down the pike at them, and even if you told them, right at that moment it wouldn't matter anyway. They wouldn't believe you."

I nod like I understand—and I do—but Dorie catches the consternation on my face.

"What, Ace, you don't believe me? You didn't like what I said, what?"

What bothers me is the offhand way Dorie said, "and her husband or whoever she's with." That's what bugs me, but I can't say that. I wonder about the way women can hold things in about themselves, can lead two lives, a hidden one and the one everyone can see, and the only clues to the hidden life are when something bubbles, however obliquely, to the surface. It's popular to ascribe this dual life to men, but being married to Dorie, I know better. But because she's so good at living this dual life with equanimity, I doubt I'll ever know what's going on in the life she's kept hidden from me. All I can do is wonder, just as I wonder now why our mother, in driving back to Chicago, would burst into spontaneous weeping soon after the border guard let her and her contraband fruit out of California.

Our mother claims that this was a singular occurrence, a stray moment when her feelings overwhelmed her—it was hot, she was pregnant with me—and she was fine after that, she just needed to compose herself. And we would believe her except our parents are great rewriters of their own history, our mother more so since she has few documents to contradict her. Our father, prompted by a ship's yearbook or photograph, can slip back into exactly how he felt when that photo was taken, and even if the memory has too much rose around the edging, you get the feeling that for him it probably did feel pretty much that way. For him everything was a big adventure.

Our mother, though, when confronted with a picture, edits. You can see it on her face, in the struggle on her lips, the slight misting in the eyes—she feels something intensely but can't bring herself to say *that*, whatever it was she was feeling. "Oh, *this*," she'll say, biting her lip, "this is from when Darlene and I went up to Point Loma and the Sunset Cliffs." The photo is of two silhouettes and what is probably a brilliant sunset, but rendered in black and white you can't tell. What you can tell is that one of the silhouettes, our mother's, is clearly pregnant. "It was before Sarah was born," our mother says, and you can hear in her voice a trace of longing, a trace of disappointment. "Darlene was pregnant, too, only you can't see it yet," and we wonder: in addition to missing their men, what did they talk about? The babies growing inside them, yes, but what else? Did our mother feel a connection to this woman, did they feel they shared something, their blood thickening, their breasts getting fuller, their bellies distending, the bloat in their hands and ankles, the dark circles under their eyes, did they feel marked, set apart, bonded? They were taking part in an age-old ritual—women great with child going up the headlands to stare out at the sea over which their men had disappeared. Yet didn't they also feel left out? Central, yet extraneous? Mere vessels, their personalities erased by their function, by the ritual itself? Wasn't our mother suffused with loss even before she knew that loss was what she felt? You can't tell unless you read into the photographs, those game grins our mother has, straining at the corners of her mouth to keep the smile in place for the camera, not letting it shatter, and the eyes, the eyes full up to bursting with squelched desires, with bitten-back thoughts.

What is it that she's leaving out? That she had no friends? That the women on the base had a camaraderie they extended to our mother only when they infrequently remembered her? That Mrs. Mapole, rather than being a comfort, was needy, dependent, and a little off, always dropping by for coffee and a monologue on her dead son, lost at sea (not exactly what our mother wanted to hear), and a different monologue on her husband, whose stroke had left him paralyzed and unable to communicate, a thin rope of drool hanging from his mouth while Mrs. Mapole talked to him, as she did to our mother, as though the listener weren't there. Our mother, therefore, had a double burden, her kids and her landlady. "Hey, can I have a minute?" Mrs. Mapole would say, and that would be the end of the morning. Is it any wonder that Nomi came to visit? That our mother was desperate for company who might inquire as to how she was feeling? That our mother was going stir-crazy, a polite euphemism for going crazy period?

"I cried all day today," our mother wrote our father at one point. "I don't know why, I suppose I must have been missing you." She goes on to other things in the letter, private things, but the tone is of a woman who has ascribed a cause to her feelings that she doesn't believe but is trying to convince herself is true.

When we ask our mother what were her happiest moments in San Diego, she will say, "Happiest moments?" as though it would be a struggle to recall any. Then she'll say, "Besides your father coming home?" and she'll pause again before telling us that the moments she recalls most fondly are the laying-in periods at the base hospital after she gave birth to Sarah and Robert Aaron. "The maternity stays at the base hospital?" Sarah asks. Our mother explains. "They had you lay in for a week back then, and there might be fifteen or twenty of us, all pregnant from the same shore leave, all giving birth within days of each other. We didn't even see the babies that much. The nurses did the feeding—this was in the bottle days, remember. We were to rest and recuperate, and we talked, and played games, and laughed." Except for the fact that they were mostly officers' wives (didn't enlisted people get married and have families?), our mother almost made it sound like it was a dormitory for unwed mothers. As though it were a bit of a lark, and once you got past giving birth essentially alone (military doctors being notorious for their requirement that births be as convenient as possible for them, the mother's comfort a distant secondary concern), it was like a party. Our mother goes misty-eyed on us. She did like parties. She'd been pretty, vivacious, gregarious, a young woman feeding on the energy of a bustling city like Chicago in the late forties and early fifties, dating a half dozen men at once and keeping track of them like beads on a string. What was it like for our mother suddenly to give all that up? To settle down with just one man and then not even to have the man? In the months before marrying him, she dropped out of school and got a job as an assistant to the ad manager at radio station WCHI. She wrote copy for supermarket ads, for car dealerships, for hardware and housewares stores, even for the big department stores. She was smart, good with words. If she'd stayed at the station she might have wound up in charge of PR. She had dropped out so she could help our father, a mediocre student at best, get through school. She wrote papers for him, double-checked lab reports. She did this willingly, believing that a little bit of her was in everything she did for him. After work she could go out for a drink with her girlfriends, or meet our father and his bandmates for dinner, then spend the evening in a whirl of music and dancing, singing and romance.

And now how did she spend her nights? Listening to the radio, turning pages in a newspaper, walking the night away with a colicky baby who spat cheese down her shoulder. Your best dresses all smelling of curdled milk. Your evenings spent sterilizing bottles and fake nipples. Meanwhile your own nipples were sore, full to bursting, and you just had to make the best of it. You had to make the best of everything, even if there was nothing special to make. Your hands chapped from wringing out diapers in borax, your hair brittle, the shine gone out of it, your figure a mess, and your insides slipping out of you every time you had to pee.

I don't think it's an accident that on the leave before our father's last trip to the Far East our mother was the only officer's wife who didn't get pregnant. This wasn't like the previous leave, when the captain decided the men could take their wives to Hawaii for two weeks' R & R and the whole ship got pregnant, even the old man's wife, and she was forty. This time our father was in port three weeks, and our mother, fertile as always, didn't pop like she usually did. "Wassamatter, Wally, your equipment ain't workin'?" fellow officers teased him as they started getting letters, one after the other, about the new bundles of joy on the way, and our father got letters of yearning that remained politely silent on the subject of buns in the oven.

Had our mother denied him access? Had she followed the old wives' advice about douching in vinegar and sitting in hot baths after sex? Our mother's not saying. She is amazingly reticent about the last few years in San Diego, as though her thoughts and feelings had gone into hibernation while she waited for our father to come home. Still, the largest gap in our family between siblings (before our mother's body started slowing down) is between Robert Aaron and myself, and I was a mandatory pregnancy—our father coming home, sick and weak, suffering from a double ulcer, his weight below one thirty, being mustered out, his time up—how could our mother not welcome him home in the one way that would surely please him?

If you asked, our mother would admit to none of this. She rarely admitted to our father that she had ever been depressed at all. She was a gamer, our mother was, and once she got over a funk she refused to admit she'd been in one. "I was just a little out of sorts." It was amazing to watch her, as we grew up, determined always to make the best of things, regardless of how she felt. She rewrote history as she went, removing the rubble from how she used to feel so the new edifice could exist quite prettily on its own terms.

One wonders: Was her weeping on Route 66 a giddiness that her loneliness was behind her, that she was now embarking on a new and real life with our father, one in which she would have, finally, a partner? Or was it that, for all her sadness, she had finally gotten used to being alone, and had our father not returned she'd have been an anomaly, certainly, a single mother in the fifties, but she also would have been her own woman, and she could have carved out a life for herself as she saw fit, and not simply tagged along behind our father's cockamamie schemes, the wedding on television being only the first? And instead she saw the future—the arrival of which she could not have waited for impatiently enough—suddenly closed to her, rendered familiar, expected, ordinary. Par for the course, our father would say about expected outcomes, be they good or ill. How our mother had once longed to be anything but par for the course!

She was better by the time they got to Chicago. Somewhere along that long drive back, with fruit by her feet, she readjusted herself to the presence of our father. Readjusted herself to the new realities. She was going to start over on new turf, and once she got used to this new fact, which is to say, to our father's way of thinking, she'd be fine.

It was, however, a long drive. One that took them past every landmark they'd seen on the way out, only they were seeing them in reverse, as though they had slipped into their rearview mirror and were seeing things from their mirror's perspective. "It's déjà vu all over again," Yogi Berra once announced. Exactly. And just as she had on the drive out, our mother threw up on every cactus and cornstalk they passed.

3. The House That God Built

SIX OF ONE, HALF A
DOZEN OF ANOTHER

The fifties don't make a whole lot of sense to anybody who didn't live through the preceding decade. For my siblings and me, that the lot of us were born in a dozen-year span starting nine months after our parents' nuptials—seven of us spat out like so many watermelon seeds—seems unfathomable. (Watermelon seeds—our father's view, not our mother's. "Watermelon seeds, Wally? Try giving birth to a water*melon*.")

Besides having us, they were also getting a house built. After his discharge our father was out of work. A lieutenant JG with a B.S. in biology and skill with an accordion was qualified for what? He was returning home to find out. Only Grandma and Grandpa Cza-Cza wouldn't have him. Or rather, they wouldn't have his wife and *her* children, as though our mother had picked us up somewhere, like a cold. They'd just bought a house in Morton Grove, a three-bedroom ranch, and there simply wouldn't be enough room for five more people—I was due any day—while our father got on his feet. Our father was welcome, provided he came alone. So our parents moved into Nomi and Artu's two-bedroom apartment on the Near North Side above a Thom McAn shoe store. While our father looked for work, Nomi and Susan Marie took the kids in a double stroller on long walks—to the Lincoln Park Zoo, to Lake Shore Park and Washington Square, to the river, to Navy Pier.

Our mother, as much as she was able, was getting her life back. It was not so different from her life in San Diego—Lake Michigan subbing for the Pacific Ocean, with more wind and snow and cold—but she had a companion now to whom she could talk about movies and plays and music. She had once shared all that with our father, but then he'd gone away, and his leaves had been so infrequent and intense—they literally launched themselves into bed upon his return and emerged only days later, stunned, disheveled, in need of orange juice and vitamins—that she'd lost it. Now she was getting it back. She felt good. Better than she had in years.

It helped, too, that she was over her nausea with me. Her belly was a fine round thing. Our father would come home in the evenings, usually after "a quick stop with the boys," and pat our mother's belly—this was the first birth he'd be around for—and our mother would beam. She ignored the raised eyebrows of her parents, who disapproved of our father's frequent nights out. Our father's old bandmates gathered at a downtown watering hole after spending their days selling insurance, or shuffling paper, or looking in people's mouths. The Navy had trained Louie Hwasko as a dentist, and now he had a private practice, which he was moving to Caledonia, out near Rockford. He'd bought five acres of land, on which he was building a dream house for his wife, who amazingly enough, was our mother's friend Helen Federstam. They'd gotten married the year previous, and our father and Louie now spent nights at the Deluxe, talking about their new occupations as country gentlemen and husbands. Our mother made allowances for this—he was just out of the military, just reunited with friends and family, he was entitled to blow off a little steam. Mostly, though, she liked having him around, liked the proprietary pat on her belly.

One of the things they liked to do in the evening was look at their house plans. Our father had found work as a detail man for Dinkwater-Adams, a pharmaceutical company based in Dinkwater Park, New Jersey. His job was to travel all over greater Chicagoland, calling on doctors, hospitals, and pharmacies, and pitch the Dinkwater-Adams line of pharmaceuticals and hospital supplies. And while the company certainly wanted him to work the downtown and Near North Side, they saw the future in the suburbs.

Which was fine with our parents. They'd been dreaming of owning their own house since they first started taking the trolley out to Butterfield and York Road. Elmhurst was perfect for them, a new suburb recently carved out of the prairie and one of the last stops on the trolley line. In picking this hamlet they thought—like thousands of other young couples making the postwar move to the suburbs—that Walter would take the trolley to work. The interstate would soon put an end to that, though, and our father would instead spend all his time on the highway.

Now the house was becoming a reality. A loan for the down payment from Nomi and Artu, a VA loan, and some help from Ernie Klapatek, who'd gone into construction with his father. It would be finished in January. Our father often drove out there, eating his lunch and drinking coffee from a thermos as he watched the house take shape before his eyes.

Charlie Podgazem, Dad's old drummer, was now working for Ernie Klapatek. He was in charge at the site. Sometimes he'd come over to our father's car, take out a hip flask, and add "a little taste" to our father's coffee. "You're in good hands, Czabek," Charlie told him, and our father nodded agreement. It was nice knowing you were in good hands. Then our father came home after stopping for "a quick one with Louie" and repeated this slogan to our mother. Our mother had heard it before. Benny Wilkerson, the Cicero Velvetones' bass player, sold for Allstate now. Their homeowner's and life insurance would be handled by him, which pissed off Bernie Zanoni, the clarinet player, who sold for Prudential. But you couldn't please everybody, could you? "At least let me do the car insurance," Bernie said. "Can't," said our father. "It's a company car. Company insurance. Some outfit out of New Jersey." "Criminy," said Bernie. Our father said he understood, it was just Benny got to him first.

On weekends our parents drove out to the home site and Walter guided a very pregnant Susan Marie around the stacks of lumber and brick. Inside they walked from one unfinished room to the next, stepping around coiled wire and cut pieces of flashing and ductwork. Upstairs they checked on the skeletons of the bedroom and sewing room, the bones of the bath. They pulled down the stair that led to the attic, and our father poked his head up inside, announcing to our mother, who was waiting below, that they'd done a very good job indeed with the insulation.

Just before one of their site visits, our mother discovered a problem. She had been going over the blueprints for the umpteenth time with Nomi and Artu. "See, here's the back bedroom for the children—it'll be huge—and the front bedroom, which I can use as a sewing room, and between is the upstairs bath and this large storage area." She started with the second floor because it contained the sewing room, which simply meant it was a room where she could be alone from time to time—something that seemed more precious now that seven and a half people were living in a two-bedroom apartment. "And here's the front entrance—we'll line that with shrubs and flowers out to the walk—and the living room, like so." Which was when she realized something was wrong. "Wally-Bear, isn't the front entrance supposed to be in front?" Her finger tapped the blueprint. Wally-Bear came over. "Yes, yes it is," said Wally-Bear.

"But when we were at the house last time, weren't the doors cut for side entrances?"

Our father closed his eyes. He was trying to picture it. Nomi and Artu exchanged glances. "Yes, I think you're right, they are," our father said, his eyes still closed. Then he opened them. "It's amazing you noticed a little thing like that."

Our mother exploded. "A little thing, Wally? A little thing? They're building the house sideways, those drunken little shits!" Our mother burst into tears. She was never very good at swearing. She always either hesitated before she said a swearword or clipped it short, swallowing whatever effect she'd intended. Sometimes when she was really angry it came out sounding like she was amused instead. How could you take a woman seriously who sounded like she didn't know how to swear? "Maybe we're misremembering," our father said. "Maybe we're the ones who have it sideways. Tomorrow we'll check and see."

The next day confirmed it. They arranged to meet Ernie and Charlie at the site. Our mother took one look at the doorless brick facing, with two windows that looked like wide-set eyes—this was clearly the side of the house, yet it was facing the street—and shrieked. She tumbled out of the car, stumbled over the packed dirt, our father ineffectively trying to guide and comfort her as she circled the house once, twice, thrice. Ernie pulled up in his Buick Skylark, and Charlie showed up in a Ford Fairlane soon after. Charlie took in the sight of our mother weeping and said, "Holy shit, I had it sideways." Then he shook out a Lucky Strike and said philosophically, "Well, it's six of one, half a dozen of another."

Ernie, in his best the-customer-is-always-right voice said, "No, Charlie. It's not."

Our father held our mother to his chest and patted her hair and said, "Hey, hey. Hey, hey, it's okay. It's gonna be okay, really." But even he seemed to know that now was not the time to echo Charlie Podgazem's "It's six of one, half a dozen of another."

Our mother was with Ernie Klapatek on this one. "No, it's not," she wailed. "It's not, it's not. My house, my beautiful house! It's ruined!"

"I musta read the blueprints wrong," said Charlie Podgazem. "That happens sometimes."

"It only happens when you're drunk," said our mother.

"Hey, that's no way to be, Susan. I make mistakes, sure, but it's not like I'm doin' it on purpose."

"You're drunk right now," said our mother.

Charlie pulled himself very erect and tugged at the belt around his waist. "Only a little."

Ernie pulled our father aside. Time to salvage what he could. Wiping his glasses, he said, "Wally, no question we got a problem. The question, though, is what are we gonna do about it?"

Our mother heard that. "What are *we* going to do about it? *We* are going to fix it, that's what *we* are going to do about it."

"It's not that simple, Susan." Ernie tipped his head, meaning our father should follow him. This was man talk. They went around back. Our mother stood looking at what should have been the back and was instead the side entrance. She was inconsolable.

Around in back, Ernie lit a Chesterfield and dragged his toe in the dirt. "Much as I'd like to help the little lady, there's not a whole lot I can do. Fact is, it's more complicated than simply taking down some bricks and cutting a new doorway. Fact is, Charlie turned the whole damn design sideways. Fact is, I can't just pick the thing up off the foundation and spin it ninety degrees to set it right now, can I? Charlie messed up, but it's not easy to fix, you understand?"

"Why don't you just say that to Susan?"

"I'm going to, Wally, but I just wanted us to be in agreement first, you see? The men wear the pants in your family, right? What I say to Susan— hey, that's only mollification. You're the guy I've got to win over here, right, big guy?"

Ernie was preaching to the converted. Fact is, even without Ernie's speech our father would have been content to let the whole thing drop. "Six of one, half a dozen of another," our father believed, as though that kind of stoicism solved everything.

"So what are you going to say to Susan?"

"Same thing I said to you, only more so. I'll explain the positives of this kind of arrangement—and hey, there are a lot of them, as you already understand." He put his hand on our father's shoulder. "And you, Wally, are one guy I knew would understand."

"You don't know Susan. She's going to want something to sweeten the deal."

"Sweeten the deal?"

"You know, to make up for turning our house sideways."

Ernie Klapatek got a hard look on his face, as though he were about to say something terrible, but then his eyes softened and he grinned. Our father relaxed a little. Whatever the terrible thing was that Ernie was contemplating, it had passed. But Ernie's grin still had an edge to it. "Hey, hey, Wally, let's make nice here. There's no reason, no reason in the world that we can't work this out to everybody's satisfaction. You got a sideways house you don't like. Fine, don't buy it. You think you're the only one wants to buy a house? I got people stacked three deep here waiting on these houses." He dropped his voice again. "Why you think I hired a Joe Schlepperman like Podgazem in the first place, eh? I got house orders to fill, I need people. It was either him or hire a colored, okay? Besides, I did this as a favor to you. And it's not the first time. The guy could barely keep his sticks straight when we were in the band together, right? But he was from your neighborhood so I said, fine, he's Wally's friend, he's in the band even if he can't tell his drumsticks from his wipehole. And now he's done a number on your house. Okay, I'm sorry. My mistake, I hired him. But it was as a favor to you, okay?"

Our father was dumbfounded. Ernie Klapatek—friend, bandmate, member of his wedding party—was threatening to sell his house out from under him! And acting like it was his own fault it was happening.

Ernie was still grinning. "Hey, hey, Wally. I see by the look on your face you're taking this personal. We can work this out, really. I want to see you in that house, I do. And I understand about Susan. She needs to feel like we're making restitution. It can't be changed, but she wants something to make up for that. I understand. It's a human enough desire. But, hey, Wally, it's not like you're gonna go to court on me because one of your friends messed up, right? Even though your friend messed up, I stand behind every one of my houses. And you are a friend. I take that serious. So here's what we're gonna do . . ."

Wally got the feeling that all this talk was just buying Ernie Klapatek time to figure out what he was going grab out of his ass next, but to our father, that was okay. In the curious world of our father's logic, a man who reached big was allowed to break the rules. This was true in the military— you got away with whatever you could get away with. And it was true, too, when he got married—Billy Ray King foisting his pregnant daughter off on a national TV audience, and giving her and her lout of a boy-friend the wedding presents destined for him and our mother. And it was true now that he was buying a house somebody else had bungled the building of. Ernie Klapatek was going to get what he wanted because he was willing to reach for it rather than simply desire it. Wanting alone got you nothing. It was the size of the reach that mattered. Our father, never possessing this quality himself, was always in awe of the people who did.

Wally was listening to what Ernie was telling him, but he wasn't really listening. He was nodding agreement. He was still nodding when Ernie led him back to Susan and started telling her how it was. How a house turned sideways like that could be a good feature. "Lots of people have carports on the sides of their homes. Haven't you seen those big places in Lake Forest and Oak Park? They have side entrances and they build a roof, even a whole room, right above where they park." Would Ernie be willing to do such a thing to make this right? our mother wanted to know. Well, no, he couldn't do that, he was already doing this house at not much above cost as a favor to our father. If he added anything he'd have to charge them, and in some ways maybe he should do that, but he wasn't going to. Not to mention it wouldn't look right. This was a nice house, but a porte cochere—that's what they called those carports on big houses—would look out of place here among these ranches and bunga-lows.

So what *was* he going to do? our mother wanted to know.

Well, said Ernie, taking off his glasses and wiping them. He was going to do something equally wonderful.

And what would that be? asked our mother.

Leave it the way it was, and let it grow on them, said Ernie Klapatek. Then if they didn't like it he could come back and do something else for them. Like what? asked our mother. Finish off the basement, said Ernie. In a few years they might want a pool table down there, and it would look better if the basement were finished.

Or, said Ernie Klapatek, if they really, really didn't like the house as it was, they could tear up the deed to purchase and wait for the next house, but they'd have to wait at the end of the line. He had people lined up as it was for houses, here and all over. People were crazy for houses outside the city. This was a nice house, sideways or not, and he'd like to see them happy in it, and frankly it'd be their own damn fault if the house ended up being sold to somebody else.

"It's a nice house, sideways or not," Charlie Podgazem echoed.

"Shut up, Charlie," said our mother. While Ernie and our father were out back, our mother had considered the other three sides from every angle. Charlie Podgazem was her shadow, his belly as big as our mother's. Our mother had got over crying, and Charlie had not said a word during her swings back and forth. He was afraid she'd either start crying again or bite his head off. Once she regained her composure, he was right to fear the latter.

Our mother turned to our father. "What do you think, Wally? And if you say, 'Six of one, half a dozen of another,' I'll scream."

That took away our father's greatest weapon: the cliché that said nothing, that smoothed over everything. Not that it mattered. Even before he said, "I think we should let it ride," our mother knew he was going to. He simply did not, could not understand. For him the sideways house was fine, just fine. The driveway was on the side. It simply meant they'd have more yard.

Ernie Klapatek shook our parents' hands and drove away. Charlie Podgazem tipped his hat to our father and half-smiled at our mother—he did not dare shake her hand—and drove away as well. Our father folded his wife in his arms and said it was going to be okay.

But it was not okay to our mother. Oh, sure, they were moving to Elmhurst. But their house was sideways! Her kitchen, instead of looking out into the backyard, would look into the neighbor's bedroom; her living room, instead of looking onto the street and the elms that lined it, would look into the other neighbor's driveway. Wally-Bear wouldn't notice because he wouldn't be home often enough to care. Wally-Bear didn't understand because his yearnings were simply for a house he could call his own. He didn't understand the concept of perfect family happiness that should exist inside the egg of that house. This was supposed to be the house that God built in the spot God had ordained they should live their lives. The house that God built, dammit, not the house that Charlie Podgazem built sideways!

Too late, too late, she realized that tears—her promises to herself that she would not cry notwithstanding—were streaming down her face. And there was Wally, telling her, There, there, there, there, it was okay, it was—all, all of it, in its entirety—going to be okay. And the thing of it was, she believed him. That was the problem: that it was going to be okay. Not perfect, not grand, not magnificent, not dreamlike, not anything but okay.

4. The Kaopectate Wars

THAT'LL PUT HAIR
BETWEEN YOUR TOES

There is a toll that marriage exacts for those who believe in it—a slow rubbing away of the individual soul—and that is perhaps why, at a certain point in a marriage, people question what the hell they are doing in it. And the union itself? I don't know. Lately with Dorie, I don't know much. But I can say with some certainty that Wally and Susan Marie Czabek moved, with three children, into a house dropped sideways at 747 Swain Avenue in January 1957, and that all their troubles at first seemed surmountable. Our mother, after her argument with Ernie Klapatek, did what countless women who have lost one of the big and intangible arguments of their marriages have done for centuries: She cried and moved on. She set about making that bare house, so new you could still smell the paint, the drywall, and the cement in the basement, a home. Her home. She hung curtain rods, sewed sheets with pleated gatherings for curtains, bought a horizontal freezer for the basement, a Norge refrigerator and GE stove for the kitchen.

They were broke, they were saddled with debt, they were happy. That, anyway, was what they wanted us to believe. And even when we had inklings that they weren't happy, our parents worked hard to keep us from knowing. They worked hard to keep from knowing it themselves, too, until the night when a dollar bill and a bout with the flu yanked things into focus.

It's easy to understand how things before that weren't in focus. In a little over eight years they packed that house with four more kids. How in God's name could they have managed to focus on anything? Here's how we stacked up:

Sarah (Sarah Lucinda—1953)
Robert Aaron (he was always called by both names—1954)
Emcee (that's me, Emil Cedric, what were they thinking?—1956)
Ike (James Eisenhower, what were they thinking II?—1958)
Wally Jr. (Walter Sr. finally gets his wish—1960)
Ernie (Ernest John, sounds like a variety of Van Camp's pork and beans—1963)
Peggy (Megan Sue, born with one leg shorter than the other—1965)

As our father observed, two girls separated by a basketball team. It was unfair to the girls, having that many boys in a row. We ganged up on them, ignored them. Sarah Lucinda, feeling romantic, wanted to be called Lucy, after the heroine in the Chronicles of Narnia, but we called her Cinderella.

She spent a lot of time hiding from us, and she was doing exactly that when Peggy found the door to the basement open and tumbled down the stairs, breaking her hip and making the shortness of the one leg more pronounced. Peg Leg Meg, we called her. It drove her to tears. Calling Sarah Cinderella drove her to tears, too. "Stop that!" our mother told us when they ran to her crying, their own cries to get us to stop having proved futile. But how could we? We loved Peg. We loved Sarah. We had to torment them beyond reason.

It was, to be sure, a male world. The neighborhood was filled with men like our father, all working nine to five, and housewives like our mother. The men were recently quit of the Korean War or WWII, and these were their first houses. They'd gotten educated on the G.I. Bill, married their high school or college sweethearts, and were happy to be affiliated with their employers, to do good work, and to come home and pump out kids as fast as their wives were able. They joined men's service organizations and clubs—the Kiwanis, the Loyal Order of Moose, the Elks, the Shriners, the American Legion—and went to church on Sunday morning. They drank on Friday night, watched the fights Saturday night, bowled Wednesdays. Their wives got driver's licenses and went to Kroger's or even to downtown Chicago. They drank coffee midmorning, watched their kids, did laundry. They spent an inordinate amount of time on the phone talking about the quotidian events of their day as though rehashing them would make them go away. It was the only therapy they could afford. They bought books with accompanying records: *How to Belly Dance for Your Husband, How to Make Love to Your Husband.* These men and their wives were pioneers on a new plain, and they watched with satisfaction as backhoes and bulldozers chewed up the sod for their homesteads and churches.

What made things interesting for us kids were the exceptions, the people not quite like us. The old folks at the end of the block who had no children. The Japanese family, the Kuras, whose kids we rarely saw—their parents kept an even tighter rein on them than our parents did. The only inkling we had that their ethnicity was an issue was when our mother, speaking to Mrs. Duckwa next door, said of the Kuras, who declined invitations to eat rotisseried chicken in various backyards, "They lost the war, you know, that's why they're so quiet." "Well," said Mrs. Duckwa, "the husband is awfully cute. It's too bad he's so short."

The Duckwas were interesting because Mr. Duckwa had served in the previous war, in the Pacific, so he was older than our father by about a decade, and they had only one child, a teenage daughter, who wouldn't speak to us. She was so far removed from us in age that she existed on another planet. The Duckwas were the true pioneers, the scouts, in our neighborhood. They'd built first, a muddy brown brick bungalow, and when things started going kablowies in the neighborhood, they were the point family, the family where things happened first.

Finally, there was Ollie Cicerelli, whose mother, Olive, was divorced. This was by far the oddest thing. In our neighborhood families did not get divorced.

It was just an accident that the exceptions lived near us. Surrounding us mostly were families like ours: large, Catholic, recent inhabitants of Chicago. The Kemmels had seven, like us, and the Hemmelbergers six. Only Olive Cicerelli and the Duckwas had single kids.

I don't know what life was like in these other families; we were rarely inside their houses. Moms sent kids out to play with instructions not to come back in unless you were sick, hurt, or it was time to eat. Ours was one of the few who relented. This leniency made her a marked woman in the neighborhood. "Go play at the Czabeks'," moms told their kids, knowing they wouldn't be back until lunch, and maybe not even then if they'd filled up enough on apples and peanut butter at our house. We also went through vast quantities of Tang, which our mother didn't like to serve because it was expensive, but Tang, having been on the Mercury flights, was like cocaine for ten-year-olds.

The reason all these women let their children run free across the neighborhood was that they believed they could. And the reason our mother became babysitter to the neighborhood was that she didn't. Or rather, she both believed and didn't believe that things were as safe as they appeared. Better if we played with our friends in the backyard, or out on the street where she could keep an eye on us. These other women had moved out of Chicago for that very reason—so they wouldn't have to keep an eye on anyone. Sure, there were other backyards where we were welcome, other moms who occasionally doled out treats, but there was a general sense among us that nobody was watching. Or perhaps it was that we never had the feeling of being watched, except by our mother. I think she was still scared that things could happen to us. That badness could reach out and grab us. So when you got that radar feeling at the back of your neck you'd look up, and there in the back bedroom window (it should have been the kitchen window, but thanks to Charlie Podgazem it wasn't) was our mother's head, a look on her face that was so filled with—what? longing? love? bitterness? despair? loneliness? tenderness? fear?—that had we known what it actually was it would have broken our hearts. Instead it made us feel creepy.

"They're asleep."

I glance over my shoulder. Dorie's right. Sophie's slumped into Henry, whose mouth is open, his head vibrating against the window. He can sleep anywhere. Woolie, headphones still in place, has his head tilted back as though his mouth is waiting for rain. "Finally."

"Finally? I thought you wanted to tell the kids the story of your parents' marriage."

"I thought I did, too. But I don't think I'm telling it for them. I mean, look at Woolie. Have you ever seen a kid less interested in this stuff? They aren't his grandparents, and even if they were, so what? And Sophie and Henry, what do they understand about this stuff?" What I don't tell her: maybe I'm trying to pull all this together in the belief that, explaining what happened with our parents, I can similarly explain what's happened to Dorie and me.

"So tell it to me, Ace."

"You're tired of hearing it from them."

"They can't tell it right anymore. Once upon a time they could, but somewhere along the way they lost it. Everything reminds your father of his time aboard ship, and your mother would rather tell you what she ate last Wednesday at Denny's than enlighten you as to how she managed to stay married to your father." Dorie pats my hand. "Maybe you'll tell it better. Not just the cutesy stuff, but everything in between."

"Right now I could use the how-to-stay-married-to-your-partner advice."

More hand patting. Sometimes I want to scream. "Don't worry, Em, we'll make it."

"What makes you say that?"

She pats my hand again. "I found a cure for my restlessness."

A cure for her restlessness. That's a good one. That's priceless. Hilarious. She's found a cure for her restlessness. Her restlessness. Her fucking restlessness.

More with the hand patting. I take my hand off my lap, go with the ten-and-two grip on the steering wheel. She leaves her hand on my thigh for a few minutes, then moves it. A few more miles like this one, the car filled with the tension of our silence.

"Hon," she says, "what's up?"

I concentrate on my driving.

"Ace, you can't have a mute marriage. You want to talk about something? Talk."

Talk. She makes it sound so simple. Talk. Now she wants to talk. What I want to tell her is, I've been thinking about when you were first "restless."

Why was everything in our conversations appearing in quote marks, as though all those words were euphemisms? Answer: Because they probably were. Her "restlessness" first appeared the year her father died. She'd been withdrawn, depressed, not interested in much of anything. Like the lights had gone off in her heart and there was nobody home. Lots of staring out the window. Okay, I thought, she needs space. Give the woman space. I just couldn't believe what she did with it. Distance, distance, and more distance. Then she suddenly got energized. Like her life snapped into focus for her, but she was in a completely new place, one that required her to be gone constantly. Up before dawn for runs, late workouts at the gym, long rides on weekends. She tells me: "Thank God I run and lift weights, Em. It's a safe way of burning off all that restless energy."

Safe?

When she gets her mountain bike, she says, "I love my bike. I'm in love with this bike."

"You said that about the last bike," I say. "What is this, serial monogamy for bikes? Still, it's good to know you're in love with something."

Says Dorie, "Don't lay a guilt trip on me for wanting to have a life, Em. Don't you do it."

Say I, "You used to have a life with me."

"You know, Em, I don't think I've ever been alone. Maybe that's where the restlessness comes from—the desire to be alone." She steps into the shower then and turns on the water. She's not bothered by the sudden burst of cold water. I open the curtain, stand there staring at her like some kid at a peep show. Once upon a time she'd invite me to join her, and even if I'd already showered that morning she'd say, "You can never be too clean, Ace," and in the immortal words of Jackie Gleason, away we'd go. But this time she tells me, "I mean it, Em. I want to be alone," and pulls the curtain closed.

And I am hurt, but not nearly as hurt as when I begin to suspect that when she goes off to be alone she winds up not being alone. This is not the time or place to open up that can of worms, however—I can picture our kids waking up just as I'm shouting at my wife about the men I suspect she may be fucking—so I say none of this. Instead I say, "I was wondering how our parents made it this far."

"Inertia," Dorie answers. "And that's not something I ever want to be guilty of."

"No? What do you want to be guilty of?"

"Oh"—she laughs—"all sorts of things, but not inertia." She fiddles with the heat vent. "Maybe they lasted because people didn't get divorced then."

"Yes, they did. Just not as often. Look at your parents."

"My mother walked out on my father; they did not get divorced."

"Are we?"

"Are we what?"

"Going to get divorced."

"Oh, Em." She raises her arms over her head in a gesture of surrender. She's taken to wearing bicycling jerseys and soccer goalie tops—brightly colored, form-fitting, sporty, boyish, except her breasts look fantastic in them. In happier times I'd reach beneath that lime green keeper's jersey with the black diamond-chain pattern and palm and massage what I found there, and Dorie would tilt her head back and close her eyes, maybe even open her legs a little so my hand would have something else to do when it tired of caressing her breast. Erotic options, she liked to call it, the key to a good sex life, which reminds me of how perfunctory ours is of late, as though she were considering wallpaper patterns and which shade of ocher would look best in the front hall while she waits for me to finish. And it is the memory of that disengagement when we should be at our most intimate that has me screaming at her, "Don't 'Oh, Em' me! I asked you a fucking question! Are we going to get divorced?"

I can't believe I'm shouting this. And it does wake up our kids. Henry anyway. Out of his sleep he asks drowsily, "Who's divorced?"

"Nobody," says his mother. "Go back to sleep." She sighs, and to me she says, "I'd forgotten, Ace, what a complete dork you can be."

"Ace dork," Henry mumbles from his sleep, as though he's concluding a blessing.

I tell this as though I were a set age and everything in our family's life happened at the same time. In memory, as in childhood, things bleed together. The only difference is how fast it bleeds. For adults looking back, each year is a tiny fraction of their time on the planet, and time washes clean everything in its wake except for flotsam and jetsam. For children, each year is a huge fraction of their time on earth, so time hardly seems to move at all. Things are running along in their normal course, then suddenly veer into left field.

It was like that with our parents' arguments. They followed a pattern that gave us comfort until the night that comfort shattered. Our parents' arguments went like this: Our father comes home late on a Friday—past our bedtime—but we're up because he isn't home yet. When he does come home, he shrugs off our mother being upset that he's late. He's home, isn't he?

"Where have you been?" asks our mother.

"What? I told you I worked all day. I was at the Office."

"It's what you were doing after work that bothers me."

A moment of silence. Our father is collecting his thoughts. Then he says, "So what did you do all day?" like she hadn't done anything. And our mother says, "Why can't you come straight home from work?" which was always news to us that he hadn't.

"Because I need to unwind."

"You can unwind here."

"Not with all these kids running around, screaming like banshees."

"They are not screaming like banshees."

"They will in a minute. A man can't think."

"So ask me again what I did all day. Who do you think stays home with the banshees?"

Along about then we slide out of the kitchen and the living room and gather on the stairs. The stairs have a closed railing, so nobody knows we're sitting there.

"Jesus, Sue, it's just . . . I mean . . . a man can't . . . I mean, I just wanted . . ."

"You always 'just wanted.' How do you think it makes them feel you coming home so late and calling them banshees? How do you think it makes me feel?"

Truth be told, we had mixed feelings. As scenes like this accumulate, we end up feeling awful, wondering why they argue every time Dad comes home with a quizzical look on his face, but the banshee business— hey, that was all right. Our father had already told us our ancestors came from Prague, Bohemia, so we were Bohemians. Bohemians, like Banshees, were a particularly fierce tribe of Indians, weren't they? A tribe of green-eyed, yellow-haired Indians with long, thin faces and haunted eyes. Very rare. Maybe our mother didn't take this news well, but we felt pretty good about it. "I'm Indian," I told a kid on my way home from school one day. "Bohemian, actually." The other kid took this in silently. Such was the power of knowing who you were. "And if I feel like it I can scream like a Banshee. Wanna hear?" He didn't.

Back on the stairs, we don't dare move. If things get quiet, if there's murmuring and then we hear our mother say, "Oh, Wally-Bear," then in just a few minutes they'll go down the hall, close their bedroom door, and all will be right with the world. Sarah will say, "C'mon," and we'll go up to bed. Or if our father says, almost calling it out, "Guess it's time for the show, *if they aren't asleep,*" we need to scamper up before our father comes in bearing both a grin and his accordion.

We think we are fooling our parents, hiding on the stairs, but they know we are there. Sometimes they call us on this and we come back into the kitchen, rubbing our eyes to make it look good. If it's still mid-argument, our father says, surly and accusatory, "You were listening." Or if the fight is settled, an affable "Mother, we have spies. What should we do with these infiltrators?" And then we're shied off to bed, our mother making sure we're washed and in our jammies and have said our prayers, and then our father (drum roll, please) enters. He's wearing—there's no other word for it, really—his accordion, the one with his name in mother-of-pearl up the side of the keyboard. This is when our father truly comes into his own. When our father seals the deal on his status as family patriarch, as good-guy bon vivant, as someone it is impossible for our mother to stay mad at. Bedtime as event, as production. Our father opens with a quick rendition of "I've Been Working on the Railroad," then lets us sip his beer. We make faces, and he says, "That'll put hair between your toes." Hair between our toes? Yuck. Why would we want hair between our toes? And isn't it supposed to be "That'll put hair on your chest"?

Says our father, grinning, "If I were your mother, I wouldn't want hair on my chest."

Says our mother, a sly smile on her face, "I don't want hair between my toes, either."

Repeated action. What comfort we take from the habitual.

The highlight after every fight, the last song, no exceptions, no encores, is "Ghost Riders in the Sky," a song that sends shivers running through us. There we are, lined up on one of our beds, our pajamas zipped up tight to our Adam's apples, enthralled as our father holds the high notes, his voice quavering with vibrato. He is way, way better than Vaughn Monroe, who made the song famous. And then the accordion squeezes shut and our father comes back from that strange place that he seems to go to while he is singing, that high chaparral where ghostly silhouettes on horseback dance against an orange sky, and we come back from there as well, and he is just our dad again, no longer possessed by some unearthly power, and he smiles and kisses each of us—wet, sloppy kisses tasting of beer and peppermint—and he says, "There, that'll put hair between your toes."

We groan at hearing it, but we are delighted just the same. Hair between our toes! How awful! How marvelous! Once our parents leave our room, we spread our toes and check. Any hair there? No, thank goodness. But we're also disappointed. Oh, to have thick, woolly feet, warm in the winter, like a dog's paws. We could be miniature yetis, leaving our prints in the snow. And with that we go to sleep, secure in the knowledge that all's right with the world.

Of late, however, their arguments had become both frequent and unsettling. More and more often they did not end with make-up kisses and sing-alongs. They took to picking up where they left off once we'd been put to bed, and in the dark we could hear their raised voices, a muffled tirade of hurt and complaint. They were taking care not to let us hear anything, but we gathered that our father's take on things was that he was out there, manning his position, and our mother's job was to man hers— hearth and home—and that was simply the way things should be. Our mother's take was that this was *not* the case, that it *should not be* the case, and she was extremely upset that it *was* the case.

Things came to a head the night we came down with a stomach flu and half of us were squirting pitifully out one end while the other half were heaving out the other. Our mother had spent the day running pots, wiping behinds, washing sheets, comforting the afflicted, and getting vomited on with more regularity than a mother had a right to expect.

And our father, once again, is late. The only child remotely ambulatory, I'm under the kitchen table holding a black thread leading to a dollar bill in the middle of the floor, a linoleum floor with little gold boomerangs floating in a sea of gold flecks and tiny black squares. A pin is attached to the bill, the thread tied to the pin. I'd seen this in a joke book. They reach for the dollar bill, you pull the thread, the bill slides from their grasp. People are lured across the floor until their heads bump the countertop. I'd been waiting for the better part of an hour. We'd already eaten crackers and peanut butter, washed it down with flat 7UP, and gotten into our fuzzy pajamas with the zippered fronts and the white plastic footies that made our feet smell.

Finally our father is home. I hear his booming "Well, what have we here?"

Under the table, seeing only his feet, I don't know if he's saying this because he sees my dollar bill or if he's responding to our mother, who's standing next to the table, the toe of her butter yellow pump going up and down. "Walter," she says. Our father booms, "Well, what have we here?" again. He is letting me get away with it, and I love him for that. I start pulling the thread—too quick, he hasn't even reached for it yet— and the dollar bill is doing its slow skittering across the linoleum. Our father steps, and *whap!* his black shoe comes down on the dollar bill. I pull, and the thread flutters toward me. The bill stays under his foot.

"Walter! He worked all day on that."

"What, and I didn't work all day?"

"He wanted to surprise you."

"So I'm surprised, I'm surprised. Here"—he reaches for the thread— it takes his hand a few tries to locate it, he doesn't even look at me—and ties the broken ends together. Then his feet go to the fridge, and there's the *pffsst!* of a beer being opened. "Okay, pull. I'll be surprised."

"You know, Wally, sometimes you're a real prick."

"What, what did I do?"

"You knew these kids were sick when you left this morning, you knew I was going to be with them all day, their behinds running like faucets and vomiting, and *still* you're late. Just *once* I'd like to see you make it home on time. Just *once* I'd like to see you sober."

Our father's feet make steps toward our mother's. "Oh, come on, honey-bunch, you've seen me sober plenty of times."

"Don't touch me! And don't think you can joke your way out of this one."

"Oh, honey—"

"Don't, Wally. Don't even try. Emmie"—our mother was the only person who called me that; to everyone else I was Em or Emcee—"has been waiting for you for hours, and the others have just about given up on you. And frankly, so have I."

I look out from under the Formica table, and our mother has her arms crossed over her chest. Our father is looking abashed and guilty and more than a little somber. A couple times he tries lifting his hand to our mother's shoulder, and our mother either shakes him off or swats it away. "I said don't touch me, Wally, and I mean it. You think you can waltz in five hours late when I've been struggling with sick kids all day and you're going to love me right up and make it better?" Our mother laughs, a high scornful laugh that scares me. "Ha, fat chance! Like you could do anything in your present state anyway."

"Aw, Susan Marie, there's no—"

"Don't Susan Marie me, Wally. You want to make yourself useful, you can go in and sing while I give them their good-night medicine. They might like that even if I don't. Or maybe you'd like to take a crack at the mound of diarrheaed-on laundry I've got waiting in the basement." Then our mother said, "Come on, Emmie. Time for bed for you, too."

We knew things had truly taken a strange turn a few minutes later, when our father stepped inside our room, accordion strapped to his chest, and found our mother dosing us with Kaopectate. "There, that'll put hair between your—" started our father before he saw what our mother was giving us. "That's Kaopectate," said our father.

"Yes, yes, it is," said our mother with forced calmness. She was trembling. Something was coming, something was about to happen. We could feel it.

"Parke-Davis makes that."

Our mother turned the bottle in her hands. The spoon was chalky from her having already dosed Ike and Wally Jr., both of whom liked medicine that left grit in your mouth.

"Yes, so I see."

"I work for Dinkwater-Adams."

"I know who you work for, Wally."

"Dinkwater-Adams makes a very fine antidiarrheal."

"I'm sure they do."

"I sell it."

Our mother said nothing to this.

"We get it for free."

Still nothing from our mother, except she placed the Kaopectate lid on the night table and poured out a tablespoonful for Sarah, who was waiting with her prim little nose in the air.

"What are people going to think, Susan, when we tell them that you bought Kaopectate for diarrhea when you could have gotten Pecarol from me for free?"

"We aren't going to tell them, are we?" She was doing Robert Aaron now. I was next.

"You're changing the subject!"

Our mother remained calm. The spoon was filling right before my eyes. If I breathed, it would be like a sudden storm on a little lake. "I'm not. You asked me what would people say—"

The spoon suddenly flew up before my face, the Kaopectate blotching my face and hair and jammies. I had seen it coming, of course. A man with an accordion strapped to his chest moves slowly even when he's angry. Even when he's furious, as our father was now.

"Damn it to hell, Susan Marie!" Wally Jr. and Ike started crying. "What in the hell do you think it says about me? A man can't even get his own wife to take what's freely offered!"

Said our mother quite evenly, "Sometimes the wife doesn't want what's offered. And," she continued, "I wish you wouldn't swear in front of the children. You see how it upsets them."

"Jesus H. Christ!" thundered our father—we knew that was a bad one—"I'll swear when I goddamn want to. I will feed my children Pecarol when I goddamn want to. I will not come home and find my wife feeding my children Kaopectate when I work for a competing company!"

Our mother's eyes narrowed. Her eyes flashed green, green like emeralds, like 7UP bottles with sunlight glinting through them. We were all lined up on the edge of my brother's bed like gargoyles, some of us crying, some of us shocked into silence. "Is that what this is about? Your need to prove yourself in my eyes? Throw your weight around? Well, let me tell you something, mister. We use Kaopectate in this household because Kaopectate is a superior product. And I will feed it to my children when and if they need it. And if you came home once in a while on time, then maybe some of us would avail ourselves of what's available in the way of *other* company products, assuming they were still *functioning* properly."

The accordion sagged ever so slightly, sighing out its harmonicalike breath.

"I think we need to continue this discussion downstairs," said our father.

"Fine," said our mother. "There are some things I'd like to say to you that the children really shouldn't hear."

We'd have heard them anyway, even if we hadn't snuck down the stairs once they got going. Shouts from our mother: "Let me do something in my life once in a while, why don't you?" and "You don't understand," and "You think money grows on trees?" and our father's heated, "Who works, huh? Who works?" "Oh," said our mother. "And I don't?"

"What's the point of being married if a man can't trust his wife while he's unwinding after a hard day of work?" shouted our father.

"Then maybe," shouted our mother back, "maybe we should think about not being married!"

"What are you saying, Susan? Susan, do you realize what you're saying?"

"I'm saying," said our mother, repeating herself now, more coolly, her voice quavering, "maybe we should think about not being married."

This freezes us in our seats. Our father has brought up the possibility of the Duckwas getting divorced before. "Ted says he and Lorna are having problems," our father had told our mother. We were eating casserole—part of our never-ending austerity measures because our parents kept having kids on our father's salary. Our father opened a can of beer with a church key and poured its contents into one of our milk cups. "He says he's thought sometimes about how maybe it would be better for everybody if they did—get divorced, I mean." Our mother had dropped her fork on her plate right then and put her hands over her ears. "I'm not listening to this," she said. "It's not right. It's a sin." "He says he's thought about leaving her."

Our mother started making this funny sound then, like a low moaning of wind in the trees. That was how our mother was for a long time early on, when our father or somebody else brought up things happening in the world that she didn't want to hear. It was just *ahoooooooo!* like wind in the trees when that stuff was mentioned. *Ahoooooooo!* Our father looked at his beer. "You know, this stuff tastes terrible when you drink it out of Tupperware." This was a safe remark and allowed our mother to rejoin the conversation. "I put the glass glasses further back in the cupboard. I'll get you one," she said. When she came back to the table with a tumbler she said, "The kids were breaking too many glasses. You have to be careful." Now she was looking at us, but we couldn't tell if she was addressing us or our father. "So many things are fragile. If you're not careful, they break."

Our father emptied his beer into the tumbler. "I'll tell that to Ted."

And yet now it was our mother raising this very same possibility to our father, and she was saying it like she didn't care who heard it. What were we to make of this? Would our house break? That was what we were told about kids (the only one we actually knew was Ollie Cicerelli) who'd gone through this—that they were the products of broken homes. I had checked out Ollie's house just to be sure. It was a bungalow, like the Duckwas', only tinier, and a zigzag crack did indeed work up the side of the porch for four or five bricks like the steps themselves.

I had already read "The Fall of the House of Usher" in the Classic Comics edition, and I imagined this steplike crack eventually developing into a foundation-shattering fissure. We would come home from school one day and find a smoking pile of rubble where the Cicerelli house had been. Was that what would happen to us? If our parents weren't married anymore, would our house come down around our ears? Would we be given to other families to be raised while our mother and father carried on with their separate lives? It seemed both utterly possible and too awful to contemplate.

It was quiet for a while in the kitchen, and then our father said, "Guess I better kiss the kids good night." We snuck back up the stairs and slunk into our beds, not daring to breathe a word of this to each other. "I feel sick," Ike told me, but that may have just been the flu. We arranged ourselves in postures of sleep, but that didn't fool our father. He went from bed to bed, giving us wet kisses from pursed lips. "You know I love you, don't you?" our father told us. "I love you guys, you know that, right?" We nodded, scared and sympathetic and hoping that he would bring out his accordion and sing, that our mother would appear behind him—even a wan, tight-lipped smile pressed into her face would still be a smile—and we'd know that the union would be preserved. But he just stood there, his hand on the light switch as though it still needed to be turned off, his eyes, glassy in the hall light, taking us in.

The next day our mother told us it had all been a big misunderstanding. Nobody was getting divorced from anybody. And we did and did not believe her. Especially since that night marked the end of the serenades— no more "Ghost Riders in the Sky" for us. No more family sing-alongs. The accordion went into the hall closet at the foot of the stairs and stayed there, coming out so rarely after that that our latter siblings didn't believe us when we told them of those once-magical bedtime serenades.

So began the Kaopectate Wars. Like the Cold War, it was about other things. A war of surrogacy. We did not recognize it for what it was: our mother's tiny, continuing rebellion against our father. There would be others. And like most of the mysteries of and between adults, it would occur mostly in code.

5. And That's the Name of That Tune

"Okay, you kids, get in the car." Trips started like that. Our father stacked us like cordwood. Big kids in the wayback if the middle seat was up. Our father had convinced Dinkwater-Adams that his company car should be a station wagon. Easy to haul around samples. So he got one, a Chevy Bel Air, with what felt like real panels of wood on the side. Only it wasn't wood, it was something better. Plastic. Anything really good was being made out of plastic—plates, silverware, hula hoops, yo-yos, telephones. It was just a matter of time before the cars themselves would be made out of this superior material.

The only provision the company put on the car's use, which our father said was for insurance purposes, was that the sole driver had to be our father. Our mother had no trouble with that. She was probably the last woman in America who believed it wasn't necessary for her to learn how to drive. There were times when we weren't sure our father knew how, either. He had a penchant for coming home and running over our bicycles and tricycles, for crunching our Radio Flyer into the gravel of the drive or pinning it underneath his car or against the concrete stoop outside the kitchen door.

"You kids shouldn't leave your stuff in the drive," he'd say. He'd have a bemused look on his face, like he was puzzled being home at all.

"Been to the Office?" our mom would ask.

"I stopped for a few with the boys."

"More than a few, if your parking's any indication."

"The kids shouldn't leave stuff in the drive. How many times do I have to tell them?"

"How many times have I asked you not to go to the Office?" said our mother.

Our father not going into work—was she crazy? Everybody's father left in the morning either for work or for the Office. Our father usually left for work, but he came home from the Office. The only exception was Ollie Cicerelli, who didn't have a father that we knew about, and whose mother was a waitress at the Woolworth's on York Road.

When we weren't envying him his freedom—he was frequently left alone until 7:00 or 8:00 P.M. and had the run of the neighborhood—we felt sorry for Ollie Cicerelli. He had only himself to keep himself company, and we had a wealth of relatives, who it seemed, we were always running to see.

We even had a relative living with us—Grandma Nomi, which meant Artu was living with us as well. Artu kept up their apartment in downtown Chicago while Nomi recovered from hip surgery, but most nights he slept at our house. In the morning, our father dropped him off at the train station before making his calls. No question, this made for a crowded house, and that might explain why our father spent so much time at the Office.

That's what we wanted to believe, anyway—that there was a correlation between Nomi and Artu being in the house and our father's being at the Office. The other explanation—that he was getting away from us kids—we didn't want to believe. According to our mother, all he had talked about while he was in Korea was how, if he lived, he wanted to be the father of a big family. So now he was—there were five of us kids and another on the way. How could he not want to be around?

It was easier to explain the friction between him and Nomi. Nomi and Artu were urban Democrats, and our father was a suburban Republican. Artu usually held his tongue on matters of politics, and outside the house our father did, too, but inside it he was lord of his castle, and the idea that this chain-smoking, bedridden woman upstairs was spouting off pieties about Jack Kennedy and what an evil man Richard Nixon was, was simply too much to bear. We didn't understand the politics of it, but there had been arguments ever since our mother had gotten a letter that made her cry. It was 1962, and after our mother composed herself she explained to us that our father might have to go away because of a bad man in Cuba. He ended up not having to go, but our father seemed to bear a personal grudge against President Kennedy in the same way that Nomi bore one against Richard Nixon.

We noticed in these arguments that our father was the only one shouting. Nomi spoke very calmly and smoked her cigarettes, rolling the tips around the inside edge of her ashtray to get the ash to drop. Then she'd hoist the cigarette up by the side of her face and cross her other arm under her chest. "Your problem, Walter," she'd say, "is you believe the crap they're telling you."

Our father would storm off, complaining that no one allowed him a chance to think. Later we'd find out he went to the Office.

For the longest time, where our father's Office was and what he did there was a mystery. He did his salesman's reports at the kitchen table on Sunday and Thursday nights. Did he sometimes do his paperwork at the Office then, too? We knew he worked hard. He must've worked even harder at the Office, because whenever he came back from there he seemed addled, as though he'd been thinking too hard.

What we did know was that the Office was the place to which our father disappeared, and from which he returned a different person altogether. The Office never failed to wreak some kind of change on him, a change our mother vociferously protested when she thought we were asleep. Their one big blowup in front of us must have scared them. They didn't do something like that again. Instead they went back to putting a good face on things when we were present, or sniping at each other in a minor way. The howitzers came out only after we were put to bed. Some nights we'd be awakened by our mother's screaming and tears. "You're not the man I married!" she shouted one night, which made us wonder who she thought she'd married, since our father had been like this as long as we could remember. Still, it was obvious to us, upstairs in our beds listening, that the world of adults was a hard place in which to live, strange and dark, and that our father's long hours at the Office were taking a toll on him, and on our mother, and the best thing we could do was steer a wide path around him, and step quietly. Our task was made easier by the fact that our father was gone so frequently, and did not much like taking us with him anywhere when he was home, unless it was all of us, and we were visiting our relatives, where we were expected. It did not seem, though, that our father much wanted to visit our relatives, either.

Perhaps this was because the relatives we saw most often were our mother's. Nomi and Artu were already living with us, and the contrast with our father's parents was striking. When we visited Grandma and Grandpa Cza-Cza, it felt like we were being put under glass. Despite her bouncy name, Grandma Cza-Cza was a serious woman, and she sat in her house knitting afghans and throws for her couches and chairs, as if she were one of those babushkas ensconced in Eastern European museums who eke out a pittance guarding the galleries while knitting scarves, mittens, and balaclavas for the coming winter.

It was better visiting Great-Grandma Hluberstead, Artu's mother, even though that house was filled with old people. For one thing, we could entertain them by showing we remembered how Hluberstead was spelled by singing it to the *Mickey Mouse Club* theme song: H-L-U-B-E-R-S-T-E-A-D! For another, they didn't mind us crawling all over their furniture, which was old and nubbly and draped in antimacassars. For still another, though Great-Grandma Hluberstead herself was old and nubbly—she looked like the Pillsbury Doughboy at age ninety-seven— she encouraged us to call her Hubie. Our mother insisted we say Grandma Hubie, at least.

I don't think our father ever felt comfortable at Grandma Hubie's house, which was a shame—and a problem—because we drove down there a lot now that Nomi was living with us.

Our mom was pregnant with what would prove to be her penultimate child, Ernie. Artu was still keeping up their apartment at Wilson and Malden, a mile north of Wrigley Field—which pained him, being a White Sox fan—but it was quiet there, with cemeteries at both ends of Malden and the lake not too far away. Artu would stay at the apartment when he was pulling a late shift as an elevator operator, but mostly he worked days, and during the week he stayed with us. Although he owned a car, he usually took the train into the Loop, and our father picked him up either at the Lowell-Wackstein building or at one of the coin shops he liked to frequent. Then he and our father would drive to Elmhurst along with everyone else heading out to the booming western suburbs. Nomi had broken her hip falling down the back stairs of their apartment. She'd just wanted to put out the milk bottles, but it was March and icy. With Artu gone all day, it wasn't a good idea for Nomi to be laid up all by herself. Dad and Artu had set up a bed in our upstairs front bedroom—the room that was supposed to be our mother's I-need-my-privacy getaway room. The back bedroom was for us boys. There were four of us at the time—Robert Aaron, me, Ike, and Wally Jr.—and we were very curious about this contraption that Artu and our father had built to help Nomi's recovery. It looked like a huge steel fishing pole with a pulley and a rope for the line. They baited it with house bricks left over from when they built our house. They were sand-colored with flecks in them like freckles. "Iron-spotted," said our mother, "the best kind." She still believed ours was the House That God Built, all evidence to the contrary. We touched the bricks and wondered what on earth they were trying to catch at the foot of Nomi's bed with this. A closet monster? Something that lived under the floorboards? Traction, Artu told us. The bricks were a counterweight for the cast on Nomi's hip, which was heavy and uncomfortable.

"Can we see it?" asked Robert Aaron. "The hip, I mean."

"It hurts her to move," said Artu. "We have to be very careful."

What did it look like, a smashed hip? Was the bone showing? Was there a scar? We didn't know. Nomi was pretty open with us about everything, forthright and plainspoken, so her reticence in this matter puzzled us.

"Why won't Nomi let us see her hip?" we asked our mother. We were downstairs now, finishing our lunch.

"It's the first time she's ever been really hurt," said our mother. "I think it pains her to be getting old." Our mother was washing dishes.

"Will they shoot her?" Ike asked. He was a year and a half younger than me, which made him not quite four.

"Shoot her? Why on earth would anybody shoot her?"

Ike said, "Daddy says it's what they do with horses."

Robert Aaron said, "Dad says, 'You know what they do with horses?' when we get hurt. Then he makes his finger into a gun"—Robert Aaron demonstrated, his forefinger extended, his thumb up in the air—"and pulls the trigger, *pkew!*" He did this right at Ike, who started crying.

"Nobody's shooting anybody!" shouted our mother. She wiped her hands on a dish towel. "Your father, really. Sometimes I wonder why I married him."

Statements like this made us wonder, too. What if she'd married the Italian? Would we look the same, only with black hair? We were all blonds except for Ike, who had auburn hair, like our mother. We didn't wonder for long, though. Your parents were your parents. Even with that one night when our mother raised the subject of the unthinkable, that seemed irrevocable. What we did wonder about was that traction business—those bricks suspended by a rope. We were in Nomi's room constantly.

Evenings we'd arrange ourselves around her pillows while she read to us, but during the day we'd sneak in while she was dozing so we could study the bricks, the rope, the bright chrome arm, the pulley. If we touched anything, Nomi would say, "Don't. Don't mess with that," and we'd jump. We thought she'd been sleeping. "Eyes in the back of her head," said our father. "Just like her daughter." We were alarmed that there seemed to be this symbiotic relationship between this contraption and our grandmother.

We got a glimpse of Nomi's hip only once, when our mother was giving her a sponge bath just before a trip to Grandma Hubie's. We were leaving as soon as Artu and our father returned from work. Artu, an elevator operator, had much the better job. Our father's work, as he explained it, consisted of calling on doctors all over Chicago and trying to get them to buy something from his big brown valise, what he called his sample case. As with Nomi's cast, we weren't allowed to examine its contents, either.

Our mother needed our help rolling Nomi up on her side. Nomi kept herself covered in blankets, and when we pushed it was like trying to get a boulder to roll uphill. It was easier to get on the far side and pull her toward us. Our mother washed her back while we stared at a mass of blankets and didn't see her hip at all except for the crazy railroad spur of the scar end, which looked like it'd been spun by drunken spiders. Its purple thickness scared us. It was like something was living beneath the cast and was sending out tendrils.

Nomi said, "I could use a beer before you leave."

"You want anything with that?"

"Sausages. Them little bitty breakfast sausages and some eggs and a nice glass of beer." Nomi was staring up at the ceiling. I thought maybe she was imagining herself back at the diner she and Artu had owned during the Depression. We had heard all those stories. Beer and breakfast sausage and eggs sounded like something you ate for dinner at a diner. A meal like that was something both she and our father loved. Except for the politics, she and our father actually got on well together. They shared the same tastes, greasy breakfast foods with beer for dinner being only one of them. At Hubie's, Nomi would not be the only woman over fifty drinking beer. She hated not going.

While our mother made the sausages and eggs, I was dispatched upstairs with the beer.

"You want a sip?" asked Nomi, pouring her beer into the short glass she always used. "It bites," she said when my face scrunched at the taste of it.

"How can you drink that?" I asked.

"It's an acquired taste," said Nomi. "Some people acquire it, some don't."

"I'm never going to acquire it."

"Don't be so sure you won't. Your father thought he wouldn't acquire a taste, either, God bless him, and you see how much he likes it now." Nomi looked out the window. She had a long thin face with high cheekbones and heavily lidded eyes that reminded me a little of a frog's eyes. I didn't realize it at the time, but once she had been very pretty.

"How do you acquire a taste, Nomi?"

"Lots of ways," said Nomi. "Out of hope, out of disappointment, out of other people's example or expectations. Mostly, though, you just keep on drinking the stuff until you like it. Me, I'm half Irish; I was born with a taste for it. And that makes you an eighth Irish, so you better watch out, or you'll acquire a taste for it, too."

That day at Grandma Hubie's *was* a special event. Our great-uncle Harold had brought his fiancée home to meet the family. Nancy was a skinny redhead with her hair done up in a low beehive and a swoop of bangs over her forehead. She had plucked her eyebrows, then drawn in new ones that looked like the way I drew crows at a distance, had the crows been flying upside down. Her skirt was too short, showing a good two inches of thigh, which endeared her to no one but Grandma Hubie. "Sit down, my dear, sit down," Grandma Hubie cried, and Nancy was left to her fate while everyone else went about their business. Even Harold eventually removed his hand from hers and went to have a cigarette in the backyard. Hubie and Tillie and Eunice took turns reminiscing to the girl about their own families, then she was released to (or rescued by) the other women, who had their own inquiries to make.

It was spring, but there was still snow on the ground and the air was chilly, especially on the sunporch behind the kitchen, which was where all the men were, playing poker. Artu; our father; Aunt Gwen's husband, Bruno; Irene's husband, Frank; Aunt Margie's husband, Alvin; and Margie's three sons, Harold, Howard, and Stephen.

Alvin was a nice man, but his face looked like he used it to stop trucks for a living. He had a bullet-shaped head and a gash for a mouth and bad teeth, which was all right because it looked like he possessed only seven or eight of them. He loved to laugh, though, like our father, and after a while you got used to seeing those exposed horrible teeth. It helped that he had a habit of elbowing his stack of winnings—the coins anyway— onto the floor. "Get that, would you?" he'd ask us, and we'd dive to the linoleum, then proffer him our gleanings. "Keep it," he'd say, and we'd snug in close to his elbows, sentries to his needs, fetching him another braunschweiger and onion sandwich, or another of the pickles he liked to gnaw on for his poor sore gums. The others took to elbowing their winnings on the floor, too, and we fanned out, each of us picking a great-uncle or grandfather whose elbow movements we shadowed.

We had one other favorite uncle, Stephen, but he played only a few hands before he said he had to get back to school. He was a sophomore at Notre Dame. "Midterms," he said as he put on his jacket. "Major parties," said Aunt Margie, sighing after he left. She'd come into the sunporch with a warm glass of milk for Alvin, who loved the food he ate but suffered from heartburn. "You'd think he'd stay to chat with Nancy."

"Why?" Harold asked. "He's not marrying her. I am."

Margie cuffed Harold gently on the back of his head.

"It's okay, Ma. We already agreed, he's going to be my best man."

"All the more reason he should be visiting with Nancy."

"Mom, give him a break. It's Friday night. I'd be out partying with my friends, too, if I wasn't here."

"The point is you are here."

"If you ask me he should be in the service," said our father, shuffling the cards in his hand. "Stephen, I mean. It'd do him a world of good."

"Nobody asked you, Wally," said our mother. The women had come into the sunporch. It was growing dark, and with Stephen's departure you could feel the day closing in on itself.

"Last fall they had me on call-up duty, you know that?" said our father. "The Cuban missile thing and they had everybody in the reserves all charged up and ready to go."

"They could have sent Wally-Bear back to San Diego," our mother said. "And me, big as a house here with our sixth."

"It seems crazy," Margie said.

"Frightful," said our mother. It sounded like our mother was confessing something, which indeed she was. This was our mother's way: something horrible would happen, and you would only find out about it later, when she had surmounted it enough to make light of it. You could tell she had been cut, but the wound was healing. That, anyway, was the image our mother wished to present to the world, an attitude no doubt ingrained in her by Nomi, whose motto could have been "Never let 'em see you cryin', girl, never ever." Inside her own home, however, was another matter. And even then it was a matter more of our eavesdropping than of her giving vent to her emotions in front of us.

That whole fall had been a tense time in our household. There had been a letter from the government, and our mother had cried when she opened it. Our parents spent a lot of time in front of the TV, which they didn't usually do, and ushered us out of the room when the news came on. Our father started coming home earlier than usual, and after we were in bed he and our mother would talk in hushed, plaintive voices. Or at least that would be our mother's voice. Our father's was calm and accepting, as though the balance of power in the family had shifted back toward him. One evening we heard our mother wail, "But they can't make you go, Wally, they can't make you go!" and our father answered, "I'd have to, Susan. I have a commission. I'd have to report." We peeked over the railing to see our father comforting her. She sat on his lap, folded into his shoulder, her just barely pregnant belly bumping into his. Our father had his arms around her, and he was kissing her hair, saying, "There, there. There, there," while our mother cried, "I can't do this again, Wally, I can't, I can't."

The whole scene scared us. Usually our mother was the indomitable one, putting up with our father's absences, or lambasting him when he did get home—but here she was weeping on our father's shoulder like a little girl who'd skinned her knee. Without a word passing among us, we agreed not to speak of this. It just settled into our consciousness, that everything could change at a moment's notice, the world turned upside down. Your parents were your parents, sure, but evidently one of them could leave and call that duty. We didn't understand this. That evening, behind the closed door of their bedroom, there was a desperate furtiveness to their noises, a plaintive urgency, as though they felt they had to use up everything inside them prior to their world coming apart. That knowledge seeped into us as well.

"It would have been my third war," said our father. "All under Democratic presidents, if you get my drift." He winked at everybody around the table. I hadn't been counting how many beers he'd had, but it had been a lot. Our father drank beer in short glasses quickly and refilled them often. He had acquired the taste.

"Wally, don't be bringing up politics. You know how I hate that," said our mother.

"Facts are facts," said our father. "You want peace and prosperity, you get a Republican. You get a recession under a Democrat, and the first thing after that you got a war on your hands to balance the budget."

"World War Two was about balancing the budget?" Artu asked.

"It got us out of the Depression," said our father. "Don't think Roosevelt didn't know that. He let Pearl Harbor happen just so he'd have an incident to get us involved."

"Don't answer him," said our mother. "It'll just keep him going."

"I thought this one was about keeping the Communists out of Asia," Harold said.

"It is. But you watch. If the economy takes a tumble, it won't be just advisers going over there. That's why Stephen should enlist now. ROTC. Life's a lot better for you as an officer, and that's the name of that tune."

"It's not okay as a civilian?" Harold asked.

"Real men serve in the military," said our father. He looked around the table. Bruno had a bad knee that kept him out of the Big One, Artu had come of age between the wars, and Howard had done a very uneventful hitch in the late fifties. That left Harold, who had a soft, serious look on his face I could identify with. Harold was a watcher and a listener. He cleared his throat.

"I'm getting married," Harold said.

"Real men—" said our father. "Enough, Wally, I mean it," said our mother. Our father poured himself another beer. As though he were speaking to the beer he said, "And that's the name of that tune." Then he put his fist to his mouth and quacked like a duck, his fist opening as he did so to let the noise increase in volume. He had this tight, befuddled little smile on his face, as though he wasn't quite sure what line had been crossed, but he was pleased one had.

Nobody said anything. Then Artu, who usually ignored our father when he got like this, said to him, "You fought the Battle of Lake Michigan in World War Two, didn't you, Walter?"

"I served my country in her hour of need," said our father.

"In the Coast Guard, wasn't it? Stateside?"

"I served my country," our father repeated.

"And in Korea, you hauled troops and ferried refugees around, right? You didn't see any real action, did you?"

"I could hear the guns," said our father.

"But you didn't see any action, did you?"

"I fucking served my country, you son of a bitch!" our father roared. He was standing now, swaying forward on his fingertips. He refilled his glass again. "And that . . . that is the name of that tune." He sat down again.

Nobody had knocked their coins to the floor in some time. This was how family gatherings with our father ended these days. Edgy. Our mother stoic but near tears. Her eyes were glistening as she got us our coats. Artu said Irene and Frank would give him a ride home.

"Are you coming, Walter?" Our father hadn't moved while our mother got our coats. He sipped from his glass, then refilled it. He held up the bottle and toggled it back and forth, meaning one of us should get him another. We didn't move. Our mother would yell at us if we did. Our father shrugged, put the bottle down. In the dining room we heard Sarah complaining. Why did we have to leave so early? Why couldn't she stay? Our mother explained icily that nobody was driving out of their way for us. And Sarah Lucinda was old enough to help with getting Wally Jr.'s coat on. Did she need to be reminded that she was part of this family, too? "I hate this family," said Sarah Lucinda. This was followed by a loud smack.

Our mother reappeared in the sunporch's doorway. She was furious and resplendent, her green eyes blazing, her pregnant belly lending her a power she didn't usually have. "Walter," she said, in clipped syllables that made it sound as though she were cutting them off her tongue with a knife. "Are you coming home with us or not?"

Our father studied his cards. "I believe I'll let you play this hand out," he said, tossing his cards into the pot and rising heavily to his feet.

A pall filled our car on the way home. "I have never been so humiliated—" said our mother, but she didn't say anything more. It was a phrase we had not yet gotten used to hearing, although eventually we would. Our mother would repeat it whenever we came home from any event our father had drunk too much at, exclusive of his many trips to the Office, which was where he would go this evening once we got home. We knew what he would say as we trooped out of the car and entered our dark and empty house: "And that's the name of that tune," he'd say, and roll up his window, and put the car into reverse, and wobble back out the drive. And our mother would want to say something to him but wouldn't, except maybe to press her lips together and breathe, "You shit," once he was already into the street, too far away to hear her or to see the fear and determination that lit up her face. "Come on inside, you kids," she'd say and usher us upstairs and make us ready for bed. Then she'd make herself tea and bring it and a beer-and-sandwich platter up to Nomi, who would listen as our mother poured out her grief.

That was the rest of our evening—the rest of our childhood, really—already spread out silently before us. For now, our parents sat in the front seat, and we sat in the middle and the wayback, and the air itself seemed permeated with silence, a silence that insinuated itself like a wraith. We kids—we all looked out the windows. Brick houses, ranches mostly, filled our view. We wondered—would life be any different for us if we lived there, or there, or there? We came to the conclusion it wouldn't.

6. The Company Car

CAPEESH?

"What is it with guys and nostalgia?" Dorie asks me. "You're so fucking sentimental about things passing—cheese in wax paper, transistor radios, pinochle, euchre, beer in short glasses. For chrissakes, everything's a little shrine with you. Even your bad memories. You want to know something? Plenty of shit happened to me, too. I just never talk about it. I don't even think about it."

Dorie's right. She doesn't look back much. What's done is done. A practical philosophy, but it also means she doesn't feel the need to apologize for anything, ever. Whatever lies in her wake is already in history's dustbin. I, on the other hand, am a sifter of shards, trying to figure out how the pieces fit, and what they might mean. My accidental discovery, for example, that Dorie was packing a diaphragm—a piece of equipment I'd thought no longer necessary given my vasectomy post-Sophie—on her bike trips. And a negligee, one I had never seen before, packed neatly around it. Discoveries I've yet to bring to her attention.

Maybe it's inevitable. I'm the longest relationship she's ever had, and she'd been through a lot of them before me. She was with Woolie's father for maybe half a year, with Henry's father less than that. And dozens more before that. A restless soul, she does not suffer boredom easily. And lately she has been bored. Distracted, both in and out of the bedroom. "Ace," she says to me, both fondly and impatiently, "what you need to understand is that sex can be okay even when it's just . . . okay. You don't need the rocket's red glare every time out." I suppose most marriages, sooner or later, settle into a kind of going-through-the-motions phase, but it still surprises me that these particular motions would be subject to the same laws of entropy. Old joke: Q: What does a wife of over seven years think during sex? A: Pink. I think I'll paint it pink. Weren't we the magical exception, though? This was a woman, after all, who was three months pregnant when I first made love to her. She had two dime-size indentations on her lower back, flanking her spine. They drove me crazy with desire. And I was in love with her in high school, too, only she ran with a very different crowd then—the oversexed dirtballs—and she wouldn't have given me the time of day. A guy named Calvin knocked her up in high school, and six weeks later Dorie disappeared. Not long after that he was happily knocking boots with Holly Gunther and referring to the still-gone Dorie as "my ex-whore." It still amazes me sometimes that we yoked our wagons together, but once we did it seemed both inevitable and right. Perhaps that's my mistake. I think in terms of familiarity, intimacy, comfort. I take the inevitability of permanence for granted. I forget about fragility, inconstancy, boredom, and change. The inevitability of things passing. Then it comes and whups me upside the head, and for months I walk around in a daze, a deserving victim of my own optimism.

This gives me pause when I think about my (our) bookstores. If Dorie decides Van Loon's is a bad business investment, it's history. If she decides I'm a bad investment of her time, I'm history. It's strange to think of our fates linked like that, but they are. Trying to keep a bookstore afloat is not unlike trying to keep a marriage afloat. You have to be possessed of a certain myopia that what you're doing is right, and you have to keep plugging away, believing in your effort, all evidence to the contrary. And even then, despite your best efforts, if your partner backs out, it really doesn't matter what you think or what you've tried or what you've hoped for. You're toast.

"Are you guys arguing?" Sophie doesn't look up from her Winnie-the-Pooh coloring book, on which she is working intently. I'm not sure when she woke up.

"Mommy and Daddy are having a disagreement about the need for preservation. You know, like in our house, saving all the old stuff because it's cool."

"There's preservation and then there's being an antediluvian pack rat," Dorie says over the backseat, though she clearly means this for me.

"You mean like Cza-Cza?" Our father is known for his inability to part with just about anything his hands have ever touched. His house is a monument to how fast paper can accumulate if you let it.

Dorie refuses to talk to our kids as though they're kids. "Yes, but what we're talking about is being an emotional pack rat. Saving up memories and feelings not because they're useful or necessary but just because you had them once."

"Oh. Can we see the planes?" We're near Oshkosh. We cannot drive past this town without one of our children, Woolie when he was younger, and now Henry and Sophie, asking if we can't stop at the Experimental Aircraft Association museum. Woolie, now a sullen teenager, no longer shows interest. He'd rather stare out the window, plugged into Rusted Root or Dave Matthews. It is no longer cool for him to show enthusiasm for anything he has not discovered on his own. But Henry and Sophie get all worked up when they see the F-14 mounted on stilts beside the highway, and the hangars at the far end of the grass airfield. They will get equally worked up when we come to the underground house at the next exit. During the early seventies someone built a house inside a berm. It looks like a coffin with windows. A string of poplars grows atop the berm. Our children measure distance by their memory of landmarks (time itself is an impediment, something that separates the landmarks and prevents them from coming immediately into view as soon as Sophie and Henry recall that they exist), and these two—the EAA and the underground house—mean that we are getting close to Cza-Cza and Mumu's house. As we come under Cza-Cza and Mumu's gravitational pull, it seems appropriate that they have two markers—one for rootedness, one for flight.

"How can you say that to her?" I say sotto voce. "Telling her memories and feelings aren't necessary."

"The downside of attachment is depression, sweetie. She should know that. And I'm not going to let that happen, not even with you." Before I can say anything, Dorie cuts me off. "Later, sweetie."

"No, wait, let me just understand—"

Dorie goes into her singsong "the kids are listening" voice: "I said LA-ter, and I mean LA-ter." And that pretty much ends the discussion. Henry is waking up now himself, and the first words out of his mouth are "Are we there yet?" which he repeats until I confirm that we are. But I don't share his enthusiasm. Nobody in a shaky marriage likes to see family. You feel transparent, your sorrow written in black Magic Marker across your forehead: WE ARE UNHAPPY. And no matter what turbulence there has been in your siblings' relationships, when your own relationship is wobbling, everyone else's seems serene. Your own hail-fellow-well-met-ness is a front, your fake serenity—yes, yes, ours too is a match made in heaven—so patently false you're simply waiting for someone to call you on it. It would almost be a relief if someone did, but in the strange geometry of our family, there's an unspoken agreement that nobody will say boo. So we will turn and twist, pretending, dissembling, and we will see in people's eyes that they know we're lying, that we're fooling no one. All this will be made worse by the occasion itself—celebrating fifty years of our parents' marriage having endured. Fifty? I think. Fifty? I don't know that we're going to see fifteen. Sophie wants to know what fifty is. "Forty-five more than you," I tell her. "Fifty is what Aunt Cinderella will be later this year." Sophie ponders this. You can see her face straining to figure it out. I try to help her. "I was forty when you were born. I'm forty-five now. So in five years I'll be fifty, too." No go. Another tack: "Fifty is half of one hundred," I say. "Fifty plus fifty equals one hundred. So when I'm fifty, what will I be in fifty years?" In the rearview mirror Sophie's face lights up. She gets it. She is joyous in her knowledge, and no doubt her mother's words of wisdom have helped her calculations. "In fifty years," she says serenely, "you'll be dead."

If SUVs, minivans, and pickups could stand in for Higgins Boats, then our arrival at our parents' is not unlike a beach landing. Villagers, Cherokees, and Explorers wash up the drive, disgorge passengers, park in uneven rows. More people arrive by the minute. And this is just immediate family. Lots more people will come tomorrow for the anniversary itself. Robert Aaron and Cinderella have children old enough to drive, and they're exercising that prerogative. Cinderella has children old enough to have children, and they're exercising that prerogative as well. Amazing: all these people have issued, in effect, from one horny couple. It is hard keeping them all separate.

But then, it was hard keeping us separate even when it was just us kids. Our mother encouraged us all to be individuals, but our father lumped us all together.

Our father rarely called us by our names. I think sometimes he'd forgotten our names, or that we even had names. To our father we were always "you kids." We were a collective plague to him, undifferentiated but bothersome. "You kids had better watch yourselves playing ball in the street." "You kids better eat that soup." "You kids better help your mother." "You kids need to make your beds." You kids. You kids. You kids. For the longest time it was hard to imagine we were complete and separate human beings. To our father we were an early version of *Star Trek*'s Borg, threatening him with our massed presence.

Our mother, on the other hand, would get us confused. "Sarah, Robert Aaron, Emmie, Ike, Wally Jr., Ernie, Megan," she'd say, rapid-fire, like she was fixing our names in her head, making sure we were still who she thought we were. She ran the list in birth order when trying to single out one of us for cautionary words or punishment, stopping when she came to the one she wanted. As though we were too much for her. As though we were a constant blur, which no doubt we were. As though she could remember the names but not the faces: "Sarah, Robert, Emmie, Ike, Wally Jr., Ernie, Ernie! Stop that. You're hurting your sister."

But it's not as though we didn't—don't—buy into it, too. When all of us have arrived, and our parents, slow-moving now, with arthritic hips and ankles, shuffle out to greet us, what are the first words out of our mouths? "Mom, Dad," we say, "the kids have arrived."

An air of jocular intensity falls over us. We hug, slap backs, buss cheeks. We talk about our cars and our gas mileage and how the drive was. How work is and isn't. I say nothing about the bookstores. To begin to explain is to own up to failure, and we can't have that. So I'm relieved that the talk quickly moves to what our kids are up to, and the funny things they've recently done or said. We tell each other we look good, though truth be told, except for Ike, Dorie, and Peg Leg Meg, we look middle-aged. Our hair is thinning, our eyes baggy, our skin pasty. I've got a spare tire I'd like to lose, though in our family that qualifies me as svelte. Most of us have followed in the fat of our father. Cinderella looks puffy, Robert Aaron rotund, Wally Jr. flabby, Ernie portly. We say none of this. "Looking good," we tell each other. "You lose a few pounds?" "Workin' on it," we reply, and we nod our heads. To eat is human, to dessert, divine. Usually fractious, despite our parents' admonitions that we are, indeed, family, we are being careful with each other. Our unspoken agreement: we will make nice. For our parents we will put aside old problems, jealousies, enmities.

Like hell. None of us wants to be blamed by the others for ruining our parents' anniversary. If things go kablowies, we all want to be able to shake our heads and sigh with relief. "Well, at least it wasn't me."

We were of one mind, too, when it came to getting their anniversary presents. In years past we have argued and bickered and agreed to disagree, and the result was that sometimes we didn't get them anything as a group. Each person made an individual offering. But on this occasion, it seemed important that we all pull together. Oddly enough, this means that we have arranged for two separate anniversary presents. One is for our mother—a twilight balloon ride over our farm for her and our father, with all of us gathered beneath them. The other is for our father—a fully restored, two-toned 1955 Chevy Bel Air Nomad station wagon. Our parents know they're getting the one but not the other. The Nomad's not here yet. We've arranged for Tony Dederoff, our father's best friend, to drive it over first thing tomorrow morning. It's actually a model year he never drove—his first company car came the next year, while our mother was expecting me—but we chose it because its detailing seemed oddly and wonderfully symbolic. Almost prophetic. Everything about it—its delta-wing jet hood ornament and the chrome side scroll, even the chrome piping of the roof rack—suggests the open road, empty highway, flight. And yet there on the rear door are seven chrome darts—one for each kid!—representing stability, solidity, staying put. The ballast that kept our father rooted right here. I suppose we're saying the same thing to our mother with this balloon ride. It's something she's been wanting for ages. "I've always wondered what it would feel like to float across the sky, but gently, not going too fast," she's told us. So we get her what she wants, but arrange for the balloon to float over Augsbury, for the flight to end in our alfalfa field. She floats away, but not too far; she ends where she's always been. And given that our father is joining her on the balloon ride but the car is pretty much his (our mother, certainly, will never drive it), gift-wise, our mother is getting the short end of the stick. But then our mother always got the short end of the stick.

I speak of the company car as though we understood what it was. But like most things that came to us from the world of adults, we hadn't a clue as to what it was or what it meant. We thought, very simply, that it meant we got a different station wagon every other year. Maybe even the same station wagon but with clever styling changes—the instrument panel, the trim and body colors, the interior color, the luggage rack, the presence or absence of the vent window.

"That's the company car," our father said. "Nobody touches it, nobody rides in it, nobody breathes on it, unless I say so. Capeesh?"

We capeeshed all right. The company car. It sounded like everything else in our house that we weren't allowed to touch, lest we break it. The company car was the car we took out when we had company. Like the company china. The company silverware. The company glasses. "That's for company!" our mother shrieked when I took out the fine porcelain our father got for her when he was stationed in Japan. "Use the everyday stuff," she'd admonish us, and I could feel we had dropped somehow in her estimation of our worthiness. I could never figure it out. Why were we saving this stuff for strangers? Weren't we supposed to reap the benefits of our father's having gone overseas? Wasn't that why he went—to make the world a safer place and to get a good deal on postwar china?

The company car may as well have been made of porcelain. We rarely rode in it. To go to church, to pick up groceries, to go on vacation, to visit relatives. Perhaps that was why, when you were allowed in it, you felt something special and magical was about to happen.

On long drives with the wayback down, the five, six, seven of us would be arranged hip to foot, hip to foot, alternating. This prevented our fighting, except for kicking, and even then we didn't mess around too much. Our father possessed a backhand of infinite reach. The arrangement also gave us the illusion of private space, which was important to us even though we did everything together. In summer we played Alphabet, counted license plates from other states, tried to get truckers to honk for us. In winter we tilted our heads back and looked at the stars, feeling the reel of the infinite above us and the thrum of the road inside our skulls. Sometimes in summer our father pulled off the highway in the middle of the night. "Look, look at the sky!" he'd rouse us, and then he'd cry, "There! There's one!" and we'd follow a tracer star streaking to its death. In winter he did the same thing, and bundled in coats we'd sit on the engine still ticking heat and watch the entire northern sky change color— pulsing, shifting curtains and rivers of white and yellow and red and green and blue and magenta, and behind that the stars in their velvet. "That's the aurora borealis," said our father. "The Northern Lights. People go their whole lives without seeing them. But we have. Now, together, all of us. Never forget that." This sounded like a prelude to his "You're Czabeks, never forget that" speech, which was pretty close to our mother's "Remember, all you've got is family" speech, which dovetailed neatly with our father's "What's said in this house *stays* in this house" speech, which scared and thrilled us with the idea that we were the keepers of deep, dark family secrets, part of some conspiracy, something that could bring down the family if it got out, or bring down a government if it didn't. We were a cabal, the Czabek cabal, and pronouncements like our father's while we huddled in our winter coats on top of the company car as the aurora borealis shimmered and danced above us reinforced the notion that we belonged to something, and that certain things belonged to us. It seemed as though our father was introducing us to the concept of spiritual ownership, and once you had something, shared in something together, then it was yours, always. So the company car was indeed something special. Inside it, we were transformed.

But it meant something different to our father.

What it meant to our father was that he never owned his own car, he never owned any car, and about the time he'd gotten used to one it was time to break in a new car.

This seemed like a fine idea to us, but it chafed our father. Ownership cut two ways for him. The world was Al Capone's oyster, after all, because he saw what he wanted and took it. A company car, on the other hand, meant something was given to him, and it wasn't ever really his. Our father believed in ownership, in the special privileges ownership conveyed—the feeling that this was yours, you'd worked for it, you'd earned it—and with a company car that feeling was impossible. A company car came with certain restrictions, one of which was that the car went back to the company when it hit the 70,000-mile mark, which usually took our father just under two years. Later, when he had a five-state territory (Wisconsin, Michigan, Indiana, Illinois, Minnesota, and occasionally Ohio), he'd put that many miles on in a single year. Still, he often wanted to buy the car back from the company, and they wouldn't let him.

Our father thought this was revenge for his requesting a station wagon in the first place. In this era of minivans and SUVs, and everything leased and traded in every two to three years, our father's desires for permanence and ownership must seem rather quaint, but at the time it was a badge of shame to our father that he never owned his own vehicle. It seemed so un-American. What were we, closet socialists? Communists? Fellow travelers? Believers in the World Bank?

It rankled our father. He wanted a station wagon, for chrissakes. What could be more American than that? But Dinkwater-Adams thought it looked more professional for their field reps to drive sedans, not to mention they got a better deal on their fleet cars if they were all the same make and model. So our father had to argue with them, exhaustingly, every winter and spring, about his need for a station wagon. I knew why. Until he started building his own in his father's basement, a station wagon was, for a long time, the closest thing our father had to a boat.

Certainly our father needed a station wagon for all the samples he was hauling around, and traveling as a family would have been impossible in anything other than a station wagon, but I think our father would have requested a station wagon regardless. I think he liked the feeling of being in a car that rode—and looked—like a boat. A beach landing craft, to be specific. The famed Higgins Boat. Something you had to moor to the curb, a car that wobbled a little from side to side and whose steering was soft enough it floated. A car with at least the memory of wood on it, something that connected this mode of transportation to his preferred transportation. Our father wept when Detroit replaced the real wood in the woodies with simulated wood-grain plastics, and he railed when Detroit announced it was no longer putting wood trim of any kind, real or simulated, along the hulls—excuse me, the sides—of its station wagons. "What is this country coming to?" our father would ask, his fingers running along the car's sides the way, many years later, I would tentatively run my fingers along the flanks of the first girl I got naked with. (The question I asked myself at the time was, of course, quite different.)

I was amazed, year after year, at our father's slight disappointment with every new car that showed up in our drive. Perhaps this was because of the haggling he had to do to get what he wanted. Perhaps it was because even then he didn't have much say in the specifics. Or perhaps it was because by the time he got his station wagon—just about when school let out—the other sales reps had had their new sedans for months, and our father was just then taking possession (and temporarily at that) of a vehicle that was already eight months old.

Still, there they were, every other spring—Oldsmobile Vista Cruisers, Pontiac Bonnevilles and Catalinas, Chevy Bel Air Impalas, Chevy Nomads and Chevelles and Kingswood Estates. Regal in their names, magical in their possibilities. And our father in them.

Can he really be blamed for hoarding that magic for himself? We wanted to go along with him on his travels, but we understood that some work needed to be done alone. His was a lonely profession—we understood that. We capeeshed. We capeeshed even as we lined up on both sides of the car as he backed out of the drive, heading to the Office for another long evening's worth of work.

"Take me with you, take me with you!" we'd cry, and our father, a man on a mission, pretended not to hear.

7. Loose Lips Sink Ships

The mystery of the Office was cleared up for us—for me, anyway—one Saturday in July. I was going on seven. Nomi's hip was better—the cast was off—but she still slept upstairs, and the steel- and chrome-armed pulley-and-brick whatchamacallit was still at the foot of her bed. The evening before our father had done a curious thing. Rather than come home late from the Office, he spent the evening cutting the yard front and back—a job he usually reserved for Saturday mornings. When we asked him why, he said he was keeping his distance from our mother. We knew he was only half-joking.

While he mowed, we ran around and caught lightning bugs, putting them in a jar with mown grass in it. The grass was for their nutrition. We did this with grasshoppers we caught, too. But they never ate the grass. They just jumped around the insides of the jars trying to find purchase, looking out at our glass-distorted faces with their sad grasshopper ones, and eventually they died of starvation or asphyxiation, despite the holes we punched in the lid. The lightning bugs fared better. We usually released them before they fell on their backs, gasping for breath with their little lightning bug lungs. Tonight we were going to keep them, though, and use them as night-lights. After all, lightning bugs were domesticated insects. They crawled over your hands, lighting up your skin with that weird greenish yellow glow before they got brave enough to fly away, and even then it was easy to catch them, and if not that one then another. So we did that as our father mowed and drank beers. He stopped every few turns for a good long pull at his bottle of Pabst, then put the empty in the case nestled up against the Weber grill and rotis-serie. We were already in our pajamas, running around the yard in the new mown grass. Our father did not particularly like an audience that moved. "Hey, you kids," he shouted, "sit on the stoop. And stay there!" We would listen for maybe fifteen seconds, then we'd be dancing around the lawn again, the grass cool against our ankles.

"You keep that up, I'm not doing for you what I'm doing tomorrow."

"What are you doing tomorrow?" we asked, but he was already head-ing the other way, and our question was lost to the bark of the mower. We didn't follow. If we trailed after him with our questions, he was liable to cut our feet off in the dark. Our mother came out and said, "Off to bed with you, tomorrow is a big day." We asked her, too, but she remained her enigmatic self. "You'll see tomorrow," she said. She seemed both bit-ter and pleased.

"We shall see what we shall see," said our father, who'd come in while we were wiping the grass off our toes. He was finishing his beer. He seemed immensely pleased with himself.

"What are we gonna see? What? What?"

"I see, said the blind man, as he picked up his hammer and saw."

We pretended to puzzle over this one for a few moments. If you an-swered him, it only encouraged him to say something about the hair be-tween your toes. Or the hair on your chest. Or how you were a day late and a dollar short. Did you really want to volunteer for that barrage?

Our father held up our jar of lightning bugs. "I'm going to let these go outside," he said. "They make lousy night-lights."

How did he know that was why we'd brought them inside? "You think you're the only ones who were young once?" That really gave us pause.

Then he sat on the edge of Robert Aaron's bed and told us again about how when he was a young boy he used to watch Al Capone's cars run down his alley, and how he used to catch lightning bugs in a jar and go to sleep watching their irregular flarings on his bedside table. He talked about how he used to build balsa-wood airplanes with tissue-paper skins, with rubber bands attached to the propellers. He went into loving detail about this, how he would spend hours making these things, cutting the struts and gluing the wings, all the bracing and infrastructure, and how careful he had to be or the tissue paper would rip, and how he'd then take his finished airplane to the attic, wind it up, stick a lit match in the nose, and sail it out the window, the whole thing bursting into flame before it hit the trees across the street.

"Magnificent," our father breathed at us in the dark, his bottle of Pabst squeezed between his thighs. "The whole thing was magnificent!"

"You did all that work, and then you burned it up?" Our heads were filled with the image of that balsa-wood-and-tissue-paper airplane afire, burning as it glided into the trees.

"Some things aren't meant to last," said our father. "Lights out now."

In the hallway we could hear our mother. "I wish you wouldn't tell them stories when you've been drinking. You always make things seem better than they are."

The next morning the family wrestle was cut short because our father said he had "big things cooking for you kids," and we should let him sleep. We kept bouncing on his belly, and when he rolled over to get away from us, we continued on his back. "What big things? What big things?" we shrieked as we kept bouncing.

"Go look in the car," our father said, and groaningly rolled into our mother as we dashed out of their bedroom to look.

In the back of the Buick was a large rectangular box. BLASTCO'S ABOVEGROUND POOL it read, 48 IN. TALL. There was also a model number that looked like something the Man from U.N.C.L.E. might need Illya Kuryakin to translate.

"All right!" Robert Aaron and Sarah screamed. This was the big time. An aboveground pool! We weren't naïve. We knew that box was too short for it to include a diving board. But there would probably be a deck we could dive off, a shallow and a deep end, and a rope of red and white col-ored floats. On these hot and humid days, the whole neighborhood could cool off in our aboveground pool! People would come from blocks all around just to see.

We asked our father when he was going to put the pool up. (Soon. Later that morning. Just let him rest now.) How long would it take to fill? (A long time. He didn't know. Go ask your mother.) How deep was deep? (He didn't know. Go ask your mother.) How soon could we go in it? (He didn't know that either. As soon as it was filled, providing we waited an hour after lunch. Let him rest now.) How deep would it be— over our heads? Would it have its own alligators? Would it be big enough for a boat? Could we go sailing on it? Could we leave it up in the winter and use it as an ice rink? Our mother, coming up from the basement with an armload of laundry she dumped on her husband, said, "Let Daddy sleep. Daddy's tired. Daddy had too much to drink last night, didn't Daddy?"

Too much to drink?

"Pool water," said our mother, separating the staticky sheets from each other to find the socks hidden within their folds. "He was testing it."

We were starting to sound like that Dr. Seuss classic *Green Eggs and Ham*. "Could we, would we—"

"LET ME BE, GODAMMIT!"

"Pool water makes Daddy cranky," said our mother, who started folding pieces of underwear and dropping them on the bulge in the blanket that indicated where our father had hid his face. "Still, he shouldn't use language like that, especially in front of his own children."

Actually, he was using that language *on* his own children, but it didn't seem like the right time to point that out. So in a rare display of family unity, we helped our mother fold laundry, making neat, wobbly piles down our father's body, stacking each pile on its own bulge of flesh, our father snoring all the while. Then we made beds, put away the laundry, swept the kitchen, washed our breakfast dishes, and stacked our *National Geographic*s. We didn't dare leave the vicinity of the driveway. From time to time we looked in the station wagon's wayback to marvel at the wonderful, unbelievably fantastic aboveground pool (48 in.!), soon to be ours.

Our father came outside at nine-thirty, rubbing his eyes and forehead, a cup of coffee in hand. By that time Artu had arrived with a trunkful of sand. Our father got plastic sheeting and his toolbox from the basement and unloaded the pool box from the station wagon. Then he went for more sand. We stared at the box, trying to imagine it unpacked, set up, the water glistening. When our father came back, he and Artu started unloading the sand from the trunk of Artu's car into a wheelbarrow, then dumping it onto the plastic sheeting. It was hard, hot work. During a break Artu opened up the pool box and took out the instruction sheet. "I see we're supposed to cut a circle for the base," he said. "Wouldn't it be easier, Walter, if we cut that first, then dumped the sand right where we wanted it to go?"

"I see, said the blind man, as he picked up his hammer and saw," said our father.

Our father said this every step of the way. He said it less frequently as the day wore on. By day's end he was using a lot worse language than when we'd tried waking him that morning.

It was getting hot. We—Robert Aaron and I—were standing on the sand pile while Artu and our father were cutting out the sod. Sarah was off somewhere, pouting over not owning a Barbie like her friends. Wally Jr. stood at the bottom of the pile with a bottle hanging out of his mouth. Ike tried getting onto the pile with us, but it was too small and we kept pushing him off.

"Hey, you kids, stop that. We won't have any sand left for the pool bottom."

Chopping out the sod and hauling it to our compost heap made unloading the sand look easy. Artu had stripped down to his athletic T and an old pair of his elevator operator's pants, which were slate gray and had dusty blue stripes up the sides. He looked like a Civil War soldier. Our dad went inside and came out wearing his Christmas present from our mom, a fishnet T-shirt he'd seen advertised in a magazine as the latest thing from Sweden to keep warm in the winter and cool in the summer.

They finished removing sod from the circle and started hauling wheelbarrows of sand, dumping each in place. Our mother called us in, no doubt so we'd stop bugging our father and Artu as they toiled under the hot, hot sun. Lunch came and went. Our mother served them lunch on the shady side of the house while we ate inside. Artu put on a long-sleeved shirt. "You should put a shirt on, too, Walter. Sun's bad today. It'll fry you."

"I've seen tougher suns than this aboard ship," said our father, for whom his time in the Navy had become the benchmark and reference point for all experience. He was taking things out of the box and lining them up on the grass. The big curl of the frame was sky blue. As though someone had taken a shears to the heavens and cut out a goofy rectangle. The lining was the same color, and there were yards and yards of curlicued white rim to keep the lining in place. Now came the hard part, stretching the lining, getting it to stay on the frame, keeping it smooth on the bottom and sides, getting the trim in place without the lining slipping. They worked on it for hours. We got bored watching them, even with our father's bad language. Our mother kept coming to the kitchen window and yelling, "Walter, the children!" as though we were meat on the rotisserie he had forgotten, and he'd yell back, "I know, I know," and then quieter, under his breath, "Jesus H. Christ, you'd think they never heard the words before."

"At least not from you," said Artu. For our part, we were pleased to be reminded that our savior had a middle name. No doubt Henry, Hank for short.

We rode our bikes around the neighborhood for a while. Nobody was out. Maybe everyone had gone to the pool up on York Road, or to Wrigley Field to see the Cubs take on the expansion Mets, who were so bad even the Cubs could beat them. Or maybe other mothers worried more about their kids being out on a day when the sky had gone white with haze and if you stopped pedaling and straddled your bike pools of sweat formed on the sidewalk.

"Hot," said Robert Aaron, and all we could do was agree.

We went home, and there it was, our oasis, with an aluminum and white plastic ladder on the side and a green garden hose looped over the railing. Water gurgling into the bottom. There was already an inch or two, enough to cover the hose's tip. We watched the turbulence of the new water coming in against the bright blue bottom. We went inside and drank a gallon of Tang and begged our parents to let us sit in the pool while it filled up.

"Your bellies will burst," said our mother.

"That water's ice cold," Artu said. "I can put you in there if you want, but I'll be taking you right out again once you cool off."

Artu was not given to hyperbole like our mother. If he said something, you could believe him. Still, we didn't want to believe him.

"Where's Dad?" Robert Aaron asked.

"Your father," said our mother both loftily and with pity, "is in a world of hurt."

Indeed he was. We found him in his bedroom lying belly-down on the bed, a thick smear of orange jelly across his back. He was moaning. It sounded worse than this morning. We were used to his morning moan. Threaded through that complaint was a certain good-naturedness; we knew it would eventually stop and he'd get up, almost playful, and start bacon and eggs snapping in the fry pan. The underpinning of this moan, however, was a pitiful whine, the sound dogs make after you've kicked them. And underneath that smear of orange jelly you could make out the source of his whine: a diamond plate pattern of boiled skin, so red it was ugly. It stood out even more because each diamond was separated from its neighbors by a white border formed by the shirt he'd been wearing. His back looked like a white window well cover had been stenciled over a slab of hot meat. As though a grill had left its marks on his back in negative.

Our mother joined us. "When he took his shirt off, all I could think of was that scene in *The African Queen* when Humphrey Bogart takes his shirt off and he's covered with leeches and the look on his face when he knows he has to go back into the water."

"What did Nomi say?" Like Artu, we trusted her judgment about things in a way we didn't quite trust our mother's.

" 'Good God.' That's what Nomi said. 'Good God.' Just like that. That's just what she said. Oh, God, he does look pitiful, doesn't he? At least Dinkwater-Adams makes an unguent."

Robert Aaron raised his opened palm. He was about to bring it down hard against our father's back, but our mother caught his wrist in its descent. I do not think Robert Aaron was simply being mean. I think he also wanted to see what it would feel like to land his hand in the middle of all that jelly. I think we were all curious about that.

It wasn't that we were callous, either. After our mother said, "I think you better leave," each of us went up to our father to tentatively touch him and tell him we hoped he was feeling better. "Don't touch me," our father said through gritted teeth as each of us came near.

When the pool was about half full we reported this to our mother, who let us change into our swimsuits. "No diving," she said. "It's not deep enough. And wipe your feet before you climb into the pool."

Artu was right. It was freezing cold despite the air's heat, and it didn't get any better the longer we tried to stay in. We kept getting out, shivering, our thighs numb, and then feeling hot with the towel over us and climbing back in. We quickly forgot about the plastic washtub we were supposed to use as a footbath, and the pool surface was soon covered with a scum of dirt and grass clippings and the pool bottom was gritty with sand. It would be several days yet before any of us felt brave enough to dunk our heads under the water and explore the texture of the bottom, to run our fingers over the ribs of the walls, to feel the liner stretched tight by the force of all that water, to explore the wrinkles in the pool bottom as though we'd just discovered the Mariana Trench. We were quite a picture: five shivering kids huddled like refugees in scummy, grass-littered water.

We were still like that when our father emerged from the house. The shadows had been lengthening for a while, and although it wasn't evening yet, you could feel the tenor of the afternoon had changed. It was the time when games become possessed of a certain fury, born of the desperate knowledge that soon you would be called in for supper, and even if you had nothing at all going on, even if you were shivering in a half-filled pool, you still didn't want to go inside.

Where was our father going in his weakened condition? The hardware store? The Office? The liquor or the grocery store? It didn't matter. We all started shouting, "Take me with you! Take me with you!" as though he were leaving a deserted island and whoever stayed behind was going to be marooned.

Our father moved gingerly. His face looked like a Christmas ornament behind his green-lensed aviator sunglasses, his crew cut a bit of fringe on top. He was wearing a pair of khakis and a light blue sport shirt made of very thin cotton. I had gotten colder quicker than anybody and had already changed into a pair of blue sailor pants, with square sewn-on pockets front and back. I had a towel over my skinny shoulders, and I was still shivering, but my T-shirt was draped over a lawn chair, within easy reach.

"You got shoes?"

I nodded vigorously. They were right under the lawn chair.

"Okay, you come along, Emcee. The rest of you—it'd take too long for you to get ready, sorry." This was our father's excuse when he didn't want to wait for us. We knew the drill. He didn't like going anywhere with more than one of us. I think Mom talked to him about this—the idea of making us feel sequentially special, of taking at least one of us each time he went out. Our turn would come, if we were patient and waited. Of course, it had the opposite effect, all of us vying for position, trying for it to be our turn, always keeping score. It was random, but we tried to make it a science.

"I can be ready before Emcee even gets his shoes on," shouted Robert Aaron.

"I'm only taking one of you," said our father. "You went last time." He meant the York Liquor Store, which was in a little shopping center just down from our church. There was a dry cleaners, the York Liquor Store, a Kroger's, a beauty parlor, a barbershop. He went to the York Liquor Store about once a week, usually for a six-pack or some scotch for Nomi.

"Where are we going?"

"We shall see what we shall see," said our father.

I sat forward in my seat. When you were the only one in the car with Dad, you got to sit up front. Place of honor. Usually only our mother sat there. If there were two or more of us, we rode in back, or even asked to sit in the wayback so we could see every place we'd just been.

Our father was sitting forward in his seat, too. The orange burn cream—what our mother called an unguent—was staining the back of his shirt. Above the collar his neck was orange and bright lobster red. It looked like it was on fire from the inside out.

"Does it hurt?"

"Like hell," said my father. He winced. "Don't tell your mother I said that."

I didn't say anything. We kalumped over the tracks for the Chicago, Central and Pacific Railroad, and then we were in the old part of town. The houses here were bigger, mansionlike. It was always special crossing St. Charles Road; it was like you were visiting royalty. You knew you didn't belong, but they let you in as long as you didn't stay long, which you wouldn't because you felt uncomfortable there anyway. Once we were downtown our father made a series of left turns, then a right back onto York. We were headed back the way we came.

"Are we going home?"

"Fat chance," said our father, snorting and wincing at the same time.

It turned out we were looking for a parking place. Our father said, "This must be the place." We were in an alley. He winced when he pulled open a door. Everything that required movement seemed to cause him pain. I felt sorry for him. He had worked hard for us all day, and now here he was taking me on an outing to the magical world of downtown Elmhurst.

Once we were inside the building, the sun, which had been so brittle and harsh I was squinting, diminished. Now it was dark, and the contrast between the harshness of the hot outside light and the cool, mute darkness inside made my eyes swim. It was like I had entered a cave. Then I could see light up ahead, some of it green, some of it yellow, some of it red. We were in a paneled corridor. Near the bathrooms, if my sense of smell was accurate. Then I could see the nameplates: MEN, WOMEN. It had always scared me, what went on inside the women's bathroom. It must be something mysterious, or why would they need a separate bathroom in the first place?

The corridor was dark, and something crunched under my feet. I felt like I was stepping on beetles, and I tried to walk carefully, but the floor was strewn with them. The corridor opened into a big room. There seemed to be four or five round tables, each surrounded by barrel-backed chairs. Everything looked heavy. Along the far wall was a long, long counter, and behind it an equally long mirror, and a whole wall softly glittery with bottles arranged on shelves that went up higher than you could reach. On the top shelf was an old radio flanked with beer cans, and above that a moose head sporting a Cubs cap. I couldn't not think of Rocky and Bullwinkle. A neon sign hung in the window, only it faced out so you couldn't read it. Men were spaced erratically down the length of the counter; two sat together at one end, just after it curved back to the wall. I couldn't see them very clearly—the window they sat against washed out their features. My father had us sit on stools right at the curve. His body blocked the sun, but when I leaned forward I caught it full in the face. A beefy man in a striped shirt and a crew cut cropped so tight his head looked like a bowling ball with stubble—which is to say he looked like my father—was leaning against the back shelving, where all the bottles were.

"What'll it be, Walter?"

This man knew my father! We must be at the Office! So this was it— where my father got all his work done, where he went to be alone, to think, to get away from Nomi's serenity and the pandemonium caused by us kids.

My father boosted me up on the chrome-legged stool, then hunkered down beside me. "We're here to unwind," he told me. "Don't tell your mother. She'd kill me." Then he lifted up his head and said to the man in the striped shirt, "The usual, Bobo."

"Your kid wants a boilermaker?"

My father grinned. "Shut up and pour. And a soft drink for the little guy."

"You know what a boilermaker is, kid?" He poured something amber-colored into what looked like eggcups, then drew a draft for my father. He put those side by side in front of my father. Then he made the same thing for the two guys sitting just down the bar. Unlike my father, they dropped the little glass inside the big fluted one and drank it down like that. "That's a boilermaker, kid, only your dad can't seem to get the hang of it."

"That's because you don't stock tomato juice."

"That's because nobody in here drinks Bloody effing Marys." Only he didn't say "effing." He said the F-word.

"Hey, my kid."

"What, he's got virgin ears?" said Bobo. "Sorry, kid. The way your old man talks in here, I figured you already got an earful. Forget what I said. It don't mean nuthin'."

Bobo had a big gut and he looked pretty serious, but the gut was hard as a rock and you could tell he liked to look serious so he wasn't grinning all the time. He liked to move the ashtrays around, too, especially when somebody was about to break the ash off his cigarette, then he'd make a big deal of wiping down the countertop and loudly complain about what slobs we all were. He also liked to turn the bottles every so often so their labels all faced front. He made me a Coke decorated with a swizzle stick and a maraschino cherry—what I knew as a Shirley Temple—and whenever he saw my glass was low he refilled it. He set a wooden bowlful of peanuts in front of me. "Go ahead, kid," he said, "it helps polish the floor." I looked at the floor. It was covered in peanut shells.

"The oils," my father said. "That Bobo, he's a smart man for a dummy."

"Takes one to know one," said Bobo.

"Hey, Bobo, you lettin' us die of thirst here or what?" said one of the other men.

Bobo said, "Yeah, yeah, it's a regular frickin' Sahara in here is what it is. I want people to find your bones bleaching in the sun come spring." But he was already making their drinks. He had a glass of Coke with a swizzle stick in it, too, which he sipped from while working a toothpick around in his mouth. He liked to wait until people insulted him before he poured them another drink. He kept busy wiping down the bar. He seemed to like everything just so, which was funny, given how the floor was littered with peanut shells. I was fascinated by that. I suppose it helped that nobody paid me much attention except Bobo, who from time to time offered me maraschino cherries straight from the jar. "I gotta get rid of these somehow," he said, like he wasn't doing me a favor.

My father was distracted by his boilermakers. Or maybe I should say he was intent on them. He would throw back the shot and say *Ah!* like my brothers and I did after we guzzled a full glass of milk in one long, deep draft. Then he'd sip his beer and say *Ah!* again. He and the other two men at the bar and Bobo got to talking about the Cubs—what a rotten team they were, but if they ever got some pitching, the men agreed, they could do some damage. Then they started talking about what branch of the service they'd been in, and where they'd served, and what a swell group of guys they'd served with, except the sonsabitches, and the old man, he was okay, too, except for when he was bustin' their balls, and it went on like that for quite a while.

When his beer got low, my father made little dancing motions with his index finger, gesturing to both glasses simultaneously, and Bobo would fill 'er up. That was what my dad said to Bobo, "Fill 'er up, Bobo, fill 'er up." Like we were at the Sinclair station and my dad was speaking to the attendant. He did this for the other guys a couple of times, too, the little finger dance—he even did it for Bobo—and they drank to his health.

"May you be in heaven half an hour before the devil knows you're dead," said my father.

I looked out the window at the people going past. Men in hats, women in skirts with boxy yokes, their arms bare, kids on bicycles. I made out what the sign in the window said despite the electrician's tape or black paint or whatever it was. Pabst, it said. I looked at the moose, who seemed to regard everything under its massive chin with benign amusement.

My father turned to me. "These are men," my father said. "These are *men*. Never forget that."

I had no idea what he was talking about, but there was something about my father's intentness that scared me. I asked to be excused. By this time I'd drunk three or four sodas and my father had had four or five boilermakers. I don't know about him, but I was really feeling it. My father excused me, and I gingerly made my way across the peanut shells on the floor, not sure if I was allowed to stomp on them or not. In the bathroom everything felt better. The urinal was a wall model shaped and sized like a bathtub, and it gave me great pleasure to relieve myself into its curved porcelain immenseness. I wrote my name, broke up cigarette butts in the bottom, chased flakes of the sanitary cake around the drain. It even came to me what my father was talking about at the bar. All these men had served in the military. That was what made them men. Although I was also pretty sure he was alluding to some other quality as well, something intangible that he could just *feel* about them, but for the life of me I didn't know what that was. Maybe I would have to join the military to find out. I decided not to let it bother me. My father said a lot of things I couldn't figure out.

Peeing by myself in a public toilet was a strangely liberating experience. Maybe this was what my father meant about being men—a steady hand, a sure aim. I shuddered, shook myself, zipped. I washed my hands and dried them on the revolving towel, yanking down hard on the edges to leave a dry spot for the next guy, the way my father always did. Then I left, empty of bladder but very full of myself, ready to take on the world. Back at the bar I opened peanut shells and discarded the husks with gay abandon.

The men were talking now about where they lived and the new highway spur and what it was like getting around Chicago these days. "Me, I wouldn't go in if you paid me," said one. "I have to," said my father. "I got a lot of clients there." "Condolences," said the other man.

"I hear you," said my father. I knew what was coming next so I started to tune out again. Our father said the number-one rule of selling was Don't piss people off. So whatever the other men said, our father would answer with one of his thousands of one-size-fits-all comments: "You can't keep a good man down." Or "There she goes," or "You're up the creek without a paddle." "Sure as shootin'," he'd say. "You betcha. You can't squeeze blood out of turnip." I wondered sometimes what it would be like to have an actual conversation with him. I wondered sometimes what it was he was thinking, what he was feeling. When he got started like this you never knew.

My eyes started looking for something to latch on to again. The moose was interesting, but its range of expression was limited. Then I saw something behind Bobo that I hadn't noticed before. It was an advertisement for Hamm's beer—the Hamm's bear cartoon figure was on the left side of the sign. In red script letters at the bottom was the Hamm's beer slogan: FROM THE LAND OF SKY-BLUE WATERS. . . . That made me hear the theme song itself, a drum going and a kind of Indian chant: "From the land of sky-ey blue-ue wa-a-ters . . . comes the beer refreshing . . . *Hamm's* the beer refreshing . . . *Hamm's* the beer refreshing . . . H-a-a-m-m-m-s-s-s-s . . ." the drums hitting really hard on the word *Hamm's*. But it was the sign itself that held me. It was a lake scene, only it seemed to be on a scroll, and as you watched, the sky blue water and sky blue sky and the evergreen trees slowly scrolled out of the frame, the sun twinkling, twinkling on water and rocks alike until you came to a couple of canoes pulled up onshore, and then you panned down the stream—it was a stream now, all pebbly with rocks—and the lake started over again. A circular universe, amazing. I got lost in it, until the front door jingled and heads turned, including mine.

It was a woman, and from the reaction of the men in the bar, this was unusual. It was hard to make her out at first, and we squinted as though we had resided too long in the dark and she was made of the light from outside, had brought it in with her. She was wearing a broad-brimmed straw sun hat and had on Jackie Kennedy sunglasses and a cotton sundress with a rose pattern—big roses—scattered all over it. She seemed a little heavyset, but she carried it well. For some reason I expected her to be wearing gloves, white kid gloves up to her elbows, but she wasn't. She sat on the opposite side of my father, between him and the two men closest to us.

"Can a body get a drink?" she asked Bobo, and Bobo rolled the toothpick around in his mouth. "A body like that can, sure," said Bobo.

"Sure as shootin'," said my father. I think he just wanted to say something to be polite. Besides not disagreeing with people, our father often said meaningless things just to break the ice, but this woman seemed to regard my father seriously.

"Well," she said, lighting a cigarette, "aren't you the eager beaver."

I thought she was talking to me. I was often described in school as "an eager beaver," so it seemed natural for her to call me that, but seeing as how I was sitting on the opposite side of my father, and he was massive, it seemed rather amazing that she had noticed me at all.

"Fill 'er up, Bobo," said my father. We were back at the Sinclair station. I always felt excited at the Sinclair station. There was plenty to watch—

the dinosaur on the sign, for example, and the attendants who scurried about our father's car, filling it with gas, checking its oil, cleaning the windshield and side windows, even the triangular vent window that we loved to have open—but we never felt we were part of the proceedings except as an audience inside the car's bubble. Things went on around us and we watched. It was like that now with the three men at the bar, and Bobo behind it, and the woman sitting among them. Things went on among the five of them, and it was like I was now in the bubble, sealed off from the proceedings but watching.

The woman's name was Shirley. One of the men sitting at the end of the bar said, "What's your name, sugar? I'm Roy, and this here's Charlie," indicating the man next to him.

"That's a nice name," the woman said. Then to Bobo, "I think I'll have one of those."

"One of what?" said Bobo.

"A Rob Roy," said the woman. Everybody was still looking at her. My father was smiling or grimacing, I couldn't tell which.

"I asked you what's your name, sugar," Roy said. He was a burly looking man with a big forehead on account of he had almost no hair on his head. He had a round face and long strands of hair that came from just above his ears and were greased onto the top of his head like colonists forced to live in a barren new country. The few indigenous strands stood up short and wild and were highlighted white by the window behind him.

"I heard you, Roy," said the woman, waving her hand at him. She had the reddest nails I'd ever seen. It was like the tips of her fingers were dipped in blood. She turned to my father just as Bobo was setting her drink down in front of her and taking the singles from the small stack sitting in front of my dad. She lifted her Rob Roy and made a little toasting gesture. "Thank you," she said to my father. "My name's Shirley. And who might my benefactor be?"

"Walt," said my father, still smiling and grimacing. He looked embarrassed, pained, and pleased to boot.

"Walt," said Shirley. "I like that name. Walt. Do you mind if I call you Walter?" She was already taking another cigarette out of her pack. She kept them in a little green purse with a clasp, and when she opened the purse it looked like a frog opening its mouth. "I never liked my name," said Shirley. "You know who I was named for, Walter? Shirley

Temple. I hate that." She had the cigarette in the corner of her mouth, but before she could light it herself my father had his lighter out. He didn't smoke anymore, but he still carried his silver Zippo with his ship and ship's number etched on the side. She bent her head for the flame, and when she straightened up she was already blowing out smoke.

"Shirley," said Roy. "I always kinda liked that name."

"Me, too," said Charlie. "I known a lotta Shirleys and I liked 'em all."

My father dipped his head and whispered to me for the second time, "These are men. Never forget that." He was creeping me out again. I knew they were men. What else could they be? Except for Shirley, of course, who looked a little like Mrs. Duckwa, unhappy and hungry. My father sat back. "And this," he said a little louder, indicating Shirley, "this is a lady."

"Why thank you, Walter. For the light and the compliment."

There was silence for a few moments then when nobody knew what to say. It was like they were waiting for the conversation to get going again after all the small talk had been depleted. I could tell Roy and Charlie would have liked for her to talk to them; they were leaning forward on the bar, hungry looks on their faces, but Shirley had turned so she was facing my dad. She'd crossed her legs, too—she had thick ankles—and was holding her cigarette at an angle in a way that years later I learned was called a "studied" pose. She looked like somebody from a 1940s movie, sort of glamorous and desperate all at the same time. She smoked for a while and just sat there, regarding my father with what I guessed was curiosity and interest. Then she leaned forward with a look of concern on her face.

"What happened to you, Walter? You look incinerated."

"I was putting up a pool for my kids," Dad answered, a little sheepishly.

"A family man, I like that," said Shirley. She let out a great lungful of smoke and sighed. "I have always depended upon the kindness of family men," she said in a fake southern accent. I don't know why she did that, but my father gave a little pained laugh. Heh-heh-heh, said my father, which was unusual for him, because he usually had a big booming laugh that you could hear clear across a room. You heard that laugh at social gatherings and invariably somebody would say, "What's Walter think is so funny?" And somebody else would say, "Walter thinks everything's funny," which was news to us, seeing as how we lived with him and the laughs didn't seem all that continuous.

My father straightened up, and that let her see me behind him. Her face lit up in a sickly sort of way. "Oh, and I see you brought your little boy with you. How sweet." She brought her cigarette up to her lips again. "Maybe your little boy could meet my little girl sometime."

Now I didn't like her. She'd called me a little boy. No boy who thinks of himself as big likes being called little, not when he's out on an adventure with his father, one he is sworn not to tell Mom about. There was something guilty and delicious about playing hooky from Mom. If Shirley had said "little man," that would have been all right. But she hadn't. She'd said "little boy," and that riled me. She kept saying it, too. "I like little boys," Shirley said to my father. "Does your little boy like to come out and play sometimes? I like little boys who can come out and play. Maybe your little boy could do that, come out and play? Unless, of course, he has too many chores around the house?" She said this last part really slowly, with pauses between each word, and her voice went all singsongy, with lots of emphasis on *chores.*

I wanted to say, no, no, my afternoon was free, but she wasn't paying me any attention.

She got off her stool. She stood beside my dad, and the way she lifted his shirt I was reminded of nurses in burn wards in the war movies, how they were so gentle around the men swathed in bandages, only the men's eyes showing, and how they cooed and ahed as they gave the men sponge baths, and the look that came over their faces when they saw the horrible burns themselves, this look of pained sympathy they got.

"You don't tan well, do you?" She seemed nicer now, and my antipathy toward her lessened. She had arms like my mother's, a little soft beneath her biceps.

My father allowed that he did not.

"Somebody is going to have to be gentle with you," Shirley said, peeking inside my father's shirt collar. She curled all her fingers except her index finger into her fist and with the tip of her blood-red fingernail started writing in the unguent smeared on the back of my father's neck. I craned my own neck to see. "S-h-i-r," she'd written in cursive. My father's back arched and shivered. Her fingernail kept going: "l-e-y." She was done. She rearranged my father's collar, pinching it between her thumb and forefinger, then wiped her fingers on a cocktail napkin. She was smiling at my father with intense interest. My father smiled sheepishly into his drink. I wanted to tell him she'd written her name on the back of his neck in unguent, but I didn't know if I should. Usually in the wayback you kept your mouth shut.

"Tell me, did your little boy get burned, too?"

"I'm right here," I said, waving. "I'm fine. Just a little red on my face." Something about how she'd written her name on my father's neck made me want to speak up, to receive the same attention my father'd received. I wanted her fingernail to write across my neck in cursive. I bet it tickled. Or maybe it felt different if you were covered in unguent. I wanted to find out.

"That's sweet," said Shirley. "You must be pleased," she said to my dad, "having a little boy who's so well-mannered. So polite. I bet he'd stand at attention if we asked him." And then again with the singsongy voice: "Or does he only take orders from *one* drill sergeant?"

I was about to leap off my stool and stand perfectly still, arms at my sides, just to prove to her I could do it, but my dad put a hand on my shoulder and squeezed. I was to stay put.

"He only takes orders from one drill sergeant," said my father. His tone had changed. He sounded apologetic, but something else was in there, too, a certain hardness, as though he had resolved to be apologetic and was sticking to that, no matter how else he felt.

"I'm disappointed to hear that," said Shirley. "I thought maybe we could do a little close order drilling some night, after the other little soldiers have all been put to bed."

"Some other time," said my father. "I need to be getting back to the base now."

"Well," said Shirley, sitting back on her stool and lifting her Rob Roy again, "you give your commandant my best regards. She must be quite the commander."

"I will," said my father. "And she is," he added, picking up his singles and putting them back in his pocket.

Shirley reached into her little frog of a pocketbook. "Here," she said and gave my dad a card. It had flowers on it. My father put it into his wallet, a wallet thick with gas cards and business cards and prayer cards and held together with rubber bands.

"Dad," I whispered as we were leaving. "You left one. On the bar. One of your dollar bills."

"That's called a tip," said my father. "And I'll give you another. Loose lips sink ships."

I had no idea what he was talking about, but I nodded like I knew, like I'd just been given a valuable piece of knowledge that would last me for the rest of my life.

8. Kids Bounce

Cumulus clouds stacked in a blue, blue sky. By rights we should not get a day like this in March. It's flirting with sixty degrees, and Ike and Ernie have set up a feast in the front yard: venison sausage and steaks, trout and bass and walleye fillets, batter-fried perch and shrimp. Coolers jammed with beer, soda, wine. Ernie's drinking too much, but then he's always drinking too much. What you hope is that he calls it quits early, as our father sometimes did, and then coasts into the evening, lubricated but pacified. To distract him, we talk about the marinades and the batter, both Ernie's recipes, and the fish, which he caught. Peg Leg Meg and Dorie and Robert Aaron's wife, Audrey, dish out potato salad and three-bean salad and Jell-O and potato chips for the grandkids, nearly twenty of them now, who then parade past the fish and meats, load their plates some more, and eat till they're stuffed. What they leave for the ants could feed a small village.

Out on the lawn now they're kicking a soccer ball around, playing quoits and lawn jarts. A Frisbee passes over our heads. There are enough of us for volleyball, but given the relative girth and/or immobility of most of the adults, we have settled for croquet. Our mother's red ball hits our father's green one, and we laugh as our mother nestles the balls together, places her foot on her ball, and on her backswing says, "Wally-Bear, I'm sending you into the next county." Her swing has within it both jocularity and vengeance, fondness and fury. We expect a great *clack!*—our father's ball rocketing off. There were times, we know, when our mother would have liked to have done this very thing with his co-jones. Only she would not have allowed them to skitter to rest under a pine tree ninety feet away, which is where she's aiming.

But a strange thing happens on the downstroke. Our mother's swing slows up, and rather than send his ball flying, she pokes it maybe fifteen feet. Our mother smiles. "Had you scared, didn't I?" she says. Then she mouths, "You owe me." Our father, flustered and bemused, shakes his head and smiles. "I know," he says. "I know, I know, I know."

It may be the first time he has ever acknowledged such a debt in public.

Our parents' turn at croquet is just for show. They tire easily these days, play one round, then shuffle back inside, our mother tilting from side to side on her rebuilt hips and bad ankles, our father listing to port as he overcompensates for his bad eye. They are starting to be a collection of replacement parts and broken down things that cannot be replaced. It's what we expect, what we dread. That they'll poop out early is also something that we count on, our father falling asleep in his chair in front of the TV, a tape of *Command Decision* or *They Were Expendable* still hissing in the background, our mother rousing him, finally—"Wally-Bear, come to bed"—and getting him to what used to be their bedroom, and then crossing the hall to the room last occupied by Nomi, where she will read the large-print edition of a John Le Carré novel until she falls asleep herself, waking two or three times in the middle of the night because her bladder isn't what it used to be and hasn't been since about the fourth or fifth of us stretched her uterus beyond recognition.

You could mistake this gathering for any midsummer picnic, only it's already getting dark. The tall stacks of cumulus and cumulonimbus clouds are turning pink and pewter in the twilight. Soon, I think, we'll talk. The kids will get tired from running around like banshees, the youngest will be put to bed, the oldest will take off, and the kids in the middle will follow Ike down to his tepee in the woods. Ike's tepee sleeps eight, with a rock-banked fire in the center (and a gas heater for really cold nights), and the kids will be crammed in there, sitting on bearskin rugs, feeding sticks to the fire, gussying up sparks. They'll toast marsh-mallows, crunch pretzels and chips, swill soda, their eyes wide, their faces orange-yellow in the firelight. They'll finger bear claws, pass around arrowheads and spear points, examine knitting needles and fishhooks Ike has fashioned out of bone. And they'll listen as Ike, Pied Piper of Czabek youth, spins a web of stories about the fate of Native Americans in this country, how they lived and hunted, raised crops and families, generation to generation, until the Anglo ax fell on them.

Why Ike has gone native is anybody's guess. When your brother decides to become a Native American, you do not question it. We know things happened to him while he was in the service. When he wanted to talk, we didn't want to listen. Our solace now is that this preoccupation is infinitely better than his previous one, which was alcohol.

Why have any of us turned out the way we have? Wally Jr. angry, Cinderella glum, Ernie drunk, me anxious, Ike stoic, Robert Aaron cheerful, Meg uncertain. As though each of us were given a faulty compass and put in a leaky boat, and even though we've steered the best we can, between the bad compass and the listing boat and the fog in which we navigate we were bound to veer off course. And bump into each other, over and over again. Our father believed that was par for the course—"Kids bounce," he'd say. Our jostling for position would make us stronger. That was why he and our mother had so many of us.

Amid such fecundity now, it's easy to ignore the fact that we still have serious business to discuss. Kids might bounce; parents don't.

Not long after my visit to the Office with our father, our mother announced that she was getting herself a pet. For companionship, she said. We tried not to understand—Why did our mother need companionship? Didn't she have us?—but we did. Our mother had a problem with companionship: she didn't have any. She had us and she had Nomi, but we were duties, not companions. And our father was not home enough to be the companion she'd thought he'd be. His absences were taking their toll. She held dinner for as long as possible before conceding that he wasn't going to be joining us. "Sarah Lucinda, call your brothers," she'd say, and fighting back tears she'd grimly serve us dried-out roasts, scorched vegetables, and pasty casseroles—dishes that could withstand frequent reheatings even after they had been cooked beyond recognition.

Other mothers had cars, and spent their days shopping, getting their hair done, having lunch with friends, taking in matinees, driving into Chicago, or just—just not being around. Our mother took a dim view of all this gallivanting about. No doubt she was jealous of their freedom. No doubt, too, she resented being the one mom at home to whom all these abandoned kids gravitated. Worse, our mother had never learned to drive, and even if she had, she had no car. She couldn't reciprocate had she wanted to go on these trips, and soon enough the offers petered out. Which was fine, our mother said, she'd rather go to the Arie Crown Theater anyway, or to the Brookfield Zoo, or to the Field Museum—places she could go with our father and us.

But the company car seemed capable of going only to certain places. "I want to go to the Botanic Garden," said our mother, to which our father replied, "You don't want to go there," as though he'd already checked it out and found it wanting. "Yes I do," said our mother. "Fine," said our father, turning the pages of his newspaper. "Get yourself a car and go."

"I don't need your car," said our mother, in a tone that made it plenty clear he was optional, too, as far as she was concerned.

Our parents did go places, but usually they were company functions, or trips to see Benny Wilkerson or Louie Hwasko—our father's friends, our mother's only by extension. She didn't see her friends anymore. Helen Federstam had moved to California, and Agnes Guranski had moved with her husband to Michigan. Benny, on the other hand, lived in the next suburb over, and Louie had bought some land and built a house outside Rockford, where he had set himself up in dental practice and was licking his wounds after his marriage had gone south. That was our father's term for it: Louie's marriage had gone south. It had actually gone west: Helen Federstam had married him two years before I was born and left him two years later. "Everyone was getting married. I thought I should, too. I liked it that Louie could whistle," Helen reported to our mother in the weeks leading up to her departure. They were having coffee in the kitchen, one of the last times our mother enjoyed that with a friend. "That's not enough to base a marriage on, though you could have fooled me at the time. What was I thinking? So how's it going with Mr. Accordion? Better?" Our mother didn't answer that one.

Just before she left for California, Helen called on our mother again. "He moved me out there to East Bumbleshoot, and now he's raising chinchillas. It's creepy. He's in the barn all the time in the evenings. I could be in a negligee with a vodka martini in my hand and he'd rather be feeding them pellets. Beware a man with a scheme. He thinks he's doing it all for you—like I've been crying for a chinchilla fur coat—when he's really just doing it for himself. I decided to leave while I still possessed some semblance of sanity."

"Good riddance," said our father. "No kids, leaving him like that, for no good reason."

"Walter," said our mother. "She had very good reasons. Reasons you don't know anything about."

"What reasons? What?"

Our mother couldn't articulate them. Perhaps they were too close to her own, and she didn't dare voice them. Our mother simply said, "She's my friend. I miss her."

"Well your friend broke Louie's heart," said our father, "and I say, good riddance."

Our father displayed the same lack of comprehension and anger whenever our mother mentioned she wanted a pet, which she'd been doing for months now. "Eight people in this house and you want to add a ninth? And I'm not even counting Artu!"

"It's not like a cat takes up the same room as a person," countered our mother.

"There's no room, no room, no room!" said our father.

"A cat can be as quiet as a mouse," said our mother.

"That's what you said about Nomi!"

"Let's go look at pet supplies," said our mother the next time we went to Woolworth's.

Such a trip was our family's equivalent of Hannibal crossing the Alps. Pregnant with Ernie, pushing Wally Jr. in a stroller that balked at every curb, our mother waddled down Madison to the York Road bus stop, accompanied by me. I'd been plucked from our fort—a ramshackle building on an empty lot down the street constructed out of two-by-fours, plywood, and paneling we'd liberated from various building sites—by our mother, who already had Wally Jr. trussed and temporarily pacified in the stroller. Sarah and Robert Aaron complained. Hadn't I just had an "out"? Our mother insisted; I was born the day after Christmas and therefore shortchanged in the celebration department. ("You were born on Boxing Day," said our father. "In England, we could return you.")

I knew what awaited us at Woolworth's: counter stools and a waitress named Madge, who looked at us as though we were an incarnation of the Holy Family. Soup for our mother and a grilled-cheese sandwich for us, the plate garnished with the strangest condiment in the world: parsley.

After a leisurely lunch, we would wander up and down the aisles looking at glassware and plate sets, small appliances and kitchen supplies, wire racks of greeting cards, wall clocks and alarm clocks, women's underthings—I averted my eyes and/or stared guiltily—and then, way in the back, near the storeroom and the employee lounge and the bathroom, the pet area.

I felt strange being on "an out" with our mother. In the wake of my trip to the Office, I thought I had something special with our father. But I was mistaken in that belief. He took us—me—on other errands around town, but after my special trip I became one of "you kids" again, and the Office reverted to being a mysterious place, a place to which our father disappeared, and from which he returned a different person altogether. I could not enlighten my siblings as to what went on at the Office because I felt sworn to secrecy—"Loose lips sink ships"—and because I was reasonably sure our mother would take a dim view of my having been there at all. I did not understand what had happened that one time, but I had the feeling that our father, when tested, had acted nobly. This was not our mother's interpretation of his behavior, though it wasn't clear whether her response was to the incident with Shirley, or to the fact that as often as not he did not act so nobly. At Grandma Hubie's, for example, I had wanted him to act noble and large and kindhearted, and he hadn't. He'd acted small and mean and aggressive. And he had been acting this way for a while now. This, too, was taking its toll on our mother.

I should have known that on an out with our mother I should not bring up our father's behavior, but I think I wanted these essentially separate worlds, our mother's and our father's, to connect. So at the end of lunch I blew it. I was softly spinning myself back and forth on my stool as our mother figured out the bill and handed two dollars to the waitress. She got her change and put a quarter next to her plate. "That's a tip," our mother said.

"I know," I said. "And here's another: Loose lips sink ships."

"Where did you hear that?" Her lips went thin. "Never mind. I should have known."

"He always leaves a dollar," I said, as though I knew what I was talking about.

"I'm sure he does," said our mother, getting off her stool as quickly as she could manage. "Come on," she said, "we're doing some shopping. And on your father's nickel," she added.

We went straight to Pets. "I should have done this years ago," said our mother. We went from cage to cage, staring the animals in the beak, in the snout, in whatever they offered us for a nose. "I want a bird, Emmie," she said, peering into the cages. "I want something that knows what I feel and can sing."

What did my mother feel? I had no idea. But I knew she couldn't sing. She had a terrible singing voice, a fact attested to every Sunday when she sang "Faith of Our Fathers" and "Ave Maria." It was a voice I was to inherit, and I felt sympathy for her, our father's tenor soaring over her cracks and croaks (mine, too, though I didn't know that at the time).

I did wonder, though, if this had anything to do with our father coming home from the Office with another woman's name written on his back in unguent. It turned out Shirley had pressed her nail down rather hard when she wrote—our father's grinning at the time must have been him gritting his teeth—and the letters of her name stood out in raised white letters against the burnt offering of his back as though they were embossed there. I know this because the day after our visit to the Office our father requested that I, not our mother, put the unguent on his back. "If Emcee's going to have a medical career, he's going to have to learn how to do these things," said our father, which was the first I'd heard of my aspirations toward medicine. Our mother skeptically raised an eyebrow but said nothing. I applied unguent, smearing it as gently as I could on our father's back, gingerly going over the raised, ghostly letters. It was not quite right, I was sure, for Shirley to have written her name like that, and it made me feel strange, my fingers tracing their raised surfaces. I tried putting on extra unguent, hoping to cover them under an orange smear, but they were still visible, like a message written in the mud of a glacial lake.

"What do you think of that one?" our mother said, pointing to a brilliantly hued parrot gnawing on its cage. I didn't like the way it was looking at me. It looked sinister, like it might come into our house, learn our secrets, and fly away with them banded to its leg. I shook my head. "That's okay," said our mother, pushing the stroller to the next cage. "It's too expensive anyway." The mynah birds were similarly expensive, which was fine with me. The orange spots of bare flesh next to their eyes gave them a tough look, as though they'd put on Halloween masks for the sole purpose of taking your candy. The canaries I didn't like because they looked like furred lemons, and it was beginning to look as if our mother was simply indulging her wish to own a pet by extending the sphere of her sighs when she stopped in front of one last cage that held not one but two parakeets. They were the color of unripe bananas, pale yellow heads and bodies, sickly green wings, the green in the sixty-four-color Crayola set that you used when you wanted to draw trees leafing out in spring. One was chattering away, the other stood stock-still on its perch, its head canted a little as though it were tired of listening to its partner.

"That one," said my mother, pointing at the still one. "It needs me."

Had I been the sullen, smart-ass teenager I would later become I might have said, "Great, Mom, parakeet intervention." Or had I been the smarty-pants college boy with one psychology course under his belt I'd become after that I might have said, "You're nesting, Mom. And really, a bird to represent your pathetic desires to get away? Get real." But I wasn't seventeen or nineteen. I was six, and what I said was fatal. What I said was "What will Dad say?"

My mother's answer chilled me. "I don't care what your father says," my mother said, clutching her belly like it was a basket full of laundry.

She must have seen the look of horror on my face. "We'll get him something, too," she said brightly, and indeed, in choosing a goldfish and a pair of neon tetras for our father, her mood noticeably brightened, as though the purpose of our trip had been to get him a present all along.

To buy my silence my mother also said I could pick out a turtle. They were all alike, but I spent a great deal of time trying to find one with the right personality, one that could contemplate the world impassively, yet also paddle around just for the fun of it when I wanted a more lively companion. This was nigh impossible since the turtles seemed to do only one thing or the other, but at last I chose one, a slow paddler that came ashore on the wading pool's hump of sand. He winked at me—I was sure it was a wink, not a random blink—assuring me that he could go a lot faster if I wanted him to. He was still resting when the Woolworth's clerk followed my finger and plucked my turtle out from the masses. "You got a good one," said the clerk, a thin, balding older gentleman with glasses slipping down his nose, and I wondered how he knew. Still, it confirmed my choice. The Woolworth's man had concurred with me, his white lab coat lending an air of esteem and wisdom to my choice.

Meanwhile our mother was picking out equipment for this mélange of wildlife she had suddenly decided to buy. She had to get a cart from the front to hold it all. I didn't look when she paid, it was too embarrassing. This pregnant woman (which, as far as I knew, was simply how our mother always looked) trying to push both a stroller with Wally Jr. in it and a cart filled with the accoutrements of her sudden whim: a fishbowl, a windmill for the fishbowl, a squat bag of fish, a birdcage (mildly Victorian with its gazebolike roof), a box of birdseed, some gizmo for the parakeet to sharpen its beak on, a little plastic tub for my turtle, and a shoebox with my turtle in it. For all this she laid out what looked like a week's worth of grocery money.

We must have been quite a sight, struggling out of the store and across the railroad tracks to where we could pick up the bus back to York and Madison. A woman with a polka-dotted housedress stretched across her middle and a determined, exasperated look on her face trying to steer a stroller loaded to the gills while clutching the hand of an eggheaded two-year-old, his abashed older brother lagging behind.

Balanced precariously atop the packages in the stroller was the bag of fish and the cage with the parakeet. I expected both at any moment to topple into the street. I could see it very clearly: the bag bursting open, the fish gasping and flipping in the street, the parakeet chirping piteously as cars struck it glancing blows until a Wonder Bread delivery van put it out of its misery with a direct hit. This seemed like the logical conclusion to our adventure.

That we made it home without incident was due only to our mother's quick hands at constantly righting the pile, and her determination to ignore the wails of Wally Jr., who was now missing his nap. "You're making a spectacle of yourself," our mother hissed to Wally Jr., as though a whiny two-year-old could be looked at separately from his milieu. To our mother, making a spectacle of yourself was one of the worst things you could do. She had an endearing sort of blindness in applying this notion to herself.

"Look what we brought, look what we brought!" our mother cried as we arrived home. She was tired, but she put on a show of exuberance so that we would all be excited with "our" acquisitions before our father came home. He would be less likely to order everything back to the store if we were wildly enthusiastic. "Walter, the children," our mother could say, and our father could concede or play the ogre, a role he played often but never consciously. To our mother's credit, she used this stratagem seldom, but she used it on this particular day, putting all the packages on the kitchen table and calling everyone in before she began the grand unveiling. The goldfish and the neon tetras were our father's, she said, but the parakeet and the turtle were everyone's. "Look, see what Emmie has in the box for us."

For us? I thought. No, for me. It was my turtle. I clutched the shoe box to my chest. We were home now; new rules were being applied. "It's everybody's turtle," our mother said. She had a hard look in her eye. I knew I shouldn't mess with her, not with what we'd just been through, but I was adamant. "But I've already named him Eddie," I said.

"Fine," said our mother lightly, definitively. "Everybody's turtle is named Eddie."

Our father didn't stand a chance of getting her to go back on this one. It turned out he didn't have to. His attention, when he got home hours later, was directed elsewhere. After everyone oohed and aahed over the animals and Nomi'd gotten her cautionary shot in ("I don't normally take Walter's side, Susan, but what were you thinking?"), our mother cleared everything away. Lucky's cage with Lucky inside was put under a blanket in the living room ("He needs to get acclimated to his new home," explained our mother), my turtle and tub were put in the bathroom ("Until he's acclimated; then he goes outside," said our mother. "Fat chance," said Nomi), and the fish, still inside their bag, were put into their fishbowl, filled now with cool water ("Until they get *acclimated*," said Cinderella). Our mother folded the bags and put them under the sink. Then she got a huge wicker basket full of whites and went downstairs with Cinderella to put them in the washer while the rest of us—except for Wally Jr., who went down for his nap—went to study Eddie as he pawed the sides of his tub, looking for a way out.

The crash and the kathumping and the screams we heard next were absolutely chilling. Shrieks of pure terror, shrieks so high-pitched they sounded like air-raid sirens. Bottomless screams, without beginning or end, ascending as they did into registers only dogs could hear. We heard them plenty well, and they froze us. We caught each other's eyes, Ike and Robert Aaron and I. Then we pummeled into the hallway, sick with dread. What would we see, what would we see? Nothing, if Nomi had her way. The door to the basement was open, and Nomi was at the top of the stairs. "Good God," she said and gestured us away. Then she hobbled her way down to where Cinderella was shrieking, quite plainly beyond reason.

Nomi's shooing gesture caused us to back up, but as soon as she was down the stairs we crowded forward. Our mother was down there, splayed at the foot of the stairs in a pool of blood. One arm was crooked over her head, and the other cupped her belly. Her head was tipped sideways. That was where all the blood was coming from. Ike burst into wailing, forming a duet with our sister. "Robert! For God's sake get them back." Nomi waved, and Robert got us to edge back from the stairway. Then we crept forward again, fascinated and sick at heart. We knew what was down there: the concrete basement floor, the open stairs, the lack of a railing. We could imagine the missed step, the grab for support that wasn't there. What we couldn't imagine was the rest of it, how our mother had tumbled, how she had landed. We had seen the results, but we didn't know how she had gotten there, and we did and didn't want to know.

For a moment we dared not look. We could hear Nomi calming Cinderella, hear the ripping of sheets. Nomi was saying that Cinderella had to run next door, to the Duckwas, and ask them to call an ambulance. I think she just wanted to get her out of there. As Cinderella came up, I peered over the threshold again. Our mother was awkwardly twisted at the bottom of the stairs, and the sheets and underwear and socks in the laundry basket were scattered about her head or draped over her like a robe. The whites were crimson. Nomi was kneeling next to our mother, lifting her head and wiping away the blood so she could see the extent of the damage. Robert Aaron asked, "Is she—? Is she—?" That was as far as he could get. My brain answered in a monotone. Our mother looked like a bloody angel, and there were these words, teletyped and scrolling off the screen of my mind over and over, like on TV when the stations are reporting thunderstorms or tornadoes. My brain kept repeating the words, as though through repetition they wouldn't mean anything anymore, certainly not what I knew them to mean: *My mother is dead, my mother is dead, my mother is dead.*

Mrs. Duckwa arrived and took us to her house. We sat on her couch, and she fluttered about, offering us cookies and Kool-Aid, pacing, smoking cigarettes, shooing us back to the couch whenever one of us got up to look out her windows as she was, holding the curtain open with one hand while anxiously watching the street. When the ambulance came, we rushed to the window and she didn't try to stop us until the gurney appeared with our mother on it. Then she shushed us back and had us sit on the couch again. Her daughter came home, and Mrs. Duckwa said, "Do something with them." The daughter whose name we didn't know—she was simply the Duckwa daughter—looked at us with something like sympathy and said, "You wanna play Monopoly or something?" We shook our heads. The sight of our mother on a gurney was enough to silence us. The Duckwa daughter shrugged and went to her room. She reappeared when her mother asked her to keep an eye on us, and sat with us while Mrs. Duckwa hurried outside. Our father had arrived, and Mrs. Duckwa told him what happened. Then our father drove off, his tires peeling. Mrs. Duckwa came in and said, "He's going to the hospital. He'll call once he knows everything is fine."

For the next five hours we sat on that couch, filled with dread and uncertainty. Five of us, arranged according to height, with identical stricken looks on our long thin faces. Our father hadn't called, and Mrs. Duckwa forgot to feed us. When she did remember, she confessed she didn't have much in the way of kid food. She wouldn't have remembered at all except her daughter came through announcing she was meeting friends for pizza. Mrs. Duckwa looked at us and said, "Oh, my, you little dears." She heated up some hot dogs and served them on dry buns without mustard or ketchup. Mrs. Duckwa did not eat with us. Evidently Mrs. Duckwa lived on cigarettes and whatever she was drinking from what our father called a "rocks" glass. Mr. Duckwa had not come home yet. Mrs. Duckwa said he sometimes worked late, sometimes he ate out, and sometimes, well, sometimes, she said, stubbing out her cigarette and lighting another, sometimes Mr. Duckwa was a regular SOB. After we ate we put the dishes in the sink, and Cinderella washed them. We went back to the couch. Mrs. Duckwa remained at the table smoking and drinking. Every once in a while she came in to where we were sitting and said, "Your mom's going to be all right. Everything will turn out fine." We didn't believe her—from the torn look of worry on her face we could tell she didn't believe herself either; I think she was afraid nobody was going to come for us and she'd be stuck with us—but we were too polite to say so. Unspoken in all this, and driving our dread, was our knowledge that there was a baby inside our mother's tummy, and we knew it was not good for a baby to be falling down the stairs. We tried to cheer each other up: "Kids bounce," said Cinderella, trying to sound like our father. "Maybe the baby bounced." "Shut up, Cinders," said Robert Aaron.

But it was true, sort of. Our father came home about eleven with the news that our mother was okay, considering. She had a concussion and a broken—smashed to pieces, really—nose and a gash above her ear that required twenty-eight stitches to close (it was the gash and the nose that produced all that blood), and they were keeping her overnight for observation, but she was okay other than that. Nomi was staying with her. The baby, as far as they could tell, was going to be all right. It was just as the chain-smoking Mrs. Duckwa had said. As Cinderella had said. As our father always said. Kids bounce.

For years afterward we were reminded of our family's near brush with tragedy each morning as we got dressed. Our underwear, our socks, our T-shirts—they all bore the once bright, now brown stains of our mother's blood.

9. You Know What They Do with Horses, Don't You?

"You can't look at your mother, can you?" said our mother.

It was true. For a little while our mother had been a bloody angel. She'd been almost beautiful, lying at the bottom of the stairs, her stomach great with child, clothes strewn about her, blood streaming out of her. She had been, for those brief moments we stood at the top of the stairs gazing at her, an icon: mythic, eternal, still as plaster.

Seeing her back inside her body again, with a big square of gauze taped to her nose and a long rectangle of it over her ear, her bandages leaking yellow ointment and stained with blood—it was creepy. She had been someplace else and come back damaged. Was she even the same person? People lost their memories all the time after a conk on the head. They were completely different people. I'd seen lots of TV shows where that happened. We had a whole religion based on something like this: He'd died, and when He came back He was a completely different person. He hung around afterward for a while, but He was different, everyone knew it, and eventually He just went up in the clouds and disappeared.

So this stranger in our living room, wincing as she served drinks to Nomi and Artu and the Duckwas and to Aunt Margie and Alvin and Grandma Hubie—it was a little celebration party for her coming home safely—I was wary of her. She seemed different, and it wasn't just the huge butterfly wings of gauze over her nose. But then she pulled me into her lap and nibbled my ear to make me giggle and I decided, reluctantly, that this woman back from the dead was indeed my mother. Still, it was unsettling.

It was a time of unsettledness and uncertainty. Our pets were dying, the town was changing, and our father was becoming more and more restless.

Lucky's quiet demeanor in the store had been misleading. He was not stoic; he was diseased. His eyes clouded with gunk, then swelled shut. His feathers turned translucent, then fell out. Raw, angry skin took up residence beneath the molt. He shat green goop, and his belly distended as though he were a child from some third world country. "Pitiful," our mother pronounced every morning as she lifted the blanket off Lucky's cage, and Nomi echoed, "Pitiful." Then she asked, "When are you going to put that bird out of its misery?" Lucky died before our mother felt she needed to answer. We found Lucky at the bottom of his cage atop page 3 of the *Chicago Tribune,* his beak posed as though he were searching for goodies up Mayor Daley's nose.

Our mother promptly got another one. She took each of us in turn, as one Lucky after another died. There were five in all. Each seemed fine for a while, chirping and learning a few words of English, fluttering about the house when our mother let her—or him; we were never strong on bird gender—out of the cage, then becoming ill or despondent, eating little, drinking less, until each one faded quickly and finally died.

The first Lucky had something like a state funeral: a shoe box lined with tinfoil, a worn handkerchief of our father's, his name lettered on a Popsicle-stick cross. Our father played "Taps" on the accordion, then "Ghost Riders in the Sky" (one of the few times the accordion had come out of the closet since the Kaopectate Wars), then took us out for ice cream. It was a fine Saturday in late September, warm and breezy, and the next day in church we prayed for Lucky's soul. By Lucky IV or V, though, we were throwing them out with the trash, folded in newspaper so it wouldn't open until the can was upended over the garbage truck.

Our mother cried, but she also thought Lucky's death was atonement for Ernie. He'd survived the fall, and if God was going to take it out on her in dead birds, so be it.

Eddie fared no better, though he died of kindness. A turtle, we believed, needed a moist environment. So we lined his tub with wet newspapers and drenched them daily. His feet grew a white cottony fungus, and the skin came off in pale white strips. When he died soon after, I buried him in a shoe box with a Popsicle-stick cross lettered: "Here lies Eddie, a good turtle."

Our father, despite playing the accordion at Lucky I's funeral, had little patience for our or our mother's demonstrations of grief. "Kids bounce, turtles don't," he said when our mother brought up the idea of a replacement turtle. And just before Eddie died our father told us, "You know what they do with horses, don't you?" He made a gun out of his thumb and forefinger. His thumb went down like a trigger and he winked. He said the same thing to us when we were sick, and he said it to our mother after Ernie was born. As though death were a comical threat you could hold over someone's head.

When his own fish went belly-up, he put this theory into practice. No shoe boxes in the backyard, no Popsicle-stick grave markers, no "Taps." It was strictly burial at sea, our father standing disdainfully over the toilet, hosing them down with his own pee. Capone, our father said, did this over the graves of his enemies. We didn't think these fish were his enemies, but they had disappointed him by dying, these fish. What did they expect? And then he pulled the trigger and flushed them out of his, and our, memory.

More unsettling, perhaps, than our inability to keep our pets alive was what was happening to our town. Elmhurst had begun its life as a sleepy prairie town at the end of the trolley line. Post-Korea, it had turned into a modest, then teeming suburb. If you looked only at what you wanted to see, you could ignore its lurchings into sprawl, its open spaces filled in, the playing fields sprouting houses. We were home one day when a bulldozer was unloaded in the last empty lot—the lot where we'd constructed a ramshackle clubhouse—our fort, our jail, our place for privacy. Years later Robert Aaron and I created another such space in the air above our house. And Dorie, I suppose, creates it when she is bicycling by herself across the country. Everyone needs such a place, and most of us will go to great lengths to protect that sacred spot. We ran over to protest. "But that's our clubhouse," we said, pointing. Said the bulldozer operator, "It's okay, kids, we're just going to move it over to the corner of the lot here."

You should not lie to kids like that. We would have taken it a whole lot better if he'd simply said, "Hey, we're going to crush your precious little fort into unrecognizable sticks of kindling." But he didn't. We watched as the bulldozer trundled into position, snuffled, huffed, lowered its blade, and without so much as a pause to indicate uncertainty, leveled our clubhouse.

We ran home crying, but when our father came home, he shrugged. "Town's growing," he said. "What can you do? It used to be Indians here. Now it's us. That's progress."

"Wally," said our mom, "destroying their clubhouse without apologizing is not progress."

"Would it have been better if he had apologized? Look, the kids just have to get used to things changing."

"Like you do at the Office every evening?"

If you wanted to, you could pretend that a sea change was not taking place, but it was. And our father, despite his stiff-upper-lipping with us, could feel it. We heard him at night, railing about how the town wasn't what it used to be. He wasn't much crazy about his job, either, spending the better part of each day stuck in Loop traffic trying to get from one doctor's office to another. He wanted a change. He didn't mind the selling, he told our mother, he actually liked that—he was good at it, he said, it suited him—it was all the goddamn driving around in traffic. If only Dinkwater-Adams would give him a new territory, and not just outside the Loop. Our father meant *territory*. "Like up in Wisconsin," our father said to our mother late one night. Let him operate out of a small town, and he could call on the doctors and hospitals in other small towns. "And the kids, Marie"—when our father got excited he called our mom by her middle name; we'd heard him sigh "Marie, Marie, Marie, Marie" during "you know"—"you think they'd be crying about a smashed clubhouse if we lived out in the country? They could build a million forts, a million tree houses." Our father was into it now. Once he started saying "a million this, a million that," there was no stopping him unless our mother physically put her finger on his lips. Our father said, "The way it's going right now there's no space for them to play in, Marie, and it's not likely there's going to be any trees left for them to climb, either—you read that in the paper, Susan—Dutch elm is wiping out the trees, and pretty soon there won't be any more goddamn trees, and who—"

"Walter?" Our mother placed a finger on our father's lips.

"Yes?"

"And what would I do?"

Our father is silent a moment. It's clear he hasn't thought of this. But then you can almost hear his face light up. "Why, you'd hold down the fort," he says and adds, as though our mother hadn't gotten the joke, "Get it, hold down the fort? And it wouldn't be just any fort, either, no, they could build tree forts, tree houses. A whole city in the trees," says our father, warming up to it again. And sitting on the stairs above them, hidden, we are carried away with him, imagining a forest of trees with big, sturdy branches, each of them supporting an elaborate, multistory tree house, with rope ladders and bridges and swings leading from tree to tree.

"You know I've always wanted to live in the country, Susan." Our father's voice was quieter now, calmer. What was happening down there?

"Well, Wally-Bear, I haven't. What would I do in the country, Wally? I'll tell you—nothing. I'll have nothing to do, and you'll be traveling all the time, and I'll go stark staring mad. I'll be so crazy you'll have to lock me up."

"I have to lock you up now."

"That's *lock* me up, Wally, not knock me up."

We could picture the scene now. Our mother had moved into our father's lap. She had her arms around his neck and she was kissing him. Then our father said, "Mmmph!" the chair got pushed back, there was a clatter, a crash, and an *ow!* from our father, and then our mother, of all people, said, "You know what they do with horses, don't you?" And then they were laughing, and there were more mmph! mmph!'s and a sighed "Marie!" and Cinderella said, "C'mon, show's over," which meant it wasn't, but as far as we were concerned, it was.

The last thing we heard before we crept back up the stairs was our father saying to our mother—and we could picture her in our father's arms when he said this, just before he pushed open the door to their bedroom with his foot and then closed it, just like Jackie Gleason with Audrey Meadows in *The Honeymooners*—"Susan Marie, you're the greatest!" And we knew then that whatever was being decided, it would be decided under the influence and afterglow of you know, which meant that it would occur in an absence of reason, that it would be undertaken quite happily by our mother, and that it would be thoroughly flawed.

He was right about the trees. Elmhurst was aptly named until Dutch elm disease denuded the city. The full devastation took place after we'd left, but the days of biking beneath those huge intertwining crowns, those days when even on hot, bright July afternoons you bicycled in a cave of dark coolness, the boughs above you a shimmering translucent green, were numbered. Already holes were showing in the crown, gaps in the firmament.

It was a sign, had anyone taken notice: in the natural world, things were not right. Any dramatist worth his salt knows what that means. But who wanted to believe the gloom and doom predictions of a couple of plant pathologists at Elmhurst College? Two plant pathologists, skinny and poorly married, the sort of geeky, eggheaded academics that it was already fashionable not to listen to. They didn't come off well in town meetings, their noses buried in the reports from which they were reading, and what they recommended would have cost lots of money—clear-cutting trees with early infestations or in proximity to said trees and squirting the bejesus out of the rest with chemicals. They said with such precautions you could save probably 60, perhaps 70 percent of the trees. But who believes that scientific claptrap? It wasn't until after the town had been denuded that they remembered the two pathologists and said to them, "Why didn't you *warn* us about this stuff?"

Our parents, no doubt, felt the same way. Threats were everywhere. There were drugs in the high schools now—marijuana, LSD. Even in the private high schools, which had once seemed so safe. Sure, terrible things happened at York High—kids beaten up, beer parties—but at Montini, the private school where Sarah wanted to go? The older sister of one of Sarah's friends had gotten pregnant there after a prom. Pregnant! How could that be? And, of course, the Duckwas' marriage was on the rocks. We pictured them hung up in a boat, so busy blaming each other over how they got there that they hadn't realized yet they were taking on water.

There was a sense now that accidents, when they occurred, were permanent. After falling down the stairs with Ernie still inside her, our mother had gotten pregnant one more time, even though the doctor had warned her that another pregnancy would be dangerous. "It was an accident," she told Dr. Wilton. "It wasn't like we were planning on it." Dr. Wilton said accidents like this could be prevented, and she and our father hadn't planned any of the rest of us, either. She did realize, didn't she, that it was possible to have sex without getting pregnant? Our mother said she understood that, and though it wasn't any of his business, just for the record she and Wally "you knowed" quite often. As Catholics, however, they practiced rhythm. Ah, said Dr. Wilton. Practiced. And did she know what you called someone who "practiced" the rhythm method? Our mother said she didn't. You called her Mommy, said Dr. Wilton. "It will be the last one," our mother insisted. "It had better be," said Dr. Wilton. "You don't have enough hormones in you to make more than one."

When Meg was born, so tiny, with one leg slightly shorter than the other and with bones that broke easily (she was two when she repeated our mother's swan dive down the basement stairs), Dr. Wilton's warning seemed oddly prophetic. Permanent accidents, Dr. Wilton called us, and our mother all but agreed with him. Our mother recounted her visit to Dr. Wilton to our father that evening. Cinderella, Robert Aaron, and I were on the stairs, listening intently—the Hear Evil, See Evil, Speak Evil little homunculi. It was like we had radar that picked up whenever they were talking about us.

"They *were* accidents, Marie, every last one of them," said our father.

"But they're *our* accidents, Wally, and I seem to remember we had a pretty good time making them." We could hear them kissing. She was probably on his lap again.

"No argument there," said our father. He was making smoochie sounds.

"We knew what we were doing, Wally. If they were accidents, they were planned."

"You mean intended?" More kissing. Our father groaned; our mother sighed. Good God, were they going to . . . you know . . . right there in the kitchen? Our mother was already pregnant. Was this how you got twins?

"Intended, planned, and permanent," said our mother. "Every last one of them."

"What if there are problems?" said our father. "These last few haven't been easy for you. Dr. Wilton's right about that."

"There are always problems," said our mother. "We'll deal with those as they arrive."

Which was what our mother did when Meg arrived with one leg shorter than the other. Was this because Meg was an accident? No, said our mother, she was a gift from God.

Still, if this was God's idea of a gift, He had a pretty perverse sense of humor.

Our father got more and more restless. He wanted his dreams to be taken seriously. He had grown up watching Al Capone's cars whiz past him in an alley, and he knew Capone had numerous getaways and lodges up in Wisconsin. These weren't just places where he could "lie low until the heat wore down." These were places where Capone went to hunt and fish, to reflect, to unwind—in short, to renew his soul. Our father, I think, wanted a new soul. He wanted to be a farmer. A gentleman farmer, anyway, and Dinkwater-Adams wouldn't let him.

For some time he'd been railing about this, particularly whenever he came back from the Office. "Jesus, Susan Marie," he'd say at night, when we weren't supposed to hear him, "they won't let me breathe. All I wanna do is just goddamn breathe. Is that so much to ask?"

"No, Wally, no. Now drink your milk and come to bed." Our mother possessed the unique ability to be distraught with and angry at our father while also pitying him.

Our father had been trying to find meaningful ways to exorcise his restlessness besides spending time down at the Office. To that end he began building a boat in the basement. Not in our basement—he didn't have the room or the tools—but in his parents' basement in Morton Grove, which offered him spaciousness and plenty of woodworking tools, Grandpa Cza-Cza having acquired them over the years in the manner that many men do: by going to the hardware store on those Saturday mornings when the prospect of spending the entire day with his wife was simply too much to bear. As our father's helpers, we were allowed to witness the phenomenon every Saturday. Whenever Grandma Cza-Cza started to harp on Grandpa Cza-Cza, Grandpa Cza-Cza zipped a jacket up tight to his chin, put on an English driving cap, and announced, "I'm going to the hardware store. We need more wood screws." Or sandpaper, or C-clamps, or pipe clamps, or a screwdriver, or a wood steamer, lightbulbs, coping saw blades, carpenter's pencils, steel wool, tack cloths, paintbrushes, turpentine, adjustable wrenches, wood chisels, a wood-splitting wedge, and an ax—these last even though there were no trees on their property and no fireplace in which to burn the wood he split. For Grandpa Cza-Cza, the hardware store was the Office.

Had it been up to our father, we would not have been designated his helpers. He would have gone up to his father's alone, worked all day, maybe spending the night if he didn't have to usher at church the next morning, and come home Sunday evening at dinnertime. Our mother did not let him indulge in his druthers. If our father was going to visit his parents, shouldn't he take his children along, at least the older boys, and give them a hobby, a lifetime skill, not to mention some time with their father?

So we were our father's designated helpers, only we weren't allowed to help. Our father was an immensely patient man when he was by himself—when he was behind the wheel of a car, say—but he was easily frustrated. His patience with us was wide but shallow, like rivers in Nebraska. He could irrigate us with his love, but we shouldn't count on a steady stream. "Here, you kids, sand this," he'd say and give us a block of wood. Sometimes it was a piece meant to go on the boat, sometimes it was a block of wood.

When we got bored there was always the rest of the basement. Grandpa Cza-Cza had a shuffleboard court inlaid in the floor tile in the next room, and we could usually while away a few hours on that. Grandpa also had a cream-colored bas relief of the *Venus de Milo*. I had seen better breasts on the Duckwa daughter. She wore a bikini while sunbathing, undid the straps when lying on her stomach. Once she forgot herself and stood up without redoing them. That something so secret could be so completely revealed and yet remain a mystery was, I thought, roughly on a par with transubstantiation. Still, the breasts of Venus were pretty good. It was a pity about her arms, though.

When our father found us staring at the sightless woman's nipples he said, "Learn to appreciate that, it's art." But we knew it wasn't—what was it doing hanging in the basement then? Or maybe he meant not the whole picture but the breasts themselves. That I could understand—the Duckwa daughter was, after all, a work of art. Sometimes when it was time to go home our father stood with a beer in front of Venus, her raised surfaces luscious enough to touch. He'd whistle and say, "Batta-bing, batta-bing, eh? Don't tell your mother I let you stare." I think he understood that the *Venus de Milo* was our escape, that we looked at her raptly not just for her anatomy but because losing ourselves in her mystery was an escape from our own boredom.

Our father never lacked for escapes. Dorie neither. She's come up with a new one. Two, actually. We're having a beer, watching the kids being marched down to Ike's tepee, and Dorie says to me, "This next year I'm going to need to be out of the house more."

"More than you are now?" I mentally tick off everything that already keeps her out of the house—the fifty-mile training rides, the fourteen-mile training runs, the classes on mountain-biking technique, trail building, the rides themselves, and—oh yeah—all the property she's managing. Twenty-some apartment houses in Veedon Park and the adjoining neighborhood. Technically she owns half the bookstore, too.

"I want to participate in some of those Ironman triathlons, and my swimming's for shit right now. And"—slow breath here—"I've decided to run for alderwoman."

"I thought you decided against that."

"I changed my mind. People are allowed to change their minds, Em."

"Feeling restless again? You could always work in the bookstore with me."

"I'd like to make a difference, Em. I can hire a manager for the properties."

"And between that, the biking, and the triathlon training, who's going to hold down the fort?"

"The kids are old enough. They won't be a problem for you."

"And what, exactly, do I get out of all this?"

"A happy wife?"

"Besides that."

"You want more? We don't have a conventional marriage, Em. We never have."

"Sure we do. It's just everything's reversed." I have a pull of my beer. This must be what our mother always felt, buried under a slurry of prepositions: being *at* home, waiting *for* our father, waiting *on* our father.

Dorie curls her arms around her legs, her chin on her knees. For the second time she asks me, "Don't you ever feel restless, Em? Don't you ever feel as though your head's going to explode?" I'd like to tell her, Sure, lots of times. Now, for instance, but she doesn't give me the chance. "Never mind, Em, I can see you haven't. Thank God I run and lift weights—it's a safe way of burning off all that restless energy." Again with the safe. I wonder if it's a line she uses at the gym, a way of flirting with the guys there. Or something she says to the guys she meets on these organized rides. See how they respond to words like *safe* and *restless energy.*

"There are dangerous ways, I suppose." Mustering up my affability.

"Don't I know it. For a while there, Em, I felt as though I was coming apart. I was a different woman for a while, when I felt that. A woman I didn't recognize. Me and not me."

I knew what I was getting in Dorie Keillor a.k.a. Dorothy Braun when I married her. She had gone through a wild streak in high school and a wilder streak after that. Voracious in her appetite. But by the time we hooked up, she told me she was ready to settle down. Only what if she was mistaken? I imagine Dorie in a future life, with some other husband, our kids grown and gone, and the thought torments me so much I can't bear it. Worse, she's talking not hypotheticals but something that's already happened. What made her not recognize herself? And before she discovered the safe ways for burning off her restlessness, what were the reckless ones? I know, of course—there's that diaphragm and nightgown in her pannier to remind me, but I can't bring myself yet to ask her. Advice for attorneys: Never ask in court a question to which you don't already know the answer. Advice for husbands: Never ask your wife a question to which you don't want to know the answer.

Our father, so far as I knew, favored the safer ways. Besides the big boat he was building at Grandpa Cza-Cza's, in our basement he was building a model of the ship he spent so much time on a decade previous. He lugged down an old red linoleum and steel-legged kitchen table of Artu's, and from a hobby store bought sheets and sheets of balsa wood in various thicknesses, X-Acto knives, and dozens upon dozens of bottles of model paint, most of them gray. Working from photographs, he was going to build a three-foot-long replica of his ship. He wanted it exact, he said, right down to the little men vomiting over the side.

Perhaps our father's one unsafe pastime was visiting Uncle Louie. Our father felt this dovetailed nicely with his desire for "room to breathe." Our mother maintained it was just another way to visit the Office. Uncle Louie lived in a sprawling ranch house on a hill outside Rockford. He had five acres of land, a creek, and a long cinder-block building in which he raised chinchillas. Then Helen had left him, despite the chinchillas he was raising "expressly for her." When we went there it was a curious mix of country holiday and pity party.

Our father, Uncle Louie, our mom, and whatever woman Uncle Louie was dating would look at the chinchillas, make sandwiches and hot cocoa for us, and sit by the fire drinking Rob Roys (our father), sidecars (our mother), bourbon on the rocks (Uncle Louie), and God-knows-what (the woman Uncle Louie was currently seeing).

Things had not gone well for Uncle Louie since Helen had left him. He was doing well financially—enough so that he owned five acres outside Rockford and could lose money on the chinchillas—though he expected to see back his five-thousand-dollar initial investment, he told our father, "just as soon as the little shits start breeding." In the blockhouse—it smelled of disinfectant and rabbit turds—we helped Uncle Louie feed the furry little rodents. They looked like hamsters or guinea pigs, and you could see in our father's eyes that there was money to be made from this. "No, Wally," whispered our mother emphatically, and our father got a hangdog expression on his face.

The women Uncle Louie was seeing had no interest in the chinchillas except as they might appear in a muff or a collar or a stole. We asked our mother what a stole was. "A stole is what these women are doing to Uncle Louie."

"Hush," said our father. "Little pitchers."

"What?" said our mother. "They shouldn't hear to steer clear of that kind of woman?"

"What kind of woman?"

"You know," said our mother. "*That* kind of woman. The kind he seems bent on seeing. Helen may have had a short attention span, but she wasn't like *this.*"

That was why things weren't going well for Uncle Louie. He couldn't find somebody "to settle down with." Every time we went to visit he was dating a different woman, but our mother was right, they all seemed the same: women with big hair and brassy jewelry, women who laughed too loud and who wore too much makeup and not enough clothing. "Barmaids and cocktail waitresses," said our mother. She and our father discussed Uncle Louie's latest "find" on the drive home, when we were supposed to be asleep or not paying attention. "If that's his 'find,' " continued our mother, "I'd throw her back. Honestly, where *does* he find them? Never mind, I know exactly where he finds them. He just looks through the bottom of a bourbon bottle and there they are."

Myself, I could see Uncle Louie's attraction to these brassy, overweight, and invariably full-chested women. They always looked slightly disheveled, as though they hadn't quite put themselves together from what they'd been doing just before we arrived. Sitting next to Uncle Louie on the limestone hearth surrounding the circular fireplace, tall glasses of Seven & Seven in their hands, they seemed possessed of a sleepy, satisfied-yet-forlorn look, as though they were wondering, having just risen from the bed, Is that all there is? And though their lips—big, generous, and outlined in red—seemed ready to take in the world as they smiled and pursed over their drinks, there was also something desperate about them, incomplete. They reminded me of Mrs. Duckwa, and of that woman we met at the Office, the woman who wrote her name— Shirley—in the unguent smeared over my father's sunburn. Women who hadn't quite gotten what they wanted out of life and felt they were due.

No wonder they always seemed to end up hurting Uncle Louie. "You have to tell him, Wally," said our mother after one such visit. "He's your closest friend in the whole world—"

"Besides you," interjected our father.

"Besides me." Our mother smiled. "You have to tell him he can't keep on letting these women hurt him. He leaves himself wide open for that. Drinking himself silly and dating cocktail waitresses is not going to help him get over Helen. Helen was one of a kind."

"Yeah," said our father, "but what kind?"

Conversations like these happened when Uncle Louie was "between engagements."

"Engagements." Our mother snorted. "That's just what he says to make himself feel better over the fact that he's sleeping with them."

"I doubt he has to make himself feel better about that."

"You know what I mean. You're just defending him because you want to see him get laid. Those chinchillas aren't the only things breeding around here. He's just lucky he hasn't been any more successful at re-producing than they have."

When Uncle Louie was "seeing somebody" (which made it sound like he was blind the rest of the time), he drank too much, laughed a lot, treated us all to fish dinners at the Rockford Moose Club. The adults sat at the bar, and we kids were essentially forgotten, which was fine with us. In high spirits, Uncle Louie or our father told stories of being in the ser-vice, and all we had to do was show up, tug on their sleeves, and in a mat-ter of moments a fresh kiddie cocktail was handed to us, the maraschino cherries impaled on plastic red buccaneer's swords, which we used in our games of make-believe or later inserted into each other's anuses in the privacy of our room. Rockford's Moose Hall was identical to the ones in Lombard and Villa Park: an open hall done in a style best described as "Tudor gymnasium"—dark polyurethaned picnic tables, a tiny bandstand, and doorways that led to the bar and bathrooms. The bar area was done up with weird green carpeting and dark green or royal blue or red drapes. Or maybe it was red carpeting, and royal blue or seaweed green drapes. After seven or eight Shirley Temples it was hard to remember. We ate our fish fry, then went to see the moose head enshrined on the far wall, wondering what it was thinking behind its glassy eyes. Then we wandered between tables, hiding under the unused ones, remaining perfectly still as our hiding place filled in around us with thick calves and peasant ankles in hose and pumps and cuffed pants with wingtips or crepe-soled shoes. Once or twice we were shocked with a view of someone's garters and crotch, but we remained quiet, and eventually snuck out the far end of the table, shaking our heads over what we had seen.

The highlight of these evenings was when the band set up—a piano player or someone with a Hammond organ, a small drum kit, an upright bass. Men in gold lamé suits with crushed velvet collars and black trim on the pockets took the platform—you hesitated to call it a stage—and started tickling the ivories, plucking the bass, and—our favorite of all—brushing the snare drum: *Ch-che-che, ch-che-che, ch-che-che.* We stood in front of the band, or sat as near them as we could, and watched them do low-voltage dance tunes, songs the beef-faced and thick-ankled adults glided over the floor to, dreaming of when these songs were new and they were young. We watched the couples, too, dancing cheek to cheek, their eyes misting over with memories. You could see it in our parents' eyes when they danced: they were thinking of a time before we came along and changed everything. Not that they regretted it, we knew, but still.

That was when Uncle Louie was in a good mood, when he was "in love" and happy. When he wasn't, when Uncle Louie was "between engagements," he stayed home, built huge fires that he let burn down to nothing while drinking bourbon and playing his *Ray Charles: Modern Sounds in Country and Western Music* album over and over again on the hi-fi, tickling the ivories right along with Ray, and shaking his head, eyes closed, plaintively singing along to "Born to Lose." He was miserable (our father's pronouncement), godforsaken (Uncle Louie's), and wallowing (our mother's). "The music consoles him," said our father. "It's his only solace, to listen to Ray sing those sweet sad tunes." Said our mother, "His only solace is when he gets his thingie between the sad sweet legs of some barmaid."

"Little pitchers," said our father.

"Really, the way he douses himself with alcohol, it's amazing he gets his bottle rocket to go off in the first place. Or maybe those women have a low tolerance for fireworks."

"The rocket's red glare," said our father.

"The bombs bursting in air," said our mother, and they laughed, and squeezed hands, and I felt sorry for Uncle Louie, all alone in his house except for when a new and no doubt temporary Alice or Maggie or Trish or Debby came over and he could serenade her with songs of how miserably the previous woman had treated him.

To be fair, he often did the same thing when he was in a good mood, when things were blossoming between him and his latest find, only then when he sang along he was just pretending to be sad and lonely, a loser. You could hear it in his voice; he was enjoying the heartbreak because his heart wasn't breaking. It was the voice of a man who'd been through all that, and who was hoping this time it would be different—it would be different this time around, baby, wouldn't it?—and the Joyces and the Monicas and the Louises would clearly be touched by his vulnerability and playfulness, and touch his forehead with their fingers, or even kiss him and say, There there, there there, it'll be different this time, sugar, I promise.

I admit I liked it either way. Uncle Louie's female problems were my own. Like Uncle Louie, who pined for his lost Helen while simultaneously pining for whatever woman had left most recently, I was in love with two women at the same time. One was nineteen, the other nine. The nine-year-old was Marie Hemmelberger. The older woman was the already mentioned Duckwa daughter. Home from college that summer, the Duckwa daughter spent every day sunbathing in her parents' backyard. She had a proud, haughty, sullen face and hair so brightly blond— like incandescent lemons—that it had to have come from a bottle. She set up shop on a lawn chair, dozing or flipping through pages of her magazines, which she kept stacked on a white rattan ottoman next to her. She wore bikinis—sometimes green, sometimes yellow polka-dotted. She wasn't even all that pretty, really, just sexy because she was so casual about baring so much flesh. Vast amounts of oiled, limber, toned, tanned, silky, exquisite flesh. She was oblivious to us, too, unfastening her bra strap when she was on her stomach, and she wasn't too particular about fastening it again when she turned over, flipping herself like an omelet, her hand holding the bra cups in place. She didn't seem to care who saw her. Maybe she was taunting us, pleased to be giving all the little boys a show, giving us tiny little erections like the first shoots off a sapling, erections we didn't even know what to do with. She was an icon, as remote from us as if she were on display in a museum, an invisible velvet rope separating her from us peons. The mere possibility that I might see something I wasn't supposed to kept me at the edge of the Duckwa driveway. When she was on her stomach dozing, her back to me, the soles of her feet filled my soul with their delicateness. She knew, I think, that I was there, my eyes the size of dinner plates, my heart folding in on itself inside my chest. For the longest time I had no name for her. She was the Duckwa Daughter, as mysterious to me as the Man in the Iron Mask was to all of France.

Her mystery only increased the day I found out her name. Our mother told us, when we were moping about the house wishing for this or that, "Be careful what you pray for. You just might get it." I did not hear the irony. So I prayed, carefully and hard, and one July day my prayers were answered. The Duckwa Daughter, who'd been lying face-down on the chaise longue, turning her face from side to side to make sure both cheeks tanned evenly, stood up. Her back was to me. Then she turned around and, yawning, stretched her arms high over her head. Then she bent for the bikini top she'd left on the chaise longue. "You're the one they call Emcee, right?" She was talking to me bent over, getting her breasts back into their cups, then she reached behind herself to fasten the thing. "Just so you know, my name's Patty, Patty Duckwa." Then she adjusted herself, smiled, and strolled nonchalantly into her house.

Several minutes passed. Had I really seen this—the curve of the breasts, their full ripe pendulousness, their nipples, the whole nine yards? Then I wanted to cry—with her eyes hidden by huge white-rimmed sunglasses, inadvertently I had focused on her face. The rest was just a lovely, lovely blur. From then on, utter the words "Patty, Patty Duckwa," and my heart would flutter, it would skip a beat and sigh.

My own little triangle surely was more complicated than Uncle Louie's: Helen, his ex-wife, was in California, and the women who occupied the other corner were interchangeable. My loves were nearby and not interchangeable. I was in a science club run by Wanda Plewa's father, who was a chemist for Corning. Wanda Plewa had asked me to join because she liked me. I had joined because I liked Marie Hemmelberger, who'd already joined because of Tim Petraglia, a handsome boy with big eyebrows and soft eyes. So it wasn't a triangle at all, it was a quadrangle, complicated by the fact that Tim liked Marie just fine. So Uncle Louie and I had something in common. We were simpatico; we knew about the vagaries of love and were trying to make the best of it, carrying our torches, putting on a happy face.

Except for those times when Uncle Louie got morose and lost it. He'd be playing along on "Crying Time" or "Born to Lose" and suddenly break down, put his head on his crossed arms on the piano top, and sob uncontrollably. Our father would say, "Hey, hey, buck up," and our mother would usher us out of the room. "Uncle Louie's just going through a difficult period," our mother would say, her voice full of empathy, seemingly forgetting that she felt he brought these periods on himself. And when he got this low, there were no jokes about his predilections in the car on the way home.

Once we went to see him in the spring, and it rained like nobody's business for three days. We couldn't go outside the whole time; the rain beat on the windows so hard it looked as though the glass was melting. Appropriate weather for Uncle Louie's misery: it rained, he cried. Our mother said he was crying not over the loss of his latest love but over Helen, remarried now. Our mother gestured at all the empty bottles and glasses and full ashtrays. Uncle Louie was in the bathroom right then. "Something needs to be done," said our mother.

Our father, both palms raised: "What?"

Our mother shook her head. She didn't know. Something. "He's drowning," she said.

Our father looked at the array of bottles, the dead soldiers and those not yet sacrificed to the cause. "I can think of worse ways to go."

"You're not helping, Wally."

Our father changed his tune. "Hell of a way to go," he said and shook his head.

Uncle Louie came out of the bathroom. With his black frame glasses and pinched face, he looked like an accountant unlucky in love. Or like a dentist, which he was. Our father kept him company, telling him to ease back, have a soda, but Uncle Louie just lit another cigarette and put his palm in his hand as "Crying Time" started for the umpteenth time. Our mother fumed, we played checkers, Stratego, Monopoly, Clue, cribbage. Nothing changed, nothing improved.

When we left, our father had to carry us to the car. Riding his hip, we looked down and screamed. The ground was alive: shiny, wet, tumescent, wriggling. It had rained so hard there was no air in the ground for the worms to breathe; they'd all gone topside. Worse, the roads were the same: Route 20 was solid worm. Our father had a hard time keeping the car on the road; we slid this way and that on a carpet of squished worms. The car squished and lurched, squished and lurched. We felt queasy, the rain beat down. Our mother worried quietly, "Wally, what if we take the ditch? We'd never get out." We weren't supposed to hear this, but we did. We made out the ditch—it was fast-flowing, torrents of water up to its brim. If we slid off the road we'd be sent to Davy Jones's locker in four feet of water. Our father said not to worry, this was a company car, nothing could happen to it. "What about us, Wally? What would happen to us?" Our mother voiced our own fear. We had a vision of the car careening off the road, greased by mud and worm guts. Water would seep into the car's cabin. We wouldn't float, as in the Volkswagen commercials. We'd sink, and lodged there, trapped by the water's force, we wouldn't be able to open the doors. Trapped like mice, we'd drown, our mouths pressed to the ceiling, eking out breaths from the diminishing air bubble while our father tried to slide out a window to rescue us. We could see him getting stuck, and if we were saved at all it would be because his girth plugged the window so no more water could get in.

We rode in silence, terrified, until we reached a wormless stretch of highway. It was our mother who spoke. Uncle Louie, she said, was in a car just like ours, careening down the highway. And unless he got some help, he'd wind up in a ditch and drown. We weren't meant to hear this, either, but no one else in the car was talking, and our parents often operated under the pleasant fiction that if we weren't talking we were asleep. Our mother's voice was full of concern; she suggested that Uncle Louie should maybe get help both for his drinking and for his self-destructive tendencies in picking out women. We had always been under the impression that our mother didn't like Uncle Louie, so her tone surprised us. "He needs help," she said. "He needs to talk to someone, preferably not someone holding a glass of the same stuff he's drinking."

Our father said Uncle Louie didn't need a shrink. Maybe some people felt seeing a shrink would do them some good, but Uncle Louie definitely wasn't one of them. "Really, Susan Marie, how can you suggest such a thing?"

"It's just he's so unhappy," said our mother. "I would think going to talk to someone about these things would do him some good."

"Right," said our father. "And I suppose you'll be suggesting I see a shrink next."

"Wally," started our mother, "there's really nothing wrong—"

"You're damn right there's nothing wrong," said our father, "and I'll ask you kindly to remember that the next time one of these damn fool ideas enters your head. Louie is the closest thing I've got to a brother, damn it, and what you're saying about him you're saying about me. We're simpatico, capeesh?" His voice dropped a little. "Louie seeing a shrink, Jeez Louise."

Our mother, as she often did, reacted to our father's reaction. "Really, Wally, maybe you *should* see somebody yourself about getting your frustrations under control."

Our father exploded. "My frustrations? My frustrations? The only thing frustrating me is I got a wife thinks she needs to doctor me up over 'my frustrations.' Jesus H. Christ, can't a man have a few frustrations without his wife calling out the National Guard?" We skidded one more time, then scudded onto wet but inert pavement and traveled the rest of the way home in silence. It was to be our last trip to Uncle Louie's for some time.

By the fall our mother had gotten over our father's reproach. She was, she said, "only trying to help." To which our father replied, "He don't need that kind of help." Said our mother, "I was talking about you, Wally." She had a point. The two boats, the trips to Uncle Louie's—it was not working. Our father remained a frustrated man, not able to breathe— whatever that meant—and his trips to the Office only seemed to exacerbate matters, not help them, as he claimed they did.

Adding to his frustration was his miscalculation regarding the size of his boat. Or rather, the size of the door the boat had to get through if our father ever wanted it to see water. Artu and Uncles Benny and Louie had come over to help our father lift the boat off the sawhorses and out the door, but the boat was too wide, even when they turned it sideways. This was unfortunate, not only because they could not get it outside but because, except in the case of Artu, who had a sense of propriety and deco-rum, they had started in on a case of Miller High Life and had drunk two of the three champagne bottles they'd planned to christen our father's boat with. Men deep in the midst of mirth-making should not, I believe, be confronted by logistical problems, or by anything that requires the figuring out of angles. In this case, the solution was clear. They had to take apart the doorframe, which they did amid much puffing, grunting, cursing, and what seemed to be genial joshing of our father, who'd con-structed that classic of American shipbuilding, the boat too wide for its container.

And even then, when they got it sideways, the demolished doorframe a pile of broken lumber just inside the door, and they were nosing the boat out the door, scraping the keel as they went, they were again stymied. Our father—and his father—had forgotten the exterior basement stairs ran parallel to the back of the house, so they were nosing the boat into a narrow stairwell that immediately turned ninety degrees to the left. The boat's nose bumped the concrete stairwell outside the door, and there they stood for a while, holding their burden, their muscles quaking— a plywood boat is pretty heavy, even if it's a fourteen-footer—until Artu let his side go and started laughing and laughing. The other guys set their sides down, too, and laughed and wiped tears from their eyes and pointed, and shook their heads, and laughed again.

"Wally," said Artu, "I do believe you're going to have to saw this puppy in half if you want to get it up these stairs."

Our father blinked, and his mouth fell open in an empty look of dis-belief. All those calculations and he'd never opened the basement door, had never thought to see what lay outside. He was mortified, stupefied, chagrined. He emitted a low rumbling of curses that sounded like a motor started across a lake and opened to full throttle as it came near.

"Wally, the children," said Artu, and our father answered him with something that I was reasonably sure was anatomically impossible. Our father was behind the boat, and I believe at that moment, had he the strength, he'd had shoved that boat into the stairwell wall until it was splinters. Instead he gritted his teeth and hissed, "The saw, get me the goddamn saw."

"I see, said the blind man, as he picked up his hammer and saw," said Robert Aaron, and for this he was rewarded with one of our father's backhands across his teeth. Blood was dripping from his upper lip, but he just closed his mouth and said nothing. Nobody else said anything, either, not even Artu.

"I said," hissed our father, "get me the goddamn saw."

"Which one?" Louie asked.

Our father reflected a moment. He walked up and down the length of his boat, his fingers stroking the gunwales as the owner of a fine horse with a broken leg might stroke its withers prior to ordering that it be put down. Our father shook his head, and we could see he was near tears, bitter, bitter tears. "Well," he bit out, "if I'm going to make a proper butchery of it, then I suppose I shall need the circular saw."

Louie fetched it, plugged it in, ceremoniously held it out to our father. Had he been able to play "Taps," I believe he would have. Then our father lowered his safety goggles, ordered his friends to hold the boat steady, and when the whine of the saw started to bite into the wood, we all had to turn away. It wasn't only the sawdust being scattered in its wake that made us flinch. That whine, that whine, I will always remember that whine. The shriek of metal eating wood. It is the sound of dreams being sawn in two.

10. The Big Halloween: We Shall See What We Shall See

BE CAREFUL WHAT YOU PRAY FOR

Roof summit. While Ike entertains our kids, we climb up the aerial tower abutting our parents' house, setting up shop with a cooler of beer and soda. That triangular tower held together by Z-shaped rebar has been the sibling escape route, and the roof has been the sibling meeting place, of choice for over thirty years. How wonderful the farm seemed from up there. You were alone on the planet, on a different plane, and for a little while you could, in the words of our father, hear yourself think. Robert Aaron and I first used it as a place where we could get away from our siblings and talk about everything in the world that scared us—our changing bodies, girls, late periods and near-pregnancies, the future, our place in the world, what we wanted or feared to want. Eventually we were discovered, and soon everyone was climbing up on the roof. It was a place our parents weren't supposed to know about, though, so even if the sib you hated most in the world right at that moment found you, you couldn't order him or her off the roof. That was our one rule: "Nobody throws anybody else off the roof." And we meant that literally. We're talking a ranch house here, one and a half stories, a low pitch, so the worst you're looking at is a sprained ankle or a broken leg, but still, it probably says something about us that we needed to have the rule in the first place. Expecting us to agree on anything is like expecting an amicable solution to the troubles in the Middle East. And for the same reason—too much history, too many pent-up animosities to untangle.

Robert Aaron, popping open a beer, is in charge. "Okay, the first order of business is nobody throws anybody else off the roof. And watch your step. I don't want anybody taking an accidental header, either. Going splat on Mom and Dad's anniversary—definite bummer.'"

"Ha-ha," says Wally Jr., who's still down below. He has a hard time getting up on the roof anymore on account of his wheelchair. We offer to haul him up with ropes and block the wheels so he doesn't pitch off, but he'd rather pull himself up, hand over hand. He's fat now, though, so it's slow going. "Now when I was a lean, mean fightin' machine," he says, "this would have been simple." He says it cheerfully, without bile or bitterness, puffing a cigar as he pulls himself onto the roof. His wife, Claire, has gone back to their house. Can't stand cigar smoke, she says. We've always suspected it was us she couldn't stand, but that's another story.

"So here we are," says Ernie, popping his sixth or seventh beer of the evening.

"Ike's not," says Meg. "Cinderella neither."

"But Ike'll be up as soon as the kids in the tepee run out of gas—"

"Or he does."

"—and what we decide isn't going to affect Cinderella anyway. It's not like Mom and Dad are expecting to move in with her." Robert Aaron is reminding us that Cinderella, having helped mother us, gave up raising her own kids about halfway through and, given the additional burden of her own poor health, is not in the host-parents-in-their-old-age sweepstakes.

"Are you sure Mom and Dad can't hear us?" asks Meg.

"Our father," says Robert Aaron, "is piloting a La-Z-Boy into oblivion, and Mom is in her room with all the windows closed. What's to hear? Besides, we're just doing the Five P's now."

"The Five P's?" Except for Brian, Meg's beau, a quiet guy who suffers our loudness well, Dorie's the only nonsibling up here. Our conversation was interrupted when Robert Aaron asked us to join him on the roof. Dorie's stretched out at the base of the chimney, eyes closed, hands folded over her belly. She's only vaguely interested in this. Her thoughts are on the hills of Pennsylvania, the sandy roads around Lake Michigan.

"Prior Planning Prevents Poor Performance."

"You get that from Dad or Dale Carnegie?"

"From me," says Ernie. "And I got it from Tony Robbins. Or Pete Lowe, one of those motivational guys. My whole office had to go to one of those seminars. You know, where they have you hugging total strangers and shouting 'I can do it! I can be happy! Today I can be better than yesterday and tomorrow I can be my best!' " Ernie does exaggerated cheerleading moves, his hands shaking imaginary pom-poms as he skitters across the roof.

"Careful," says Robert Aaron. "I don't want you throwing yourself off the roof."

"Will you relax? It's a party, goddamn it, a party!" Ernie drains his beer, slings the bottle into the alfalfa field.

"Hey, pisshead!" says Wally Jr., never exactly Ernie's buddy. "Stop being an idiot."

"Too late," says Ernie. "I'm hap-hap-happy! Act happy, feel happy, be happy! Let me hear you say Amen! I said, Let me hear you say Amen!" He's dancing, eyes closed, spinning first on one foot, then on two. The spirit's within him. He spins again and dances right off the roof.

"Amen," says Wally Jr.

In what was to be our last autumn in Elmhurst, our mother decided to throw a costume party for Halloween. Of course, we didn't know it was to be our last autumn in Elmhurst. We—we kids, that is—still thought we were entrenched there. Cinderella was in eighth grade, already dreaming about life in high school. Robert Aaron was trying out for seventh-grade football. Horrible things were happening in the world, but our parents, at least in front of us, were pretending that everything was okay. "The static quo," Nomi called it. "You can do worse in life than maintain the static quo." A veteran of several bankruptcies and the Great Depression ("She doesn't look sad anymore," said Ike), she was allowed to pontificate in our household, even to our father, to whom her remark was directed.

Of course the static quo was not okay with our father. After months of silence on the subject and no visits to Uncle Louie, our mother took a different tack. Uncle Louie was to visit us. Our mother maintained the party was to cheer up Uncle Louie, but we guessed that it wasn't only for him. Our mother was hoping that a real celebration, a party on a day usually reserved for the kiddies, and at our home, would make our father feel better, would make him forget about the sawn-in-half boat that was sitting now in our backyard. It also would bring Uncle Louie back into the fold, and reestablish our mother as hostess and peacemaker, not the distraught harridan who was forcing our father into his nightly pilgrim-

age to the Office. Our mother was no doubt aware that these were am-
bitions no party should bear, but she was also grimly determined that it
be all these things. In the weeks before the party, our mother wore on her
face an expression of aggressive niceness, as though her fierce good cheer
would be contagious. Were it not for the fact that it was Halloween and
we had our own desires, we'd have been creeped out by the alien, its
smile fixed firmly in place, that had taken over our mother's body.

The year of our parents' costume party it was a warm Halloween. We
were ecstatic. No winter coats covering up our costumes, and our hands
wouldn't freeze. Not quite ten, I was the Indian brave I had always
thought I was. Down the outside seams of my jeans our mother had
sewn strips of diamond-patterned cloth and had made a breechclout,
vest, and headband out of the same material. Two pheasant tail feathers
completed the headdress. My war paint was streaks of lipstick in three
colors, and I was probably the only Indian brave east—or west—of the
Mississippi who sported a blond crew cut.

I was looking forward to being out all evening. Out in the gloaming,
as Artu would say. "The homer in the gloamer," said our father, recalling
a day when the Cubs still won pennants.

Oh, to be a ten-year-old at dusk in America!

Our mother had other plans. "Short night," she said. "Patty Duckwa
is going to babysit you." Patty Duckwa? My heart did its lurchings. My
brain twittered with an image of the bas relief *Venus de Milo* in Grandpa
Cza-Cza's basement, only she had Patty Duckwa's arms and Patty Duckwa's breasts. Flutterings in my stomach now, twitchings and tinglings in
my groin. I barely heard our mother explaining that Cinderella, our
usual babysitter, would need help later, and Nomi and Artu, who didn't
want to be in the house as the party got going, were going out for dinner
and a movie. And our mother, who had a party to prepare for, wasn't
going to walk with the little ones. We had to. Patty would be over later.
More tinglings.

We went outside. "Criminy," said Robert Aaron. He had friends waiting for him. He and Cinderella and I were each assigned a sibling. Cinderella, a witch, had Peg Leg Meg, dressed as a princess. Robert Aaron, a
pirate, had Ernie, a pumpkin. Ike and I (Ike was a sheikh, my costume
from last year) had Wally Jr., whom Mom had dressed as an Indian brave,
too. Great, I thought, just what I needed: a towheaded Indian in tow.
How was I to maintain my ferocity and seriousness if a rotund, jolly,

dimple-cheeked Indian was holding my hand? I could already hear the jokes: "Oh, are you blood brothers?" "Abner, come take a look at this— one little, two little Indian boys." And then they'd start singing that song.

Wally Jr., Ernie, and Peg Leg Meg had plastic buckets with jack-o'- lantern faces. Our plan was to get those buckets filled as quickly as possible, then get these kids the hell home. Once we got out of earshot of our mother, the soft night air would belong to us.

It didn't play out that way. We walked our charges around our block once, and around the block behind us, but when we got back our mother wasn't ready yet, Patty Duckwa hadn't come over yet, our father wasn't home yet, and we had to take them on another round of the neighborhood. They were tired. They were whiny. Their hands were hot. We circled another block and brought them home. "Oh, good, you're here," said our mother. "Dinner's ready, then it's off to bed with you." To bed? This early? On Halloween night? But we were just getting started. "I can't help it," said our mother. "The party's going to start soon, your father isn't here, and I can't have you wandering around the neighborhood. Of course I don't mean *to bed* to bed. I mean you have to be in your rooms, where Sarah and Patty can keep an eye on you."

We begged, we pleaded—Just one more block, Mommy, *pleeeeeeeease!* just one more block? She relented. She was wiping her hands on a dish towel—her most characteristic gesture. "You'll be the death of me," she said, but she had given us her blessing. We took off like a shot.

It was already dark. We had no intention of going only a single block. We'd already visited every house in a three-block radius. Robert Aaron suggested we split up. "We'll cover more ground that way. It's getting late."

"It's already late," countered Cinderella. "You're just hoping to run into your friends."

They would have argued this point longer, but Robert Aaron pointed out they were wasting time. "So fine," said Cinderella. "How do we meet up again?"

"Who says we need to meet up?"

"What'll Mom say if we come back one at a time, and somebody stays out late?"

"What *can* she say about it?"

"Remember that time Emcee got 'lost' in the snowstorm and he was just sledding?"

"All right, all right. How about in an hour?"

"But what about Ike and me?" Up until this moment Ike and I had said nothing. But he and I didn't have wristwatches. Robert Aaron and Cinderella did.

"You guys stay together," Cinderella said. "And when you think an hour is up, ask somebody what time it is." Now that Robert Aaron had suggested something out of bounds, Cinderella was only too happy to explain the new rules, to draw up the loose new parameters.

They were already walking away. "And where will we meet?" I called after them.

"How about the corner of Madison and York?"

"But that's way past where Mom will allow us."

"And who's going to know?"

"Mom!" This was Ike's contribution to the conversation. It almost sounded like he was calling after her, as though she were the one walking away.

"Only if you tell, you big baby."

"We only have an hour." I felt obligated to bring this up. Once Cinderella and Robert Aaron got started on breaking rules, there was no stopping them.

"So run."

Which was what they did when they reached Madison. They took a left and burst into a windmill of legs. Ike and I followed them, calling out "Wait! Wait!" but they were too fast for us, and they'd already split up themselves.

They were heading into a new country, Robert Aaron and Cinderella, and it made me angry at having been left behind.

"What do we do now?" asked Ike. We were about three blocks from our house. Kids our age were still out in full force. Little packs of them, like costumed lab rats, scurried from feeding station to feeding station. All we had to do was join them.

"Split up ourselves," I said.

"But how will we find them again?"

"You heard what they said. We meet at the corner of Madison and York in an hour. That's not so hard. It's right by our church."

Ike's voice had started to tremble with his very first question. I should have heard it when Robert Aaron and Cinderella were abandoning us, the plaintiveness in his voiced "Mom!" Now he was close to tears.

"But I can't read," Ike said.

"What do you mean, you can't read? Of course you can read. You're eight and a half years old. You're in third grade, for God's sake."

I was repeating a conversation Ike had had with our father. Our mother crying. Like our father, I didn't want to believe Ike, but I knew he was telling the truth. He could not read. He had dyslexia. It hadn't been diagnosed at school, and it was Ike's report cards that had set our father off. The teachers said he was slow, stupid, that he wasn't putting forth enough effort. If only he'd try harder. Our mother didn't believe them. She had spent the summer on a crusade to find out why Ike couldn't read. She found out. One of the theories at the time was that dyslexic children hadn't spent enough time crawling, developing the right focal distance to read. So part of Ike's therapy, besides phonics and word flash cards, was crawling around the living room on his hands and knees. It was humiliating, and I knew that, and I knew, too, how hard it was for him to confess to me now that he couldn't read.

He stood there trembling, waiting for me to say something else. He'd already said all he was going to. We were standing in a pool of streetlight, and it was like we were—I was—on trial. I thought of my loyalty to my brother, and I thought of Robert Aaron and Cinderella taking off on us. I wanted to be like them, alone and free. Breaking rules and happy to be doing it. It was liberating, I knew, my anger at him right at that moment. Renounce him and earn your own freedom. There he was, in a coat of many colors, sewn by our mother as his sheikh's robe, a fez bobby-pinned to his auburn hair, a tiny devil's goatee inked on his chin with eyebrow pencil, the curlicues of his pencil-thin mustache already starting to run as the tears trickled down his cheeks. His cheeks, still plump with baby fat. I hated him. Hated him for depending on me, for being foisted on me, hated my mother for expecting me to watch him, hated Cinderella and Robert Aaron for leaving him with me, for leaving us, for leaving me. But Ike was the only one I could leave right then, and I took full advantage of the opportunity. How I hated that baby fat. How I hated those plump cheeks. "You can't read, you whiny little baby. Who wants to hang around a whiny little baby who can't read?" And I took off running myself.

It did not take me long to feel remorse for what I had done, but by then I was blocks away. I had not looked back once. I trick-or-treated at a few houses, but my heart wasn't in it. The elation of betrayal had lasted only as long as the words were coming out of my mouth and I was first running away from him. Then guilt sat in my mouth, heavy as mashed potatoes. A few more houses and I went back for him, but he wasn't where I'd left him. Good, I thought, momentarily relieved and feeling vindictive. He's fine and good riddance. About time he learned to fend for himself.

Then I started calling his name. "Ike, Ike, it's me, Emcee! Come out, Ike! I'm sorry!" I don't know why, but I thought he was hiding. I thought it'd be easy to find him. How many trick-or-treating sheikhs could there be? There weren't any. Not one. I went up and down blocks for what seemed like hours. How long had it been? Which was when I realized that when we'd left nobody'd said what time it actually was, so what was an hour past a time you didn't know?

I started calling his name, louder, then louder. I was shrieking. Other kids gave me strange looks. What kind of idiot misplaces our ex-president? "You looking for Eisenhower? Check the golf courses, dummy!" I realized then that a lot of kids my age had gone home. It was mostly older kids now—teenagers, even high schoolers. Their costumes were scarier—gruesome rubber masks and lifelike blood. The ghosts and the vampires seemed particularly disembodied, the Frankenstein's monsters all too corporeal. I was scared, and then I really started to worry.

This was worse than losing myself. I had lost Ike, my brother. I went back to the rendezvous point. Robert Aaron and Cinderella were waiting. The buzz-cut pirate and the blond witch. "I lost Ike." I ran up panting.

"No shit, Sherlock," said Robert Aaron, who had recently discovered the delights of profanity. He cuffed the side of my head.

"What do we do?" I wailed.

"What do we do?" Robert Aaron wailed back, mocking me. "We split up is what we do. We each check a set number of blocks, then we come back."

"Mom's waiting."

"Mom's waiting. So what do you want to do, go back empty-handed and tell her?"

"I think we should," Cinderella said. "At least she'd know only one of us was lost."

"Yeah, and who was supposed to be watching him?"

"I was," I said glumly.

"That's what you think. What Mom'll think is it was all of us who should've been watching him. We're up shit's creek if we don't find him." Robert Aaron checked his watch. "Fifteen minutes. We meet up here again in fifteen minutes. If we haven't found him then—"

"What? What?"

Robert Aaron got a strange look on his face. He looked like Dad right then, befuddled and bemused, but seemingly in control of the situation. "Then we shall see what we shall see."

I didn't waste any time. I tore off straight for home. I was not in luck. The party was not in full swing; our mother had not forgotten about us. She grabbed my wrist as soon as I came in the door. "Where is everybody?"

"Still out. I lost them." My voice trembled. I had told a general lie, afraid of the more specific one.

"Where's Ike? Is he with the others?"

"I think so."

For a moment luck was with me. Too anxious about the party just starting, she pushed me out the door again. "Go find them. Patty Duckwa will go with you."

I hadn't seen Patty. I waited in the gravel of our driveway. When she emerged she was backlit from the lights in the kitchen. This was more than a young boy should be expected to endure. She was dressed like a harem princess—like Jeannie from *I Dream of Jeannie*. Her tummy, still mildly tan from the summer, was bare, and she'd pulled her hair up into a ponytail. She had on a poofy, slit-sleeved blouse you could see right through, and a red satin bra, from which her breasts rose like two scoops of ice cream.

Unfortunately, Patty Duckwa was pissed. She was pissed about being made to babysit us, pissed about being at a party with a bunch of "old fogies," pissed about life in general. And here she was out, half-dressed, looking for a lost kid on a now coolish October night.

"Christ," said Patty Duckwa. Unlike Robert Aaron, who was still learning, Patty Duckwa could swear elegantly. "So, where we going? And which of you is lost?"

I explained. We were at the corner of Swain and Madison. A car full of high schoolers screeched by us, its occupants catcalling at Patty: "Hey, sugar, how about a ride?" "Yeah, toots, I'll give you a ride. The ride of your life!" "Trick or treat: your trick, my treat."

"Christ," said Patty Duckwa.

She would say that a lot as we walked up Madison. I had thought for a moment that maybe we would share this intimacy of the dark, maybe hold hands as we crossed streets even though I was too old to need my hand held. But we walked a gauntlet. Hidden behind masks and costumes, high school guys took liberties they wouldn't have dared take if they'd seen her in her backyard. Like me, they would have been struck dumb. But not so at night, out here, under the stars. The trick-or-treating was winding down except for the older kids up to no good. They were traveling in cars now, or roamed the streets in gangs—gorillas, commandos, vampires, werewolves, ghouls. Predators, every one of them. They said things. Suggested she ditch the Indian chief, come with them. At the corner of Madison and Kent a guy in a gorilla suit reached into the gap between the halves of the jean jacket she was wearing and palmed a breast. She slugged him. He laughed a gorilla laugh and ran.

It was no fun, I realized, being Patty Duckwa.

It was even less fun once we found Ike and made it back home. Cinderella and Robert Aaron had been waiting for us at York. We fanned out, Cinderella and Robert Aaron taking one side of the street, Patty Duckwa and I the other. We found Ike lying at the corner of Euclid and Oneida, a block north and west of where he was supposed to be, curled up into a ball behind some bushes that formed a capital L. He'd been weeping, but he was only mewling now. Patty squatted down and said, "So how are you, soldier?" I was immediately jealous. Her tone softened with Ike. He was her little soldier. I wanted to be Patty Duckwa's little soldier. Why couldn't it be me who'd gotten lost? I could have been Patty Duckwa's brave little brave. Oh, the curse of having a decent sense of direction! Ike sat up, and his head collided with Patty's chest. His fez was askew. The bobby pins had come undone on one side, and the fez flipped over. It looked like Patty Duckwa's breasts had knocked his hat off and the hat, refusing to leave, was now asking for donations. Oh, to be Ike's head right then! He didn't seem to notice.

"Tell me what happened," said Patty.

Ike's story was a simple one. Abandoned by me, he had gone to Madison and York almost immediately. He was already on Madison, so he just had to walk up to the busiest street. He knew that. The problem was the busiest street was also where the high school kids congregated. They took his candy, cuffed him around a little, sent him on his way. They didn't want him hanging around their street corner. By the time we got there they'd moved on, maybe afraid that the little sheikh would come back with his parents. Ike, crying, had wandered off, sat behind these bushes—he was afraid of other bullies finding him—and cried himself to sleep.

"Sons of bitches," said Patty Duckwa. She patted his head, hugged him some more, got him to his feet. Again I thought maybe Patty Duckwa would walk with me back to our house. Given her newfound sentiment for Ike, I wouldn't begrudge him his place. He could walk on one side of her, I the other. Holding hands, we'd form a human chain on the sidewalk and sweep away any who dared give us—give Patty—grief.

Again, it wasn't like that. Patty held Ike's hand all right, but she hogged the sidewalk. I couldn't walk beside her without making it obvious I was trying to do just that. I fell in behind instead and consoled myself with the vision of her behind swaying inside her harem pants. Cinderella and Robert Aaron had already put their speed-walking into overdrive and were heading for home. They couldn't wait to tell Mom what had happened.

I didn't care anymore. I was the third wheel, the jilted brave, his squaw claimed by a neighboring tribe. But then my luck turned again. Ike asked if he could run after them, and Patty Duckwa said if he promised not to get lost again, sure. He tore off as fast as his fez and his flowing robe would let him.

"So," said Patty Duckwa, crossing her arms over her chest again. I could imagine her saying "So" in just that tone of voice to somebody her own age immediately before kissing him.

"So?" I didn't think I had a role here except as parrot or monkey.

"So we're right back where we started," she said. "I'm pissed and you're in trouble." She was walking briskly. I had to trot to keep up. "Not that you're the only one in trouble." I couldn't figure out how she could walk so fast with her arms crossed over her chest. But she was right. We were all going to get it. Probably Ike was the only one who'd emerge from this unscathed, and he'd spent the last hour curled beneath some shrubbery balling his eyes out.

Right then another car went by and the driver—a cowboy with a ten-gallon hat—and a guy in the backseat dressed like a doctor both hung their heads out the window and yelled, "Hey, Jeannie! Three wishes! Guess what the first two are!"

"Sons of bitches," said Patty Duckwa under her breath.

But they weren't done. The car pulled a U-ie and came up alongside us. Now it was a pencil and a can of Budweiser. "Come on, sugar," said the pencil. "Give me something to write home about." The can of Budweiser said, "Sit on my face. I'll guess your weight." Then they peeled off, all exhaust and laughter and chants of "Piece, piece, give me a piece!" in their wake.

"Bastards!" Patty screamed after them. "Fucking sons of bitches!"

Patty had stopped walking. I had never heard her—or anyone—use that kind of language. I knew those guys were saying mean and dirty things, but it was all code to me, and what wasn't code was Greek. But shocked as I was, I didn't blame her. I blamed myself. If I were a bigger, more imposing brave, they wouldn't have been so mean. The car drove down Madison and turned right. I watched to see if they'd come back. They didn't. If they had, I'd have suggested we go down a side street. It would have been easy to cut across backyards and lose them.

When I turned back to Patty, her head was down and her shoulders were shaking. I recognized those heaving shoulders—my mother owned them. Why was Patty Duckwa crying? She could have taken any of those guys in a fair fight. "Are you okay?" I asked. This was the stupidest question on earth right at that moment. But it was what I asked my mom whenever she was crying, and you should lead with your strong suit, even if it's dumb.

"N-n-n-o-o-o-o," Patty quaked. She was hiding her eyes behind one hand. Her forearm was crossed over her belly. I grasped that hand and squeezed it. She took a few great gulps of air, settling herself. Her voice was still shaky, though, when she said, "It's not enough they've gotta dump you. They've gotta knock you up first. Christ, oh, sweet Christ," and with a groan she was back to holding her stomach and weeping. She bent way over, nearly doubled, like she was folding in on herself. She was clutching her stomach, and her ponytail hung down one side of her face like a rope. I didn't know what to say, or do. I had no idea what she was talking about. I put my hand on her back, trying to comfort her, and she put out her hand like she was trying to push me away. But she wasn't. She was trying to steady herself. Suddenly she sat down on the sidewalk, pulling me with her. She was clutching me like a favorite teddy bear. Her head was resting on my head. My one arm was around her back, my other was around her tummy, and she was clutching my shoulders. I was suddenly in the position Ike had been. Her breasts were nestling my cheek—or was it vice versa?—and I could hear her sighs, hear the clanking of her heart. Her bra was scratching my ear, making me all tingly inside. I liked it, but I felt extremely uncomfortable, too. I was there under false pretenses. She was clutching me because I was handy. It could have been anything—her jacket with the embroidered peace signs, for example—if I hadn't been there. We rocked like that for a while, she sniffling, muttering "son of a bitch, son of a bitch," over and over, sometimes punctuating it with "bastard, that bastard," and I paralyzed in her arms. Finally she wiped her cheeks, and getting up, she said, "Well, come on," as though we'd sat there because I needed to and she was tired of waiting for me.

We were only a few blocks from our house now, and she was wiping the sidewalk grit and bits of grass off her bottom and running her index fingers under her eyes. "Do I look okay?" she asked. Like my opinion mattered. What could I say? She looked beautiful. She'd used eyeliner past the corners of her eyes to give her face that curvy, almond-eyed Cleopatra-I-Dream-of-Jeannie look. Now it was a blur down her cheeks. But what did that matter? My heart rose and lodged in my throat. "Great," I managed to croak out. "You look great."

"Bullshit," she said. "My mascara is running, isn't it?"

"You look like you've been crying," I admitted.

"Shit," she said again, elegantly. "Shit, shit, shit." She shriveled her arm up her jean jacket and wiped at her cheeks with her cuff. It just smeared more. I offered her my sister's blouse, which I was wearing. She thanked me and managed, with spit and the sleeve of my sister's shirt and some crumpled tissues in her pocket, to wipe up most of the damage.

"How do I look now?" she asked. "Better," I said, and she managed a little smile. Then she took my hand and we headed off into the night.

The party was in full swing when we got home, and it was readily apparent why our mom had hired Patty Duckwa when normally she'd have thrown us upstairs under the semiwatchful eye of Cinderella. In order to get everyone in the neighborhood to come, our mother had promised free babysitting. Our mother hadn't told us, hadn't even told Cinderella, whom she also hired on the spot, because she knew we'd be bouncing off the walls all day if we knew fifteen or twenty kids were going to spend the evening at our house. Patty and Cinderella were now in charge. Cinderella took a bunch of kids downstairs; Patty had the upstairs contingent.

Our mom didn't notice that we were an hour or more late, that Patty had been crying; she didn't notice anything. She was flushed, her party was a success, she felt pretty, everything was turning out okay. She didn't even say anything about my running away from Ike. Robert Aaron came up to me just before he disappeared upstairs. "You're lucky, numbnuts. We got home and Mom was in such a hurry to get us out of the way she didn't ask a single question." Our mother's instructions to both Patty and Cinderella were "Unless there is death or an awful lot of blood, I don't want to know about it. Settle it among yourselves. I'm granting you full authority to spank, smack, or ground people as you see fit." The conferral of authority was just for effect. Nobody took it seriously except Cinderella, and we were too much for her. Patty had her own concerns.

That the party was in "full swing" is a bit of an understatement. The house was booming. Windows were shaking. Patty and I could tell that from outside. Inside, pandemonium reigned on three floors. Kids were running around downstairs unsupervised, playing hide-and-seek, hiding beneath the pile of dirty clothes under the laundry chute as though it were a pile of leaves. Kids were also climbing into the barrels storing our out-of-season clothes, which were now scattered in great heaps on the floor, mingled with the dirties. Our father had moved his model-building stuff out of harm's way, but his train tracks were getting a real workout. The model railroad looked like a miniature tornado had touched down on it.

All the real action, though, was on the main floor. The doings of adults in general were strange and mysterious, and this was doubly true on social occasions, perhaps triply so for a Halloween costume party. Our mother, certainly, was not acting like our mother, and I wanted to see if the other adults would take similar leaves of their senses.

So many people came! It was hard to believe our house could hold so many. It was such a swirl of sound and color and music that I couldn't understand how anyone could possibly want to spend time downstairs covering themselves with our dirty clothes when they could be up here, on the stairs, watching this marvelous scene unfold. For one thing, there was this meeting of our parents' various worlds that heretofore I had assumed were separate and autonomous. Now everything was a mishmash. The Kluzarskis were talking with Aunt Gwen and Uncle Bruno, Uncle Alvin was laughing with Charlie Podgazem, Agnes Guranski and her husband were dancing with Mr. and Mrs. Hemmelberger, Marie's parents. Some of the costumes were so elaborate we didn't even recognize our friends' parents. Other people you could tell from a mile away just by the shapes of their bodies. Mr. Izzo, for example, with his stubby barrel of a body, was recognizable as a fire hydrant even with his black crew cut and his glasses painted red. His wife came as a springer spaniel. She kept nosing him, circling him, like she was looking for a place to pee.

Our house was filled with human dogs and cats and sea captains and Errol Flynn look-alikes (if you excused the belling of flesh at the waistband and the florid cheeks), mobsters in pin-striped suits, southern belles, a life-size G.I. Joe, a Ken and Barbie. Batman was there, Robin (Mr. and Mrs. De Bochart; Mrs. De Bochart was a very sexy Robin), Superman (Mr. Plewa), a twenties flapper, a king, a queen ("Catherine the Great!" shouted Charlie Podgazem. "Where, pray tell, is your horse?"). Zorro made his appearance, as did a gorilla, an organ grinder and monkey, a doctor (Uncle Bruno drinking vodka and lemonade; he claimed to be a urologist), a nurse, a two-part horse, witches, goblins, ghouls, and all the rest. Our parents had coordinated their costumes with the Duckwas, of all people. They came as the Honeymooners. Dad, as Ralph Kramden/Jackie Gleason, in a bus driver's uniform. Mr. Duckwa—"call me Ted"—as Norton. Mom and Mrs. Duckwa—"call me Lorna"—were Alice and Trixie, though they wore the same kind of dress with the same checkerboard apron. They had their hair done up like they wore in the fifties, and Mom had exaggerated her eyebrows extensively.

The Audrey Meadows–like eyebrows came in handy when I finally recognized Uncle Louie's date, the woman welded to Uncle Louie during all the slow dance numbers. It was Shirley, the woman who had written her name in unguent on the back of my father's neck at the Office! I couldn't contain myself. I leapt off the stairs, shouting, "Dad! It's Shirley! Shirley came!" I couldn't believe it, couldn't believe she was Uncle Louie's date—his latest "find."

Evidently our mother couldn't believe it either. She came over, the Audrey Meadows eyebrows going, her lips pursed. "How does he know who Shirley is?"

"At the Office, Dad, remember? I saw her at the Office!"

"She introduced herself," our father said. "I thought Louie might like to meet her."

"I'm sure he would."

"She wrote on your neck, Dad. With her finger, remember?" I was too excited to know what I was saying. Loose lips sink ships.

"So that was Shirley," said our mother.

"Best thing your father ever did for me," said Uncle Louie. He and Shirley had heard their names and come over. Uncle Louie was a Confederate general. Shirley was wearing a belly dancer's outfit. I knew because I had seen an album in the hi-fi's album well: *How to Belly Dance for Your Husband*. The lady on the album had nothing on Patty Duckwa as Jeannie, but she was pretty enough. Shirley, though, was pushing it. She had a lot of veils on, and those poofy pants, like Yul Brynner in *The King and I*. She also had a lot of belly showing, and given that she was a bit hefty, this appeared as a white snowdrift of flesh, soft and voluminous. Like Patty, she was wearing just a bra on top, only this was crocheted, so it looked like her breasts were being held in place by a couple of pot holders. The effect was startling, even for a boy like me. Figuring it was Mom's record, though, and that therefore she knew all about belly dancers, I was surprised when she asked Shirley, "What are you dressed as?"

"A harlot," said Shirley, who had lipstick on her teeth. This was greeted with stunned silence and the arching of the Audrey Meadows eyebrows. "No, actually," said Shirley, arranging her veils, "I'm the queen of Sheba."

"You were right the first time," said my mother.

"Best thing your father ever did for me," repeated Uncle Louie. "I couldn't have found Shirley without his help." He gave her a squeeze. Shirley squealed. "Ooo, Louie." Her breasts rose some out of their halter.

"I think you'd best be getting upstairs, little man," said our father.

"Yes," echoed our mother. "I think our little man should be getting upstairs."

"Little man, little man," sang Shirley, "oh where, oh where, should my little man go?" I had a feeling this was a rhetorical question on Shirley's part, not directed specifically at me.

"Wait," said Uncle Louie. "Since he was present when his dad first met Shirley, he should be present for our announcement."

"Announcement?"

Uncle Louie curled his thumb and his middle finger into his mouth and issued an ear-piercing blast. "Hey, everybody!" For a moment, everything came to a standstill. Uncle Louie gestured for people to get into a circle, and he waited until there was some semblance of one. Somebody lifted the tone arm on the hi-fi, and the music stopped momentarily. Then Uncle Louie grabbed Shirley's hand and clasped it to his chest. "I want you to know! This fine lady here and I are getting married!"

A cheer erupted, which I thought was very nice seeing as how two-thirds of the people there had no idea who Uncle Louie or his fine lady were. I found myself buried in a crush of big people and standing next to Bruno Gulch, who had a highball resting on his stomach. His lower lip was stuck out. "When's it due?" he asked, taking a sip from his glass, but the music had already started up again, and nobody heard him.

"Champagne! Champagne!" Uncle Louie cried. "I've got some in the car, Wally. Help me bring it in."

Our mother caught me standing there taking all this in. Since she couldn't officially be mad at Shirley anymore ("The nerve of that woman, really," she said to our father late the next morning, when they both appeared in the living room. "And what possessed her to wear that outfit?"), she had to find another target. "To bed," she told me curtly. "And I don't want to hear another peep out of you." Our mother was pointedly ignoring the assorted screeches and *bump-thumpings* emanating from the basement, but that was okay. She didn't really care right then if I was in bed or not. She just wanted me upstairs. That I could understand.

"C'mon, I'll take you," said Patty Duckwa. She had been hanging out downstairs, too, but now she was tired of that. There was no mistaking the looks she was getting from some of the men. When we'd first arrived, Patty had excused herself "to go fix her face." "It doesn't look broken to me," said Batman. And timid Mr. Boxtein kept trying to see down her bra. It must have been like being outside again, only the comments weren't so crude. But the message was the same. I don't think she wanted to hear that message anymore.

The message, though, was pretty clear. In keeping with the *Honey-*

mooner theme, Dad was playing on the hi-fi a steady stream of hits from the Jackie Gleason Orchestra. Dad and Mr. Duckwa and the guys in the band would croon along to "I'm in the Mood for Love," our father often sounding as good as whoever was singing on the record.

"You know, Wally, we coulda done better than that," said Charlie Podgazem.

"We *can* do better than that," said our father. He was busy pouring champagne for anybody who wanted any.

I was sitting at the top of the stairs now. It was weird, seeing the tops of all these heads milling about. The exodus from upstairs, which began as soon as kids realized there was stuff in the basement to mess around with and no one down there was going to supervise them, continued. They didn't want to see their parents this way—ten, fifteen years into their marriages letting down their hair, pretending their kids didn't exist. I wondered hard for the first time what it meant when the door to our parents' bedroom closed. What happened downstairs when we went to bed, or when our parents got dressed up—infrequently, granted—and left us in Nomi's care while they went to a party? Was it like this? You really didn't want to think about it too much.

The number of kids upstairs had really dwindled. Pretty soon it was just me and Marie Hemmelberger and Tim Petraglia and Patty Duckwa. Marie and Tim were playing checkers—one of the few games that Robert Aaron and his minions hadn't hauled off to the basement. Patty sat down next to me. Our thighs were touching. Here I was, so close to my belusted, but I now knew something I guess I'd always known but hadn't wanted to believe—that boys like me really were insignificant chunks of matter floating in orbit about her. She had lots of boys like that in orbit. They—we—didn't count. We couldn't do her damage like the other ones. She seemed exhausted. We probably were too much for her, even though most of the banshees were in the basement. Also, she was probably still feeling terrible about being "knocked up." She had said that earlier when she'd started crying. Crying, I knew, took a lot out of you. Our mother almost always looked the most done in after she'd been crying. "Knocked up": I didn't know what this meant, but I had the feeling I wasn't supposed to ask. And if I did ask, the news that Patty Duckwa had been "knocked up" would be all over the neighborhood, and I had the feeling she wouldn't want that, either. Some things you can just feel.

I decided I'd ask my mom the next day. If anybody could tell me, she could.

Coming to an intellectual decision about such things, of course, doesn't help you at all when your beloved is sitting right next to you. Or in the next room, playing checkers with Tim Petraglia, who used to be a good friend of yours. Sitting next to Patty and thinking about Marie and Tim (at some point they had discreetly closed the door to my room), I wondered if this was what it felt like, to really love two people simultaneously. Could you do that? Certainly my own feelings were not equal. Patty made Mr. Wiggly stiffen. Marie made me feel warm. That wasn't the same feeling, was it?

I wondered because of what I saw unfolding before me. Under the urgings of Charlie Podgazem and our father, the Cicero Velvetones had brought their instruments, and they were playing now, and people were dancing with as much abandon as people that old can muster. The whole house seemed to be throbbing. It had gotten so loud, so hot, and so packed that the party had spilled out our living room door, which was open, and into the driveway between our house and the Duckwas'. Nobody complained; most of the neighborhood was there anyway. You couldn't really hear anything but the music and, over that, this loud huzzing of human voices punctuated by high-pitched laughter. Such a sight: our parents—dancing! But not with each other. That was what I wondered about. Unlike at weddings, where it seemed everybody danced with the people they were married to, here everybody seemed to be dancing with everybody but.

Mr. Duckwa, for instance. I knew he and Mrs. Duckwa did not get along—you'd have had to be deaf not to hear them screaming at each other some evenings—and that would explain why, for this party, they spent hardly any time together, but why did he spend all his time with Mrs. Plewa? They were below us now, standing in the doorway leading to our side yard and the Duckwa driveway. Mrs. Plewa was dressed as a cat, in black leotards and a pipe-cleaner mustache and white mittens on her hands. Mr. Duckwa had his hand resting on the doorjamb above Mrs. Plewa's shoulder. He looked like a plumber chatting up a slightly chunky Felix the Cat. People had to duck their heads to get outside.

Patty had an answer for why her father was with Mrs. Plewa. "He's randy," she said.

"Randy? I thought his name was Ted."

"His name is mud if my mother catches him." At that moment Mr. Duckwa lowered his head, obscuring Mrs. Plewa's face. "C'mon," said Patty. "I don't want to be a witness to this."

It wasn't any better in my room. Tim and Marie were sitting on the floor, kissing. My throat closed tight. Fearful they had been caught by adults, they stood up immediately. Tim pointed out the window. "We were just watching them." We looked. The backyard was filled with couples. Some were standing, jabbering away, others sitting on lawn chairs. Superman was chatting with Barbie; the rear end of a horse was having a heart-to-heart with a dalmatian. Each half of our father's boat had a couple in it, and they were curled up as though at any moment they expected to be hit by lightning.

Uncle Louie and Shirley were lying in the sand circle left by our pool. They looked like they had fallen there. Shirley was on her back, gazing up at the stars, Uncle Louie on his side, stroking her tummy. From time to time he leaned over and pecked her cheek. He also tickled her, causing Shirley's belly to wriggle and her face to scooch up. It was warm enough in the house that the window was open. We could hear the fainter sounds of the music here, the laughter, and Shirley's "Oooo, Louie," as she giggled at the work of his hands. They got up, Louie offering her his hand, and walked to the opposite side of the house with their arms around each other. We went to the opposite window. They were right beneath us when they stopped and kissed. Shirley's hand, I noticed, was on Uncle Louie's neck, and it appeared to me that she was writing something underneath his collar with her fingernail. I thought of the labels that came inside my shirts—Van Heusen, Fruit of the Loom. Was Shirley's insistence on writing her name in cursive on the backs of men's necks sort of like that?

"Well, they're all lovey-dovey, aren't they," said Tim as they walked down our drive to Uncle Louie's Chrysler Imperial. I was too jealous to point out that just a moment ago he had been, too. Uncle Louie and Shirley got in the car and closed the door, but they didn't drive away. The seat folded back, and then they pretty much disappeared from view.

"What are you kids doing by the window?" It was Mrs. Hemmelberger, Marie's mom. She had a couple of jackets over her arm.

Patty answered for us. "They're watching," she said. "What did you think?"

"Well, no doubt you've seen enough."

"No doubt," said Patty Duckwa.

You could tell Mrs. Hemmelberger was about to say something, but she stifled it. I'd always wondered about the things adults were about to say but chose not to. I got the feeling those were the things that would let us know that they were human, that they were more than parents and old people. What Mrs. H said, though, was standard Mom talk. "We need to get going. Your brothers and father are waiting."

"I guess I need to get going," Marie said to Tim. It was like I wasn't even in the room.

"Thank your host," her mother said.

"Thanks, Emcee," Marie called spacily over her shoulder. I think she was still in a daze from having kissed Tim.

I could hear Mrs. Hemmelberger on the stairs on the way down. "What were you doing in that room with two boys?"

And Marie answering, "It wasn't two boys, Mom. Patty Duckwa . . ." I didn't listen to the rest. It didn't concern me. And I had the feeling that it never would.

The party was starting to wind down. You could hear the good night, good nights shouted from the front doorway. Mingled in with those were the voices of children. "Aw, Mo-o-o-o-m . . ." It was time to go home.

"I'm pretty tired," I told Patty Duckwa.

Patty rubbed her eyes with the tips of her fingers. "I'm pretty tired, too." She flopped backward on my bed. "Go to sleep," she said. What was I to do? I crawled in beside her, tucked myself up against her side. Her arm came down over the crown of my head and rested on my shoulder. To shield herself from the eyes of the men at the party, Patty had put on her jean jacket. A peace sign was embroidered over her left breast, a much larger one was embroidered on the back. This was as close to the sixties as I was likely to come. "You have a crush on her, don't you?" she asked. The lights were still on in our room. I studied the river lines of cracks in the ceiling plaster. "Who?"

Patty Duckwa punched me lightly on the arm. "Who? You know who."

"Yes," I admitted. I didn't want to say I had a crush on Patty as well. I didn't think she'd laugh, but who knew what a tired woman in your bed was capable of?

She lay back down. "I wanted to thank you for being nice to me," Patty said to the ceiling. "I've had a pretty tough day, you know that?" And it was then that I found out what a tired woman in my bed was capable of. Sleep. Patty Duckwa was sleeping, her luscious warm belly and *I Dream of Jeannie/Venus de Milo* chest rising and falling as though there were a tiny bellows at work inside her. I rolled up on my elbow and watched Patty Duckwa go on breathing, quietly and evenly, and when I lay down to fall asleep myself, I counted myself a lucky man.

When I woke up, it could have been fifteen minutes or three hours later. I couldn't tell. But the lights were still on in my room and my siblings hadn't joined me yet, so it couldn't have been that long. It had been long enough, however, for me to get a tiny erection, no doubt because in her sleep Patty Duckwa's hand had found its way to my groin. I shivered with this new, unexpected pleasure. The Bohemian brave takes a wife! Patty was still sleeping, her belly gently undulating, her breasts doing their rise and fall. I could have watched that for some time, but I had woken up to the clankings of metal and the steady poundings of what sounded like a hammer against steel and steel against the wall. It was coming from Nomi's room. I knew what it was. My siblings were taking advantage of Nomi's absence to have a rumpus in her bed. Nomi's bed was adjustable—a hospital bed with a metal frame and cranks to help her sit up, or to elevate her feet, or to give her back some relief. We weren't supposed to play on it, but I was sure Robert Aaron and Cinderella and Ike and Wally Jr. were anyway. No question Nomi's bed was really getting a workout.

I sat up, gently moving Patty's hand to her side, though if I could have walked down the hall with her hand placed exactly where it was, I would have. Still, I didn't want us to be found like this. Some things should just remain private.

I went down the hall, hoping to peek in on my siblings acting crazy. Then I would leap into the room, scream Boo! and scare them all half to death. The door was closed but not completely. The noise inside had settled into a rhythm, the clankings hammerlike, and there was the sound of someone in distress breathing hard. Robert Aaron, no doubt, wrestling Ike into submission. He liked to do that, put a hammerlock on you or sit on your head or back and rock you into the mattress, facedown, until you slammed the mattress three times to indicate Uncle.

I swung the door open, just an inch. I couldn't see anything. Just the side of the bed and a bit of the iron railing headboard. Then I heard Nomi come home downstairs. The noises of the party had subsided. There was a Glenn Miller record playing, but that abruptly ended with a *brrrrzipppp!* when Nomi or Artu took the needle off by hand. Nomi said she was going upstairs to sleep, Artu said something about having a beer. I could hear Nomi's foot on the stairs. If they didn't get out of here this instant, there was going to be hell to pay. There was just enough time if I warned them for them to scamper back down the hall. Nomi would see them shooting by, but unless they'd really made a mess of things, she wouldn't know what, exactly, my siblings had been doing. I swung the door the rest of the way open.

Some things should remain private. Supporting herself from the crane was Mrs. Plewa, stark naked except for her mittens and the crushed Norton hat Mr. Duckwa had been wearing. Her black leotards were trailing off her calves, and she was furiously raising and lowering herself atop Mr. Duckwa, who was thrashing and bucking as though he were undergoing a seizure. Both appeared to be hurting themselves, only it didn't seem as if they knew whether they were or weren't. A groaned "No! No! No!" was followed by an exuberant "Yes! Yes! Yes!" I had seen Mr. Duckwa in shorts and a T-shirt before while he was cutting the grass, so I knew he had a very hairy body, but I didn't realize the hair covered his belly and chest, even his back, like fur. Mrs. Plewa I had only seen in a housedress before, and the sight of her without any clothes on, the hat bouncing on her head, her spare flesh and bulbous breasts jiggling—she was quite a bit larger than Mr. Duckwa, actually—well, it was like seeing the *Venus de Milo* come to life riding a lemur. I would have laughed except that at that moment Nomi came up behind me.

"Good God!" she yelled, and this put an end to Mr. Duckwa's and Mrs. Plewa's exertions. They threw sheets on themselves and I didn't see any more because Nomi spun me around to get me out of the room and she spun me smack into Patty Duckwa's warm soft belly. "Dad?" she cried, and her face crumpled like a shredded balloon. But the carnage was not complete. In the silence we heard a rustling from the hall closet, a closet large enough to step inside, and Nomi, muttering "Good God, Good God" under her breath, opened that door, too. "Good God!" Nomi screamed again, and this time Artu came bounding up the stairs. "What is it? What? Have you hurt yourself?" Nomi only pointed, her cane quivering. I nosed my way in to see, and such was Nomi's shock that she didn't stop me. Our father's balsa-wood boat model was in there, crushed beyond salvaging, but the startling thing was who had done the damage. It was Lorna Duckwa, her dress open neck to belly, and Mr. Boxtein's pale pimply back covering her, his baggy khaki shorts (he'd come as an African explorer) incompletely covering his pale and skinny behind.

"Good God!" said Nomi.

"Mom?" wailed Patty Duckwa.

"Jesus H. Christ," said Ted Duckwa, draped now in a sheet. Mrs. Plewa had disappeared. Patty Duckwa ran down the stairs and out of the house, weeping profusely. I couldn't stop her. I couldn't stop anything. My parents were coming up the stairs now, siblings in tow, and Nomi shouted down, "Don't bring them up! Don't bring them up!"

"What?" Cinderella and Robert Aaron cried, pushing up the stairs. "Let me see! Let me see!"

"You're not seeing anything," said our father, grabbing hold of the two of them.

Nomi said to Artu, "Get him to bed," meaning me.

I was not allowed to see anything more, but I could still hear them. Mr. Duckwa saying, "Jesus, Lorna, Boxtein? Frank De Bochart I could understand, but fucking Lyle Boxtein? What were you thinking?"

"Like you have such great taste," hissed Mrs. Duckwa, laboring to extricate herself. "You'd fuck anything that moves." She started buttoning her polka-dotted dress while she lay on the floor, but she was mismatching the buttons and holes.

"So this is what you do while I'm gone all day," Mr. Duckwa spat at his wife.

"Don't be sanctimonious with me!" snarled Mrs. Duckwa. "I'm tired of 'Ed Norton' checking out other women's plumbing and laying pipe for Francine Plewa."

"Get up!" Mr. Duckwa screamed back, at his wife or at Mr. Boxtein or maybe both. Mr. Boxtein was still facing the floor, his hands underneath him as though he were protecting himself even before he rolled over. "Get up!" yelled Mr. Duckwa. "Get up and take it like a man!"

"Enough!" screamed my father. "I have children in this household. What in God's name were you thinking? Downstairs, we're settling this—everything—downstairs."

And away they went.

That was the end of our parents' social life in Elmhurst. Winter was coming anyway, and it may have been that the last gasp of nice weather and the party's explosiveness caused a recoil. People nest in the winter, after all. But there also may have been a tacit agreement among our neighbors to give our parents a wide berth. They had hosted a party where everyone had cut loose a little, and several people had cut loose a lot, and a natural response might have been to disassociate yourself from the site of your misdeeds. Shoot the messenger, and all that. Of course I didn't know that at the time. What I did know was that our parents felt isolated, shunned, and our mother spent the winter tight-lipped, as though she were afraid to breathe, as though in the very action of inhaling and exhaling she would either take in or expel poison.

Things may well have gotten better if we'd stayed, but the blowup and aftermath of that evening fueled our father's desire to move away. Far, far away. He wanted to raise his children in the splendor of nature, where modern life was not imploding on itself. Our mother would have been happier moving back to Chicago, or to a different suburb, but our father wanted wide open spaces. If you're going to dream of remaking your life, he reasoned, dream big. Always, always dream big.

Of the night in question, nothing was really settled. I don't know what transpired in our kitchen that evening after the couples were separated; I don't even know who still remained in the house when it occurred. I can imagine, however, our father in his bus driver's uniform, all Ralph Kramden/Jackie Gleason eyeballs and outrage, trying to talk sense into the Duckwas, the Plewas, the Boxteins, the De Bocharts, and whoever else remained, and failing miserably, his own ire exacerbating the situation he was trying to help. And our mother—calm, sensible, her Audrey Meadows eyebrows arched—exasperated with our father's mucking things up again, telling him, telling them all, to go home and forget about it. Work on their marriages.

And still the carnage was not complete. Things festered over the winter. Mr. Boxtein was a mild soul, henpecked to death by Mrs. Boxtein, it was widely believed, and in some quarters (we found this out years later) it was maintained that the events as described couldn't have occurred; Mr. Boxtein simply didn't have it in him. Wags would point out, no, Mrs. Duckwa had it in her. Everyone waited for the inevitable—for Mrs. Boxtein to divorce Mr. Boxtein and throw him out on his ear, but it didn't

happen. People in our neighborhood did not divorce. They stayed together and were miserable, or they lashed out at each other with wildly
inappropriate behavior, such as semipublicly fucking their neighbors'
spouses, or they medicated their desires into submission, finding relief
from each other in an assortment of prescription drugs and Jim Beam, or
they turned it all inward, where it went off with a muffled yet devastating explosion.

Kind, quiet, gentle Mr. Plewa responded to his wife's infidelity and
some setbacks at work—being passed over for promotion was one rumor,
receiving a lateral move that effectively ended his career was another—
by going into his basement laboratory one fine March day, and while
Wanda was out bicycling and Mrs. Plewa was out shopping, drinking a
sulfuric-acid-and-arsenic highball.

"A chemist doing that? That combination? Jesus, he must have really
wanted to suffer," said our father when our mother told him, sotto voce,
over dinner.

"Wally, please."

"I mean, I can see punishing her for wanting a divorce after she was
the one that went and cheated on him, but punishing her for wanting a
divorce by drinking sulfuric acid? Jesus."

"Wally, please."

"What happens when you drink sulfuric acid?" we wanted to know.

"Horrible things," said our mother. "Now be quiet."

"But what things?"

"Your throat and stomach are completely eaten away, and so are the
rest of your insides. It's a terrible way to die."

"But why would Mr. Plewa want to die like that?"

"Because his wife cheated on him, then wanted to divorce him."

"Wally!"

"Okay, okay," said our father. "Beats me. He wanted to die, and he
wanted to suffer."

"Doing that to your wife and your little girl, my God," said our
mother.

"He killed Mrs. Plewa and Wanda too?"

"I mean for him to kill himself like that, knowing they'd find him. He
thought he was punishing Mrs. Plewa for wanting to divorce him, but he
was really only hurting himself and Wanda. It's a terrible thing, thinking
things are so bad you want to kill yourself. You must never think that,

never. You must never give up hope, Emmie," said our mother. Her eyes were glistening. "All of you. You must never give up hope."

Besides never giving up hope, there was another lesson in this for us: if people were unhappy, they downed tranquilizers and stomach antacids and sulfuric acid, but they did not, repeat, did not divorce.

Ah, but they did. The Duckwas that spring were getting a divorce. We had heard about it, but our parents hadn't said anything to us directly. The extent of their explanation about this series of tragedies that had occurred in Nomi's bed and in the hall closet and who knew where else on our property—the severed halves of our father's boat?—was our father taking us aside one Sunday after a Mass in which one of the readings had been about the woman accused of adultery who'd been saved by Jesus—the famous "he who is without sin" speech—and asking us if we knew what adultery was. We didn't. Our focus during the readings had been on wondering what it felt like to get stoned. To actually die from rocks being thrown at you. Our father explained to us that adultery was cheating. It was wrong. Cheating on your spouse was wrong.

Said our father, "I want to make one thing clear to you. I have never cheated on your mother, and I'm not about to start now." We were relieved to hear this. It would have been terrible, after all our father had said about playing fair, to find out that he cheated on our mother when he played cribbage or Parcheesi or euchre. It was good to know that we now had a big-league word for this. When our friends tried to miscount in Monopoly and land just beyond Park Place with our hotel on it, we could accuse them of committing adultery.

Mr. Duckwa had moved out, but Patty and Mrs. Duckwa were still around. Patty looked different. Haggard, haunted. She had dropped out of college. All that winter and spring her belly swelled and circles grew under her eyes. Pregnant and alone (our mother explained to me what "knocked up" meant; Ollie Cicerelli helped me understand, in a crude way, the mechanics of it), Patty Duckwa had entered the pantheon of instructional tragedies. Even as her belly swelled, we bonded. We had shared something. I had been there when Patty had her little breakdown while trick-or-treating, the two of us had both heard Nomi's "Good God," and I had been there when Patty saw both her parents in flagrante with other people. And I had said nothing. I never told my siblings—never told anyone—what I'd seen, or what Patty herself had told me that night. As Nomi said, some things are best left private.

One of the things Patty told me that winter: "I just wanted someone to like me. I thought they—he—cared."

I didn't ask about the shift in pronouns. I didn't say anything. That was our deal. She'd come over to the little hedge that separated our back-yard from her driveway, kick at the snow, a coat pulled loosely over her burgeoning belly, and try to smile. "Hey, Emcee," she'd say, and I'd say, "Hey, Patty," and then she would talk and I would shut up about it.

The baby was going to be put up for adoption. That was what she and her mom had decided. She didn't look too sure about it. "I just thought I wanted a baby," she'd say. "I thought if there were something to love in my life, then my life would be filled with love. That makes sense, doesn't it?" She'd get this faraway look in her eyes then, as though the answers to her questions were to be found someplace beyond the backyards and the Monopoly-house-looking garages and the diseased elms. There sure weren't any answers coming from me. What I could offer came from my father, and it wasn't something I could say: "Be careful what you pray for."

That spring while Patty Duckwa was waiting for her baby and Mrs. Plewa and Wanda were burying Mr. Plewa, our parents were taking trips to Wisconsin, leaving us on the weekends in the care of Artu and Nomi. What were they doing? we wondered. And what was with all the hushed and drawn-out conversations in the kitchen?

One day in April we found out. "Okay, you kids, get in the car." We piled in and started driving north up Highway 41, the same route we took for our family vacations.

"Where are we going? What are we going to see?" we kept asking.

"We shall see what we shall see," said our father.

We looked at farmhouses, windswept fields. The land undulated like the back of a snake. Most of the snow was melted. The earth was bare, brown and black. What pockets remained looked like white scabs.

"What are we supposed to see?" we wondered.

Our father and mother looked at each other and smiled. Or at least our father did. "One of these—someplace—is your new home," our fa-ther announced, grinning. Our mother looked out the window, her lips puckered back inside her mouth.

"Which one?" We had been through this before, on vacation. Our fa-ther pointing out houses in the woods, telling us that one of these could have been Al Capone's secret hideaway.

"We don't know yet. We're still looking." Our father looked at our mother. "Should we tell them, honey?"

Our mother, still with her lips tucked inside her mouth, nodded assent.

"I'm changing jobs and we're moving. To Wisconsin. We're going to be Wisconsinites!"

This announcement was not met with the general acclaim which our father expected. Cinderella groaned. "My life is over! Daddy, how could you?"

"How could I what?"

"I'm starting high school next year. How could you do this to me?"

"Do what?"

"Tear me away from my friends, Daddy! How could you?"

The teary accusations and the flustered, then angry, parental defense that followed is an old conversation, and need not be given here. Our father was rendered nearly speechless. He was about to do what he had always wanted to do, what he had dreamed of doing, really, since those days he stood in an alleyway in Cicero, Illinois, and watched Al Capone's cars speed by, off for grand adventures in the great north woods. How could we not want what he wanted? How could our mother not want it? It was what he'd prayed for. That was how he ended that discussion. "It's what I've prayed for, goddammit!"

His own dictum hung heavy in the air. Which made us wonder: How careful would we need to be? And would the rest of us get what we prayed for? We hadn't even picked out a place to live yet and our mother was unhappy. So we wondered: Did God answer only some prayers and not others? Were prayers answered equally? And what if the answer was no?

Part II

GOD'S GREEN ACRES

Suppose the salesmen are the real explorers
at the eroded shores of absence . . .

—CHARLES BAXTER, from "At the Center of the Highway"

11. Another County Heard From

We rush to the side of the roof and peer down. Ernie's on his back, sprawled out beside Wally Jr.'s chair. He's lucky he didn't hit it. His belly's great with hops, and the baseball cap he wears over his receding hair has popped off. It's like looking down at a younger version of our father. As soon as he dropped, Wally Jr. said, "Christ," pulled himself over to the edge, shimmied down the aerial fireman-style, and now is bending over him.

"Is he—?"

"He's breathing, if that's what you want to know. Funny—it used to always be me taking the knocks. I don't remember passing the baton to Ernie. Must have been when I entered gimpdom. I preempted myself from more stupidity."

"What did he land on?"

"Heels, butt, back of the head. He knocked himself cold, but he's all right." Wally Jr. turns Ernie's head this way and that, patting his cheeks. "Your problem," he says to the unconscious Ernie, "is you cannot stand prosperity."

Ike materializes out of the dark. "What happened? You clock him again?"

"The drunken sot spilled himself off the roof." Wally Jr. gets back in his chair.

"Well, bro," Ike says to Wally Jr., "that's no worse than we used to do." And they recall for each other the story of when they used to windshield-walk. During their *Dumb & Dumber* days—how's this as a cure for restlessness?—they used to climb out of a moving car from the passenger side and work their way across the windshield to the driver side—hand over hand, three sheets to the wind. They performed right in the middle of rush hour—all those paper mill workers going home at 3:30 for an early dinner and a six-pack. Wally Jr. and Ike did it shirtless, pantless, naked—whatever idiocy struck them at the moment. Then they got two friends equally bored and reckless, and they drove side by side, only they weren't racing. Instead of trying to beat each other, they tried to stay perfectly even, door handle to door handle, and not only did you walk across the one windshield but then you climbed into the passenger window of the car to your left, and slid over as the driver of that car windshield-walked across his own windshield and entered the car to his right through the driver's window. The driver of that car slid over to the passenger seat, climbed out, and did the same maneuver. In this way they performed figure eights—the symbol for infinity—from one car to the other, and kept it up for twenty miles, from Appleton to Oshkosh. Their big finale was doing it over the Lake Butte des Morts Bridge at sixty-some miles an hour.

"Lake of the Dead is fucking right!" Wally Jr. screamed as he threw the dead contents of a minnow bucket out the window. If he'd had a good night fishing the night before (a good night on Lake Butte des Morts at the height of the whitefish run was a couple hundred fish), he'd toss the fish themselves. Some sailed over the bridge to freedom far below, but most smacked the windshields of the cars following them.

This would have been all right—a naked teenager hurling fish at you while crawling across his windshield was idiosyncratic and perhaps unnerving but mostly something you shook your head over ("Kids these days")—had not one of those fish struck the windshield of an unmarked county cop car following them. And even he might have let them go with a verbal warning—a dressing-down followed by an admonition to get dressed—had Wally Jr., still riding the effervescence of his own hydraulic lunch, not tried to beat the rap with an insanity plea.

"We are fishers of men," Wally Jr. told the cop once they were pulled over on the bridge's far side. He offered a whitefish to the officer. "Behold the miracle of the loaves and the fishes."

The officer looked in the backseat, where a collection of empty Pabst

Blue Ribbons and Red White & Blues nestled on the floor like puppies. "And I suppose those are the loaves?"

"Drink beer for Christ," offered Wally Jr.

"Get some clothes on," said the officer. Rubbernecking had slowed traffic. A naked man standing by the side of the road as the traffic hummed by—it bothered the officer, you could tell, but he had seen worse things than reverse streaking. Way worse.

"We are clothed in the spirit of Man," said Wally Jr.

"I'd rather you were clothed in the clothes of man," said the officer. "Can you walk a straight line?"

"Make straight the path of the Lord," said Wally Jr. He performed a wobbly, loose-kneed prance, but he did it in a straight line.

"Have you got any I.D.?" asked the officer.

Wally Jr. started singing the "And they'll know we are Christians by our love" song, his voice descending the scale very dramatically for the last phrase.

"Love?" said the officer. "What, son, you think this is 1968? You're late by almost a decade."

Wally Jr. started singing again.

"Knock it off with the love, son, you're getting on my nerves."

"Make love, not war," said Wally Jr. That was when Wally Jr. blew it. He didn't know his audience. This cop was pushing forty. He'd been in Vietnam. This was no time to be trotting out political slogans. He should have stuck with the bastardized Christianity he'd been offering.

"Hands behind your back, son."

"You're arresting me?"

"I'm making war on you, son, if those are my choices. I told you, I never went in for that love crap."

"What fools these mortals be," said Wally Jr.

"And don't quote Shakespeare, either. I was an English major before I got drafted." The officer put on the cuffs. Then he motioned for Ike to get out of the car, too. Ike was shirtless and shoeless, but he had his pants on. "You're the quiet one, is that right? The strong, silent type? You let Nature Boy be the idiot and you're just along for the ride, am I right?"

Ike swallowed, nodded. His own craziness was yet to come.

"Well, your compadre here needs to work on his French. When he was bare-ass naked on your windshield yelling 'Lake of the Dead is fucking right!' at the top of his lungs—I don't go in for that kind of talk, by the way, especially from somebody doing a weak-ass impersonation of an addled Jesus freak—he got it wrong." He cuffed Ike and turned to Wally Jr. "*Lake Butte des Morts* means Lake *Bluff* of the Dead, son, and yours has been called."

They displayed remarkable loyalty in not ratting out their windshield-walking buddies, who'd disappeared in traffic. But then, their friends hadn't been lobbing fish at police cars, either. Our mother was mortified, our father shook his head—boys will be boys—and Wally Jr. and Ike neither stopped nor learned from their mistake. Wally Jr. drove without a license; Ike found a new brand of foolishness to pursue. And after kicking around a couple of years after high school, Wally Jr. pursued it with him. They joined the military.

Only not just any military. They joined the Marines.

"Why'd we do that?" asks Ike.

"Which—walk across a windshield at sixty miles an hour or join the Marines?"

"Either."

"You think it matters now?"

"No, I was just wondering."

"Well," says Wally Jr., "I'm sure we had a fucking good reason."

"And what reason was that?"

Wally Jr. laughs. "I forget. But it was a fucking good one, I know that."

If you pressed them on it, they would tell you they joined the Marines for the bucks, and because there was nothing to do in Augsbury. While both those reasons were true, particularly the latter—how else do you explain naked windshield walking as a participatory sport?—it wasn't just that. Like our father, Ike had musical talent up the wazoo, but he turned down scholarship offers from two or three music schools—granted, none of them was Juilliard, but they all would have paid for college—to play in the Marine Corps Band. Which would have been fine had he not forgotten that the Marine Corps Band was a combat unit, too. And Wally Jr. after high school had a decent job welding at the Neenah Foundry. It was hot, dirty work, but it paid well. So what was the real reason?

Well, patriotism, of course, but Robert Aaron's wife, Audrey, who being outside the family could see us more clearly than we saw ourselves, laughed when she heard that. "They're trying to outdo your father, you nitwits. He was in the Navy and the Coast Guard. He was in

WW Two and Korea. And it's not just them. It's all of you. All of you boys think you're the black sheep—you know that? Every family has at least one black sheep, and each of you thinks you're it. And you know what? None of you is. You're all too busy pleasing your mother"— she looked at me—"or your father"—she looked at her husband—"to be a black sheep. Even when you're not pleasing them you're still worried about it. I'll tell you something, you numbnuts—black sheep don't feel guilty. That's why they're black sheep."

We felt abashed. I had to admit I liked Audrey. She was one of those big, no-nonsense, rutabaga-like midwestern girls, the kind who take their men in hand and mold them into the men they want their husbands to be.

What a pathetic, nervous, striving pack of siblings were we. "Look at me, look at me!" Flailing our arms in the only ways we knew how— getting ourselves or our girlfriends pregnant, marrying early, running off to join the Marines. *That'll show them. They'll pay attention to me now.* Pay attention to what? Show them what?

Ike toes Ernie on the arm. "Don't you think we should tell Cindy?" Cindy—Ernie's wife. Like most spouses, she takes a dim view of her mate's excesses. In the Czabek family, that covers just about all of us.

Dorie at the roof edge: "She told me she was going to bed, she was pooped."

Wally Jr.: "How pooped can she be? She doesn't have any kids."

"She's pregnant."

"I'll be damned." Wally Jr. rolls to a cooler and opens a Mountain Dew, the only thing he'll drink now that he's on the wagon. "Kids wear you out even when they're still inside you? I thought they had to be running amok outside to do that."

"We wore out Mom, didn't we?" Looking down, I see a bald spot is taking root on the back of Wally Jr.'s head.

"Speaking of kids, your own are way hungry. I came up for hot dogs." Ike squats by Ernie. "This puppy all right?"

Wally Jr. glugs down his Mountain Dew. "Just counting stars in his sleep."

Dorie announces that she and I will bring down the hot dogs, make sure the kids are fed. Then she turns to me. "What do you say, hon? You want to come along?"

The history of our marriage writ small: Dorie decides what she and I are going to do, then asks if I want to come along. It's petty of me, I know, but I don't much want to be alone with Dorie right now, even for only the few minutes it would take to walk down to the woods. "No thanks," I say. "If you want company take Audrey. And Jake and Jennifer." Jake, four, is Audrey and Robert Aaron's youngest, a surprise baby they had after they thought they'd stopped having kids. Jennifer, twenty-two and engaged, is their oldest. I heard about her conception the same night Robert Aaron did, up on this very roof. Audrey and Robert Aaron were just dating then. Jennifer's wedding will be in September.

Dorie goes down the aerial tower a few steps. I love the way her biceps jump, the way her forearms flex. For a second I reconsider. Her head even with my knees, she looks up and grins. "You sure you don't want to come along?"

I do but shake my head. She gets this look on her face. I'm being petulant. She knows it, I know it. "Suit yourself," she says (translation: "fuck you"), and down she goes.

Wally Jr. shakes his head. "Man, what is wrong with you?"

"What? We were having a powwow here, weren't we?"

"Right. Your wife wants to take a walk in the dark with you, batta-bing, batta-bing, and you turn her down?"

"Another county heard from. Can we start or not?"

"Cinderella's still out with her Prince," Robert Aaron says. Her Prince—that's what we call her beau, Mel. Owns a catering firm, seems like a nice enough guy, but like Meg's beau, makes himself scarce around us. Cinderella and the Prince left at the end of the croquet game.

"So we just need to get Sleeping Beauty here awake and we've got everybody," says Ike.

"I can handle that." Wally Jr. *pffssst*s open another Dew and pours it on Ernie's face. Ernie comes to with a start, his chest heaving up from the deck like those of patients in hospital shows when they apply the heart resuscitation paddles.

"Ow!" he says, sitting up. "I think I broke my butt!"

Wally Jr. keeps his arm moving in a spiral. Mountain Dew splashes off Ernie's head. "Another county heard from," says Wally Jr. He sounds remarkably like our father.

Piled like cordwood in the wayback and beating on each other as only kids in cramped confines can do without drawing the wrath of their parents, we had not noticed the slow dissolution of our mother from stoic wife and mother to weeping, distraught woman keening over her loss. Such was the hubbub of chatter that it took some miles before any of us heard her. The center of our attention had been Cinderella, who unlike her namesake was bereaved about being yanked away from her ball. "My life is over," she kept repeating. "My life is over."

"Your life is not over," said our father irritably. "It's just beginning in a new place. You'll make new friends. You'll have a ball." Stony silence from Cinderella. "Look, you'd have to make new friends regardless of where you went to high school."

"I'd at least know *somebody*!" Cinderella protested, then went back to muttering about hick towns and Hooterville Junction. *Green Acres* and *Petticoat Junction* were both popular shows then, and the idea of moving into a sitcom seemed to please only our father. Myself, I was curious about the girls in the water tower, and what you might see there—they left everything to your imagination in the opening credits of *Petticoat Junction*. I couldn't wait to get there.

But then, like our father, I was thinking about only myself. We were leaving our friends, sure, but we were all in the same boat on that score, and we were all close enough in age that we could keep each other company if worst came to worst. Except for Cinderella, who was too busy experimenting with hemlines and makeup and huddling with our mother over deep, dark secrets to have time to play with us. Cinderella's feelings about the move probably ran parallel to our mother's, only our mother had put on a happy face while we were packing and Cinderella had balked at every step, even claiming, "You don't love me," as though putting everything we owned into a Mayflower truck was an exercise designed to prove exactly that.

It wasn't until our father launched into the *Green Acres* theme song nearing Oshkosh that we actually heard our mother weeping, and we probably wouldn't have noticed that had our mother not done the unthinkable. She asked our father to stop singing. "Wally," she wailed, "would you please stop that infernal racket?" Our mother? Asking our father to stop singing? The man who wooed her with song? Telling him to shut up? This was a breach. Our father was trying to inject some levity into the drive. He was trying to calm Cinderella. Granted, he'd gone about it all wrong, teasing her and spewing out facts as we drove— "That's the Evinrude plant," he'd said a while ago as we passed a building that looked like the world's largest pole shed. "Our boat's motor came from there"—but at least he was trying. He just wasn't particularly sensitive.

That was when we heard it. Quiet sobbing from our mother. Who knew how long she'd been holding a tissue up to her eyes, staring out her window, sniffling as the scenery passed by?

"What?" our father asked. "What? I was just—"

"She doesn't want to hear that song, Wally, and neither do I." Our mother blew her nose, and I thought that was going to be the end of it. But then our father did a curious thing. He drove in silence for a bit, then he began to sing, very quietly, "I've Got Sixpence." The song is meant to be a round, and our father's sotto voce "jolly jolly sixpence" was meant to entice us into singing along. Our father no doubt thought he was teasing our mother, but this was a rebellion, boys against the girls (the ratio in the car was two to one in favor of the males), and if we joined in the singing it would soon become a crashing, crescendoing wave of rebuke. Gleeful and naïve on our part, more pointed on our father's, the message would be "Lighten up, we win." Of course, we didn't know this at the time. Or we thought it wasn't the battle it actually was. We were just teasing, too. No cares had we. Poor wife, poor wife.

We didn't realize the seriousness of the game until our mother screamed, "What are you teaching them? The same irresponsibility that you enjoy, is that what you want?" She was huddled up against the side door weeping, "It's over, it's all over"—just has she had done a dozen years ago when they drove away from San Diego, but none of us knew that. She was weeping so hard our father had to pull off the road to console her. "It's over," our mother kept repeating as she wept. "It's over, it's all over."

Once again our father hadn't a clue. "What?" he asked. "What in Sam Hill is all over?"

Between bouts of weeping our mother sobbed, "E-e-e-e-e-ver-ry-y-y-y-thi-i-i-ing."

Our father was exasperated. "Everything is not all over. Everything is just beginning. You'll see, honey, you'll see."

"Yeah, Dad, everything is all over," said Cinderella. "Why don't you just turn this beast around and head us back home?"

Our father's backhand caught her flush on the cheek. "Another county heard from, and yet we didn't hear a thing." And with that he put the station wagon back into drive.

In the wayback, you always see most clearly where you've been. We knew why we were moving, and it wasn't just that Halloween party, the Duckwa marriage exploding in our upstairs hallway. It wasn't just Mr. Plewa's suicide, either. It *was* everything. Our father's frustrations, his desire for more space, his fear of what the world was becoming. Our parents tried to pretend that none of this mattered, but it did. The summer before their Halloween party, Richard Speck had murdered eight student nurses in a Chicago dormitory. He'd used a knife, and he would have gotten away with it except a ninth nurse had managed to escape. The night was no longer safe. The streets were no longer safe. There were people out there loaded up on drugs and armed with knives and they meant to do you harm. Cities were burning, emptying out. The suburbs were getting more crowded, and who knew who these new people were? And people in those suburbs were leaving for suburbs further out, one ring around another, where the houses were newer, the garages more spacious, where the backyards rolled into fences and the treeless streets curved from one bulbous cul-de-sac into another. Our parents said the hell with all that. The steady progression of sprawl sprawling—it solved nothing. So they leapfrogged all of it, quitting their suburb of Chicago, where there were drugs and divorces and even suicides, where the last lot had been purchased and built on two or three years previous, and quite literally bought the farm.

This made our parents back-to-the-landers and put them unknowingly at the vanguard of a hippie movement they vehemently disdained. It fact it was partly because of the hippies—"Hippies, yippies, zippies, whatever the hell they call themselves, I don't like 'em," pronounced our father—that we were moving. "Their free love stuff is probably what got Patty Duckwa in trouble," said our mother. Given the trouble Patty had gotten into, I wondered how you could call it free. She had been sent away to have her baby in the middle of May. When she came back she was puffy in the face and sullen. She didn't hang out in the backyard anymore. She was gone a lot at night. We could hear her and her mother screaming at each other all through June on hot nights. "You can't make me, you can't make me" was Patty's refrain. Mrs. Duckwa's was "You little tramp, as long as you live in my house—" Then Patty would yell, "Dry up and blow away, you old biddy!" and there'd be a slap, then silence, then the banging of the screen door as Patty went out once again to join her friends, who came to pick her up in a Volkswagen van. We didn't see her much anymore, just witnessed the fury of her comings and goings.

We moved in July, midway through the Summer of Love, though you wouldn't have known it by us. Like lots of families that got started in the fifties, we missed the sixties entirely. Or at least our parents were hellbent on our avoiding it. We were just old enough to know something was going on, but too naïve to know we wanted to be a part of it. Sarah was the exception, but at fourteen, what did she know, really? She tried, of course—a few years earlier she and her friends got taxis to take them into the Loop to see *A Hard Day's Night* and *Help!* when they first came out— but Cinderella was a compliant soul, and her heart wasn't in it. Later, when *Yellow Submarine* came out, we were already in Wisconsin. Sarah went to visit friends in Elmhurst, and for old times' sake they took a taxi to the new Oak Brook Shopping Center. They could just as easily have ridden bikes. "I rode my bike to the revolution"—that doesn't sound so hot in comparison with Watts burning, or marching for civil rights or to protest the war, or to espouse free love and "contemplating your navel," as our father put it. No Molotov cocktails for Sarah. No storming the barricades, no protests, no tear gas, nothing like that. She ironed her hair flat as a sheet and let it hang down one side of her face like a curtain. "Veronica Lake," said our father. "Except her hair was wavy." Sarah cut her skirts as short as the nuns would allow (Sister PMS—Peter Mary Stephen—checked with a ruler when the girls entered school), she wore paisley or giant daisy jumpers, and sometimes she didn't wear hose to church, but that and lipping off were the extent of her rebellion.

But why single out Cinderella? Sure, she was the oldest, seven already when the decade started, but by most people's accounts the decade didn't really start for a few years after that. So it's probably wrong to put everything on her, as though she could lightning-rod the decade for us, let us know it was coming, and ground the rest of us. At fourteen she was with the crowd of quiet, "good kids"—what Nixon might have called the silent majority of teens—who kept their rebellions to themselves, who didn't make public nuisances of themselves.

We had gone bucolic by the time the decade really exploded. Our parents watched Uncle Walt—Walter Cronkite—on TV as the marches grew in vehemence, as the riots grew worse, as the cities burned and King was assassinated, and then Bobby Kennedy, and the kids went crazy with their music and LSD and marijuana, their clothing bizarre, their hair unbelievably long, and they would say to each other, "Thank God we're out of that mess." As though by moving us to Wisconsin they had caused the decade to skip over us. When people say they miss the sixties, they usually mean they long for them. We simply missed them—historical Passover.

Our parents' thinking exactly. With "room to move, room to grow," we'd be safe. It was a noble, misguided idea, postponing the inevitable by a decade at most (in the case of some of us not even that), but credit the audacity of their undertaking. Our parents left everything and everyone they knew and hiked us two hundred miles north to give us a chance to play in unbounded space, the only boundaries being fences you crawled under or through, or creeks too wide to leap across.

It was a farm we had not seen. Our father had discovered it on one of his weekend drives without our mother. He was now working for Dinkwater Chemical, headquartered—like Dinkwater-Adams—in Dinkwater Park, N.J. ("If you ask me," Robert Aaron whispered to me after our father had announced his new employment, "Dad's problem is he just can't get away from the Dinks.") Dinkwater Chemical made water additives and defoaming agents for paper mills so they could comply with newly written government standards regarding the purity of industrial discharge. They also made paint, paint removers, thinners, varnishes, and shellacs, the leftovers of which *were* industrial discharge. Our father was in the Specialty Chemicals division—paper mills, not paints. He started with three states—Wisconsin, Minnesota, and Michigan. For his job he now had to haul around not pharmaceutical samples but five-gallon pails of gloppy chemicals and sample bags and collection bottles and pipettes and petri dishes and a heating oven and a small chemistry set and God knows what else. Dinkwater Chemical had no problem with our father's request for a station wagon.

Since March he'd been living in small-town motels during the week and driving around on the weekends trying to find us a home. Sometimes, if his workweek ended in Racine or Kenosha, he'd come home, get Mom, and they'd go looking together. Once or twice we joined them, but the strain of looking at houses with seven kids put that low on the totem pole of possible options. Finally, one Sunday night our father came home and said he had found the perfect place. Subject to our mother's approval, of course.

"I'd like to have been consulted before you get everybody's hopes up, Wally."

"It's ninety-nine acres, honey! Think of it! Ninety-nine acres!"

"What's it like? What's it like?" we shouted.

"We shall see what we shall see," said our father.

"But we wanna know *now*!"

"Oh, all right," said our father. He got out a map. He pointed to a tiny black dot. "It's three and a half miles from here," he said. The town's name was Augsbury.

"We're three and a half miles from town?" said our mother.

"We're going to own ninety-nine acres," said our father. "Think of it—for the same price as this house, we're going to have ninety-nine acres."

"How big is Augsbury?"

"It's got a high school and an elementary school and churches of three denominations," said our father. "It's got a grocery and a chiropractor's and a bowling alley and a funeral parlor. It's got a Dog 'N Suds and two garages and a car dealership. It's plenty big."

"How big?"

"Appleton, which is nearby, has almost fifty thousand people," said our father.

"Wally."

"Green Bay, home of the Green Bay Packers, is forty-three miles away. Eighty-seven thousand people."

"Wally, I'll scream."

"Augsbury, Wisconsin, has a population of one thousand, three hundred, and sixty-three people," said our father, sounding like the voice-over to one of those documentary filmstrips we often saw in school.

"So all by ourselves we're going to raise the population by"—she quickly did some math in her head—"six-tenths of a percentage point." Our mother got that look on her face she often had when our father came home from the Office with a definite weave in his walk.

"Honey, please, just come and see. If you don't like it we'll keep looking."

Our mother hesitated. It hadn't been her idea to leave in the first place. "I'm sure it's fine, Wally, it's just—"

We waited, not saying a word. It some ways it was like we weren't even in the room.

"What, Susie Q? What is it, lamby-kins?"

"It's just—" Our mother hesitated again. Something was warring inside her. We could see it on her face. She was torn between expressing her own feelings and saying what she thought was right for the family. Our father looked at her expectantly. She said quietly, "It just seems so far away, Wally."

"It's not so far," said our father. "Early on, until you get settled, we could make weekend trips back down here."

Whatever our mother was going to say next is lost to us. She opened her mouth, started, then stopped. Her throat constricted. She put a smile on her face that looked as though she was keeping her own feces warm inside her cheeks. "I'm sure it's very nice, Wally."

Nothing more was said on the subject until moving day. As it got nearer, Cinderella got more and more petulant, but our mother ascribed that to "growing pains," and aside from lecturing her about being more thankful for our parents' sacrifice, she let Cinderella sulk to her heart's content. Our own friends wished us well, expressed envy, gave us a few parting jabs—"Criminy, a farm. What are ya gonna do up there, Czabek, sleep with chickens? Hope you like the smell of cow shit"—and that was about it. What had attracted people to the neighborhood wasn't in the neighborhood anymore.

Our mother did visit the farm with our father once, but she said nothing about it. She was taking the company line. Her mouth had settled into a thin gray line, and she packed and got us ready with a brusque efficiency that let us know that if this were the Charge of the Light Brigade she'd go ahead with it, but she had severe misgivings and thought the person in charge was misguided if not out-and-out delusional. The most she let slip to us was one evening as she was sorting clothes and putting them in big Mayflower boxes. She sighed, folded a pair of pants, and sighed again. "Your father has his dreams, doesn't he?"

And that was all she'd say on the subject until Cinderella got snotty in the car. Then she vented a little—but not much—and everybody fell into a contemplative silence. We knew this was bad. Our parents were sociable people. If they were being quiet it was a sign of enmity between them. It could only be worse if our father kept talking and our mother remained silent. Fortunately our father decided that discretion was the better part of valor and shut up.

For the next fifteen or twenty miles we concentrated on the scenery. It was mostly rolling farmland. Black-and-white cows and brown cows and brown-and-white cows appeared in the fields. So did pigs, horses, even sheep. The corn was thigh high. I thought of the words to "Oklahoma!" but dared not sing them. There were other fields growing green stuff, too. We had no idea what they were. Our father, who'd studied up on these things, asking around at the diners he ate in, called them out as we passed. "Oats, wheat, alfalfa. That's probably soybeans." One field was thick with sunflowers. "You wait, that's going to look gorgeous in another month." Other fields didn't seem to be growing anything but stubble. "They're leaving that fallow so it regenerates. It's a way of letting the fields recuperate." Some hillsides had two or three crops on them, done in rings like colored Easter eggs. "Contour planting," our father explained and told us they did that to stop erosion. In one plowed field that hadn't been planted, he pointed out the gulley that had washed out because there were no plant roots to hold the soil. He was feeling okay again. He knew things. He was heading to his new life and taking us with him.

Our father pointed out the cows as we passed them. "Holsteins," he said. "Gurneys. Swiss chard, I think."

"Wally," said our mother, "stop making things up." She sounded a little better. She was trying to put a good face on things. "Really," said our mother. "We won't be too far away. We can go back and visit on weekends."

Our father said nothing to this.

"Really," said our mother. "What's three, three and a half hours?"

"We'll be pretty busy when we first get up there," said our father. If you weren't listening for it, you might not have heard the sound of another thin line being drawn in the sand.

"We'll get back," said our mother, trying to cover up the edge in her voice. "We have to visit Nomi and Artu." They weren't coming with us. Artu had gotten a job managing a Thom McAn store in the Loop, and they were moving into an apartment on Fullerton Avenue. They were city people. They didn't have that great a desire to see what ninety-nine acres looked like.

"I want green I'll take the bus over to Grant Park," said Nomi.

"But this is ours," said our father.

"So's Grant Park," said Nomi. "I pay my taxes."

The landscape was starting to seem familiar. Maybe it was just that we'd seen so much of it. "There certainly are a lot of signs," said our mother. Evidently Wisconsin had decided to opt out of Lady Bird Johnson's "Beautify America" campaign. There were billboards every twenty feet or so—Harn's Barn Furniture, Shakey's Pizza, Jane's Curl Up and Dye, Hovelings' Waste Removal, Bolar's Pest Control, Ariens Snowblowers, Frigo Cheese, Nate's Marina, Aid Association for Lutherans, Catholic Insurance. "Is that insurance against Catholics?" asked Cinderella, who was still feeling bitter. "Shut up," said our father. "I don't want a bolt of lightning hitting us twenty miles from our new home."

"You're not supposed to say 'Shut up,' " said Ernie, who was just innocent enough to say this to our father without getting bopped.

"It's like the old Burma-Shave signs," said our mother. "Remember, Wally?"

"I remember."

Our mother cast her voice into the wayback. "You kids wouldn't remember this, but there used to be Burma-Shave signs alongside the road every few miles. They'd tell a little story, or a joke, or a jingle. You'd drive and wait for the next one to come along. Remember, Wally?"

"I remember."

We could see our mother's hand slide across the bench seat and our father drop his right hand from the steering wheel. They were having a moment. All was forgiven.

Tucked in among the motels and gas stations and rolling green fields was a concrete blockhouse painted the color of a grape. And up above was its sign, which Ike, who had trouble reading, read anyway: "The Night Palace. Naughty Things for Nice People." Then he asked, "What are naughty things for nice people?"

Said our father automatically, "I don't know, ask your mother." So Ike repeated his question. "What are naughty things for nice people?" The rest of us wanted to know, too.

Our father waved the question away with his hand. "You know," he said.

But we didn't. Our imaginations were woefully inadequate for the enormity of the task at hand. What was inside there, waiting for us?

Candy, treats, comic books, all the G.I. Joe paraphernalia we would need for a platoon?

Then our mother weighed in with the right intonation. "Well, honey, you . . . *know* . . ." and for those of us older than Ike, everything clicked in, more or less. "You know"—the phrase meant to encompass all the answers to all our questions. It belonged, we understood, to that ungovernable and mysterious territory of marriage, to what occurred after our father kissed our mother, or pinched her butt in the kitchen, and our mother said, grinning, "Stop that, Wally," but she didn't mean it. What she meant was, "Later, after the kids are asleep."

So there we were, thinking abstract thoughts about the particulars of "you know," when we turned onto Highway 45—"It's only twenty more miles now," said our father—and came upon a butter yellow sign with black lettering. It was the exact same color and shape as the state license plates, and except for the painted cross and lily, it was the same general design. JESUS IS THE ANSWER, the sign proclaimed. WHAT WAS YOUR QUESTION?

"That's quite a juxtaposition," said our mother, and if by juxtaposition she meant that the pleasure we had been experiencing as we mentally contemplated "you know" had just turned to guilt and dust, she was certainly right about that.

Just beyond that was another twenty-four-hour sex toy emporium, advertising itself as exactly that: SEXY TOY EMPORIUM 24 HR. in bright red lettering on a white sheet that snapped in the breeze. "They must have just opened," said our father.

"How nice," said our mother. "Business is booming. There must be a lot of nice people with naughty needs out here."

"Mom," asked Ike, "what's an emperneum?"

"Emporium," said our mother. "That's a fancy word for store."

"Oh," said Ike.

"It's a world for head scratching," said our father. And on we drove, slightly amazed that in between the three signs and the worlds they represented were the same green clover and cloudless blue sky.

We were even more amazed when we crested a hill twenty minutes later and our father said, "There she is. The new homestead. Our answered prayer. God's green acres."

We were staring at a washed-out-looking ranch house set back about two hundred feet from the road. At one time the house must have been a deep oxblood color, or a reddish mahogany. Now it looked like a dry scab, the wood where it was bare a weather-beaten silvery gray. The house was set into the side of a little hill, so part of the basement was exposed and the driveway ended in a rise. The garage was underneath an L-shaped porch on what we would come to call the second floor. The Mayflower truck was already there, unloading.

"A ranch house?" asked Cinderella. "We thought it was going to be a farmhouse." By that she meant the kind of farmhouse in picture books: a stalwart foursquare with a large attic and root cellar and well-tended vegetable garden out back. This was a split-level ranch that hadn't been painted since it was built in the middle of the previous decade.

"Another county heard from," said our father. "Let's just start unloading, shall we?"

But we didn't. Before going into the house we had a look around. The air smelled dry. It hadn't rained in a while, and the fields, a dusty green, showed it. You could feel sand in the wind, taste it on your teeth. Our father stood with us on the rise behind the house. The land sloped away below us toward a line of scrub trees, beyond which was an open field.

We started to run, just to experience the feeling of moving over our land, but one after another we tumbled and fell. That was how we discovered why the air was full of sand. The previous owners had hit upon a curious way of rendering their fields fallow. Or maybe they knew they were selling the place and, their hearts no longer in their work (we had heard they had moved to California), they had decided to do everything that last spring half-assed. What they had done was set the plow blades to turn up, but not over, each furrow, so that the field had the look of a baby's curlicue, row upon row of upright waves, like Mohawk haircuts suffering osteoporosis. Every step you were liable to stumble.

Just as we were picking ourselves up, a very pale pastel green Chevy pickup pulled into our drive. A farmer got out. He was short and wiry, and wore those heavy black glasses favored by accountants, governmental officials, and orthodontists. He was wearing green chinos and a blue-and-green plaid shirt. His arms were deeply tanned, and so was his face except for his forehead, which when he took off a dusty Kafka Feed and Seed baseball cap, was lily white. He was possessed, like our father, of an easy and infectious smile. He stuck out his hand.

"Name's Tony Dederoff. I'm with the Farm Bureau. Plus I got a farm of my own other side of the hill. I heard you were moving in today, wanted to get a look at you. Is what I heard right—you're city folk? Moving up from Chicago? Whoo-ee, that's a long way to go. Most we've got usually is somebody hightailing it from Appleton. It's not like we even get people from Milwaukee, usually, except if they stop in town for a bite on their way up north."

Tony Dederoff was a talker. This suited our father to a T, and we could see they were going to be at it quite a while. We took off to explore.

It was a bit like discovering yourself in Oz and the enchanted monkey forest at the same time. The barns had fallen. There were two of them, and one was completely gone except for the fieldstone walls and wooden window frames and the stanchions; the other was leaning like the Tower of Pisa, only worse. There were also two outbuildings—sheds, really, probably pressed into service after the barns collapsed. One contained a decrepit-looking tractor, the other had its corrugated sheet-metal roof partially torn away. A two-tone Chevy was listing on its side in a thicket of weeds next to the Tower of Pisa barn. It was white and the same washed-out pastel green as Tony Dederoff's truck. Its tailpipe protruded from the trunk as though that was where it belonged. This had our clubhouse beat all hollow.

In the abandoned silo we heard the *hloo hloo* of pigeons and threw rocks at them, though our throws were pitifully short of the mark—the pigeons were high up, on a ledge, unperturbed and unconcerned. I was scouring the barn floor for more rocks when I heard a voice creaky with age saying, "You boys stop that." I looked up. It was an old woman in a faded housedress, the kind our mother wore. Wisps of white hair danced around her head, and her eyes were thickened with what looked like fish-belly flesh. They were both piercing and blind-looking at the same time. And her teeth! She had maybe eight in her entire mouth, and as her lips flapped at us the teeth still remaining in her jaw protruded every which way and took up residence outside her lips. And then there was the grapefruit-size lump underneath her chin, distending it and making her head tilt back. In the sunlight it looked white and purple, like an eggplant.

"There are barn swallows up there," she said. "Don't be tormenting the barn swallows. They, too, are God's creatures." She gave us a horrible, knowing smile then, like she knew exactly what we were thinking, and what she was going to do with us. And that huge lump beneath her chin seemed to swell and breed, twitch and glow as we watched. No doubt she was a witch. And like those cacti in the Southwest that explode from overwatering and give birth to a thousand tarantulas, something evil was about to break loose from her neck. We ran screaming over to the woodpiles—all the lumber from the collapsed barns—which we jumped on.

"Hey, you kids, there's rats in those piles," Tony Dederoff called, and we jumped off the piles as though the rats were making for our pant legs. We ran back to our parents, breathless, wanting to tell them we had moved inside a Grimm's fairy tale, complete with witch. Our father was telling Tony that we had bought the farm for the land, not for the house or the buildings.

"That's a good thing," said Tony Dederoff. "It's real pretty land, but frankly, it's not much for farming. You only got about fifty tillable acres—more, I suppose, if you drain that marsh"—he pointed—"but mostly it's sand. The soil you want blew away years ago over to your neighbor's. You knew that, right?" Our father, a little abashed, allowed that he'd seen it only in winter, when there was snow cover. Tony continued, "Well, anyway, you're down to lake bottom now, which is what this was about two million years ago. More recently, the folks who had this before you—the Hovelings?—they did everything half-assed—pardon my French—and it shows. No soil conservation at all. Plowed vertically down this hill so what didn't blow away eroded into that lower field. Fact is they weren't really farmers. They half-turned these fields years ago, then left them sit for soil bank. You can take advantage of it, too, if you want."

"Soil bank?"

"The government pays you not to grow crops. You don't make as much as if you were farming it, but you don't make a whole lot less, either. The Hovelings put just about everything into soil bank. Given the way they plowed, that was probably a good idea."

"We saw their billboard on the way up," said our father. "Did they own a waste removal business?"

"Septic tank cleaners. Those were cousins. They had enough trouble dealing with their own shit—'scuse my French—let alone handling somebody else's. What wasn't fallow they had in corn, which takes a terrible toll on soil, especially soil like this, if you let it. They depleted the hell out of it, then got a contract with their septic tank cousins to dump what they pumped out of the tanks onto the fields here. The bowel movements of half the county are probably fertilizing your fields even as we speak."

"I'm not sure I wanted to hear that," said our mother.

"Of course, you could always grow potatoes. Potatoes do well in soil like this. They like it sandy." Tony Dederoff wiped his glasses. "Real pretty land," he repeated, "but I wouldn't want to make a living off it. Even if it was good soil and it was all tillable, you got about half what you need to make a go of it. You got other employment?"

"Sales rep for Dinkwater Chemical."

"A peddler, eh? What do they sell?"

"Industrial defoamers. I sell to paper mills."

"You're in the right place then." Tony looked at each of us. "I count seven," he said. "Five on the school bus come this fall?"

"That sounds about right," said our father. He turned to our mother. "It's seven, right? You haven't had any I don't know about yet, right?" Our mother only smiled.

"I drive this route. These don't look like they'll give me any trouble." He flicked Wally Jr.'s nose. "I've got five kids myself. I'd have more, but then I'm younger than you."

"So you have an extra job, too."

"Most folks do. For me it's farm, Farm Bureau, and school bus driver—in that order. I play a little accordion on the weekends, too."

"Really?" said our father. "I used to play accordion and sing."

"We'll have to get together sometime." At that moment a rather docile and arthritic-looking dog appeared from somewhere and Tony bent down to pet him. "This is the Hovelings' dog, Charlie. Looks like they left him. He's a good dog, but I wouldn't let him inside the house. Like most things they owned, the Hovelings didn't really take care of him." He kept petting the dog. It looked like a beagle-Lab mix and was very appreciative of Tony's attention. It hadn't barked once since we'd arrived. Once we started petting the dog, Tony stood up. "Church?"

"Catholic. There's St. Stephen's in Augsbury and St. Ambrose in Chetaqua, right?"

"Don't forget St. Genevieve's in Holton. That's where me and the missus go." Tony Dederoff shook our mother's and our father's hands and got back in his truck. He leaned his head out the window. "Hope to see you there. It's a nice crowd no matter how you slice it."

"I like him," said our father as Tony Dederoff backed his truck down our drive.

"You like everybody," said our mother.

Before Tony Dederoff was even out of our driveway we were imploring our mother about Charlie. "Please, Mom, can we keep him? Please, please, please, please, *please*?!!!"

Our parents exchanged looks. Our mother sighed. We cheered.

"But he stays outside!" said our mother. "In that barrel over there. That must be where they kept him."

Like everything else the Hovelings owned, the fifty-five-gallon drum Charlie lived in was rusted, full of holes, and obscured by weeds. There were some blankets in there, a smell of must and wet dog, and probably half a million fleas.

"We'll start by burning that blanket, and getting this mutt to a vet."

"Today, Wally?"

"Okay, maybe in a couple of days. Kids, don't touch the dog, or at least don't let him get in your lap. And wash your hands after you've touched him." Our father regarded the dog, whose rheumy eyes were those of a St. Bernard. "He's not going to be much of a watchdog, is he?"

Evidently not. While we were talking a tall, rail-thin man came over carrying a couple of grocery bags, and Charlie didn't even sniff his pants. The man wore overalls, and his T-shirt flapped on his thin but muscular arms. There was a silvery wash of stubble on his chin and some longer hairs further down his neck. He was carrying housewarming presents: a bag of apples and a bag of tomatoes. "Them apples is last year's from the fruit cellar," said the man, "but the tomatoes are fresh." He handed a bag to each of our parents. "I'm Alfred Bunkas. I live over there." He pointed at the original farmhouse, which must have been pretty in its day but had succumbed to an asphalt siding salesman in the late forties or early fifties. It was now a nondescript blue with a pine green trim that did not match. "I seen you already met my mother."

"We did?"

"Your kids did. Probably scared them." He turned to us and pointed at his throat. "My mother has a goiter. That's what you seen on her neck. And her eyes"—he pointed to his own—"them's cataracts. It makes her eyes look funny, don't it? All milky? Well, she sees things milky, too. It's no fun being old when your body's breaking down on you." He turned back to our parents. "Not enough iodine in her diet. I told her she could get that and her cataracts taken care of, but she's stubborn. You know how it is with old ladies." He turned back to us. "Her name's Tillie. You can call her Grandma Tillie if you want. She'd like that." Alfred Bunkas then bent himself double to talk to Wally Jr. and Ike. "She won't hurt you," he said. "She's a nice old lady. She just looks funny." Wally Jr. and Ike kept their wide eyes on Alfred Bunkas as they slowly backed away and sidled themselves in behind our mother's legs. Alfred Bunkas laughed. Our parents thanked him for the gifts, which Alfred Bunkas waved off— " 'tweren't nuthin' "—then he shook their hands and loped across the field back to his house.

"What a nice man," said our father.

"These apples are a little soft," said our mother, "but it was a nice gesture all the same."

Said our father, putting his arms around our mother, "I think we're going to like it here."

"We'll see."

"We shall see what we shall see," sang our father.

A fine sand blew from the bare gulleys between each furrow. When the breeze picked up, you had to squint to keep from getting a faceful. "Let's get started," said our father.

The Mayflower movers had been working the whole time we'd been out exploring. They'd been consulting with our mother, too, about where she wanted things. Now they were almost done. We stayed out of their way as they brought in the big items, which they set against the walls or in open areas between the boxes. We would be days getting everything to rights, but it was July and we had eight weeks before school started to set up house, to learn our way around the place, to make friends and put our farm in order.

The house was hot, and our mother thought we should start by opening the windows. Only we couldn't. Sand was everywhere. The window tracks were clogged with it. It was like the Dust Bowl, said our mother. "Does this all come from not knowing how to plow right?"

"Contour farming," said our father. "Crop rotation. I bet they teach that at the high school. The Hoveling kids must have been absent that day."

Once we got some boxes put away, we could see where the Hoveling kids had probably been instead. They'd gone through the entire house before they left, kicking in doors and ripping out woodwork. Our wood-work. The house had been built without any. Closets were open caves, the windows glassed-in holes, and floors met walls without moldings or toe rounds. Our parents had authorized workmen to measure, cut, and tack up all the trim. We'd stain, varnish, and do the final nailing ourselves. Our first family project. Trusting people, our parents had no idea what sort of people they'd bought their house from. Any trim not already nailed to the wall the Hoveling children—or, could it be, the adults?—had broken over their knees like kindling. The wreckage was total—floor moldings, toe rounds, sliding closet doors, hinged doors, edging—all of it snapped or kicked in. An obscenity in red Crayola sug-gesting what we could do with ourselves adorned the living room wall next to the fireplace. Our mother had missed it earlier.

Our mother put her hand over her mouth. She stood like they do in those pictures of people suffering in Asia or Africa, or standing over the ruins of some Mississippi Gulf town devastated by a hurricane. "I have to get some water," she said, but she didn't move. Then Charlie, who had nosed his way inside, came up the steps from the landing, put his snout between his paws, and promptly threw up at our mother's feet. Something was alive in the vomit—a mass of tiny white worms, blind and wriggling. Our mother cupped her hand in front of her mouth, but her vomit soon joined Charlie's.

Our father had our mother sit on a Mayflower box while he got her some water. "Jesus H. Christ," we heard him shout from the kitchen. There was a tremendous rattling and kathunking of pipes and metal. Now what? We ran to see. Our father was holding a glass of tap water up to the light. But it was no use; you couldn't see through it. The pipes were rattling and bonking, and orangey-brown water was shuddering out. Then the tap closed up completely. Our father unscrewed the faucet cap, and a burst of sand and water and rust cascaded into the sink. The particulate in the glass he'd set on the countertop was settling now. What we were getting from the tap appeared to be a forty-to-sixty ratio of sand and grit to well water. Our father handed this glass to Cinderella with the instructions "Give this to your mother."

The next day we would find out that the well pipes had caved in and that we'd need to dig a new well. A week after that the septic system would back up and we would have to hire the Hoveling cousins to locate our septic tank and dig that up. At the first good rain we would discover that the flashing around the chimney leaked, and that sand was not the only thing the basement windows could not keep out. Water filtered in between the storm and the interior windows, filling the space and turning the downstairs windows into filled-but-vacant aquariums like you might find in a seafood restaurant down on its luck. Water continued to pour in after that and belled out the pink bathroom wallboard like the tummy of a pregnant cheerleader.

Given the horrors to come, our mother's reaction—crying over a glass of tap water—was not unreasonable, particularly if she was prescient, which from time to time she claimed to be. She was no Jeane Dixon, mind you, but at various times she'd get a presentiment and tell our father, "I feel good about this," or "I have a very bad feeling about this." When pressed, she never elaborated, but we were given to understand that something mystical had happened inside our mother, that she simply knew something was going to happen before it did. If she'd had any such feelings about our move, she'd not voiced them to us. What she might have said to our father, of course, is another story. But we thought it telling that he could not face her with a glass of tap water just after she had vomited on her own shoes.

Reluctantly, we filed into the living room, where her crying escalated from muffled sobs to outright keening. The albino sea snakes were still wriggling in the vomit at her feet, and our mother was screaming, "I can't take this, Wally, I can't take this, I can't, I can't, I simply can't take this," just prior to running into their bedroom, where she threw herself on the naked box spring and cried for hours.

"Let's clean this up," said our father. He supervised for a little while, then he went back to our mother. The door closed and there was screaming from our mother, things we couldn't make out, and then our father reappeared, a look of anger and purpose on his face. He didn't say anything, but when he left we had a pretty good idea where he was going. We knew he wouldn't be back for hours, and we hoped to be in bed by the time he was.

12. This Will Reflect
on Your Merit Review

Was it really like this, our mother crying all the time? Pandemonium and sorrow, shrieking and recriminations, slammed doors, loud silences, our lives constantly in the balance? No. Our mother was a trouper. But when you are a child, it is not the moments of motherly strength you recall much, for they are expected. What you remember are the lapses, the moments when things break down—when she breaks down—and the world as you know it grinds to a halt. Your mother, crying her eyes out.

Oh, she cried for joy, too, plenty of times. When we sold the old house, when our father got a larger-than-expected sale just before Christmas, when we gave her handmade Mother's Day cards, when Nomi announced she was again coming to live with us. But it is when she is sobbing, keening, and then afterward, when she is wrung out like the proverbial dishrag, her emotional insides displayed like a skinned rabbit—that's the image engraved in our eyes. Our mother clutching her stomach, bent over, trying to keep her grief inside and failing, and Ernie or Peg Leg Meg saying, Momma, no cry, Momma, no cry.

Tugs at your heart, doesn't it? Pitiful, a mother so bereft she breaks down in front of her kids, has no one else with whom she can find solace—an audience of two- and four- and six- and eight-year-olds.

But what of those moments of strength, the default mode of our mother's existence? She had us all week, twenty-four hours a day in the summer, seven of us, rambunctious and high-strung, hellions each to each. All of us pulling for our moment of attention, all of us screeching out our hurts, our needs, our laments, the injustices done us by our brothers and sisters, our denials about the injustices and hurts and lambastings we visited upon them. Our mother acting as referee until she got tired of it and screamed, "Enough! Settle it yourselves. I don't care who did what to who. Whoever tattles is getting the same spanking as he who hits. And he who hits is getting spanked twice—once by me and once when your father gets home."

When our father gets home—the great empty threat in our household. At one time—when our father came home at night—it might have carried some weight. But now, when our father was gone all week? When he called from Ishpeming or Thief River Falls or Duluth-Superior? Fat chance. By the time he came home on Friday, he'd already visited Banana's Never Inn in Holton or the Dog Out on Highway 45 and JJ—his new Offices—and he was in no mood to settle petty disputes that had been accruing since Monday. What did he care that Robert Aaron used Ike's plastic tank as a target for his pellet gun? Or that Wally Jr. crayoned inside my Silver Surfer comic books? And what of my own malfeasance, squashing Wally Jr.'s Play-Doh elephant to a squishy turd under the heel of my foot?

"You're driving me to drink!" our father yelled, hands up in the air.

"No, Wally, you already drove yourself to a drink. Then you came home." Which as likely as not sent our father out again, "just so I can hear myself think, goddammit!"

So how about our mother's default mode? How about the time she drove into Augsbury on a tractor to get a prescription filled because there was no car and she couldn't drive one anyway? Or all the times she dealt with our mashed or sliced fingers, broken arms, cracked skulls, poked eyes, or sprained or broken ankles all by herself because our father was in Ypsilanti, Michigan, or Cloquet, Minnesota? Or what about the time the sheep or the cows got loose, or the chickens all took sick at once and died? Or what about our school plays and music lessons and concerts, our ball games and parent-teacher conferences—nothing our father could ever make it home for? Or what about all the illnesses, the measles and chicken pox and flu and mumps, the strep throats, the asthma attacks, the pneumonia, the fevers, the diarrhea and the vomiting, sometimes both ends at once, sometimes three or four children at once, one child puking into a stewpan while diarrhea drips down his bum and another child is crying piteously for saltines and flat 7UP and another announces, "Mommy, I don't feel so good," just before vomiting all over his pajamas, sheets, and teddy bear, while another is fouling the sheets because the pent-up gas he thought was a fart was really the same lower intestinal bug his brother had? Oh, and did we mention our mother didn't have any friends, not being able to drive into town or a neighboring farm to meet them, not to mention not having time for friends anyway seeing as how she had to keep the house running in our father's absence? You think that didn't take balls?

So she allowed herself her periodic cry to console herself, and we, blind and selfish and desperate to keep ourselves at the center of her universe, tried to understand.

What has been harder to understand is Dorie's yes-I'm-here-no-I'm-not disappearing act. She's been almost defiant about it. The clincher was this evening during dinner, before she asked me to take a walk with her down the field. We've got paper plates balanced on our laps and she tells me, "You know, hon, I'm going to be traveling a lot for this city council thing. It's supposed to just be our district, but the way it works these days is you've got to have a larger presence for effective fund-raising. I'm going to be all over. Which is why this trip out East is important. I need to get away before I throw myself into all that. And," she adds, almost as an aside, "I think we need to think about how we're going to pay for all this." I can feel it coming, the linkage between my books and her council, but I ask anyway. "Pay for all what?" "Oh, you know," she says, "doing a little belt tightening, rethinking what we like but can live without, showing some—what do the Republicans say?—*fiscal responsibility.*" "Are we talking about my bookstores here?" She pats my knee. "We can talk about this another time. I just wanted to put it on your radar." I suggest that her two trips this summer—the lap around Lake Michigan and her solo trip out East, consuming six weeks between them, might fall into that category of "things we like but can live without," but she just laughs. "Ace," she says, "be serious."

There is a history here. A bit of overheard conversation, Dorie to a friend on the phone: "You may as well do as you like. The consequences are going to come later whether you want them to or not, so you may as well at least have fun in the meantime."

"Who was that?" I wonder, hoping she was just offering advice to one of her recently divorced friends, not making a statement of personal philosophy.

She gets this look on her face. "You know what the bad thing about marriage is, Em? Being married to just one person."

Don't go there, I tell myself. Don't say a word. But I can't stop myself. "What's that supposed to mean?" and she says, "Don't you think it'd be great if there were time bubbles?" "Time bubbles?" I say. "Like one of those Mylar balloons," she says, "or one massive soap bubble, nicely appointed," and she goes off on this whole riff about how with time bubbles you could go away with someone you were attracted to and romp to your heart's content, and meanwhile, outside the bubble, time would have stopped, and you'd return to your life with no time off the clock. With no time missing, no gaps in your life with your spouse, you could feel perfectly safe doing something for yourself without hurting anyone else. "Time bubbles," I say.

"Oh, come on. Tell me you haven't thought of it." We've been putting away groceries, the phone rang, and the next thing I know we're talking about time bubbles and Dorie's saying, "I don't think there's any difference between wanting to fuck somebody and fucking them. If you're married and you want to sleep with somebody else, you may as well sleep with them."

The logic here astounds me. "You really don't think there's any difference between the thought and the act? Isn't that what got Jimmy Carter ridiculed?"

"He thought it was a sin, didn't he?"

"But don't you get any credit for wanting to do something and choosing not to?"

"Why should you?"

About a year and a half later—right before this past Christmas—she tells me, "Remember that argument we had about the difference between wanting to fuck someone and doing so? I think you're right. Wanting to do something and actually doing it are two different things."

Which begged the question "What made you change your mind?"

"Nothing. I just thought about it some more and decided there really is a difference."

I wanted to believe nothing had happened, that our life together might have lost its magic but we could find it again, simply from the will of wanting it to return to us. I did not want to imagine or believe—but I was tormented by the thought—that my wife was finding that magic somewhere else. With someone else. That was the mystery of our life together—that Dorie had turned elsewhere for magic in her life, but she had chosen to remain with me, and so she lived a double life, and I did, too: the life of a man who acts as though nothing is wrong in his marriage, and the one of a man who believes—knows—otherwise.

Not long after that Dorie announced that she was going to visit her friend Mia in Darien, Connecticut, this coming summer and that she was going to get there by bike. Dorie and Mia go way back, to when Dorie had first left Augsbury when she was seventeen and had recently been impregnated by one of her dirtbag boyfriends. Mia was her confidante and partner in crime for a good half dozen years. Probably was also, for a brief while way back when, her lover. Mia is married now, the mother of two, and having an affair with her supervisor at her brokerage house. Dorie tells me this, and immediately I know it was to Mia that Dorie was speaking when she offered up her advice/philosophy about the limitations of marriage. "So, what, you're going out there to compare notes? Want to see what the difference is between the wanting and the doing?"

Again with the look on her face—exasperation, impatience, maybe even loathing. "It's a two-way street, Ace," Dorie says. "People in affairs don't get there by accident. Whoever they're married to is at least partly responsible for the affair having happened."

Then comes the clincher, the thing meant to undo me, which it does. Something so dripping with scorn and condescension that when she says it I flinch. "What, Ace, is this going to 'reflect on my merit review'? If I had an affair would that reflect on my merit review?" Our father's phrase. But coming out of Dorie's mouth it is meant as a reproach against the long-suffering of my mother and the antics of my father. It is a reproach against the kind of marriage our parents had, against me, against, even, the kind of marriage I thought we had. And we are a long way from the kind of marriage my parents had. Or maybe we're not, it's just that the roles are reversed, and I am only beginning to understand just how hard everything was for our mother, living with a man who was so frequently elsewhere, so completely caught up in his own desires.

Our father, coming home after a long week, a little soused and perhaps feeling guilty over having stopped at the Dog Out for three or five or eight quick ones before heading home to hearth and family, tries to make light of everything, even his own intoxication. "This will reflect on your merit review," he tells our crying mother. Or he will ask her, a little abashed at himself, "This is going to reflect on my merit review, isn't it?" before he collapses on the sofa and falls asleep.

But mostly he will say it to us. When we screw up, when we break something or do something so badly that we need to redo it, but especially when we do ourselves harm—cutting ourselves on broken glass, trimming under the electrified fence with a hand sickle and knocking ourselves on our asses when the blade makes contact, smashing our thumbs nailing bluebird houses together—he will try to cheer us up, make light of our anguish and pain by saying, "This will reflect on your merit review." And after we're bandaged he'll say, "Back in the saddle again," and find some other work for us to do. Perhaps we will measure instead of hammer, or paint instead of saw—whatever, he will keep us busy.

There was plenty to keep us busy. That first summer we had to replace all the doors and trim inside the house, sand, stain, seal, and varnish (three coats) all the wood, then hang or nail it all into place. With our father we put up fencing. He bought a tractor—a small gray Massey-Ferguson— and a posthole digger, and at the Farm and Fleet store he'd gotten rolls and rolls of barbwire and electrical fencing. He'd also purchased wire cutters and wire stretchers, fence staples and insulators and fencing nails and insulating wire and heavy gloves for all of us. He bought chain, circular, and crosscut saws. Our father was taking no chances in the tool department. He loved gadgets and gizmos of any kind. Having a farm gave him license to buy just about anything his little heart desired. The one thing he didn't buy was a wagon. The Hovelings had left one behind, one with wood sides and open ends that could be linchpinned to the tractor, and it was the generally decrepit—antique—appearance of this wagon that enticed our father to keep it. It rode on a couple of bald truck tires, and he could throw just about everything he needed for fencing, including a couple dozen split rails, into its bed and still have room for us kids to sit on the back of the wagon, our feet dangling over the side.

Fencing is slow, hard, hot work, at least the way we did it, with cedar split-rail fence posts. Tony Dederoff tried to dissuade our father. "Use steel posts. They're straight, easy to drive, and they don't rot. Those posts you got there—they'll rot."

"They're cedar," said our father. "They won't rot." He and Tony were taking a break. It was early evening. Tony had come over on his way home from the Kafka Feed and Seed, and our father was standing him to a beer. Robert Aaron and I were cleaning out a hole with a clamshell.

"Termites or wood borers will get 'em, I don't care what they told you at Farm and Fleet. If they ain't slathered with pine tar, same as the telephone poles, they'll succumb to insects or rot—one or the other. Three, five years, maybe, they'll start going, and then where will you be?"

"Right here, putting a new fence in."

"Exactly. You don't want to be messing with all this. With steel you can go electrified or not, either way. It's easier maintenance, too—you go out each spring with a wire stretcher, some spare insulators, and insulator wire. Scythe down the weeds, stretch, replace, you're done. You got time to pop a cold one. This—this'll take you weeks, especially doing it just on the weekends, like you've got to." Tony raised his beer to his lips. "Of course, if you're doing this as a character-building exercise for your boys, that's another story." He grinned.

We were not amused. The cedar posts were our father's idea of picturesque fencing.

We had no idea at the time, but this was the first (or second, if you counted moving up here, too) grand, misguided idea he'd had since the boat, which rested now behind the house on matching sawhorses, a two-piece puzzle that he hadn't quite gotten around to solving. And like all of his other misguided ideas, he was determined to see it through, at least for a while.

Our father raised his beer bottle and indicated the two of us. "This'll put hair between their toes."

"But, Dad," I panted. "What if we don't want hair between our toes?"

"Then this will reflect on your merit review." He removed a pocket spiral notebook from his bib overalls and made a notation.

"You have to write it down?" asked Tony Dederoff. "For my kids I keep it all up here." He tapped his temple with his forefinger.

"You're not on the road all the time like I am. I don't write it down, I forget. Then where would I be?"

"Then where would you be," agreed Tony Dederoff. They were having a gay old time. Robert Aaron and I hated them.

But you could not hate him—our father—for long. And you could not hate Tony Dederoff at all. Tony was our father's guide and spiritual mentor, at least in regards to farming. And Tony was a good guy, cheer-

ful and blunt. His wife was happily pumping out babies, just as our
mother had a decade ago, and at the age of thirty, with his own farm and
the respect of his peers, he had the world by the tail. But he was always
well-meaning. "Wally," he told our father now, "I gotta tell you, Wally,
you bought the least promising farm I can think of."

"Will that reflect on my merit review?"

"Not if you fork over another beer."

"Done. And done," said our father, and in the dark we heard the *pfsst*
of the church key doing its work. We kept doing ours, taking dirt out of
a hole we could no longer see, while Tony instructed our father as to the
order of the projects needed to make the farm a paying enterprise again.

"Nobody's done jack on this place in ten years," said Tony, "but you
could. You got the horses."

"Horses?"

"Five boys, if I'm counting right. You got another couple stashed I
don't know about?"

"Naw, that's the full complement."

Tony Dederoff found this very funny. "The full complement. I like
that. You got a big family, you gotta see everything as a military campaign." The suck of a bottle. "Well, General—"

"Admiral."

"Admiral. The first thing I'd do, Admiral, is replow this field and plant
alfalfa. You get a good root system with alfalfa. You won't get a crop this
year, but if it takes, with any luck you'll have three cuttings a summer for
the next seven, eight years. And the first thing I'd do before that is take
that wagon of yours and clean out the rocks."

"The rocks?"

"You can't plow till you clean out the rocks. You hit a boulder with a
plow blade, you'll break the blade. These fields haven't been cleaned in a
decade. You're gonna have yourself a bumper crop of rocks. Take this
ship of yours"—Tony's hand slapped the wagon—"drive it real slow over
the fields with your troops fanned out behind it, and throw anything
bigger'n a quarter into the wagon. You'll have yourself quite a harvest.
Course you'll have to do it again next spring—the freeze and thaw cycle
pushes 'em up every year like flowers. It's amazing, really, the world
don't run out of rocks."

We liked Tony. He was a sober, happier version of Uncle Louie. He'd
come over, have his one or two beers, then leave. Of course, we never

saw our father have more than one or two beers, either. It was what he was drinking when he wasn't around us that was the problem.

But in those early days, our father's enthusiasm for all things rural kept his drinking more or less in check. And he heeded Tony's advice. We hauled rocks. The fields were littered with them. Our father did a slow *ka-bump, ka-bump* over the fields, and we fanned out in a line and threw rocks in the wagon. We found dozens of arrowheads, too. We felt we were gleaning sacred earth. We were in touch with our Bohemian ancestors, that mythical tribe of blond-haired, green-eyed Indians in which I, only too recently, had believed.

Borrowing Tony's equipment, our father plowed, spring-toothed, dragged. He planted seed in the now-level earth. With our father watching the furrow ahead, we rode the Ferguson's fenders and kept a close watch on the seed spilling out behind. When it stopped we'd yell, jump off the tractor, and muscle—with our father's help—another bag of seed into the bins.

If you discounted our mother—and all too frequently we did—it was a time of great family happiness. Every week we had a project. We took lumber and corrugated sheet metal from the barn that had collapsed and reroofed the sheds. Lumber, tar paper, tin—it took two days. The rusty tin heated up something fierce, and you had to be careful not to cut yourself on the sheet metal or Mom would insist on a tetanus shot, but it was glorious work. We were fixing things, making things! This! This is what farmers do! After we pulled all the usable lumber from the leaning barn, our father looped a chain around a corner pole, hooked the chain to the tractor, and pulled down the barn. That was glorious, too, watching it collapse with a great *woof!* of exhaled dust. So this was why that bulldozer driver merely shrugged when he destroyed our clubhouse. He was having too good a time to be disturbed. Destruction could be as much fun as—maybe more fun than—construction was. Who needed a balsa-wood airplane burning out an attic window when you could take down an entire barn and watch it woof chaff and smoke?

Or set fire to an immense pile of rubble and lumber?

We did that in the fall, when farmers burned their ditch lines and leaves. The air smelled wonderful. Acrid, pungent, sweet—there are few smells that can transport you to another time quite like the smell of burning leaves. The smell of an ex-lover's perfume glimpsed on a city street, perhaps, but what did I know of that then?

Our contribution to the fall burning would be our lumber piles, swollen with torn out fencing. Our father ran a hose—two hundred feet of it—out to the piles and stationed us around them with pellet guns and twenty-twos and pitchforks and spade forks and scoop shovels. Our father wielded a pistol and a four-ten shotgun—what he called his squirrel gun. The idea was we'd kill all the rats and mice as they ran out, not give them a chance to relocate in the newly sided sheds, where we hoped to keep chickens and horses and sheep and some beef cattle someday.

Although our father had trained us in gun safety, and was a dues-paying NRA member, the notion of seven or eight or nine people in a circle all shooting at the same objects running out from the center did not raise any red flags for him. I mention this only in hindsight. It didn't occur to anyone else at the time, either.

Our father circumnavigated the piles with five-gallon cans of gasoline. He sprinkled liberally. He added an oil change's worth of old motor oil for good measure. We stood back, our weapons poised. Tony came over to help. He had a twenty-two rifle; his oldest son, Matt, had a Daisy BB gun; and Borowski, his hired hand—a kid not much older than Cinderella—had a sixteen-gauge shotgun. There was soda and beer in a washtub of ice water back at the house. It would be a party. When everything was ready, our father took two empty pop bottles and filled them halfway with kerosene. Then he took two strips from an old bedsheet and poked them into the bottles, leaving three or four inches of wick sticking outside. We recognized these—Molotov cocktails. We'd seen them on television. We just didn't know you could use them for this. And we were surprised our father knew how to make them. We thought only student radicals and Negroes in inner-city ghettos knew about these things. But maybe it was something you learned in the Navy, too. He lit them with a Zippo lighter, then handed one to Tony. The flame was long and smoky. Our father said, "Ready?" and Tony Dederoff nodded. "On three," said our father. "One, two . . ." And they lofted them together.

Elsewhere, it was the tail end of the Summer of Love. In Augsbury, on the old Hoveling farm, we were gathered like extras for an updating of *Frankenstein*—the villagers-storming-the-castle scene, ready to burn or shoot or pitchfork to death anything that moved.

Of course, there were casualties. This began when the bottles were first thrown onto the piles. Our father's didn't break. Tony Dederoff's did, and a huge roar went up from the pile on the east. Our father was just reaching into the pile to retrieve his cocktail when the heat and some flicker of flame from Tony's pile set off the kerosene-gasoline–motor oil mix in our father's. The concussive *WHOOOMPH!* of all those inflammatories going off at once knocked our father backward, blackened and seared his face, and burned off his eyebrows and most of the hair on his knuckles. He lay there stunned. The cocktail was in his hand, still burning, as he sat up, dazed. Given our father's girth, sitting up in itself was an ordeal. By the time he noticed the cocktail in his hand, the fire was running down inside the bottle. Our father had barely launched it when it struck a board projecting at an odd angle from the great jumbled pile and exploded a few feet from his face. Glass erupted everywhere. Our father screamed and fell back, his second wounding. Blood was pouring from his face and hands from a thousand tiny and not so tiny cuts. And underneath the smell of burning gas and wood, the stench of burning oil, there was the smell of burning protein—hair, fur, flesh. Something alive was going up in flames.

"Here they come," yelled Tony Dederoff, and I felt like I was that guy at the end of the movie *Wake Island,* where the last you see of the doomed Americans wearing World War I–issue helmets is a lone guy spraying death from a machine gun, twisting and turning to ensure the largest field of fire.

The rabbits were first. They bolted, zigzagging as they leapt, and we let them go. The rats came next. They were big and quick, some of them like house cats. We had mowed around the piles to give us a clear line of fire, but that was good for only thirty feet or so before the long grass started, and behind us was the drop-off into the ruined barn, with its nooks and crannies, into which a rat could disappear. We had to be quick or they'd escape. Fortunately, the bloodlust was upon us. Or at least upon my fellow villagers. They fired and hacked and beat with efficiency. I watched as Wally Jr. speared one with his pitchfork and flung it, trailing blood, back into the fire, the rat making a little *fliiiiip* sound as it came off the pitchfork. I watched the rats dying and tried firing, but it froze me, seeing them scurry and die. My aim, with a pellet gun and a bent sight, was pitiful. I led them too much, I aimed too high. Invariably, just as they were about to reach the grass, or had reached the grass, Tony Dederoff or Borowski or my older brother, Robert Aaron, or my younger brother Ike would swing and fire, and the escaping rat would die, or lie there wounded, or turn little circles in the dirt, like Curly from the old Three Stooges shorts, or turn and do flips and cough its death throes. Wally Jr. or Ernie had the job of impaling the survivors or scooping up the dead and throwing them back into the flames.

The flames, the flames. Perhaps I shouldn't admit this, but the other reason I was not doing my part in the great rat hunt of 1967 was I was as mesmerized by the flames as I was by the rats running their invisible mazes as they tried to escape. Given the broadness of the two piles and their intersection, it was amazing to me that the flames shot up not in twin columns but in a single conflated pyramid of fire that narrowed as it reached the sky. A good Catholic boy, I recognized that imagery: the flames—red, yellow, and edged in black—traced, inverted, the sacred heart of Jesus. Joan of Arc died in flames like these. Joan of Arc—not much younger than Patty Duckwa. And if I could hold the image of those two women in my head simultaneously, it must mean that, yes, indeed, we were in one of the lesser rings of hell.

The fire and the heat were tremendous—you could feel them as a physical presence. The shimmering waves kept you at bay, and we worked on the outside edge of that, killing and killing and killing. Surely God would reward us for this glorious and necessary evil.

Suffice it to say I was all mixed up. I felt bad—rats, too, were God's creatures. They wouldn't have survived this long if Noah hadn't brought them on the ark, but I felt good, too. There was something beautiful about the way the flames leapt into the sky, the air shimmering around you, distorting everything you viewed into elongated sine waves—the trees, the clouds, a bird flying, your father lying on the grass.

Our father. We had forgotten about him. Crazed with bloodlust, heady with our accomplishment, we had not noticed that our father was still on the ground. He was no longer bleeding profusely, but he was bleeding, and his face looked scorched, the eyebrows missing, his forehead a great red bullet. He was still stunned, still looking up at the sky. It had been only a few moments, really, since he'd first been blown backward. Everything was happening in a nether time, both quickly and in slow motion. Was it like this at Custer's Last Stand, I wondered, things winding down in a frenzy? We were still killing things, and I was celebrating what might have been my only kill, a rat I'd caught in the teeth, spinning him around where he lay very still, facing what he'd been fleeing, when I saw a baby rat leave the pile and make a beeline for my father's trouser leg, which was big and loose and open and inviting.

Of course no one saw this but me. And I knew why we were killing these rats in the first place. They were evil. They ate chicken eggs and carried disease. If one were to bite my father, he could get rabies or bubonic plague and die a horrible, slow, lingering death, and there would be nothing anybody could do for him except amputate the parts that turned green and comfort him in his misery while he lay dying. It would be against everything we knew and held dear to put him out of his misery. We could do that for rats; we could not do that for a rabid and gangrenous father. So I had to stop this panicky rat from inflicting a slow and painful death on our father. One problem, though, was that I panicked. The other was that I was a lousy shot. I led the rat too much. The first shot entered just above our father's heel, in the fleshy part of his ankle. He had ignored the advice he had given us about wearing work boots or Wellingtons. He had on a pair of canvas deck shoes offering no protection from a well-meaning son with lousy aim. The second shot, when the rat was going up his trouser leg, hit his calf, the third, his thigh. My father was screaming, the rat was burrowing—no doubt both were in panic as to where my next shot might go—and it was Wally Jr., little Wally, who solved matters by skewering the rat with his pitchfork. Only a single tine pierced our father's leg, but it went deep, and our father jittered and danced like one of the wounded and dying rats before Wally removed his pitchfork from both the rat and our father's thigh.

"Jesus, sweet Jesus," choked our father, trying not to scream. All about us the carnage was nearly complete. We gathered around him. He was still looking up at the sky, his great bulk of a stomach heaving like a stone that had acquired the ability to breathe.

"Wally, you okay, Wally?" asked Tony Dederoff. With a hunting knife he cut open my father's trouser leg. The rat fell out—it's entirely possible that it died of a heart attack before my brother skewered it—and we examined my father's wounds. Fortunately a pellet gun does not create projectiles with a whole lot of force behind them. The wounds in my father's leg were tiny, round circles that bled a little but not much, the pellets not having penetrated deeply, so near the surface that Tony Dederoff dug them out on the spot with a needle-nose pliers he kept in his truck—the same needle-nose pliers he used to dig hooks out of fish gullets. Tony also produced a hip flask of Jack Daniel's, which he first poured over the wounds and the pliers and then offered to our father. Tony had a drink himself before he commenced digging. Our father winced and grunted and gritted his teeth, but he did not scream, and for that I was grateful.

"Who was the wiseacre who shot his father?" Tony asked nonchalantly as he plucked first one pellet and then another from my father's leg.

"That would be me," I managed to choke out.

"Well, you're lucky. Your old man is going to live. He'll need a tetanus shot for these pokes"—he indicated the wounds Wally Jr. and I had made in our father's leg—"but he'll live. Just remind me never to go hunting with you. I'm liable to wind up gutted on your kitchen table and my head mounted over your fireplace before you realize your mistake."

It was several minutes, I think, before I heard my father calling to me, and by that time Ike had run to the house and come back with our mother and a first-aid kit. He would still need to go to the hospital, where maybe they'd need to take a stitch or two in his face, and they would need to bring the rat in and check it for rabies, but it did look like he was going to be all right. He would not lose his foot or his leg or have it swell green with pus and require amputation. He was even smiling/grimacing, like a man who'd survived his own chemistry set explosion—and he'd done that as well. Tony Dederoff and Robert Aaron helped him to his feet. I tried, but I was afraid to touch him, afraid he wouldn't let me, so I trailed a little behind, my arms out but not quite touching (not unlike Ira Hayes at the flag raising on Mount Suribachi). I was in such a state I did not hear him calling my name.

"Emmie," my father said. It was one of the few times he called me by the name our mother always used. "Emmie, Emmie, Emmie, Emmie."

Finally it dawned on me that he was speaking to me. At that point, though, after shooting him three times, I couldn't manage speech. I could barely look him in the face. My father, I think, understood this. Despite having been shot by me, he felt sorry for me. He wanted to make me feel better. He wanted to let me know it was okay, that everything was going to turn out all right. He clamped a hand on my shoulder. I do not think that anything he could have said right then would have made me feel better, but he tried, and despite my best efforts to the contrary, I did feel better. He gave my shoulder a little shake, which was meant to make me look at him. I did. His face was bleeding from a dozen tiny cuts, his nose and forehead had the look of rare beef, and his remaining hair was cooked and curlicued, but he was grinning, and I have to give him credit for that. And credit, too, for making me grin back.

"Emmie," he said, giving my shoulder another shake, "this will reflect on your merit review."

13. Observations from the Wayback

OUR MOTHER, THE TROUPER

"I used to be a lean, mean fighting machine," laments Wally Jr., hauling himself up the tower again using only his arms. He has massive, slablike arms, but what's more impressive is the body he's trailing, shaped like a cross between a barrel and a pomegranate. "No more," he says. "Not since I achieved gimphood." He flops like a potbellied carp when he gets to the roof. Ernie's the same when he heaves himself onto the roof. Both lie there for a moment, as though a fifteen-foot climb up an aerial was on a par with scaling the Matterhorn.

"This," Ernie puffs, "will reflect on our merit review."

"Fuck our merit review," says Wally Jr. "Whose idiot idea was it that we meet on the fucking roof? This ain't even close to being in compliance with the handicap laws."

"It started the night I told Emcee I was going to marry Audrey." Robert Aaron hauls up Wally Jr.'s wheelchair and blocks the wheels while Ike tethers it to the chimney.

Wally Jr. pulls himself into his chair. "Oh. So we do this for sentimental reasons."

Below us, the screen door opens and out come Dorie, Audrey, Jennifer, and Jake, all carrying grocery bags. Audrey calls to Robert Aaron that they'll bring the kids up after they've been fed. Dorie doesn't look up. Jake, carrying a flashlight, keeps turning it on and off under his nose.

"Can we just get started?" I ask.

Meg says we shouldn't start until Cinderella gets here.

"Like that's going to make a difference."

"What's bugging you, Emcee?"

"You know we're just like Mom and Dad. Dinking around, frittering away time, never getting anywhere—"

"And getting somewhere would be what, putting them in a home?" asks Wally Jr. "That's what this is about, right? Puttin' 'em somewhere? What, you just want a vote and that's that?"

"That's not what I meant. Christ. Can we please just discuss this rationally for once?"

"Rationally, he says. In this family he expects rationality."

"I'm not expecting, I'm asking. I think we can do this. Even if we can't, it needs to be done, dammit. How much longer do you think Mom and Dad are going to be able to care for themselves? And then what?"

Wally Jr. fishes around in the cooler for another Dew. "I say we drive off that bridge when we come to it."

"Driving off a bridge is not going to help them or us, Wally."

"Don't knock it till you tried it, pantywaist."

I should have known. I fucking should have known. Our making nice lasts only as long as we're talking about things that don't matter.

"Shut the fuck up," says Wally Jr. "Or I'll make you shut the fuck up." He backs his wheelchair off the blocks and executes the first half of a Y-turn so he can make a run at me. I'm puzzled. Wait, did I say that out loud? You don't do that around Wally. Even from a wheelchair, Wally will take on all comers and eat them for lunch.

"Don't," says Robert Aaron, stepping between us. "Just don't get started on all that. We'll be here all night."

"Don't get started on what?" Our mother's outside on the deck, leaning on her cane. She's a compact woman now, and her face has the look she used to get when she listened to our father's wilder stories. "What are you out here talking about?"

Silence. Finally somebody says, "Nothing." Somebody else says, "Stuff."

"Nothing and stuff. Look," says our mother, "don't take me for a simpleton just because I'm old. You're talking about your father and me, aren't you?"

"Where is Dad?"

"Sleeping. Your father poops out early these days. Don't try to change the subject. And get down here. I don't want to get a crick in my neck talking to you."

"Christ," says Wally Jr. "I just got up here again."

"Well, you shouldn't have been up there in the first place, Mr. Smarty-Pants."

We climb down. Wally Jr.'s wheelchair first, then Wally Jr., then the rest of us. We stand around the way we used to after fights, all hangdog and guilty. What would it be this time—yelling, a spanking, or something icily controlled and distant and devastating? Yelling we could handle. It was that calm, bitten off "Well, I'm disappointed in you, children, I expected better" that ripped our guts out.

Our mother looks around the circle, shaking her head, her eyes glistening. She takes a deep breath. A tear spills onto her papery cheek, but she's smiling. "What lousy liars you all are. I used to say this about you playing with balls, but it's true of cabals as well: don't have them so close to the house." She sighs. "No balls or cabals close to the house," she says as she shuffles back inside. "You're bound to break something. Windows, hearts—something."

The soundtrack for our first summer in Augsbury was the continuous, nerve-racking hammering of a new well being drilled. Two hundred and fifty-one feet of it. Most wells in the area, we found out, usually hit water at about fifty-five to sixty-five feet. A few went to eighty, a few more to a hundred, a hundred and ten. But day after day the drill rig pounded and pounded right behind our house, and nothing. Sand, then clay, then rock.

"We don't know what the deal is," the crew chief told our father. "Usually by now we're just gushing water." They were at one hundred and eighty-one feet and counting.

Our father managed to escape this pounding entirely—they weren't drilling on weekends, the only time he was home. And we kids escaped it by playing army. The enemy was shelling our base of operations—listen to that bombardment!—and day after day we fought for control of the ruined barn, poking our submachine guns out windows framed in rotting wood. We were Vic Morrow in *Combat!* with stubbled chins and candy cigarettes dangling from our mouths as we went from one bombed, burned-out building to the next, spraying death to the Jerries

every step of the way. We fought up the rise and attacked our own backyard, whooping and hollering and spewing death to all who stood in our
way. The crew drilling in a futile search for water in our backyard were
not amused. "Hey, you kids, go play somewhere else."

Why? we wondered. It was our yard. They were the interlopers. What
were a few dirt hand grenades between friends? We swept and secured
the area, retired to the trees. Time for a new mission, even deadlier than
the last one—secure apples from Tillie Bunkas.

Tillie Bunkas scared the bejesus out of us. She was a nice old lady who
gave us apples, rhubarb pie, and her son Alfred's dandelion wine and
honey, but to us she was still a witch, an old crone with a goiter who lived
with her sixty-something-year-old son because she'd put him under a
spell, and she'd put us under one, too, if we let her. That evil eye would
get us, turn us into frogs or toads or stones or she-goats or something.
And all that poison she kept stored in the bulbous lump on her throat. If
any of that poison got you, you'd wind up just like her—blind and tooth-
less and cackling, with your own gourd of poison on your neck.

Tillie liked us, I think, even when we staged commando raids on her
orchard. But we didn't trust her generosity. She shouldn't have been so
accommodating during a commando raid. There we were, liberating apples, and Tillie Bunkas would appear in our midst, apples in hand, ruining it for us. What lousy commandos we were. How did she sneak up on
us? "Boys, boys," she'd say, "come out of the trees. See what I have for
you." And like that witch in "Hansel and Gretel" she'd wave her wizened
brown stick arms, the apples shiny in her claws.

It shouldn't have been so hard to take them. But the wind screwed her
hair around her head like a web and her dress blew like loose rags about
her and we could see her nylon stockings only came up to her knees and
the sun had turned her cataritic eyes into fish scales and her tongue
flapped around her five remaining teeth, and there was no way in hell we
were coming near this sweet old lady who simply wanted to keep us
from ruining her fruit trees.

Our mother had no such diversions. Her job that summer was the utterly mundane one of painting a ranch house that had been built in 1956
and hadn't been painted since. Actually, we were supposed to help her,
but that was not how it turned out. The boards on the west side of the
house were the color of old blood and so weather-beaten that the paint

we applied soaked in as though each silvered, blood-colored board was one of those sponges they compare paper towels to in the Bounty commercials. Gallon after gallon of primer disappeared into the side of the house. We got discouraged, tired, and our mother took over for us. Inside we cleaned up, then felt reenergized enough to roam the fields and woods, leaving our mother to the hot, lonely work of painting, her brain under a constant and inescapable sonic assault.

Our mother did most of the finish painting as well. Our father was gone Sunday night to Friday night, and when he returned after a ten- or twelve-hour drive, taking brush in hand was not an option. A seven-ounce fluted glass at the local tavern was, however, a different proposition. Our mother muttered about this and kept painting. The blood-red house slowly became off-white. "Like what a bride wears for her second wedding," said our mother.

Second wedding? Could you do that? People got married once, forever, and that was that. Uncle Louie was the exception, but his unhappiness ran deep. Already we were hearing that Uncle Louie and Shirley's marriage was not the match made in heaven he said it was. And our mother, while certainly sad for Louie, took satisfaction in having her premonitions proved correct. Yet here was our mother suggesting that people could get married more than once, and saying it with a disturbing wistfulness. People could start over. Which made us wonder: In trading the House That God Built for God's Green Acres, was that what our parents had done—embarked, metaphorically, on a second marriage? And what if that one didn't work out?

These days, when people move from one identical subdivision to another, every tract mansion the same combination of mismatched architectural styles and missized styling elements, the idea of being wedded to a single, particular place seems quaint, almost comical. But our parents were of a generation for whom mobility was a new and only semi-desirable thing. Mostly it was scary, engendered by a sense that they had to move out or lose what they had worked so hard to build in the first place. This was a generation that came of age during the dislocations of two wars, each preceded by a depression. The Korean War and its depression were littler than their predecessors, true, but the déjà vu sense was very strong in them. And after each dislocation, they wanted nothing more than for the boat to stop rocking.

No wonder our father was a company man. He needed someplace for all that loyalty and rootedness to go. Dinkwater Chemical helped him leave Elmhurst when everything seemed to be spinning out of control. They allowed him to realize his dream of living in the country. They also gave our father a company car—a Buick Skylark station wagon—and all the mobility he could stand. Seventy thousand miles a year worth. Therefore, Dinkwater Chemical deserved his loyalty. It was the simple arithmetic of a new marriage—get divorced from Elmhurst and Dinkwater-Adams, get married to the northern cousins.

This new marriage required, though, getting used to a new set of in-laws. Again, it was easier for our father. He no longer had the Office, but you couldn't walk a hundred feet in Augsbury and not find a bar, a tavern, a saloon, a bar and grill, a restaurant, an inn, or a tap enticing you with its open screen door, its cool dark, its hunched patrons and grinning barkeep. Our father had done the math—thirteen bars, thirteen hundred people.

It was after our first Sunday Mass that our father decided St. Gen's would be our regular church and Banana's Never Inn would be his regular bar, and living here would be a very good life indeed. Immediately after the ten o'clock High Mass, everyone left St. Gen's and went straight across the street to Banana's Never Inn. Our parents thought a brunch would be a nice treat for us, but as new parishioners they first wanted to introduce themselves to the priest. Monsignor Kahle was a stiff-backed, grim-visaged priest with absolutely clear gray eyes behind rimless glasses. He wore his hair in a pure white brush cut and lacked, I thought, only the dueling scar on his cheek to be a full-fledged Prussian officer. During his sermon he had railed about vice and immorality, stuttering out images of hellfire and damnation like bursts from a machine gun. It had scared me, this white-haired old man with his purple face and plosives. But now Monsignor Kahle was calm, affable, almost jovial. In welcoming our parents, his eyes twinkled, and he rubbed my and my brothers' crew cuts as though he were an uncle. He placed his fingers under Peg Leg Meg's chin and cupped Cinderella's cheek. He said we looked like a fine, fine family. Our father said it seemed like a nice community, and he thought it wonderful that the bar across the street offered a brunch. They certainly seemed to be doing a very good business. Monsignor Kahle said Banana's Never Inn had no brunch. They had a toaster oven for pizza, they served pickled eggs and beef jerky out of jars, and if you could convince Banana—when he was around—to fire up the grill for a hamburger, you were a lucky man indeed.

"But those people," protested our mother, "right after Mass—they streamed right over."

Monsignor Kahle shrugged, the shrug of a man who's seen everything twice and who is not going to get all worked up over changing what he can't. "Sometimes," he said, "sometimes after my sermons what everyone wants is a good stiff belt." He leaned in close, his eyes twinkling, his lips pulled back in an abashed to-err-is-human grin. "Me, too," he whispered.

The place suited our father. It suited us as well. It did not suit our mother. We kids had each other, and our father had Tony Dederoff—Uncle Louie was "nesting" right then—and when he came home he could buy a round at the Dog Out or Banana's and acquire a lifetime of friendship for that afternoon. But who did our mom have—Tillie Bunkas?

Our mother could see this more clearly than we could. In Augsbury we were the odd birds, the queer ducks, the flightless fowl. We had come from the city at a time when no one was doing that, and it would be another ten to fifteen years before people did that in numbers large enough to make a difference (which meant they came and changed everything to make it seem more like the suburbs). In 1967 the only people "moving back to the land" were beatniks and hippies (the terms were still interchangeable), and the farmers of Augsbury, with the notable exception of Tony Dederoff, did not want us city folk in their midst any more than they'd've wanted a bunch of unshaven hippies and beatniks. It would take our parents a good dozen years before they were accepted as locals. I could tell the change had finally occurred when I went into town to get some U-bolts. Art at Art's Hardware squinted at me and said, "You're Wally Czabek's boy, aren't you?" Wally Czabek's boy—we were in. Up until then he'd have said, "You live on the old Hoveling place, don't you?" as though the Hovelings, gone ten years by then, were anytime soon planning on returning from California and claiming what they'd left behind.

Our mother understood this long before we did, how attitudes in the Midwest changed slowly, if at all. When you're in, you're in. And when you're not, you're our mother.

It didn't help that all day, while she was painting, she was subjected to the well diggers' incessant yammering, nor did it help that our father's propensity for buying tools he thought we needed, along with the expense of putting in a new well, and the fact that our house in Elmhurst hadn't yet sold, was driving us into the poorhouse. Our mother was keeper of the finances, and while our father was buying rounds for new friends he'd never see again, our mother was calculating how little we had to buy groceries.

What made it worse was that after the Hovelings moved out, our two-hundred-foot-long driveway had become a lovers' lane. And because we were one of the few farms in the area without a yard light, our moving in had not discouraged the amorous. Once our lights went off, cars crept down our drive, gravel crunching. Our mother would wake us. She wanted us ready to bolt in case something awful happened—say a man with an ax came to the door. She had horrible night vision—night blindness, really—and she was terrified that she wouldn't be able to protect us. "What's going on?" she'd whisper. "What do you see?" The headlights on the car had just gone out. We were at the windows, just barely peeping our heads over the frames while our mother danced furtively behind us. Our lights were doused, the storm windows open. Our faces pressed against the screens. From our windows we saw jerky, furtive movements, the kind of wrestling people do in confined spaces. It was summertime; the car windows were open. Over the hum of crickets and the buzzing of June bugs, we heard the engine ticking heat and the heavy sighs of people administering love to each other. Also the occasional clink of a bottle being dropped onto our drive, which we would find in the morning, glass testimonials to love, or something like it.

Our mother wanted a crime light put in. This seemed odd to me. I had only the vaguest idea of what the occupants of those Dodge Darts and Chevy Camaros were doing, but it wasn't a crime, was it? They just sat there, faces welded tight, bodies writhing like snakes in a blanket, and after an hour or so they started the car, backed out our drive, and were gone.

"Look," our mother whispered to our father those nights he was home. "They're at it again." Our father got the same half grin on his face Monsignor Kahle got on his, and then he, too, shrugged. "I'm sure it's nothing, Susan. Just harmless fun." "They can be harmless somewhere else," said our mother. "Do you want your children—your daughter Sarah—looking at that every evening?" That clinched it. The crime light went in. Nobody parked in our drive anymore. We were safe. We'd moved from Chicago, and now nothing could hurt us.

That idea was undone twice just as our mother was finishing up the house painting. We awoke one night to a terrific series of crashes and thumps. Something metal was being torn from its moorings and ferociously bumping its way down our field. A big hulking Buick—one of those 1950s jobs with the clipper ship steering wheel—had leapt the ditch, plowed through our fence line, and come to a rest two hundred yards down the field. "Good God, what is that?" shrieked our mother, doing a very good impression of a startled Nomi. Although we wouldn't know this for some minutes yet, it was our neighbor Ernie Ott, driving himself home from the Dog Out. Our father threw on a blue terry-cloth robe and boots and struggled across the field to where Ernie's Buick sat, the cone of its headlights still wobbling in the fog that had settled over the field, its wheels deep between two furrows. No doubt Ernie Ott had a broken axle.

We watched from the upstairs window as our father helped Ernie stagger across the furrows back to our house. There was a clumping up the stairs of our mudroom, and then there he was, in our kitchen. Our mother was making coffee.

Ernie Ott was huge. Imagine a bowling ball in overalls, with another bowling ball, much smaller, sitting on top of that, and three rubber donuts for the chins which connected them. He was wearing one of those plaid Canadian baseball caps, the brim of which was pointing toward the corner of the ceiling.

"What happened?" our father asked. Our mother eased a cup of coffee across the kitchen table to Ernie Ott's waiting fists. Ernie looked dazed. Even the coffee didn't seem familiar to him. His eyes were marbled with tiny broken veins, and they rolled slightly in his head the way those of cartoon animals do when they've been whupped upside the head with a two-by-four or a crowbar. His head tilted slowly to take in Cinderella, who'd recently turned fourteen. Ernie's eyes got big, and I suddenly understood what the word *leering* meant.

"I've got a son about her age," he said, his eyes cutting across to our father and then centering back on our sister. "Maybe you and me can work out a deal. My boy and her boy, eh?" Our father nodded in stiff-lipped agreement even though Ernie Ott had misspoken the deal. This was the nod our father gave in bars when somebody said something particularly heinous and our father, being a salesman, didn't want to contradict or offend anybody. Our mother shooshed Cinderella a little farther back behind her brothers. There were five of us; we made a pretty uneven picket fence.

I was in the front row now, and I could see how heavily Ernie Ott sat. Like a sack of concrete, sagging. "So tell me what happened," our father said affably, as though he would really like to hear the story. "Wally," our mother said. Our father held his hand up, meaning it was all right, he could handle this.

Ernie Ott waited a minute. Two minutes. He bit his lip. Clearly he was gathering himself. He couldn't understand it, either. Finally he said, more to himself than to us, "The red house. I always turn at the red house." He shrugged and grinned like the idiot he was.

And this is what has always puzzled me. Our father clapped him on the back, helped him to his feet. "Well," our father said, "that happens." And that was what I couldn't understand, our father's conviviality in the face of man who'd torn out our fence, left his car wheezing in our field, and suggested his son mate with our sister. Yet here was our dad suddenly as affable as Monsignor Kahle telling us about his parishioners drinking right after Mass on Sunday. It was horrible for me to see these three men yoked like that, and our father and Monsignor Kahle went down a peg in my esteem for consorting, philosophically, with the likes of drunken Ernie Ott. It was not until I had to deal regularly with drunks myself that I realized what a great salesman our father was, and I think now that part of his success was this ability to nod pleasantly at other people's inanities as though he agreed with them. He suffered fools lightly.

"We're not safe here, Wally," said our mother after our father had gotten Ernie Ott out of our house and back to his own.

"We are perfectly safe. We are more safe here than we would be in Elmhurst."

"In Elmhurst we did not have people driving into our fields."

"In Elmhurst if this had happened they would have driven into our living room."

"I don't know if I can take this, Wally."

"Sure you can." Our father kissed our mother's forehead and held her. He was still in his blue robe. Ernie Ott's car was still in our field. "You're a trouper."

"Oh, Wally." Our mother collapsed against our father's chest and belly. They were sharing a moment. It was one of those times when we as children disappeared for them, and they could be wholly themselves with each other, loving and vulnerable, two people, not parents. We did the decent thing. We retreated, at least as far as the mudroom, which was on the landing before we went to our bedrooms downstairs.

"I don't have any friends, Wally."

"Sure you do. Didn't you just say you'd made a friend last week?"

"One, Wally, one. And that was an emergency."

"Does it matter how you make them? We made babies during a national emergency." He kissed her forehead again; the sound was different from when they kissed on the lips.

"That was different."

"How was it different?"

"We didn't know what we were doing. And lots of other couples were in the same boat."

"We're all in the same boat, honey. Still. It's just that there's more space between us."

"What does that mean, Wally-Bear?" Our mother was sniffling.

"It means you'll find friends. You'll make friends. It'll just take time is all."

"Easy for you to say. You aren't cooped up here all week not knowing how to drive."

"Sarah Lucinda will have her license soon."

"Not soon enough."

"You'll make friends," repeated our father. "It's just it's a big ocean out here. Ships don't go bump in the night so easily. But we do, honey."

"We do what?"

"You know—go bump in the night."

"Oh, Wally." Our mother blew her nose, and then they were quiet for a time, just making the *mmmm, mmmm* noises people make when they are tied up and have duct tape across their mouths. It sounded like they were both trying to escape, but who could set them free? Then we heard our mother gasp. "Oh, Wally, Wally, not here, the children might hear us," and then they made more escaping noises, though it didn't seem to us like they were getting anywhere. Then our mother started screaming, "More! More! Oh, Wally, more! More!"

"What's going on?" I asked, though I knew it was a stupid question. Years later I would ask the same question to myself, and feel the same way about the answer, when I discovered that Dorie was packing her diaphragm on her bicycling trips even though I'd been snipped years before. You know the answer to your question before you ask it, even if you don't know or understand the particulars. I knew that what our parents called "you know" referred to the great mysteries that occurred once their bedroom door was closed. We knew it had to do with our mother being "the greatest" in the same way that Alice Kramden in *The Honeymooners* was "the greatest" to Ralph. When Ralph and Alice disappeared into what we assumed was their bedroom, something happened in there, and what happened was so awesome, mysterious, and mystical that, like the name for God in the Jewish religion, it could not be stated directly.

As for Dorie, I wanted to believe it was force of habit, meaningless, the way some guys, monogamous twenty or thirty years, still carry condoms in their wallets, an impotent ode to possibility. With Dorie, though, I knew better. You don't pack a negligee and a diaphragm in your pannier unless you plan to use them. There was no mystery as to why. It made me think of when I first met her. Then as now, she was curious but indifferent regarding the consequences of actions, other people's in general, her own in particular.

Our father was right, our mother had found a friend. Sort of. The week before Ernie Ott stranded his car in our field our mother was still painting the west side of our house. She wanted to finish the trim for our father, who was coming home in the middle of the week—a rarity for him—as a present for his birthday. Robert Aaron and Cinderella had taken the little kids into the woods on a hike. They were going to find "natural gifts" for our father—birds' nests, pheasant tail feathers, interesting rocks, et cetera. I'd opted to go bike riding instead, on the big hill to our east. I wanted the plain, unadulterated thrill of going very fast, the wind roaring in my ears.

I had not counted on the gravel. Nor had I counted on the movers having removed the front wheel of my Schwinn to make it fit in the truck and bolting it back on loosely. I'd hardly ridden the bike since we'd moved; there'd been so many other things to do. So when I hit the gravel, and my arms shook trying to hold the bike steady, the last thing I expected to see was the front wheel parting company from the rest of my bike.

Our mother heard me screaming from a half mile away. I found this out later. What I remembered came in fragments. Feeling with a thickened tongue the stump of one front tooth, the bloody cavity where another had been. The shock of standing up and not being able to see anything, then feeling my face where it hurt and feeling large, wet breaks in the skin. My fingers coming away all bloody. Looking down at my white T-shirt, now crimson. Staring at the back of my hand, which had no skin covering two knuckles. I started screaming.

A woman in jeans and barn boots and a paisley blouse came running up the drive I was now staggering down, half-blinded by my own blood. She didn't say anything. Just took my wrist and with her other hand between my shoulder blades guided me toward her house. In her kitchen she used one washcloth after another to clean me up. "Whose boy are you?" she asked. Once she got a part of my face cleared, she pressed the washcloth hard on it. Whenever she took one away I could feel the blood pulse out of me. In sucking back my blood, I could feel my lip all ragged and swollen and split. I glanced down my arm where I felt blood trickling off my fingers. On the silver and gold squares of the yellowing linoleum, a pool was forming from the patterings of my blood. I felt faint. I hadn't answered her question yet. Over the woman's shoulder I saw a girl, about my age, staring at me. She didn't seem shocked, just curious.

"Dorie," the woman said, "either help or get out of the way."

"I'm not in the way."

"You will be soon enough unless you help. Here, rinse these."

"It's got his blood on it."

"Everything's got his blood on it." She hadn't taken her eyes off me. Her face bore a look of calm efficiency, slightly puckered. She was impatient in the same way our mother was when one of us was hurt. In the face of that you did what you were told. The girl took the washcloths to the sink.

"We're going to get you to a hospital," the woman said, the heel of her hand pressing down on a washcloth located near my temple. "Whose boy are you?"

"He's mine," said my mother. She was at the screen door, all out of breath, then the door was banging shut behind her.

"You're those new people took over the Hoveling place, aren't you?" said the woman. "I've been meaning to get down there." She and my mother switched places.

"Have you got ice?" asked my mother. The woman was already getting it. I could hear the refrigerator door open behind me, and the next thing I knew another washcloth, cold, with a lump inside, was pressed against my lip. My tongue felt the nubbins of the washcloth, the torn flesh of my lip. I was trying not to whimper. My mother's face had that same look on it: panged efficiency, wounded concern.

"He's banged up pretty good," said the woman. "You've got your car here?"

"I don't drive," said our mother.

"We'll take him to St. E's, it's closest," said the woman. "You get him outside, I'll turn the car around. Dorie, you can stay or go. Your mother won't be home till dinnertime anyway."

"I'll go," said the girl and went out with the woman.

The woman had an old brown-and-white Rambler idling outside her kitchen when my mother got me on the stoop. The woman held the door open for us, then jumped into the driver's seat and roared off as fast as the gravel in the drive would allow. We fishtailed out the drive, and in the sweep of the back end I could see my bike, its front wheel missing, the frame askew.

"When I saw that bike—" started my mother.

"You thought he was dead."

"I could hear his screams clear on the other side of the house, where I was painting."

"I heard them in the garden. He's got a healthy set of lungs."

"I thought somebody was pulling his toenails out," said the girl. She was blond. The woman driving was no taller than she was. Across the back of the Rambler's bench seat, their heads were even. The woman's hair, though, was the color of straw, with orange and gray woven in. She looked like a banty rooster, small and feisty. She drove with mean efficiency. We were going very fast, I could tell, but she kept up a calm patter with my mother.

"It's nice you're painting that house. The Hovelings didn't put much stock in niceties."

"I have to thank you for driving us like this."

"I was going to let your son bleed all over my kitchen while we waited for an ambulance? It'd take too long."

"I'm Susan Marie Czabek."

"Matty Keillor. This is my granddaughter, Dorie Braun."

"My son Emmie."

Dorie turned around. She had a sharply oval face and green eyes that were both flat and piercing. She was wearing a T-shirt, like me, and her hair was cut bluntly at her shoulders. "Emmie, that's a girl's name. Where'd you get a name like Emmie?"

"Dorie—"

"Have you ever heard of Emil Zatopek?" I knew she hadn't. Nobody had.

"Should I have?" I wanted to think she was doing a pretty good job of talking to a kid with a torn-up face without showing the slightest distaste or squeamishness, but really she was just doing a fantastic job of sounding bored beyond belief.

"Emil Zatopek," I said through swollen lips, "was a Czech runner who won four gold medals, three of them, an unprecedented triple"— I was quoting my father here—"in the 1952 Olympics." That was pretty much exactly what my father had told me when I said that kids at school were teasing me about my name. I wasn't named for Emil Zatopek, and really, nobody cared about a Czech running to glory in his underwear. Still, it was the sort of thing that made possessing such a name easier to bear, and when anybody asked, this was what I told them.

"I know an Emil," said Dorie Braun, who was cute in a tough way and was already wiping away my memory of and pangs for the worldly and forlorn Patty Duckwa. "Emil Brauneiger. But Emil—that's an old name. Like Oscar. Or Irene. Or Matilda."

"Don't go there, Dorie Braun. Or I might tell somebody what your real name is, too."

"What is it?" I asked the ceiling, thickly. My mother had me leaning my head against the seat back, which was covered with an old army blanket. My blood was seeping into that.

"Dorothy," Dorie answered before her grandmother could say it. "Like in *The Wizard of Oz*. As in 'I'll get you, my pretty. And your little dog, too.' "

She did a pretty good job imitating the Wicked Witch of the West's speaking voice. Her regular voice had a roughness to it as well, which I liked.

Her grandmother observed, "Nobody's naming their daughters Dorothy anymore, either."

"My dad says that's because I broke the mold."

"Given a chance, you'd break anything."

The conversation changed then when Matty Keillor asked our mother what it was our father did. The cautious exploration of each other's family history and background was something that connected the two women, and left Dorie and me out of their conversation. All this talk had distracted me from the fact that my face was broken, but now as we neared the hospital I realized how I hurt all over. They got me inside, stitched me up while I writhed and screamed, told my mother I'd need to see a dentist about yanking that shattered front tooth, filled me full of painkillers, and sent us on our way.

Our mother was downright fluttery by the time Matty Keillor pulled into our drive and let us out. She thought she'd made her first real friend. Granted, she had met a number of other women from church, but at least so far they were taking a wait-and-see approach to friendship. It was as though friendship with these women was a kind of exclusive club, with a limit on the number of members, and though they were cordial to our mother, they had all the friends they currently needed, thank you, but do keep in touch, and should one of our members move away (unlikely) or die (only slightly more likely), we'll certainly keep you in mind.

It didn't help that the women gathered in groups—the Women's Guild, the Craft Union, the Women's Auxiliary of this or that—in which our mother didn't feel comfortable. She preferred intimate gatherings—another housewife over for coffee, a shared trip to the fabric store. The one informal place for meeting women was the mothers' room at church, but being bonded by the fact that you had a crying infant or unruly toddler and therefore had been relegated to the back of the church in a separate room with a sliding glass window that was usually closed was not conducive to real friendship. A few pained looks, shared exasperations, yes, but friendship?

Not even Matty, who was friendly and open and the most accepting of the women our mother met, could offer her that, though our mother entertained hopes. Matty had seven kids, too, and a husband (and a daughter) who drank too much, but Matty was also a decade older, had been a grandma for a decade. That may have been why our mother liked her so much. She'd already been where our mother was heading. But Matty had her hands full, and being some unhappy city woman's mentor was not her idea of an occupation. She felt sorry for our mother, that her husband had dumped her in the middle of a cornfield, but it wasn't her fault things had shaken out as they had, and it wasn't her job to make everything all better, either.

Our mother knew this, but she couldn't help getting attached to the woman. Despite what she'd said the night Ernie Ott plowed into our field, our mother wanted to believe she'd found a friend. She found all sorts of reasons to go up the hill to visit. There were eggs and milk to get, and next year's garden to plan, and what fared well in sandy soil—she wanted to tell Wally—and would Matty like to come over for tea, or would it be okay if our mother just sat for a spell, she got winded easily, this was such a pleasant kitchen to sit in, not like her own at all. The Hovelings had put in their own kitchen, and like most things the Hovelings had done, it was a botched job. A peninsula with cabinets over it cut the kitchen in half, the drawers didn't fit, the doors didn't match, the counters were small, you were always turning around for things that should be handier but weren't, and when Wally-Bear got a nice commission they were going to put in a new kitchen—this was our mother's fervent, constant hope—and frankly if I were Matty Keillor and this woman was talking my ear off, I'd keep her at some distance myself even if I did like her.

Like our father, our mother was a person of enthusiasms. Unlike our father's, hers tended to leave her feeling scalded rather than renewed. When an idea or enthusiasm fizzled for our father, he just embraced a new one. Our mother was enveloped by the ashes of her defeat.

So it was with that fall's Halloween party. Held just a few weeks after the bonfire of the rats, it was meant to wipe away the bizarreness of last year's Halloween party and to introduce our parents to everyone who hadn't gotten around to introducing themselves. And our mother was hoping to make new friends, maybe find people who wanted to make trips down to Chicago.

"Hon, are you sure a Halloween party is the way to go for this sort of thing?"

"Of course," said our mother. "Everyone will be in costume—what better way to meet people? We'll talk, discover common interests. And I'm sure there won't be any excesses."

And there weren't. Excesses or interests. As we found out in later years, it wasn't because these people didn't know how to have fun. They just didn't feel like having it with people they didn't know well, people recently moved up from Chicago who could decamp just as quickly as they'd arrived. Although our mother's invitations said "Costumes optional, but encouraged," few people felt encouraged. Tony Dederoff and his wife, Marcie, had come as hayseed farmers off for their first trip to "the big city," and Matty Keillor came as a scarecrow, but her husband, Ben, had come as himself, as had most everyone else. Our mother, dressed as a flapper even though her breasts were too big for the sleeveless sequined shift she wore, and our father, a gangster, complete with pin-striped suit, fedora, red carnation, black shirt, and violin case, were adrift in a sea of street clothes: plaid sport shirts and ironed jeans or slacks for the men, flowered dresses for the women. Our mother, with her feather boa, white feather headdress, and kohl-heavy eyes, looked like some exotic dancer from New York or L.A. delivering a candy-gram in the middle of Wisconsin. Not the right thing for what the neighbors thought of as a courtesy call, a perfunctory Saturday night neighborly get-together. The men talked about the weather, the Kafka Feed and Seed, and stock prices (pigs, heifers, steers, and Holsteins, not stocks, bonds, and Wall Street); the women talked about kids and child-rearing, knitting and gardening. Chicago did not come up except as a punch line in jokes. People came, were quiet and polite—our parents were given a wide berth—and excused themselves early. Our mother sat in the ruins of her get-together. It was not yet nine-thirty; there were cases of beer and soft drinks still in the hall, waiting to be squeezed into the refrigerator, and Jell-O salads and little sausages on toothpicks and cheese cubes and rafters of hard liquor opened and unpoured, and cracked ice melting back into solid blocks in buckets, and unused noisemakers, and all the detritus of a party that never once, not even for a moment, got off the ground. She had thrown everything she had into this party, and it had lasted all of an hour and twenty minutes.

She started cleaning up, then froze. "Kids," she called down the stairs, "there's plenty here to eat. Why don't you come finish this off?" Then she went into her room and locked the door. She did not unlock it when our father knocked and said in a low voice, "Susan? Susan Marie, honey?

Come on and open the door." You could hear something stifled happening in there, maybe whimpering into pillows, but that was all. Our father turned around to face us.

We were lined up in the hall, arranged from biggest to smallest like an exercise in perspective. The crescent rolls and frankfurters we'd been eating were dry in our mouths. Solemn. That was how we felt. Like we were witnesses to something, some small but critical failure on the part of our parents. We didn't even know what kind of failure, or what it meant, or why it mattered. We only knew we had witnessed something, and forever after our parents were going to be slightly diminished in our eyes. We knew that, and our father knew it. He took us in, a slow, sad sweep of his head, full of the grandeur of disappointment. Said our father, "You try being married sometime. I'd like to see you try," and then he was outside and driving.

Her aspirations having collapsed like a cardboard box left out in the rain, our mother considered the alternatives, one of which was paralysis. I say this as though it were a conscious choice, but it wasn't. Our mother had always been sickly as a child—rheumatic fever, double pneumonia—and having seven kids in a little over a decade had certainly debilitated her. Still, her health was reasonably good until our move to Wisconsin. Her body rebelled against this move even though she, consciously, did not. She got sick, developed allergies to dust, fur, pollen, mold, and grass. She discovered she couldn't breathe. Her lungs would seize up on her, she'd try to take a full breath, and all she'd get was a closed-off *uuuuhhHHHhhh* that peaked in the middle before she realized she was making it worse by sucking in so hard.

Ironic that we moved to Wisconsin so the kids could breathe country air and it turned out our mother couldn't. She developed asthma, hay fever, bronchitis, lung infections. Seeing her as an early candidate for emphysema, her physician that winter put her on huge doses of prednisone, among other things, which he neglected to tell her would suck all the calcium out of her bones and make her blow up like a puffer fish. Suddenly she didn't even look like our mother.

The house went to pieces. She had never really unpacked the master bedroom. Our father, gone all the time, had left that chore to her, and the prospect of actually taking everything out of the boxes and truly starting a new life here proved too much for her. The bed and the dresser came away from the wall so we could paint behind them, but they never went back against the wall. The sheets we used as drop cloths stayed where they were, dangling half on, half off the furniture. And the Mayflower boxes stayed where they were, only they were unstacked so our mother could get at their contents. Nothing was put away. Washed and folded clothes were precariously stacked and balanced on the corners of the boxes, and whatever fell in fell in. Not that it mattered, since our mother, dazed on her medication, frequently forgot what box something was stacked on, or came to believe it was still in a box (entirely likely), though she couldn't remember which one, and her mornings were spent rummaging and pillaging boxes, then leaving the mess as it was when she couldn't breathe anymore.

It was the same thing with paper. Our mother couldn't throw anything out. Neither could our father. The result was that our house was soon inundated by years' and years' worth of paper. Paper piled in uneven, tottering stacks, which fell and slid together, forming larger, more uneven stacks, which grew and formed the base, the genesis, for even more stacks, the paper breeding underneath the piles, paper increasing incrementally and exponentially until the paper itself linked staples and paper clips and self-sealing return envelopes and became one single, hulking, impenetrable mound, a mountain range of paper cascading from living room to dining room to kitchen to hallway to bedroom to office and back again. There was no beginning and no end to it; it was a Möbius strip of clutter and waste, and any attempt to meet the enemy, to attack it, to put a dent in the mounds, was greeted by either our mother or our father with a crescendoing denial that it needed to be dealt with by anyone but themselves.

No doubt there was something comforting in all that detritus. When the world is a shaky place, feathering—papering—your nest must seem like a comfort. No doubt that urge explains why I am spending more and more hours now at the bookstores. They're havens from the sadness occurring at my home. Though there's sadness there, too. And frustration. If Dorie and I split up, I don't want to think about what's going to happen to them—it was, after all, Dorie's money that made them possible. Even if we stay together it's possible that one, two, or maybe all three of these stores aren't long for this world. And she might make that call for me, as she so graciously informed me this evening. Could I buy her out? Only if I leveraged myself to the hilt. And even if it doesn't come to that, the stores might not make it. In a down economy, books, for a lot of people, are a frill they can live without. Independent bookstores are right up there with restaurants in rates of failure. So I shuttle from one store to the next, my heart filled to bursting with the fragility of what I've accomplished.

It doesn't help that when I get there I'm confronted by a customer who says she was told by a staff member that her choice of a book—the latest legal thriller—was poor and she should read instead this "serious" story collection by a promising but unknown writer. "Who told you that?" I ask, and it is, of course, my best employee in terms of energy and exuberance, Jillian Kowalska, on whom, I am sure, I am developing a crush. After I deal with the customer—no, no, we really want her to have the thriller—I speak with Jillian. "It was my Pick of the Month," Jillian defends herself. "It's right there." She points to the wall of "Our Staff Recommends" books. "I tell them what to buy, and they always ignore me." "Well, that's their prerogative." "Yes, but their prerogatives are stupid," Jillian says, leaving me to wonder how I'm going to keep this afloat when my employees are haranguing the customers. I briefly wonder, too, under what circumstances a harmless crush might turn into something else, but I abandon the thought on account of its general stupidity and impossibility. What I really would like right now is simply to build a wall of books around me and not have to deal with another living soul for a very long time.

Still, what was at our parents' house was junk. And there was no end to it, no matter how much we tried to help get rid of it. We'd fill a few shopping bags, maybe a Hefty garbage bag or two, stack newspapers and tie them with twine, and then the litany of protest would begin. "Not that. I was just looking at that. Let me handle that."

We felt ashamed, living with all that junk. It was a failure of character. And of course we blamed our mother. She seemed to be competing with our father for "most debilitated while serving a parental role," but we granted our father indulgences we never granted our mother. Our father was the mystery in the center of our lives. The absent center, but still the center. And our mother? Our mother was . . . ordinary. Commonplace. How dare she collapse like this! How dare she not be able to breathe! She would pick at the papers for a little while and then give up, the dust was affecting her, the mold spores, everything. I don't think we ever quite forgave her for falling apart on us like that.

It would be safe to say that our mother gave up, except that she didn't. She was rebelling.

We did not know this at the time, but like any crafty, small, benighted country threatened by powerful neighbors—and our father, a larger-than-life blustery and blustering man, tormented by his own smallness, was in his infrequent visits to the kingdom of his family more like an invading neighbor than a principal ruler—our mother was resisting through surrender.

She never breathed a word of protest, at least not in front of us, except sometimes to say, "Your father seems to think money grows on trees" or "Your father sometimes gets possessed by strange and costly ideas." She might cry, she might weep for her lost and always-promised-but-still-far-off kitchen (the once and future kitchen, we liked to say), she might rail at him in private, and we might overhear the heat and passion of her anger, but in front of us she kept up a brave front. When he realized, from time to time, just what a shit he was, he'd say to us, "You know, your mother is a trouper," and then he'd feel better, having sainted her. He would not change his own behavior, of course. Saints, after all, have fewer material needs than sinners.

Was it any wonder our mother collapsed, took to her bed, came down with a thousand and one ailments? She was being buried alive, she was drowning in a sea of paper, and after a while her resistance was to give up breathing itself. Asthma, bronchitis, bronchial asthma, pneumonia—if TB were still possible to catch, she'd have come down with that.

That Christmas we all piled into the company car, our bloated mother up front looking froglike, the rest of us stacked in the familiar feet-to-hips arrangement. The seats were down. It was a Friday night, and we were going to spend Christmas visiting the relatives in Beverly, and bouncing from one household to another. During the long drive to Chicago I pretended, for the sake of the little kids, that the red lights on the high-tension electrical wire towers were the winking lights of Rudolph, the red-nosed reindeer. Our mother usually took on this role, and we were simply required to play along, but on this drive she was strangely silent. Cinderella was moody, too, and Robert Aaron had gotten a smart mouth and for now couldn't be trusted with the family myths. So it was up to me to explain to the littler kids how if they saw lots of lights in procession—a field of high-wattage lines—then what we were looking at was the whole crew: Dancer, Prancer, Vixen, Blitzen, et cetera. They had received the red noses as badges of their courage. For it took a lot of courage to navigate these night skies with all those planes about. "What else could it be?" I asked Wally Jr. and Ernie and Peg Leg Meg.

"Yeah," said Ike, "what else could it be?"

"It could be they're warning lights on the tops of high-tension towers," said Robert Aaron.

"Shut up," I told him. "It's reindeers' noses. What else could it be?" I repeated, and Ernie and Wally Jr. silently nodded agreement. Peg Leg Meg was already asleep.

"How do I look?" my mother asked my father as we coasted to the curb in front of Grandma Hubie's.

"You look wonderful," said my father, and I watched the look that passed between them, a look I could not decipher except to understand that part of it was founded in love, and that part of being in love was agreeing to take part in a deception.

"You did a good thing," our mother told me once we were on the sidewalk. I did not believe her. We were standing outside a house where we would be greeted by our relatives and told how much we had grown, how good we were, and what a fine, happy family we were, and where people would take one look at our mother, her face so puffy it looked like she was trapped inside some horrible genetic experiment gone awry, and tell her, "Country life agrees with you, Susan Marie," and I did not believe any of that, either.

Just as our parents had done, just as our relatives were about to do, I had told my younger siblings a convenient lie because it was easier than dealing with the unhappiness of the truth. I had even managed, for a little while, to convince myself. Though I knew I was lying, I had looked up in the cold night sky, my face craned to take in the distant bright stars and the flight patterns of passing planes, my breath fogging the window, and for the briefest of moments, I had believed. There was a Santa Claus. He was out there, making his appointed rounds, and the behavior of little boys and girls all over the globe was duly noted and gifts were given accordingly.

But Robert Aaron was right. The truth was plainer than that. This did not stop me from believing, but it made me angry at myself for so willfully participating in the lie. And what I saw clearly was that it was best if

I continued doing it. Pretending was expected of me. It would reflect well on my merit review. And what made me so angry right then, I think, looking up into the kindly, sad, bloated face of my mother, whom I loved, was the sudden knowledge that adults did this all of their lives, and that I truly had signed on for the duration.

14. No Guts, No Glory

FLYING PUMPKINS AND THE LATE
GREAT DREAMS OF OUR FATHER

"Great," Ernie says. "Now what?"

"Don't you feel like a perfect shit or what?" It's been several minutes since our mother shuffled back into the house. We're still on the deck. The temperature's dropping. We can see our breath. Clouds are moving briskly across the stars and half a moon, and down the field we can see a straggly line of kids, and kids carrying kids, making its way back to the house. "Just as well," Robert Aaron says, going down the field to help Audrey. "I was starting to freeze my tush up there."

I call after him, "But we haven't talked about a goddamn thing yet!" Dorie is holding hands with Henry, our middle child, and walking alongside Woolie, who's carrying Sophie on his back. Woolie is seventeen, about to start his senior year in high school. He is, I'm guessing, starting to resemble his father. Curly dark hair, a serious, handsome face, eyes that light up when he infrequently smiles, though he smiles more now that his braces are off and the fits and starts of adolescence are nearly over. It probably doesn't hurt that he's got his first girlfriend, either, a lithe young woman who swims and plays midfield on the soccer team. I remember when she was awkward and gangly, a manager for the boys' swim team, and it heartens me a little that she takes an interest in Woolie, who is just now emerging from his own awkward, gangly phase.

It also makes me feel jealous.

"Tepee'll be free soon. Nice and warm in there." Ike's got his arms around his wife, Sam. He's standing behind her, and they're slowly swaying back and forth. He's so content right now, so filled with equanimity I want to hit him.

"Good," I say. I want things to be decided, over. I want—as our father always wanted—for there to be a plan. A master plan just waiting to be executed. Funny choice of words—to execute a plan. When you execute people, they're dead. Given what happened with most of our father's plans, perhaps the wording was appropriate.

We agree we'll meet in the tepee—just the sibs—once the kids are put down. There are good nights to those not staying, then Dorie takes our kids inside, Sam takes hers and Ike's back to their house, Audrey takes hers and Robert Aaron's to her parents', just a few miles away, et cetera.

I'm the last to leave the house. Woolie has settled in on the living room sofa with his Discman and a Rusted Root CD; his head bounces as he clicks on the TV and picks up a large-print *Reader's Digest.* How does he manage to concentrate? I wonder, but maybe that's the point—awash in stimuli, you coast over the surface of it. Is this what concentration will be like for the new millennium—the ability to juggle multiple sources of information simultaneously, paying just enough heed to each to say you "got it"?

"Turn that thing off," I say, and I sound just like our father when he used to complain about whatever I had playing on the stereo. I want to laugh, it's too ridiculous—what does it matter to me if he's watching *Sports Center,* glossing over another installment of "My Most Unforgettable Character," and listening to the tribal drumming of a neo–Grateful Dead band all at the same time? And yet I'm furious.

He lifts up one end of his earphones. "Eh?"

"Off, turn it off!" I'm nearly shouting.

"Turn what off?" he asks innocently.

"One of them. It doesn't matter which."

"Why does it matter at all?" He's right, and I'm angry because he's right.

"Honey, could you give me a hand with Henry and Sophie?"

Henry is already asleep—Henry could fall asleep on a roller coaster if he wanted to—and Sophie is already tucked in, her Winnie-the-Pooh and Eeyore dolls nestled under her chin.

"What is wrong with you?" Dorie hisses at me. "You sounded like an idiot out there."

"Is Daddy in trouble?" Sophie, turning the pages of a Berenstain Bears

"I Can Read Book," looks as serious as her mother does when she is disassembling her derailleurs and chain.

"He will be if he doesn't start acting like a human being."

"Good night, honey." I kiss Sophie on the cheek.

"Read me a story, Daddy?"

"Mommy will. Daddy has to talk to his brothers and sisters."

"It would go better if you talked *with* them, not *at* them. That would be true with other people around the house as well."

"Present company excepted?"

Dorie holds her thumb and index finger half an inch apart. "You are about this close, Ace, to becoming a male soprano."

"Read Sophie her story, why don't you?"

"Yes, Mommy, read me a story."

Dorie sits on the trundle bed. "Ah, the Berenstain Bears," she says. "A good one. The daddy is an idiot in these stories, too."

I do not get away cleanly. Woolie barely notices me—I half-wave going past, and he lifts his head in acknowledgment—but in the kitchen our mother is minding a kettle that's just starting to whistle. I get a beer from the refrigerator, and she puts a hand on my shoulder.

"Is something the matter with you and Dorie?"

"No, Mom, nothing's the matter." I open the beer, take a swig.

Our mother turns me around. The look on her face is kindly, concerned. "You were always an atrocious liar, Emmie. You and Ike, you had no facility for deception, ever."

"I'd rather not talk about it, Mom."

"Honey, I'm not the one you have to talk about it with."

Even as our mother was sinking into her personal quagmire of ill health and depression, our father embarked on an ambitious series of schemes to get rich, make his mark, and become what he'd always dreamed of being: a gentleman farmer, a man who tilts his chair back on the veranda and, cigar in hand, watches as the industry of his land brings forth new fruit. Our mother, desperate to break out of her funk, signed on to almost all his harebrained ideas. Their beauty was in not looking harebrained until they had foundered, sunk, crashed, or burned.

They were also predicated on the assumption that his dreams required only his foresight and our labor to succeed. His brains, our backs—a simple equation. Gone Sunday night to Friday night, driving seventy thousand miles a year, he had plenty of time to wear his thinking cap, particularly if he watered it regularly, which was more or less a point of honor with him.

He never mentioned these harebrained schemes when he first thought of them, or rather, when he first came home. We'd have recognized them for what they were if he had, if they'd been delivered to us still wet from stewing in his brain's pickled juices. Perhaps he knew that. Perhaps that was part of his genius, that even stewed, his dreams knew when to lie low, and when the time was propitious to spring forward, newly hatched, clean and shiny and new.

Saturday mornings our father cooked and kidded his way through breakfast, and while we chowed down, he told us about his dreams. Only he never called them dreams. They were his "ideas," and while he kidded us about how much or little we were eating—bacon by the panful, eggs cooked in the bacon grease—his conversation was threaded through with how he saw his idea working itself out to the benefit of us all.

"We're a family," he never tired of telling us. "And this is a family operation. We rise or fall together. What are we?" he'd ask, his voice rising in inflection at question's end.

"We're Czabeks!" we'd chorus, some more lustfully than others, our enthusiasm usually in direct opposition to our years. You can call out your identity with gusto only so many hundred times, particularly if your surname sounds like some sort of Central European cookie.

"Never forget that," said our father, as though we could.

After breakfast our father would gather his ratty blue terry-cloth robe about him, sit at the kitchen table with a cup of coffee the size of Rhode Island, and go into detail about how this latest idea of his was going to make us money.

"Venture capitalism," said our father, "is always about adventure." This might have sounded better had our father not been dressed like a cowboy Buddha with three bellies and a walrus mustache (he'd grown one soon after we'd moved north), sitting with his robe open to his boxers, his feet shod in the rubber-soled cowboy boots he wore as protection against the cold cement floor of his downstairs office, to which he would retire in a little while to sketch out his grand ideas in more detail. Then he would call us downstairs and make the closing pitch: here was where we stood financially; here was where we were gonna be.

A veteran salesman, our father knew how to close. It was all about *pre-*

sentation, and toward this end he had visual aids, hooks: aerial photographs, charts, price lists, sketches on graph paper done with a mechanical drafting pencil, the lettering precise and sure.

He showed us where the outbuildings were, including the lumber piles we'd already burned and the barns that had already collapsed. We saw the woods and the creek and the ravine and the marsh, where he thought we could dig a pond—a swimming hole, stocked with fish, where deer would drink and geese would land and we could shoot at both. He pointed out where we'd already strung fence and where we still needed to. He sketched the outbuildings we were going to build. We were going to have horses, chickens, sheep, cattle. Tony Dederoff had already informed him that we had only half the acreage we'd need to make a go of it as dairy farmers, and besides, dairy required you to be around all the time. You never got a vacation.

"My advice," said Tony, who did dairy himself in addition to his other two jobs, "is to go into veal. They're cute little things, and then you kill them all, but they're only with you three, four months. Then you get a couple weeks' break before the next batch are ready."

Our father was particularly taken with the idea of a cash crop. Uncle Louie's chinchillas had given our father the idea that breeding itself got you things. He had gotten a labor force by breeding with our mother, after all, and the math was simple and progressive: $1 + 1 = 9$. If you could do that with humans, imagine what you could do with sheep, cattle, chickens, or seed, none of which wore out like our mother.

Our father's first notion in this regard was pickles. Cucumbers, actually, though nobody called them that. Cukes, maybe, but most everyone in the business called them by what they'd end up as: pickles. Our father discovered this rather arcane way of getting rich when he picked up some chives and leaf lettuce at the Randolph, a tiny family-run grocery in Augsbury given its rather formal name as a joke by its owner, Randolph Muncie. Randolph ran the grocery, but that wasn't where the money was in their business. His wife, Naomi, ran a greenhouse attached to the end of the frame house, and they had a shed and another greenhouse behind that. Randolph also did a booming bait business, registered deer during hunting season, and dickered with local farmers for their produce, which was why his was a lot fresher than Buss' Foods, the big grocery just down the street. And he had a pickle-sorting machine, which meant that anyone who wanted a pickle contract went through him.

That's not quite accurate. Actually, Randolph, charming and disarming—he had an "aw, shucks" manner and a limp from breaking his leg on a cargo net at Normandy—sweet-talked people into taking on pickle contracts. I prefer *sweet-talked* to the more vulgar *suckered*. This was in March. Our father was restless for something to do. Randolph explained to him how it worked—you contracted with a pickle company through him. If you were just starting out, five acres was about right. You plowed and dragged the field, planted the cucumber seeds in long rows, hoed around them to keep the weeds down. The vines grew quickly, yellow flowers bloomed. The cukes grew behind that. Those little dots you see on the ends of cucumbers? That was where the flowers were. Now, here is where the work comes in. Pickle companies pay the most per hundredweight for the tiniest pickles—those little baby gherkins you see stuffed into jars. But cukes grow really, really fast. If you want baby gherkins, you gotta be out there every day, picking that whole field. You leave a cuke on the vine, and in two days it's the size of a baking potato. The cukes you buy in the store for salad? Worth almost nothing. You can pick bushels and bushels and make three dollars. The point, Randolph was saying, is that anybody can leave a cuke on the vine. Every day, pick the littlest ones you can see. Pick 'em twice a day.

"Thirty-one fifty a bushel for the little suckers," said our father. "It's easy money."

Why did we believe him? Well, for one thing, he was our father. For another, he still wore a scapular with its brown string and itchy plastic sheathing and a St. Christopher medal. He was marked by the signs of belief, as were we. And as were we, he was touched by greed. We could believe in the future, and what it would bring us. All we needed to do was block out all evidence to the contrary. Things like a man in boxer shorts, cowboy boots, and a ratty robe telling us about easy money. "We'll plant them close together at first. We can always thin them later," said our father. "Put straw between the rows once they're up. That'll keep down the weeds."

We believed him about the pond in the marsh, too. And about the pumpkins, the sheep, the mushrooms, and the chickens. We believed him about the horses, about the beef cattle, and we believed him about the black walnut plantation. We did not believe him or his friend, Ben Keillor, about the crops grown into the shapes of liquor bottles that would appear as aerial photographs in magazine advertisements, but that was only because we were adults by then, and painful experience had taught us to be leery of just about anything our father cooked up.

As with any of our father's dreams, we had no idea what we were getting into. Nor did we have the first inkling of how to go about doing it. The actual time, money, and labor we'd invest in each of our father's get-rich-quick schemes? We hadn't a clue. Everything for us was a maiden voyage, and the ship of our dreams was invariably named *Lusitania*.

How, exactly, did we fuck up? Let us count the ways, starting with the cucumbers. First off, unbrined cukes are surprisingly easy to grow. Plant and wait. A little rain, a little heat, and poof! delicate, twin-bladed shoots appear, the world's tiniest propellers. They grow slowly at first, then faster. The shoots become vines, the propeller-like leaves become thick, irregularly edged, their undersides and the vines, too, scratchy and rough with cilia. Then the buttery yellow blossoms appear, and behind them, the little buds of the cukes. You are now in business.

One of the things we knew nothing about: weeds. Weeds grow faster than whatever crop you plant. They choke out plants, steal nutrients from the soil. They must be stopped. So even as we enjoyed watching our little plants grow, we had to hoe and pluck weeds. Every day. Five acres. By hand. In a field that had grown nothing but weeds for the past, oh, twenty years or so. Hardy brutes, weeds. You can pull them, pluck them, yank them, chop them, whack them, hack them, deliciously decapitate them and spread their stalks and their veiny little leaves out under a hot, hot sun to sear them a pale white green, but unless you get the roots, they are back at their posts the very next day, tender shoots of evil. Our hands were blistered, our fingers cramped and green from pinching and pulling, and every day there would be more.

Which would not have been so bad if the crop itself were more cooperative. Oh, it was plenty cooperative in growing, and growing quickly, but Randolph Muncie down at the Randolph did not tell us what a god-awful thing it is to pick cucumbers. He did not tell us that cuke vines grow close to the ground, that the little cukes seem to grow closest to the main stem, and that you'd scratch your arms reaching for them. Nor did he tell us that daddy longlegs and wolf spiders like to hide among the vines, or that slugs gather on the wet soil after a rain, and while you were picking you were likely to discover all of them. He did not tell us that those bumps you see on pickles, the smooth bumps on the cukes you buy in the produce department, are what are left from the translucent green thorns that exist on baby cukes when you pick them. They are not on the cukes later because they break off in the pickers' fingers, and it is not too long before your fingers are bleeding, sore and stiff, caked with dirt and cucumber juice and blood, and your fingers pads wear brown- and red- and brine-colored helmets. And every day you do this for three hours in the morning and three hours in the afternoon because cukes grow that fast, and if you want to make any money you pick twice a day.

He did not tell us any of the obvious things, either, such as it rains quite a bit in the summer, particularly when you don't want it to, and mud is not a nice thing to be kneeling in for six hours a day, and that we would come to loathe the pickles and our five acres, and that after a while we would actually pray for rain to inundate the field, to make it so god-awful gloppy that our mother would give us a reprieve, and that when we returned to the field what we wanted was for the cukes to have exploded with heat and moisture into bulbous yellow gourdlike tubers, unfit for human consumption and therefore not worth picking, and for their rapid growth to have exhausted the vines' ability to put out any more flowers.

But those feelings would come later. At first there was the happiness of seeing the seeds sprout. Our fingers in the warm soil, the early joy of seeing the propellers turn into leaves, the stems into vines, then the thick canopy of leaves close to the ground. We never grew tired, at least, of watching this miracle. The growth, day by day, which seemed to occur only when you weren't looking right at it, as though there were elves in the field, cucumber fairies, who touched the vines with magic wands to make the buds appear, and touched them again to make the little cukes grow behind them, cukes no bigger than a fingernail at first, then no bigger than your little finger, so vulnerable until you tried to pick them.

Then pick them we did, day after day, until we were praying for rain and an early frost to put us out of our misery. When our father had local calls, he would take us in the evening with our haul to the Randolph, and we would dump our bushel baskets on Randolph Muncie's sorting machine, and the cukes dropped, some right away, too many farther down the way to our liking, and Randolph and his son weighed our gleanings, and Randolph consulted his chart, did a little math, hitched up his pants, sniffed, rubbed a finger under his nose, and announced our pathetic total in a drawl that seemed stuck up his nose. It would accumulate, of course, so by week's end it might actually amount to something like a hundred and thirty dollars. Good weeks he might cut us a check for one hundred and fifty-six or one hundred and eighty-five dollars. One hot week it was for two hundred and sixty-two, another week it was for three hundred and twelve. We whooped, we celebrated. "Now you're cooking with grease," said Randolph Muncie. Our father was elated. "See what you can do?" he kept saying over and over. "See what you can do? This'll put hair between your toes, goddammit." Then we went to the Dog 'N Suds and gulped down enough root beer to make us forget the pain in our fingers and knees.

When our father wasn't around, Tony Dederoff took us, or if he was too busy we dialed up Mikey Spillsbeth. Mikey Spillsbeth was sweet on Cinderella. Tall, gawky, and skinny, with black glasses and hair like an Airedale's, he would do anything for anyone who gave him the time of day. And Cinderella, gangly herself, still ironing her hair straight and putting on too much eye shadow and mascara, was eager to try her new-found wiles on anybody who might prove susceptible. In a year she would be sixteen and have her license, so it was really for only this summer and fall that she would need Mikey Spillsbeth. She played him accordingly.

It was amazing to me what a little misapplied mascara, a touch of rose pink lipstick, and a finger twirling stick-straight hair can do. She actually had a crush on a guy named Guy, the tight end for the football team, but given that Guy didn't know she was alive, any attention was welcome. Even from Mikey Spillsbeth, who most people agreed was a little weird. He had a high-pitched laugh, and when he chuckled it sounded like a girl's giggle. His normal speaking voice wasn't so hot, either. It seemed to buzz in his mouth, as though he were speaking through a microphone with too much reverb. Add to that a very long and skinny neck and you had the whisperings of . . . Well, let's just say it was good for Mikey to be seen driving Cinderella around, even if she was just using him for his car.

It didn't matter to us who was driving as long as those cukes were going to market. On good days with our father we might need two trips, and with Mikey's old Rambler we might need four or five. It was greed that drove us, greed and our inability to tell our father we hated the work and didn't think the money was worth it. Not that this would have mattered one iota to our father. Even when we did manage to tell him, along about August, he didn't want to hear it.

"No guts, no glory," he told us. And "In for a dime, in for a dollar."

Finally he told us, "Look, you're just getting started. It's normal once the bloom is off the rose to have second thoughts. Just stick with it. Perseverance is all about persevering. If it's still terrible next year, we'll try something else."

Perseverance is all about persevering. That was the lesson our father wanted to teach us. That there were easier ways of earning a pittance did not seem to matter to him. He'd already chosen this way. This was what made our father a good company man. He was willing to lower his head and plow along, and while he might grumble, he would finish what he started. Our father, had he been in the Charge of the Light Brigade, would have insisted on carrying the flag.

We caught a break the next spring, when it rained uncontrollably for weeks on end and washed the seeds we'd planted into the far corner of the field. When they finally erupted, it looked like Linus Van Pelt's Great Pumpkin Patch. The concentration made it impossible to harvest, and the vines that did grow choked each other out. By the end of the summer we were hauling in all of seventy-one dollars a week, and our biggest week had been one hundred and thirty-six. Divide by the four of us picking, with two others toddling around and stepping on plants, and you weren't getting much for all the muddy pain and effort. Our father said, All right, enough, he would come up with something else over the winter.

In addition to the family garden, we were each given a vegetable to raise on our own. The theory being that we would take a special pride in seeing what became of what we had planted. The littler kids got the non-food vegetables—gourds, pumpkins, Indian corn. Ernie took to the Big Max—a pumpkin that, when mature, regularly weighed over a hundred pounds—in a big way. He wore OshKosh B'Gosh overalls and an engineer's cap whenever he was working on "his garden." And who could blame him? To encourage entrepreneurship, our father announced that whatever wasn't consumed by us could be sold for profit, and the child responsible could keep his or her money. There was a logic to this, but it was the logic of a suburban man who doesn't understand yet where he's living. Our neighbors did not want our vegetables. They had their own. Though their plots were far more modest than ours, they had all the vegetables they needed, and once they found a family like ours, they would lie in wait after church and heap their unwanted zucchinis, peppers, tomatoes, and cucumbers on us as though we were one of those unfortunate families whose home has been borne away by a flood or tornado. We got big honking cukes thrust on us even though our fellow parishioners knew we were growing them for Randolph Muncie. "Well, we just thought," they'd say and hand us another sack full of something we already had too much of ourselves. And because our parents were pioneers, the first little lapping wave of what, in twenty years, would become an exurban flood, there weren't many people yet like our father, nostalgic for roadside stands staffed by semicherubic farm offspring, a neat little row of blond children in white T-shirts with manure on their pant legs. Oh, you'd get asparagus thieves, people who'd drive out from Appleton and feel quaintly rural hunting the ditches with a paring knife, but on a week-to-week basis we probably would have done better selling our blood.

"This is no way to make a living," said our mother. "It's not supposed to be a living for anybody but us," said our father. "Whatever extra comes in is gravy. Pure gravy."

It is hard to think of it as gravy when you are putting your finger through the mush of a rotten starter spud, or when you see that the row of weeds you had so energetically hoed the day before were actually pepper plants, and that where you had weeded correctly had reseeded itself in weeds so quickly you'd swear the weeds had mastered time-lapse regeneration.

It was not a good time to be one of the older kids. Robert Aaron's corn got blight, which grew like tumors on the stalks and ears, Cinderella's cantaloupes and watermelons put out nice vines but miniature fruit, and my potatoes did too well. I had to keep asking everyone to help me stay ahead of the weeds, and I had to keep mounding the potato hills so the potatoes wouldn't see the sun and turn green, and my requests, except when our mother ordered everyone to help, were frequently met with jeers of "You volunteered, sucker!"

It was a wet summer, though, so by July the more waterlogged vegetables never flowered. But the zucchini went wild. We took a special joy in pelting each other with overripe zucchinis and cucumbers. They burst open on your back, a mushy spray of seed and goop. When we got tired of that, we threw them against fence and telephone posts, enjoying the splatter. We shot skeets with them, too, and stabbed them with pitchforks or halved them with shovels, or heaved them into the field and listened for the *plunk, thunk, splat* of their landing.

It didn't matter, though. There were always more vegetables. In just a few short months we had gone from shivering with delight at being able to grow our own food to being hardened vegetable murderers, eager to find a Final Solution to the Vegetable Problem.

The littler kids did not share our bend of mind. Not raising anything you'd want to eat, or needed to pick, they could watch their stuff grow all summer long. Pumpkins, ornamental squash, Indian corn—you left that stuff alone. The only work they had was with Ernie's pumpkins, which at a certain point needed to be thinned, and as the summer wore on, turned occasionally so they got orange all over. Ernie, Wally Jr., and Peg Leg Meg were just waiting for the fall. With little kid certainty, they knew they were going to make a killing. And they did, at least compared to the rest of us. The three of them wound up covered in gravy.

Ike ended up doing fine, too, with his Indian corn, but he didn't seem that interested in the money. He was fascinated with the idea that this multicolored corn, these red and orange ears, these starburst purple and white kernels, connected him back to an ancient culture that used to roam our land, fishing it and harvesting it and hunting it, long before white settlers came this way, long before, even, Columbus "discovered" this country. When we field-picked rocks, Ike walked with an eye toward finding arrowheads and spear points, and what he found fueled a lifelong love affair with Indians. When Tony Dederoff told us (after Ike had shown him the arrowheads) that there were burial mounds in our woods, we believed him. We felt special, to be living on holy ground. The whole farm was holy. And when we went running in the woods, or worked our way through the trees playing army, we could feel the spirits of the Indian warriors who had trod this ground before us. Ike felt it more than we did, though, and he kept feeling it long after we found out the burial mounds were actually dredge mounds from when they'd cleared the creek bed thirty years previous.

In the fall our father took some of Ernie's pumpkins to county fair weigh-ins, and the size of these pumpkins—one weighed in at one hundred and eighty pounds and took two men to lift—plus the photos our father took of Ernie sitting inside one of his hollowed-out pumpkins, drummed up a lot of business for the little kids. Ike seemed not that interested in selling his corn, but Wally Jr., Peg Leg Meg, and Ernie basked in the glow of their successes.

So did our father. For the next spring he planned a scaled down vegetable garden and a huge field of pumpkins, half in Big Max, half regular. Lots of ornamental gourds and Indian corn, too. The cucumbers again, of course. "We had one bad year with them," said our father. "It can happen to anybody." As a concession to our mother, he didn't protest when she announced she was putting in flower beds, both around the house and in parts of the vegetable garden. "The kohlrabi and Brussels sprouts," she announced, "are not long for this world."

"I grant you permission to deviate from the master plan," said our father. He was grinning but only half-joking.

"Fuck you, I don't need your permission," said our mother. It was the first time we'd ever heard her say "Fuck." She was joking, but there was an edge there, too. Our father dutifully sketched in the flower beds on his graph paper. Little rectangles at the ends of the huge squares that were his—and Ernie's—pumpkin patches.

The weather, of course, was under no obligation to cooperate. The next year started wet, and things got bedraggled and moldy. A drought followed. We ran hoses, lugged water, gave each plant its own drink, and saved those plants that hadn't gotten too yellow or white green. We felt pretty good about being the garden's Red Cross. Then came the tornado warnings.

"It doesn't rain but it pours," said our father as we stood outside our house, looking to the southwest. The sky had gone from deep gray to deep slate to a yellowy purple green—the color of an old bruise. The wind had been blowing very hard, and then it had gotten quite still. Although it was a mid-July day, it suddenly felt chilly.

Our mother came out of the house hugging her arms. "Wally, I'm freezing."

Our father said, "That's because the temperature's dropped twenty degrees in the last ten minutes."

"Can it do that?"

Said our father, "It can do anything it wants. Feel that stillness?" He wet his finger and held it up, checking for a breeze. "And you can practically taste the electricity in the air." I stuck my tongue out, expecting to feel the tang of metal. "We better get downstairs."

The southwest corner of our house was Robert Aaron's room. His windows faced the road. We packed in there, on the bed and floor. Because one of my chores was changing sheets every week, I knew about the *Playboys* under his mattress. If things got really bad, I wondered, would it be a sin if you spent your final moments contemplating the parabolic breasts and the discreet pillow placement on a sable-haired, sapphire-eyed beauty from Greece?

Our father brought in the fifty-four-band overseas radio, the one that could receive Argentina, and, more important, Cubs games from Chicago. Our mother opened the windows an inch. She and our father went through the house, opening windows. The sky was a boiling darkness. When the wind started shrieking, our mother said, "Let us pray, children," and we did, our heads down, our eyes closed. I pictured the sloe-eyed woman from Greece, whose pendulous breasts might be all I would remember of this life as we were carried into the next. I pictured Patty Duckwa, whom I recalled now only when I touched myself, and I pictured Dorie Braun—who favored cutoff jeans and T-shirts—wearing only the former. Dorie was just beginning to get breasts, pointy things under her T-shirts, and I'd noticed that some days she wore a bra—the straps were visible under her T-shirts—and some days she didn't. While we waited for our house to be lifted up around us, and were praying to Jesus for our safety, I was getting a boner.

The house did not lift up around us. No twirling house in the sky, no witches going past on bicycles, not even Tillie Bunkas with her goiter. The winds became fierce, and rain lashed at the house, and then we heard the hollow stinging of hail, little *tip-tippings* on the window that sounded like someone quietly rapping, over and over. "Close the windows, close the windows!" yelled our mother, and she and our father left to shut what they'd just opened. We dared to look out. The hail was pea-size and bounced when it hit the ground. It almost looked like it landed and then jumped up again, for joy. Then there was a shift. It was not rain with some hail mixed in; it was hail with a little rain mixed in. And the hail was marble-size, and larger. It sounded like both a drummer and a jackhammer had gone to work on the south and west sides of the house. Furious poundings, hard brutal thockings, thousands of them, as hail met wood. Upstairs a window crashed and our mother shrieked. The sky had gotten so dark our crime light went on. Then the lightning struck, immediate and furious, a flash so bright it lit up everything before it knocked out the power. We shrieked, too, then were plunged into darkness.

Rain followed. Great buffeting gusts of it, and once the crime light came back on and we could count "one one thousand, two one thousand" between the lightning and the crash of thunder, we could make out in the gray half-light the shapes of trees bent double by the wind.

"Are they going to live?" asked Ernie, his eyes wide with wonder and fright.

"What?" I asked, wondering if he meant the trees, the crops, the animals, what?

Answered Ernie, "Everything."

There is something about coming outside after a storm into gorgeous sunshine, the wall of slate receding behind you, the sun brilliant, the air crystalline and clear, the trees, the eaves still dripping, that makes you feel as though you have survived something. And you are glad. You count fingers and toes and walk around in a daze. We felt that way as we surveyed the damage with our father. Our mother, our father said, was "still putting herself together," whatever that meant. We checked the house first. The siding on the west side, where our mother had spent so many hours getting the wood to drink up paint, was ruined. The wood looked like it had been sandblasted and beaten on with ball-peen hammers. We touched the indentations with our fingers. Our father whistled. Three windows had been cracked in the hail assault, one had shattered. While our father checked the roof for damage, we threw hail at each other and examined the trees. Branches were stripped of their leaves, and on the smaller trees the bark had been shredded. "Will they live?" Ernie kept asking. "Will they live?"

"I don't know, honey, I don't know," said our mother. She'd come up behind us, and we were surprised to see the fingers of her left hand wrapped in gauze. There was a cut on her cheek as well, a fine line beaded with blood. "I was trying to close the window when it shattered," she said. "It's okay. They bled a lot, but they weren't very deep."

"Was that why you screamed?" asked Peg Leg Meg.

"We all screamed," said Cinderella.

"I didn't," said Robert Aaron.

"Well, hooray for you," said Cinderella.

Ike and Wally Jr. maintained they hadn't screamed either.

"It doesn't matter who screamed," said our mother. "Has anyone checked the garden?"

We hadn't. We'd been having too good a time playing with the hail. Cool lucent stones. You could see the layers that formed them once you split them open. We'd also been quietly celebrating the destruction of the pickle field. It was an almost total loss, leaves shredded, vines trampled. The hailstones still there, gleaming, almost phosphorescent. Oh, happy day.

It wasn't until we heard our mother's sharply inhaled "Oh! Oh, my!" that it dawned on us the damage would not be limited to what we wanted destroyed.

The garden was shredded, too. Poking up from the mud were fingers of stems, in some cases not even that. The petals of our mother's flowers lay strewn about, driven into the mud by the rain's fury. We did not even know their names, except for the common ones like the snapdragons and petunias. Our mother wept. Our father put his arm around her.

"It'll come back," said our father confidently, breezily. "A lot of this will come back. It looks bad now, sure, but give it time. You wait, a lot of this is going to come back."

Our mother had one hand clapped over her mouth and another over her belly. "Oh, Wally" was all she could say to him.

"It'll come back," repeated our father, and you could tell he believed it. But his voice's quaver told us he wasn't sure *she* believed it. And he needed her to. Like it wasn't just the flower beds he was talking about but something in their marriage, their own enterprise of being here together. It's like in a relationship, when one party says, "I love you," and the other replies, "I know," rather than "I love you, too." A sign that something is seriously wrong. When our father says, "It'll come back," our mother is not supposed to answer, "Oh, Wally."

We waited to see how this was going to turn out. Our mother quivering, our father quavering. The seven of us lined up like cheerleaders: Quiver, quaver! Quiver, quaver! Kiss him, Mom, do us all a favor!

She did, the union was saved, and as soon as they fell into each other's arms we went back to throwing hail at each other like it was confetti, like it was rice.

———

It was not the rain that did in our pumpkins, no. And it wasn't the hail, chopping like a butcher's knife. A surprising amount of stuff cut to ribbons in that storm came back, at least partially. Three or four plants in a row here, half a row there. Because of the hail we didn't have the two or three gargantuan pumpkins that would make people's eyes pop with disbelief, but we had several one hundred and fifty pounders, and really, when you're dealing with one-hundred-and-fifty-pound pumpkins, how many do you need?

We got an early frost that year, and a pumpkin field after an early frost looks both trampled and beautiful. The vines have all gone limp, the pumpkins' umbilical cords wither and dry, the leaves surrender to death and decay. But the pumpkins themselves look gorgeous. There is something about their orange, potbellied robustness in the midst of all that fragility that reminds one of the grandness of life and all its cycles in a way that the indiscriminately breeding pickles do not. When pickles have run their course and the last cukes on the vine have exploded into yellowy green tumors, all you want to do is smash them, stomp them with your boots, hurl them into fields, throw them against fence posts and barn walls. They are to plant growth what cancer is to cell growth. Pumpkins, on the other hand, perhaps because they are so few and so squatly ostentatious, seem like the fulfillment of something, a promise made and kept.

After the hailstorm that summer, our father said that pumpkins might indeed be a better cash crop than pickles. Next year we'd plant twenty, thirty acres of the beasts. And after we planted them, our work would consist of rolling them over in the sun.

We would, our father said, make a killing.

The tornado that came a week before Halloween made a prophet out of our father. We were at school that day, on the playground. It was a crisp fall day, one of those days that dawns bright and cold, the temperatures just below freezing, and then the air warms to a brisk forty-three or so. The sunshine so bright off the colored leaves and the air so clear it feels as though time itself has stopped, as though it could stay exactly that way forever and you wouldn't mind at all. The clouds moved in that morning, heavy, scudding, a solid wall. The wind picked up. Little dust devils whirled away madly in doorways and across the playground, picking up leaves, swirling them off the ground and up. Then we got a blast of air, and something seemed odd. It was warm air. Very warm air. We were on the playground in zippered sweaters and corduroy coats, and the next thing we knew we were hot. Most kids took off their jackets. And then time did seem to stop. Balls rolled away from their owners, and conversation, the laughter and shouting, died away. We were enveloped by stillness. The sky, so gay and bright and inviting a moment before, took on that ominous old-bruise color. It was like a light had suddenly been switched off, plunging us into twilight. We knew what it meant. A second later the siren on top of the school started its high-pitched, crescendoing whine, and the teachers were herding us into the school's boiler room even as the wind began its furious whip and howling.

Our mother, home with Peg Leg Meg, reported on what we could not see. She watched it from Robert Aaron's room. From radio reports, the tornado formed southwest of town, and the funnel stayed off the ground until after it had passed over the town and past our school. It first touched down about a mile from our house, exploding our neighbor's barn and killing thirty-four dairy cows that were trapped inside. It was tearing branches off trees, upending tractors and corn pickers, shattering corncribs, ripping off roofs, dropping power lines. Poultry, pigs, horses, sheep—if it was in the tornado's path it became airborne, and everything in the air became a missile. Our mother could see it coming over the rise from our neighbor's. It was on the ground now, not bouncing as it first had, and was making a beeline for our house. That was when our mother covered Peg's body with her own, crouched on the floor, and began to pray.

The roaring, our mother reported afterward, was tremendous. She could hear windows shattering upstairs and the walls *thump-thumping* as debris pummeled the house. She could feel the suction of air on her body even though she was below grade and inside a house. She was quite certain that she was going to die, and she prayed that her children would be taken care of. Then the roaring stopped, and she realized she was still on the floor, protecting a child who was complaining, "Mommy, get up, you're hurting me, I can't breathe!"

Our mother and sister were saved because tornadoes rarely make a beeline for anything. They meander, they wobble, they zig, they zag. This particular tornado passed, as we could see from the wake of its destruction, about fifty yards west of our house. It took out our neighbor's trees and our toolshed. It picked up one of our cats and heaved it into the house. Curiously, although the toolshed was gone, its walls distributed among the trees along our creek bottom, the tools themselves were still on the benches, the lawn mower still on the floor. Coming home from school on the bus, we passed one scene of destruction after another—cornfields flattened, trees split in two or completely uprooted, barns missing their centers, houses with their roofs peeled back, lumber and barn siding and bark stripped from trees littering the road and fields. A huge oak that stood near the corner of our property and our neighbor's was not missing more than a branch or two, but sheets of green-and-gray metal roofing from the Myerses' barn were embedded deep into the trunk and into the crotch of branches that formed the crown. When we got home we found a lot more of the Myerses' barn roof, sheet by sheet, littering our ravine, wrapped around trees as though corrugated sheet metal were nothing more than wet toilet paper. Standing on the rise behind our house, you could see a couple of exploded areas in our creek bottom where the tornado had touched down, and then it must have skipped over our hill and done its final damage to the farms on the other side. We heard about those in the coming days, once the power lines were up and phone service restored. Miraculously, no one was killed.

Given the severity of the storm, it was easy to overlook what was missing. We came home to find our mother crying with relief, a little dazed, still clutching Peg Leg Meg's hand. "Mommy, you're hurting me!" Peg kept squealing, and our mother said she was sorry. But she didn't let go. It wasn't until we'd walked around the house twice, looking at broken windows, the dead cat, torn up shingles, broken tree branches, the tools residing in bare air, that Ernie asked, "What about the pumpkins? What happened to the pumpkins?" He was standing in the field behind our house. The ground was bare. It was as though someone with a push broom had swept it clean. The wilted vines, the fat orange pumpkins—everything was gone.

Flying pumpkins. It seemed almost too comical to be believed.

"Where could they be?" Ernie wondered, and as we gazed down the field, looking for a flash of something orange, we wondered the same thing.

In the days that followed, we found out. Like everything else lifted by the storm, they had become missiles, fat orange bombs thrown like fastballs at the objects they ultimately hit. Cars were destroyed by them. Cows up to two miles away were killed by them. Pumpkins had wiped out chicken coops, flown through bedroom windows, taken out dining room tables. Barns had been aerated by them, tractor engines caved in, apple trees knocked down like bowling pins. We got calls every day for weeks as people found out who the projectiles belonged to. They couldn't sue, of course, act of God and all that, but the callers asked our father to stop growing them. Avoid the near occasion of pumpkin sin seemed to be their message. "How often are there going to be flying pumpkins, for chrissakes?" our father asked them.

"One time was too many," they answered.

The next year the pumpkins were gone, at least as a cash crop.

"We were putting too much emphasis on the summer growing season anyway," said our father the next spring. "We need a year-round crop. And what grows year-round?" asked our father. "Animals," he said, not giving us a chance to answer. "Chickens, sheep, cattle. Also mushrooms. We have moisture in the basement anyway. We may as well take advantage of it."

Our father was nothing if not an optimist. Often his chest pocket—which held a pocket protector filled with mechanical pencils and pens and a palm-size circular slide rule—was decorated with a button that said "Accentuate the Positive" or "Ask Me Why I'm Smiling" (we had our own theories, none of which would have reflected well on our merit reviews). To his credit, he did not let our family's failures in agriculture get him down.

He also didn't always explain his intentions. His first experiment with beef cattle was a calf we named Molly. We assumed it was a pet. We fed it supplements, let it suck on our fingers, groomed it like a dog. Come September it was gone. Our parents exchanged looks when we asked what happened to Molly but didn't say anything. Later that month we had a cookout. Our father was doing up a big stack of hamburgers. He also had a few pounds of hot dogs and some Polish sausage, each sausage linked to its compatriots with a little twist of intestine, though we didn't know that at the time. One by one we were served. Clutching our paper plates and our hamburger buns, trying to keep the potato chips from flying off in the breeze, we were suddenly seized with dread as it dawned on us what our father might be serving us.

It was Peg Leg Meg who voiced the question on our lips. "Is . . . is that Molly?" she asked, her head nodding at the burgers sizzling on the grill, their juices spittering the coals below. Our father exchanged a look with our mother, who was stirring potato salad. "You may as well tell them, Wally," she said. He nodded. "It's time you knew where your food comes from," said our father, not at all unkindly. "We raise animals so they can feed us. It's okay. It's what nature and God intended." Our father leaned down farther, his round face slightly obscured by smoke. "Yes, honey, this is Molly. And it's okay for you to eat him." (We were, it turned out, shaky on cow gender.)

Meg's lower lip quivered and her mouth opened and her jaw worked, but no words came out. Then she managed a quavering "I-I-I-I-I'll have a . . . a . . . a . . . ho-ho-hot do-o-og."

One by one we echoed her. Our father was left with a good ten pounds of thawed hamburger patties that were drawing flies and a clutch of kids all sitting as far away from the scene of the crime as possible.

"The pig your hot dogs are made out of, the pig's name was Rupert," called our father to us disgustedly. "You didn't know him, but his name was Rupert."

The black walnuts were in some ways our father's deepest disappointment. He had the idea that a black walnut, started from a seedling, would in twenty or thirty years, be ready for harvest, and given what black walnut was going for on the open market once it was sized and cut for lumber, a mature tree was, he had read somewhere, worth a good twenty thousand dollars. That was *per tree,* he liked to point out. "When you kids are ready for college and tuition is due," he said, "we'll just go out to the woods and harvest one of those black walnuts. Presto, four years of college paid for in one stroke of an ax." It was a lovely thought, but like most lovely thoughts, it ignored the facts. The trees would be mature closer to our children's college years, not our own; inflation would make his idea of how much a college education cost quaint if not laughable; and we were not miniature Paul Bunyans, felling trees with one stroke of an ax. We would use a chain saw, like normal people. Although for all those black walnuts grew, an ax, and one stroke at that, would have been plenty. Two other things our father didn't take into account: soil that was too acidic for black walnuts, and a deer population that seemed to love the black walnut seedlings as though they were champagne and caviar. Our father had us plant four hundred black walnut seedlings. In a few years less than than thirty were left, and most of the ones that made it to maturity were too misshapen to use for lumber.

But should one be judged on one's success, or on the size of one's dreams? Our father's plan was to start out small and end up big. In actuality, he started out too big and things ended up small. He wanted to be an entrepreneur, he wanted the farm to be his monument, but he wasn't around enough to make his dreams a reality. He couldn't be there for the day-to-day of it that might have kept things humming. And we blamed him for it.

There was also that fact that he was not a robber baron like his idols. He was not driven like that. He was driven to dream, not driven to succeed. He was no Al Capone, hiding out in the Wisconsin north woods, and unlike Dillinger, he would never shoot it out with police. He was too nice a guy for that. He didn't cut corners. He played by the rules— a quaint, almost outmoded way of thinking.

I remember being taken to the Dog Out once. It was a Saturday afternoon, the time of day when men in bars, if they aren't pathetic, take on a kind of heroic stature. Especially if you're still a kid. While our father jawed with Mike the bartender and a couple customers, I became fascinated by a cardboard sign that jutted from a metal clip above the cash register. Like the Hamm's beer signs of a few years before, the sign pulled me into its universe:

Y.C.H.J.C.Y.A.Q.F.T.J.B.
T.Y.

What did it mean? I wanted, *needed* to know. It was a code of some kind, the deciphering of it the entrance requirement for some secret society, and only the elect would be admitted. I wanted to be among the elect.

But I couldn't make hide nor hair of it. Meanwhile our father had been lured into a game of pool by a sharpie, a stocky guy with a pencil-thin mustache and wavy black hair combed tight to his skull. He wore a polo shirt under a gray suit coat. When he smiled you could see the gaps between his teeth, and he smiled a lot. He looked like a gangster on holiday. I paid only fleeting attention to the game. I wanted my father to win, but I'd seen *The Hustler.* This guy looked like a professional who went town to town, setting guys up for big falls. My father was an earnest mark. And besides, I was trying to figure out what those initials stood for. But twice during the game I happened to look over after my father had scratched and the sharpie was putting the cue ball down at the wrong end of the table. "We broke here, right?" he asked my father, but it came out sounding like a statement, not a question. And you could see why he wanted the break there. He'd have an easy shot. The man, I realized, was a fraud. If you were a really good player, you didn't need to change ends of the table like that. My father's scratch should have been all the help he needed. He was no sharpie. He was a guy who liked to dress like a sharpie and pretend he was a sharpie, but he lacked a sharpie's skills. So he resorted to tricks like pretending he didn't know what side of the table the break was on.

"Dad," I stage-whispered. "He's cheating."

"I know," said my father. "He's going to lose anyway."

I don't think I had ever seen my father so confident before. He let the guy switch sides of the break so he could put the cue ball down where he wanted, and he acknowledged the guy was cheating, and he didn't seem bothered by it at all.

"But, Dad," I stage-whispered again. "He's *cheating*."

"It's okay," said my father, "cheaters never win."

I don't know if my father believed that or not at the time. In later years he railed quite a bit about all the cheating and fraud and backstabbing that went on at his company, the methods guys used to get ahead, to make more money, to make sales, and our father made it clear he was being screwed by other people's shenanigans, and certainly by the age of fourteen I had seen plenty of kids cheat with great success, but he said it in the Dog Out that day with the surety of a choirboy, with all the earnestness of a young Horatio Alger, with all the aplomb of Lord Baden-Powell uttering his code to his first troop of Boy Scouts.

Clearly our father's unruffledness nonplussed the sharpie. He missed his next shot badly, even with his homemade advantage, and soon after that left the bar. "No two out of three?" asked our father. "No guts, no glory?" The sharpie had lost five straight to our father after taking the first two.

"Fuck you," said the sharpie, and that was the last I ever saw of him, though the Dog Out was one of our father's favorite bars.

"How did you know he was going to lose?"

"He's a salesman, like me," said our father, resettling himself at the bar. "Peddlers always talk a better game than they play." He sipped his beer. "Once he started asking for special dispensations from the pope of pool, I knew he was lousy."

The pope of pool? I wasn't going to ask. But my curiosity about the sign was overpowering. I pointed at the top of the cash register. "What does that mean?" I asked.

Mike the bartender was grinning. "Go ahead, Wally, tell 'im."

"Your Curiosity Has Just Cost You a Quarter for the Juke Box, Thank You," said my father. "Cough it up."

My father paid for my curiosity, of course, and even let me choose the songs from the jukebox. Simon and Garfunkel, Bob Dylan, the Monkees. Our father winced, muttered something about kids today, you couldn't take them anywhere, but he was grinning at Mike when he said it.

We left the bar that day with me feeling closer to my father than I probably had in ages. My father was a genial giant among men. Fair, strong-minded, indulgent of his children, and a damn fine pool shot.

We came home to discover that Nomi was coming to live with us, and though our mother announced this with a smile, she soon broke down crying. Nomi was coughing up something of a different nature entirely.

15. Accidents and Acts of God

The summer Nomi came to live with us we didn't get a whole lot of wet, and what we got came at the wrong time. Nomi came in May. Artu would stay in Chicago, working, because that was the only way to keep up the insurance for her treatments. "What treatments?" we asked. Our mother stumbled for a circumspect way to tell us. Finally she just came out with it. "Cancer treatments. They're not sure, but they think maybe they'll help."

May. Maybe. Things should have been growing but they weren't. The corn, the alfalfa—everything was a pale green, heat-seared as though it might be August. Nomi, supporting herself on our mother's arms, looked over our fields and said, "Looks like the only thing blooming around here is inside me."

Asked Ernie, "Is it like a Big Max is growing inside her?"

"Something like that," said our mother.

"So if the weather inside her changed, the Big Max inside her would shrivel up and die?"

"That's what they're trying to do, dear."

"Just don't give her any water," said Ernie. "That'll take care of it." For the rest of the summer he scowled whenever he saw Nomi drinking iced tea.

In his eagerness to understand and to help, Ernie was confusing the roles of God and Mother Nature. It is a common enough mistake. Most children are paganists before they become theists. And adults confuse the two as well. We found this out when our parents tried to collect on the toolshed the tornado had blown down our fields. Said the insurance agent, "Sorry, Wally, but acts of God are not covered by this policy. And tornadoes are acts of God."

"Everything," said our father, "is a goddamn act of God."

"You need a policy that will say so," said Og Tieken, our insurance agent. "For a little bit extra you can be covered for acts of God."

"With or without flooding?" asked our father. "Have you got a Noah policy, a forty days and forty nights rider?"

"Oh, flood insurance is pricey," Og said. "You're on high ground, you don't need that."

"Oh, you never know," said our father. "I might get me some of that extra insurance just so God can do what He likes. And so can Mother Nature. The two of them can go sky-bowling with our pumpkins any time they feel like it."

There it was, that confusion again. As near as I could figure, for things like tornadoes and hail, big events, God and Mother Nature were in cahoots. For regular weather, it was strictly Mother Nature, and for anything unpredictable and freakish, like a calf being born with two heads, it was an accident, an act of God that threw Mother Nature for a loop.

Which meant, I guess, that what befell Nomi was an act of God. Although it wasn't completely unpredictable: Nomi smoked a pack, a pack and a half of cigarettes a day. The surgeon general had years before come out with his warnings about smoking maybe sort of possibly being harmful to your health. Our mother was more succinct. "I guess what they're saying is true. Those things can kill you."

Nomi was given Ernie and Meg's room across from the bathroom, and they moved into the downstairs rec room with Ike, Wally Jr., and me. Although Nomi was, when she wasn't in pain, her usual acerbic and jocular self, we avoided that room a lot. Something was going on in there that we did not understand and wanted no part of. Unless you had business in Cinderella's or our parents' room at the end of the hall, you avoided going down that hall entirely.

I couldn't avoid going down that hallway. I was curious about Nomi, for one thing. What was happening to her was scary, but my guilt at neglecting her was far greater than my fear of her pain. For another, in the past couple of years I had discovered a great many things of a private nature, two of which happened to be my parents' shower and my penis. It was a curious, perhaps necessary dual discovery: my almost obsessive desire to be clean twined with a powerful inclination toward self-abuse. I won't elaborate on the obvious intersection of the two except to say that the shower stall in our parents' bathroom was metal and the staccato thunder of water on metal masked my groanings.

"My," said Nomi, "you sure take a lot of showers."

"I like to be clean," I said.

"I understand," said Nomi. "You like your privacy when Mother Nature pays a visit. Some changes," she said, "are best explored in private. I trust everything is where it should be?"

"Huh?"

"Is everything going okay with you, Emcee?"

"Yeah, I guess. Is everything going okay with you, Nomi?"

Nomi sighed and lit a cigarette. "No, everything is not going okay with me. But it's my own fault, I suppose. I like these too much. Always have." She looked small and shrunken in the double bed, more so than she had when she was recovering from hip surgery in the House That God Built. It creeped me out, but she was Nomi, whom I'd known always.

"Are you going to be okay, Nomi?"

"I'd like to believe so, Emcee, but no one can say for sure."

"Not even the doctors?"

"Not even God," said Nomi, looking out the window. Nomi said she was tired then, she needed to rest, and I left, looking for someplace where I could ponder what was happening to me and to her in private.

If it was Mother Nature regularly visiting me, and an act of God visiting Nomi, then why did everything seem so accidental? The assigning of a personality, a willful presence, to the nature of accident threw me for a loop. But for the past couple of years everything was throwing me for a loop. And more than anything that summer I wanted to be by myself, largely because I'd made other discoveries.

I shouldn't have been snooping. We all knew better than to be checking out our parents' dresser drawers. But snooping is an addiction. Once you find one thing mildly curious you keep looking, and once you find the mother lode you simply cannot stop yourself. All the guilt in the world won't keep you from looking where you oughtn't.

The first few times we snooped in Augsbury, it was Cinderella, Robert Aaron, and me. We discovered a Frederick's of Hollywood catalog and snapshots of us as babies. We also found baby teeth in coin envelopes with our names on each one and the dates the teeth were lost.

"That blows the Tooth Fairy theory," said Robert Aaron.

"Shut up," said Cinderella. "Like you believed any of that stuff."

"I used to."

"Yeah, well you used to a lot of things." Cinderella had recently gotten cynical, her hair a blond waterfall over her face, her breath smelling of cigarettes and Life Savers. She pawed through the drawers: lipsticks, compacts, a bundle of letters written on onionskin paper from when our parents were first married. "I've read those," said Cinderella knowingly. "Like you'd really be interested in where you should put things." I made a mental note. Cinderella never let us read those letters. Next time I was alone I would. We looked at more photographs—First Communions, Halloweens, Christmases, Easters—and at our father's boxers, printed with tiny diamonds or those fat commalike things called paisleys. We discovered our mother's lingerie, gauzy things we'd never seen her wear. The way it was stuffed into the drawer you couldn't tell if it had been hurriedly hidden or just forgotten. Cinderella was competitively curious. "I wish I had nice stuff like this," she said, holding up a sheer black jacketlike thing with a tie at the throat and black fluff at the hem. "It wouldn't go to waste, if you know what I mean."

We didn't know what she meant, but that hardly mattered to Cinderella these days. She had a boyfriend, a guy who was out of high school already. And it wasn't poor, sweet Mikey Spillsbeth. This worried our mother and pleased Cinderella. "She's got to stop thinking of me as a Goody Two-shoes," Cinderella told us, holding up one of our mother's black lace underwire bras. "I wish I had Mom's chest. Why didn't I get Mom's chest? Mom's chest is wasted on her," said Cinderella, the bra comically empty as she held it pinched to her shoulders.

That was one of the great mysteries of life, I thought, though I didn't tell Cinderella. Life was full of mysteries and secrets, and you could ponder all you wanted, but that didn't mean you were allowed to figure anything out. Like how come our dad was so big and we were all skinny? And how come our mom had what she described as a voluminous chest and Cinderella's were petite little mounds? Or why did peanut butter toast always land peanut butter side down? Or why was I drawn to the letters and our mother's lingerie drawer like a bee to honey? I knew I was bad, and that I would be punished, if not in this life then in the next, but

I couldn't stop myself. I had to know, I had to see. And the opened boxes and drawers in our parents' bedroom, as though everything had just been thrown together or taken apart, made it easy.

One of the many reasons I spent a lot of time by myself that summer was I was getting boners at the drop of a hat. Had been, actually, for the last two years. It didn't help that the magazines—*Time, Life*—were running more and more risqué pictures: fashion layouts with models wearing about what we found in our mom's underwear drawer, and through the sheer tops the models' inconsequential breasts but dark nipples were clearly visible. But it wasn't just that. Anything could trigger it. The swoop and dip of a barn swallow, the cold taste of Tang on a hot day, smelling clover in the fields, watching Glenn Beckert, Don Kessinger, and Ernie Banks turn a double play, pulling myself up on the chin-up bar, seeing Dorie Braun with the right insouciance in her eyes, a bit of rounded flesh peeking out over her swimsuit cup, a bit of belly over her hip-huggers' waistband—anything at all could set my stem rising, and then it was a question of what to do with it. Peeing with an erection was tricky. You had to push the little fellow down and stand further back, so gravity came into play, allowing the arc to find the porcelain. I wondered if this was why the urinals at school smelled like they did. Was there a whole nation of men and boys out there, all walking around all day with stiffies, and none of them disciplined enough in their aim to hit their intended targets? It certainly gave me a different picture of America. Not an America I wanted to belong to, although I was already a part of it.

I worried, too, about the eagerness with which I crept past Nomi's room and stole into our parents', reading and rereading those letters, savoring their incomprehensible deliciousness, fingering the lingerie with the same luscious, lewd thrill of those border guards lo! those many years ago. What it felt like under my fingers! I got goose bumps just touching it.

And then I wanted to wear it. There I was, standing amid the water-spotted *Reader's Digest*s and *Popular Mechanics*es, the accordioned copies of *They Were Expendable* and *A Bridge Too Far*, my fingers running up and down the silky length of our mother's scarlet nightgown. Surely no boy in America was doing what I was doing right then. I showered, our mother's panty hose just above my head. I toweled off, Little Jr. (I was picking up terminology from our mother's letters) stiffening under the terry cloth. Then I wrapped the towel about my waist like Yul Brynner in

The Ten Commandments. Little Jr. strained to peek through, but the towel's weight was more than it could lift.

No matter. Something besides how much cloth my penis could bench-press was calling me out of the bathroom. Something I'd discovered on one of my first forays to our mother's lingerie drawer. I was always looking for new stuff, things I'd missed last time. Everything was tangled up, tossed together; you couldn't be sure what belonged with one outfit and what with another. I rationalized the intrusion on the grounds that putting things away was one of our chores, so my being there had a kind of logic to it: I was trying to find out what belonged where. Armed with opportunity and motive, and needing only courage to run the Nomi gauntlet, I was back there every chance I could get. It was wrong, I was going to hell, I was racked with guilt, tormented by what I saw, but I was also thrilled and curious, and that thrill of being admitted to the hidden mysteries—even if they remained mysteries—was worth the price of admission.

What I found were pictures of our mother without any clothes on. In the pictures, our mother's torso was white and blocky, like rough-cut marble. Beneath her belly was a stippling of skin that reminded me of bread dough, and one breast was lower than the other, more rounded, and canted to one side. Its nipple was larger, too, more oblong, and her areolae, had I known to call them that, were huge and dark. She was sitting at the kitchen table, as though waiting for coffee to be served, leaning forward, her breasts flattened and spread out, her cheek resting in the palm of her hand. She looked whimsical and amused. When she was sitting back she looked bored, the same look our faces got when our father fiddled with the camera too much. "Hurry up and take the picture," our mother's face was saying. "I'm not sitting here naked just so you can get your jollies with the camera. Who cares if it's too light or too dark? What's it going to matter? Who's going to see them besides you, and you can see them any time you like?"

I imagined this conversation between them, our mother bored and a little impatient, but willing to play along if it pleased our father, and our father frustrated that the equipment wasn't working right, the flash failing to fire, or firing too early, or the photo tearing when he pulled it from the back of the camera, and then the fixer, that pink tongue of chemicals you had to wipe over the picture to keep it from fading, something could always go wrong with that, and meanwhile our mother is sitting there naked, nipples stiffening in the cool of the house, and it was this moment of easy yet awkward intimacy between them, stolen from the rest of their day—we were outside, playing, likely to return soon, sweaty and demanding Tang—that made me realize what a fragile, wonderful thing marriage is, and to what lengths one will go to preserve it.

There was one other photograph, and it revealed mysteries I couldn't even guess at. The photo shows our mother reclining on the bed in the House That God Built. Her legs are spread, and the photo is taken from the foot of the bed, by her feet. Our mother looks vulnerable and inviting. Looking at the dark bush of hair where her thighs met, I can't believe our father didn't put down his camera immediately after this photo was taken. Who could resist? Certainly not me, and I didn't have a clue as to what was going on. I just knew I wanted to climb up there. I had the feeling it was home; it was where I needed to be. I touched myself. Little Jr. was a hard branch grafted into my groin. It felt as though it might burst into flame if I kept touching it. I kept touching it. I was driven by some force that seemed both inside and completely outside myself. Satan, I was given to understand, did his best work through ecstasy.

We had stopped going to parochial school once we moved to Wisconsin. It was simply too expensive. To make up the difference, every Wednesday we went to Sunday school (Sunday school on Wednesdays—another contradiction of the Catholic Church), which was run at St. Gen's by a nun with all the charm of a drill sergeant. She delighted in instructing us in the wages of sin by telling us stories that illustrated her point, stories that scared the bejesus out of us.

Sister Henrietta's favorite story was of the boy who went to a cabin with a group of friends (he was eighteen, an age remote enough from us to give it the proper moral weight and glamor)—including some girls (Sister Henrietta called them "girls"; she called anyone under fifty "girls")—and come Sunday morning the boy in question went waterskiing rather than to church to take our Lord Jesus' Holy Body and Blood into his soul to nurture him morally and to give him strength to resist the temptations of the Evil One. That was her name for Satan: the Evil One. "But he did not go to Mass to take our Lord Jesus' Holy Body and Blood into his soul to nurture him morally and to give him strength to resist the temptations of the Evil One," said Sister. "He went waterskiing with his friends. With those *girls*." Sister Henrietta raised a bony finger. I stared at the three dark hairs growing from a mole on the underside of her chin. Did she know they were there, and if so, why did she choose to ignore them? Didn't nuns own tweezers?

"Had he prayed," continued Sister Henrietta, "had he been in church where he belonged, taking our Lord Jesus' Holy Body and Blood into his body to nurture his soul and to give him strength to resist the temptations of the Evil One, he might be alive today." Sister Henrietta let that one sink in a little while. Her voice dropped to an excited whisper. "Do you know what happened, boys and girls? Do you know what *always* happens to boys and girls who do not find the strength in Jesus to resist the ways of the Evil One?" Another pause. "He drowned. The boat swung him around too fast and he lost his footing. And he was a silly boy, a proud, silly boy, and he wasn't wearing a life preserver, and when the boat came around again, his own friends, with their boat, clunked him on the head and he slowly sank to the bottom of the lake." Sister Henrietta paused yet again. "And we can only hope, and pray, that that dear, sweet boy, who missed Mass only that once to go waterskiing, regained consciousness enough as his lungs filled with water and as the blood vessels in his chest burst, we can only hope and pray that as he was drowning he regained consciousness long enough to pray a complete Act of Contrition before he died. Otherwise he is in Purgatory, was sent there as soon as he died, and he is still there, to this very day." Again Sister Henrietta paused. Her voice sweet now, sugary with moral righteousness. Another group of thirteen- and fourteen-year-olds stricken with a deep-seated fear of God. "Can we all say an Act of Contrition, dears? Both for our own souls, that we are spared making such choices as presented to us by the Evil One, and can we also offer up our prayers today for that sweet, good boy who chose wrongly just one time, and to this very day suffers eternal torment and longing in Purgatory for that one sin he was never able to confess or wipe away with an Act of Contrition, thereby damning himself for all eternity?"

And while we prayed I kept picturing, as I'm sure everybody else did, this poor boy slowly floating to the lake bottom, his arms and legs loose in death, blood-tinged bubbles escaping from his mouth. But I thought of something else as well: that girl in the boat, what was she wearing? A bikini? A peach- or lemon-colored bikini? And did he sleep with her the night before? Did he die happy, knowing, at least, that he'd had sex with her the night before he died? And was that what God was punishing him for? Was he really being punished for that? And that girl—did she like it?

Was she pining for the loss of this boy who'd maybe made her happy? Was she cognizant that every boy she'd ever be with after that would have to compete with this memory, and they would always fail, for who—ever—can compete with a ghost and win? And what about that girl, who I pictured looking like Dorie Braun—what did she look like under her bikini? Were her breasts tan and creamy? Was the place where her thighs junctured a lovely white? Would I be the boy who years later would finally wipe away the memory of that boy lost forever at the bottom of the lake? Could I be that sweet and kind and gentle, could I please her? Would she let me reach inside the cup of her peach-colored bra and palm what I found there?

It was all a tangle, all of it. There I was, contemplating sex and death, sin and salvation, touching myself while looking at a picture of my mother naked, and imagining a girl in a peach-colored bikini, a girl I would never meet, though she had Dorie Braun's face and Dorie Braun's body. I went back into the bathroom, where our mother had left her panty hose draped over the shower curtain rod. I took down the panty hose. I put them on. I was all scrunched up inside the panty hose and there was a tingling throughout my loins that surely had to be what that boy and girl felt when they'd pleased each other the night before he drowned.

But something was missing, too. I wanted to feel manly. So I went into the back of our father's closet and put on one of his helmet liners and on top of that the slate green steel helmet, which was so heavy it made my neck wobble like that of one of those NFL dolls you see mounted in the back windows of Chryslers. I took his twenty-two rifle, too, the one with the scope, and I stood in front of the wardrobe mirror that had never been mounted on the wardrobe. It sat on the floor, amid the detritus of our parents' lives, their clothes and papers and magazines, their Sansabelt slacks and terry-cloth robes, their bank statements and survivalist-spiritualist books, their *Reader's Digest*s and *Outdoor Life*s, their catalogs and cosmetics and purses and briefcases, their shotguns and their rosaries—all the clutter that our mother would not pick up because doing so might indicate she was settling down here, and she still wanted to believe this move was temporary—and I stood there, too, in panty hose and helmet, brandishing a twenty-two, sure I could do damage to somebody.

Doing it to myself would have been a pretty good guess. Especially since I *was* doing it to myself, the gun in one hand, the other inside the panty hose, and it was right as I started to spasm, my first real come, with an emission and everything, that Nomi's face appeared in the mirror behind me. She was at an odd angle, bent over her walker, so her face appeared between my legs. "Good God!" thundered Nomi. "What are you doing?"

I could have died. I pulled my hand out of the panty hose as fast as I was able, the goop on my hand smearing on the panty hose, a dollop landing on the mirror. I had a sudden inkling of my mother putting on these son-spackled panty hose and getting pregnant by me. That was the way girls got pregnant in our high school. There was never any intercourse. Too many kids crowded in cars going to drive-ins, that was the problem. The girls sat on the boys' laps and the boys came in their jeans, but fluids leaked through. Immaculate conceptions all. The ways of the Evil One were many and various. A warm lap now, an eternity of hellfire and damnation later, flames licking at the very laps you once so innocently sat on. Girls! Sit on those phone directories! Do not give in to the pleasures of the Evil One!

But it was too late. I already had. The evidence was everywhere—in what I was wearing, in what I was doing, in what I had expelled from my body in excruciatingly sweet and sinful relief. I cried out to Nomi, "It was an accident! I swear!"

But Nomi was already backing up in her walker, and closing the door on me as soon as she felt it was safe to do so. "I'm sure it was," she told me. "I'm sure it was."

I washed and rinsed and washed and rinsed those panty hose before I put them back on the curtain rod with their brethren. Brethren—should I even think thoughts like that? The little seedlings milling around in that pat of ejaculate were microscopic—ninth-grade biology told me that. What if one hadn't been washed away? What if one made it? What rough beast, what abomination would result from that? And what ring of hell was specifically reserved for boys who knocked up their own mothers? Would it be Oedipus and me sitting in the box seats, munching on dried dung beetles and mealy worms and grubs like they were popcorn, watching the murderers and rapists at hard labor? Or would it be the other way around?

I had plenty of time to think about what I had done. I thought about it every shower, and every waking moment outside the house. Nomi had said nothing to me, bless her; but still, I knew how she'd found me. And even if Nomi hadn't caught me, I knew what I was doing was a sin. All my bad thoughts were sins. And I was caught between the guilt of doing them and the desire to do them again, as soon as my privacy allowed me. Horror—that my blind worm could stiffen at the drop of a hat. Delight— that it was so easily appeased.

Like most good guilt-wracked, masturbating, and wet-dreaming boys of the period, I started having accidents with such regularity they no longer seemed random. It began with my bike accident. A year later, I tumbled off the barn roof and broke my forearm. The year after that, Wally Jr. and Ike dared me to climb to the top of our mercury lamppost. I slipped. A nail caught me underneath the rib cage and the nail head opened me up like a zipper. After each accident our father said to me, "You know what they do with horses, eh, Emcee?"

I knew. But I couldn't stop it. My yearly present to him, it seemed, was somehow doing damage to my person. A leg broken falling out of a tree house, a broken nose, a dislocated shoulder—our father surveyed the wreckage of me in my hospital bed as though he were a carpenter checking for knots or worm marks in a length of lumber. He shook his huge head, disappointed in what was obviously an inferior product. "We should have put you out of your misery years ago," he said, chucking my shoulder, assuming my shoulder was not in a sling.

This was how our father handled Nomi's illness as well. He was uncomfortable around Nomi, and he thought by telling jokes he could make everyone feel better. Mostly, though, he was trying to make himself feel better about things he had no control over. But a woman with lung cancer does not want to be asked by her son-in-law each time she sees him, "You know what they do with horses, don't you?"

Said Nomi, "Wally, shut up already."

This didn't stop him from saying the same thing the day the sheep stampeded our mother.

Sheep are not normally marauding animals. We kept them in a pen attached to one of the sheds, but the box-wire fencing sagged with vines, and their ringleader, a dry old ram called Bucko, kept pushing it over and they'd step through. Then we'd play tag with a half dozen sheep in an open field, trying to direct them back toward their enclosure. Most of the sheep complied willingly. Bucko didn't. He resisted herding, taking off like a spooked fire hydrant whenever one of us came near. We finally got a rope around him and dragged him back. A Massey-Ferguson tractor was equal to his stubbornness. At that point we should have sold him. Tony Dederoff told us, "Once a sheep goes bad, it's bad. There is no re-habilitation for sheep. They become hardened criminals. They go after the cow feed, they start scattering chickens. Pretty soon they're all hang-ing out at one end of the pasture, smoking unfiltered clover and making lewd baaing noises at the passing heifers."

What we had on our hands, according to Tony, was the Cool Hand Luke of sheep. Wally Jr. had the job of feeding the sheep, and every time he stepped into the pen Bucko backed up a couple steps and charged him. He played havoc with the backs of Wally Jr.'s thighs. Bruised the hell out of them. So after the first couple of Bucko's charges, Wally Jr. went into the pen with a scoop shovel, which he cocked and brought down like a baseball bat across Bucko's forehead. This would stun Bucko, who'd stand there for a minute, dazed, shaking off the cobwebs, and allow Wally Jr. to break open a fresh bale of hay for the other sheep. I feared the blows were making Bucko retarded. A likelier theory was they were making him mean. Regardless, he kept breaking out and get-ting into the clover just beyond our garden. Wally Jr., shovel in hand, went to get him.

Our mother was positioned at the top of the rise near where the old lumber piles used to be. Sheep normally veer away from humans and, given some direction, trot docilely toward where they're supposed to go. With the small cliff of the ruined barn on one side, and our mother on the other, the sheep's natural course would be down the path and back into their pen. This might have worked fine had the sheep not been led by a sociopath like Bucko. He came up the rise, chased by Wally Jr., Ike, and Robert Aaron, and instead of veering away from our mother and trotting down the path, he lowered his head and charged her. It looked like a bad scene from the streets of Pamplona. Bucko bowled over our mom, breaking her forearm, and the other sheep followed. It was a sheep stampede, and all our mother could do was cover her head as the sheep ran over her and crashed through the garden.

Our father was traveling. When he came back and saw our mother's arm in a cast, her eyes blackened, the first words out of his mouth were "This will reflect on your merit review."

"Piss on your merit review," said our mother.

Our father tried to keep it light. "You know what they do with horses, don't you?"

Our mother had ingested several painkillers, and her self-editing function must have short-circuited. "Fuck your horses," said our mother. "I want that sheep dead."

"Shouldn't it be 'Hold your horses'?"

"Shoot him, Wally. Shoot that goddamn sheep."

But our father could do no such thing. The job was given to Wally Jr. It was a reward, I suppose, for having driven the animal into criminal insanity with his scoop shovel. He walked into the pen, the infamous shovel in one hand, a shotgun in the other. He brained Bucko just as he stepped back to charge, and shot him as he was shaking out the cobwebs. "Take that, you fucker," said Wally Jr. He used a sixteen-gauge and fired a second round into Bucko's forehead even as the first had him sinking to his knees. Wally Jr. was taking no chances.

There was a certain zeal to Wally Jr.'s murder of Bucko that should have told us something, but we paid it no heed. Wally Jr. was defending his mother and redeeming the family honor, which had been blackened by a deranged sheep. Zealotry in defense of your mother is no vice.

What *is* a vice is trading places with your mother because you are scared shitless of Bucko, and she offers to take your spot on the ridge, and you get her spot at the pen, ready to close the gate once the runaway sheep are inside. So what happened to our mother was my fault. Everything was my fault—I had gotten my mother's arm broken, shot my father, nearly given my grandmother a heart attack at the sight of me, cross-dressed and ready for battle, pumping my little stem into spasms of ecstasy and panty hose spackling that might very well result in my having knocked up my own mother.

Not to mention that the true object of my little spasms didn't even know I was alive. Dorie Braun's interested disinterest from when I'd smashed up my face had settled into plain disinterest. She was entering Patty Duckwa territory now, off with older boys—a boy named Calvin Brodhaus, mostly—and she was leaving me behind. Not that we'd ever been an item, but she knew I liked her, and that should have counted for something. It didn't, of course—she was forgetting I existed at an alarming, almost a record, pace—but I'd show her, I would.

I ran for class president. I lost, badly. I joined the cross-country team, figuring to impress her with my Emil Zatopek–like accomplishments. I may as well have been running on the far side of the moon. In an ill-fated bid to demonstrate my masculinity, I briefly joined the wrestling team. In practice I was matched up with Calvin Brodhaus, even though he outweighed me by a good fifty pounds. Calvin pinned me in six seconds, a record that I believe still stands at our school as the fastest pin ever. The only way Dorie would have noticed me at that point was if she owned a copy of that imaginary book *A Short History of the Geeks,* in which contributions by people like me to the records set by people like Calvin were duly noted. It was no use and I knew it.

The only thing that saved me from making a complete ass of myself was the fact that I'd already done so. Two years previous, when it was first becoming clear to me how little Dorie noticed me, I had concocted, with the curious logic of a twelve-year-old boy, what I was sure was a can't-miss method for making her mine. I would root for the Chicago Cubs. I'd will them to victory, and the mystical power I wielded would imbue me with desirability, at least as far as Dorie Braun was concerned. Never mind that year after year the Cubs swooned better than a femme fatale in a Jimmy Cagney movie—that year it was going to be different. I could tell. There was an air of inevitability about the '69 Cubs. They couldn't lose. Our father said they were cursed, they'd fall apart, it was just a matter of time, but this was their year. Santo, Williams, Hundley, Kessinger, Beckert, my beloved Ernie Banks, plus a pitching staff that included Ferguson Jenkins, Bill Hands (a pitcher named Hands, believe it!), Ken Holtzman, even the submarine-throwing Ted Abernathy—it was a team of destiny, a team of greatness, a team that had a nine-and-a-half-game lead on the hated, pathetic Mets and it was already August. I'd always believed in the Cubs; now I became them. Their drive to the pennant would redeem me in Dorie's eyes. I would become the boy I'd always hoped I'd be. My shaky status in the male gender would solidify; I'd become accepted, manly. Dorie Braun would notice the change in me. I'd be a winner.

Our father would come into the living room after one of his sojourns to the Dog Out and look at the TV for several minutes. Then he'd announce, "They're losers. You watch. They'll tank. They'll choke. They're no good." The way he spat it out he may as well have been saying it of me. Of course he had no idea how closely I identified with the team. How could he? He was never around. But his pronouncements made me will them to victory all the more. I'd show him. They were *so* good. They were the forces of light, battling the forces of evil. I—they—we would triumph. Over history, over adolescence, over the various demons bedeviling them, me, us.

History has chosen to record the success of the Amazin' Mets of '69 more so than the late season collapse, the total breakdown, of the Chicago Cubs, who in a matter of some six or seven weeks, managed to blow a nine-and-a-half-game lead and finish the season eight-and-a-half games behind the Mets, finishing, in fact, in third place. They weren't even runner-up. This is as it should be. The Mets were winners, and history is written by the winners. And our father was right. The Cubs were losers. Choke city. Complete collapse. "They're bums. They're *looooosssss-eeeerrrrs.*"

I was crying. I was crying and I could not stop. If only he'd just shut up, let me watch the stupid game in peace. But he kept it up, fueled by Miller High Life and the joy of his own invective. "You watch," he said. "They'll find some stupid, boneheaded way of giving it away."

"Wally," said our mother, who'd been listening to the diatribe for seventeen years now.

"What?" barked our father.

"He takes it seriously," our mother said quietly.

"How can he take these losers seriously? How can anybody take these losers seriously? They're a joke."

"Wal-*ly.*"

"Oh, right. Sorry." For the next inning our father tried to be on his best behavior. "That Banks kid can hit. Only decent player on the team. Been that way since the fifties. You know that? Always a gentleman. *Let's play two,* he used to say. And whoa, did you see that? Another single for Ernie. What is that today? Three singles? He keeps dinging them in the exact same place. He must have cut a groove out there."

He was trying, but it was too late. I couldn't stop crying, and my father—old habits die hard—couldn't stop berating the Cubs. When Abernathy gave up a bases loaded double in the ninth and the Cubs lost both halves of the doubleheader—they hadn't even come to bat yet but you knew that they were going to go meekly—my father lost it. "*Loooosssseeerrrs! Looosssseeerrrs!* They're nothing but a bunch of fucking losers!"

I lost it. Something welled up in me and burst out, and I tore out of the house, completely hysterical. The back-door screen had its storm window down. My arm went through that. There wasn't a lot of blood until I yanked my arm back through the broken glass.

"Good God," screamed our mother as the shattered glass continued to fall. "What was that?"

My parents came lumbering from the living room, but the door had already banged behind me, more glass shattering, and I was running, out into the field. About two-thirds of the way down the field I sank to my knees, my arm throbbing. I had it clutched to my T-shirt. And there I gave vent to all the anguish inside me, turning my insides out as I screamed until I grew hoarse. There were some sheep in the next field over, and their "*MmBaah!*" was either assent or disagreement, but then they, too, fell silent. I screamed to the bright blue sky and the cottony white clouds drifting like ships in that sweet open immenseness. "I'm a failure! I'm a failure! I'm a failure! Why? Why? Why? Why? Why?" All my rage had turned into defeat, and the clouds, the green grass, the sky, God—nobody, nothing answered. It was mockery. It was worse; it was indifference.

Nomi, two years later, would be right. Not even God could help you.

They found me like that, beyond hysteria, my right arm covered in blood, my T-shirt soaked crimson. They carried me back up to the house, where I continued moaning, "I'm a failure, I'm a failure," until they were able to pump enough bourbon and elixir of Benadryl into me—red juice, we called it (a Parke-Davis product, much to our father's chagrin)—to calm me down. They got me into a warm tub of bathwater and started cleaning me up. I would need stitches for some of the wounds, but most could be butterflied closed. Our mother washed the tear-streaked dust from my face, washed my arms, held a washcloth to the worst of the wounds, looked with concern at me and with an expression that could melt steel at our father.

Our father tousled my hair and said he was sorry. He didn't know I had taken things so seriously. He said he wouldn't do that again. "You have to understand, Emcee," he said. "The Cubs will always be a day late and a dollar short. It's no accident they're so bad. It's an act of God, and you just have to accept it."

I was down to whimpering and could breathe again. I looked at both my parents. Our mother with her concern and flared anger, our father stupefied with beer and filled with, yes, fumbling, awkward love. I suppose in a perverse way I had won that round. In breaking down, I had almost broken through our father's wall of clichés. He had had to say something to me that wasn't simply a truism. He had used a truism to get at an elemental truth.

And he was right. The Cubs were a day late and a dollar short. And so was I. The only good thing that came out of it was that a couple of years later, when I again tried to woo Dorie with acts of gallant stupidity, it hurt less when I failed.

I have told this story over the years to Dorie—she knows all about my Cubs obsession—but I've never told her that it was connected to her as well. She thinks it was purely Cubs-related, and I've never had the courage to let her know how much of my breakdown back then was related to her, or how much I desired her even before I understood it to be desire. Nor have I told her that I've always been afraid of losing her, both well before she was mine, when the loss wasn't really consequential, and—more heartbreakingly—after. It is that I am losing her now, or perhaps have already lost her, that is driving me nuts.

Not long after Bucko's attack on our mother, Nomi took a turn for the worse. Our mother joked with Nomi about anything that touched on the borders of what was going on without ever getting to the heart of the matter. Artu visited often, was always cheerful, yet on more than one occasion on a Sunday afternoon as he was getting his car ready for the long drive back to Chicago I found him in our driveway, a gallon jug of water in his hand (he was topping off the radiator), his eyes glistening as he looked out over our fields. I thought I knew what he was thinking, but I did not. He shook his head, closed the hood of his car, looked back at the house, and drove away.

Inoperable was the word whispered by our mother before she collapsed in our father's arms, begging to be held. What she meant was "terminal." Like sex, death had its own euphemisms. For example, the doctors explained that, given the advanced state of the cancer inside Nomi, "aggressive" treatments were called for. *Aggressive,* we found out later, meant "experimental." They pumped her veins full of mustard gas, which never reached the cancer but did kill off a number of those veins. You could see the dead rivers and their tributaries beneath her skin: muddy, ghoulish, purply brown. Scars of the doctors' handiwork.

Nomi, indomitable Nomi, became a wizened sack of bones, whimpering, groaning, dozing in and out of consciousness. It was not pretty, and our mother kept us from her room now that she was "sinking." She was still in the house, but we no longer saw her except for when our mother ushered us to her doorway when she was napping. It was a little like looking at a mannequin, only the waxy lips were open and the head was tilted to one side. "It's only a matter of time," our mother would say. "I pray to God He's swift with her."

"Maybe she'll die in her sleep," I said.

"Yes," our mother said. "Maybe she will." And turned away, her hand over her mouth.

But then Nomi got better. She "rallied," the doctor said. When she had been groaning and whimpering, he said she "lagged." It was a language of nuance and things unspoken or glossed over. Nomi herself wasn't like that, and her rally meant she was her old self, giving our father hell, laughing with our mother, questioning us kids about our homework and our friends and our aspirations. Having graduated high school, Cinderella was now enrolled at the tech, in a field called "fashion merchandising." Nomi sniffed. "Is that a degree in clerking for Montgomery Ward's? Sarah Lucinda, you don't need a degree for that. Just good shoes."

Cinderella had brought home her tech school boyfriend. He had sandy orange hair, freckles, and bug eyes. He kept licking his mustache. Cinderella said she was going to marry him. He had a name—Oswald Grunner—but everyone called him Okie. "Is that because of the size of his root or because he has an acorn for a brain?" Nomi wondered out loud.

"He spent time in Oklahoma, Nomi. He was in the Air Force and he broke horses."

"He broke horses. Now there's an occupation to support a family. Did he get paid when he broke wind, too?"

"I love him, Nomi."

"You love the idea of being in love. It's not the same."

Our mother stayed out of it. She was afraid that if she voiced her displeasure it would alienate Cinderella, might even drive her toward the boy in a fit of romantic it's-you-and-me-against-the-world passion. And when his unsuitability did dawn on her, our mother didn't want to have said something that might cause her to feel she couldn't come home to lick her wounds. Our mother was counting on reason and good sense prevailing. Besides, Nomi was good at doing the dirty work. You couldn't be mad at Nomi.

She asked to be introduced to Okie and said in his presence to Cinderella, "Anybody can have a fool for a friend. You can even fall in love with one. That doesn't mean you have to marry him."

"Mom wasn't much older than me when she married Daddy."

"Your father wasn't a fool. Your father probably doesn't know this, but I've always been rather fond of him."

"Begging pardon, ma'am, but I ain't no fool. And we ain't getting married till it's time."

"And how do you reckon it's time, Okie?"

"I ain't figured it out yet. I'll know when I get there."

"Ah," said Nomi, "a boy and his dream. Remind me to get you a Timex for a wedding present."

"I love her, Nomi, and I promise I'll do right by her."

"What I'm afraid of," said Nomi, "is that you'll have to."

"Why don't we go outside and let Nomi rest?" our mother suggested.

It was a fine October day, warm and windy. Cumulus clouds were stretched out and racing across the sky. "It's a shame we can't bring Nomi outside," said our mother. "She'd enjoy this."

"I thought she only went in for blood sports," said Okie, not as stupid as he seemed.

"It's part of the family hazing," said Cinderella. "If you can get past Nomi, you're in."

"So did I get past Nomi?"

Cinderella grabbed his forearm. She was smiling. "The jury's still out." I didn't know squat about love at the time, but right then I had the notion that Nomi was right. Cinderella was in love with the idea of being in love. She liked the commotion she was causing; she liked showing off her beau. She was both oblivious to the outside world, hermetically sealed inside her feelings for Okie, and watching everyone for reactions to her being inside this bubble. They looked like a couple that had already "you knowed," and had found it pleasing. They made a strange couple— Okie all blunt edges and squares, Cinderella thin and whiplike. And she and Okie were enjoying their moment, their starry-eyed double solip-

sism, the wind ruffling their hair—take a picture, somebody, please—
until Nomi called to our mother, "Susan, I need to pee!"

It would be safe to say that Okie never got past Nomi. Our mother
went inside the house and was gone for several minutes before she
started screaming, "Help, help! Somebody help! Help me! Help!"

We took off running, only to be barred from coming inside the house
by our mother, who told us to stay outside, an ambulance was coming.
Her face was ashen. She admitted Cinderella and Okie; the rest of us sat
on the front stoop or milled around, waiting to find out what in Sam Hill
was going on.

We didn't find out until the ambulance arrived, lights and siren blazing. They went in with a wheeled gurney. Father Reardon, Monsignor
Kahle's replacement, arrived all harried moments later, clutching a black
valise that looked like a doctor's bag. The paramedics came out several
minutes later, their gurney now holding what looked like a zippered gray
garment bag. They put this in the back of their truck and drove away
slowly, almost casually, pausing at driveway's end to put on their turn in-
dicator. There were no lights or siren. Our mother had come out with
Father Reardon and Cinderella with Okie while they were loading up
the gurney and its burden. Okie had his arm around Cinderella, who
curved herself into his chest, and Father Reardon had his arm around
our mother, who stood stiffly, the wind ruffling her hair and causing her
tears to curve down the slope of her face, which she batted at with her
cast.

"She was saying she needed to pee," our mother said. "And I said, 'I'm
coming, I'm coming,' and she said I needed to hurry, or she'd be sitting
there in her own juices. And I laughed, and she laughed"— our mother's
mouth fell open as she was saying this, and she put her hand to her open
mouth as though trying to keep something in that had fallen out—"and
it seemed, for a moment there, just like old times. And then while I was
getting her to sit up so I could scoot the bedpan beneath her"— again our
mother's mouth fell open and she gasped for breath—"she opened up
her mouth and everything just came out." She gestured with her casted
hand to indicate the arc of the hemorrhage out of her mouth. "There was
just so much of it, all at one time, and there was nothing I could do to
stop it, and then she was gone."

Our mother's voice had gotten very quiet, and was choked by her crying, which was a queer happy-crying, like she felt better about things now that they were over. "At least it was quick, at least she didn't suffer. It was just everything, all at once"—she made her gesture again—"and then she was gone, so soon, so soon, oh, my God, she went so soon!"

Six months later, when our sister married Oswald Grunner in a ceremony that came only weeks after the hushed disclosure that she had been impregnated by him, the impregnation itself was classified an accident. That was how Okie maintained it had happened, by accident, and if Nomi had been alive she would have proclaimed Okie was right. It was an accident from the word go.

16. Hook, Line, and Sinker

STONE SOUP AND
THE NATURE OF BELIEF

That was the beginning of the end, but what it was the end of nobody could say. The clock struck midnight on Cinderella—we knew that much. We knew, too, that our father had wanted to believe our move out of Chicago and into the country had made us impregnable. So maybe Cinderella's pregnancy put an end to that. And though our father was quietly furious, he was also stoic. After all, she wanted to marry the lout, and the lout was amenable to marrying her. Maybe it would all work out. "We shall see what we shall see"—even with a pregnant daughter, our father was a Zen optimist.

He believed, for example, that the itty-bitty creek that ran through our property held fish. Or could hold fish. He had seen a few minnows hanging out in the shade of the culvert one hot day and decided that, yes, though ours was an intermittent creek—some summers it dried up completely—it was part of a great drainage basin. It was a feeder creek for Bear Creek, which fed the Embarrass River, which met up with the Wolf, which flowed into Lake Poygan, which slid into Lake Winneconne, which joined up with Butte des Morts, which flowed into Winnebago, which spilled off into the Fox River, which flowed north—*North, goddammit, north! Can you believe it? The only river in North America that flows north*—up to Green Bay, where it became Lake Michigan, which ultimately joined the St. Lawrence River, which joined the mighty Atlantic, which was one ocean of four, but *Look,* he'd say. *Do you see any boundaries? In all of that water, do you see any boundaries? No, you don't. It's all one ocean, it's all con-*

nected. That creek out there—he'd jab his finger out toward our woods—*it's part of the Atlantic Ocean if you think about it. We could be catching tuna out there some day. Or eel. Or albacore!*

This exuberance of our father was not unexpected. His capacity for great dreams was not yet exhausted. His belief in the brotherhood of fish—that we could hook an albacore in our creek—was greater than his belief in the brotherhood of man. This confused us, but it should not have. Leaps of faith were not without pitfalls, and though our father, trained as a biologist, subjected to the rigors of Navy discipline, wanted to believe there was a logic to his leaps, they were leaps all the same. Some hurdles of logic he cleared; others he didn't. That a sea bass could make its way upstream, past locks and dams and predatory birds and a drastic change in its environment's saline content, and eventually find its way into our backyard was more believable to him than the notion that all men were brothers under the skin. We'd left the suburbs because they'd gotten ugly, and with more people fleeing to them they were apt to get uglier. A man who dealt with people all day, our father wanted to get away from people. This put him at odds with his adopted religion, but Catholicism itself is a bundle of contradictions and—at least as it is practiced in America—quite tolerant of hypocrisy. That whole notion of "practicing Catholic" appealed to him. You were never a perfect Catholic; you were always practicing, always falling a little short, and with a wink and a nod and a few Our Fathers and Hail Marys you were back on the schneid. Al Capone, our father was sure, was a very good Catholic when he wasn't killing people.

When our father married our mother, he'd gone from being an agnostic to being an indifferent Catholic, lapsed almost from the moment of his First Communion. But then a strange thing happened. After we were born he transformed himself into a Super-Catholic, the SC emblazoned on his chest. He wore a scapular, a St. Christopher medal, joined the Loyal Order of Moose, had a St. Christopher statue mounted on his station wagon's dash, put up crucifixes in our rooms. He kept prayer cards in his wallet, a rosary in his Dopp kit. He loved St. Christopher, patron saint of travelers and peddlers. Years later, our father never forgave Rome for taking St. Christopher off its official saints list. And for the flimsiest of reasons—just because the famous ferrying never happened? "So what?" said our father. "None of it is true. It's all stories. You think that sliver of wood in the glass compass they have us kiss on Good Friday is a piece of the true Cross? Give me a break." But he believed in that, too, just as he believed in the Shroud of Turin and Mary of Lourdes and Fatima and transubstantiation and the stigmata and the forgiveness of sins and life everlasting. What he loved was ritual. The belief in belief. He loved the Latin Mass, with its chanted Kyries and its incense and the priest at the altar with his back to the parishioners. A clear chain of being—God outside, above and behind the church spires, the priest at the altar, the parishioners in their pews, the mothers in the back with the whiny little ones, and ushers moving among the faithful, directing traffic, taking up the collection, bringing up the gifts, selling the Sunday paper on the steps of the church afterward. Our father liked the idea of being one of God's ushers—solemn, serene, in charge. A universe that made sense, that was orderly. He saw all that slipping away after Vatican II. The handholding, guitar-playing "Kumbaya shit"—he didn't trust it. A garrulous man, our father was uncomfortable with the rite of peace. He believed in hierarchy, and this new equality among the community baffled him. Still he believed, and what he believed, we believed, at least for a while.

So we built a pond where we had a marsh. This was not quite Moses striking the rock to get the water to flow in the desert, but it was along the lines of Ponce de León searching for the Fountain of Youth, or any number of French voyagers seeking the famed Northwest Passage. Our father, like the King of Spain or France, had entrusted Wally and Ike, eager minions, boys young enough to thrill to the chase, to find the spring that he believed issued there. It would be a burbling beneath the marsh grass, he believed. He would have liked to have found it coming out in a pool surrounded by granite rocks, but there were no rocks in the marsh. So he told the boys, "Just look for the water under the grass," and off they went in their Wellingtons, canteens on their backs, slathered in deet to keep away mosquitoes.

They never found a thing, but our father believed it was there anyway, and borrowing a backhoe and a bulldozer, he dug a small lake in the marsh's middle. It kept turning back to marsh, but no matter. Someday there would be geese and ducks and walleye and northern pike and bass—largemouth and smallmouth—and bluegill and perch and sunfish and gar and maybe—who knew?—in the fullness of time we might be fishing for muskies, forty-eight-inch, sixty-four-pound fish we would land on treble hooks and deertail lures. It was all a matter of believing.

This was particularly true when our father lost his job. Without telling us, he'd changed companies, only it turned out the new company didn't need him like he (and they) thought they might, and until our father could catch on with Dinkwater Chemical again, or with a more established competitor, things were going to be tight around our house. Things had always been tight anyway, nine people on a salesman's salary, but it was worse now. How much worse we would find out soon enough, though our parents strove mightily to conceal it from us. The extent of the damage to our family's finances, the resultant belt tightening, the blows to our father's self-esteem, the hits our parents' marriage took—we were told none of this. We were instead led to believe that our father was traveling less because of a "restructuring" of the company. We were also led to believe that casseroles, served six nights a week, were not an austerity measure but a move calculated to improve our diet.

At the risk of insulting the great chefs of Europe, there is no finer culinary art than that practiced in large midwestern families whereby the "chief cook and bottle washer" (our father's phrase for our mother) makes one pound of beef or two cans of tuna serve nine people. And makes them believe they are eating something good and special and different every night. Casseroles. We ate thousands of them, in seemingly endless variations: tomato or cream of mushroom soup, elbow, flat, or spaghetti noodles, meat or fish (fish for the mushroom soup; the promiscuous burger went with anything).

It was belief that kept us eating those casseroles. Belief that what our parents told us was true. That everybody ate like this, glops of casserole mounded high on our plates. That our father wasn't spending his time at the Dog Out, however glazed his eyes and addled his walk when he finally got home, late in the evenings, when the younger kids were already in bed. Belief that things between our parents weren't getting worse, their "discussions" more heated, that our mother's patience with our father wasn't wearing thin even as she worried about him, about them, about us. We were better off not knowing that our father had lost his job. If we believed all was well, all was well.

I think Dorie is counting on this same culture of belief being present in me. Alas, she is right. My need to believe in Dorie is greater than my doubts. The diaphragm, the packed nightie—surely there's an explanation. I am my father's, my mother's son. I am cursed with faith.

When things looked particularly bleak—the year I turned sixteen our father was out of work eleven months—our father was still trying to get us to believe. To stretch the family food budget, he announced, he was making stone soup. Ike had found a large, irregularly shaped hunk of granite that spring during the annual rock gleaning, and our father started to boil that in a huge soup kettle half-filled with water. "This is going to take a while," he said. "Rocks take forever to cook. Go do your chores."

We were suspicious, determined to find out what the trick was.

Our father added salt, pepper, cut up a few carrots, stirred. He read our minds. "There's no trick," he said. "It's a rock." He held up a stalk of celery. "I'll add this and some garlic. You want to watch? Rocks don't do anything exciting when they cook. They don't turn red like lobsters or split open like clams. They don't get bigger or much smaller."

"So why are you cooking it?" asked Peg Leg Meg.

"Minerals," said our father. "The minerals leach into the water and make the broth. It'll be the main source of our vitamins and minerals tonight."

"I don't believe you."

"Come take a look." Our father brought a kitchen chair up to the stove. We took turns peering over the side. There was a scummy froth on the surface and cloudy water beneath.

"Looks like it's going to be a pretty thin soup," said Ernie.

"Well, it's all we've got. You know how it is in this family. We make do with what we've got. Now go do your chores unless you think watching a rock cook is interesting."

We went outside. Sheep, the cattle, the horses. Ran water in the troughs, distributed hay, watched for a while to see if Pat and Mike would copulate. Mike's doohickey (our mother preferred this word over *dong,* Tony Dederoff's term) was amazing in its boa constrictor–like turgidity, and even though Pat was not interested, Mike's interest rarely waned. A mating dance involving hooves and a snake that long deserved some attention.

We watched for a while—Pat shaking her head *No way, Jose* as Mike nuzzled her flanks—and wondered if this was how things were these days between our parents. Then Robert Aaron and I climbed up the aerial. We'd recently discovered that climbing the aerial got you on the roof. Up there we felt rather lordly, the rest of the household literally beneath us, and all the farm spread out before us. It was way cooler than the tree house, which we'd outgrown, and we got a thrill out of putting something so unremarkable as a roof to a new and almost magical use. We were hiding out in plain sight.

"You think size matters?" I asked Robert Aaron, pursuing a recent topic of debate in the locker room. The possessors of big doohickeys said size was the only thing that mattered; those of us on the short end of the stick, as it were, thought that wasn't the case, but we owned no experiences that would allow us to mount a counterargument (nor much of anything else). Dorie by this time was dating Calvin Brodhaus, a wrestler who'd won sectionals and took third at state wrestling at one hundred and seventy-three pounds. He claimed he got down to weight by filling Dorie up with his jism. Even if it was just locker-room talk, and I wanted to believe that was all it was, I knew right then I didn't stand a chance, would never stand a chance, with Dorie Braun.

"Ask Cinderella," said Robert Aaron, who was flicking pebbles off the roof. "When she first started seeing Okie that was the word—that he was the owner of a big dong. See what she says now. How important a big dong is once you're already knocked up."

We would never ask Cinderella. Since her wedding she'd been walking around all hangdog, like getting married and carrying a child were the exact opposite of the greatest happiness she could experience, which was what our mother told us it should be. But it was an unhappy wedding, Cinderella's. It was like she'd gotten to the doorway of the room where all the secrets are kept and what she'd found was a big empty sadness, and that sadness had seeped into the center of her being. The look on her face was that of someone who'd just taken a blow to the stomach, or eaten a bad bit of beef.

"Maybe it's just the morning sickness. It's supposed to make you feel awful." I was wondering two things: what it was like having a baby inside you, and how those pebbles had gotten on the roof. Balls and Frisbees were up there, too, but you could account for those. But the pebbles, and that baby that was now distending our sister's belly—these were mysteries.

"Mom says she's far enough along she shouldn't be having morning sickness anymore. Christ, Emcee, she's big as a fucking house. She looks like she doesn't know what hit her."

I didn't know either, but I had an inkling. Those twin sons of a Catholic childhood, guilt and grief, had taken up residence in Cinderella's heart. She had done something unfettered and free, something that she had wanted to do (though perhaps also the result of one of those "if you really loved me" scams), something that felt good (though from what Cinderella let drop in idle moments that wasn't necessarily a sure thing, either), and the consequences had been almost immediate. God was punishing her. She had liked sex (maybe), or at least had thought it would get her something she wanted, and it had backfired. She would take it all back if she could, but it was too late. Those nuns had another success story: another woman—a girl, really—who was terrified of sex, of her own body and what it had done.

"She fell for that boy's promises hook, line, and sinker," we overheard our mother say on the phone to Matty Keillor. "Belief in a boy's promises is a terrible thing." I thought of Dorie right then—what had Calvin Brodhaus promised her? I didn't want to think about it, but I did anyway. Especially when I heard that Dorie, too, had gotten knocked up—she was all of, what, seventeen?—and though she didn't keep the baby (and Calvin was an SOB, disavowing any responsibility while bragging about how he did it), by the following spring Dorie was gone, off to Chicago, some said, and it would be a good decade and a half before I would see her again. The only thing she told me about that time was that she was young and stupid and that falling for a guy hook, line, and sinker was something she would never, ever do again.

Hook, line, and sinker—another of our father's phrases. He said it without cynicism, without despair. If the bait was good, the fish bit. They might know a hook was buried under that worm, might know they were going to be reeled in, no matter. The attraction of the bait, the promise of what's to come is too great. They block out consequences, the surety of their own death. They mouth the bait, suck it down, gorge themselves, and the hook buries itself deep in their gullets. It happens with people, too. We are driven like salmon up the river of our desires.

This may be a uniquely American phenomenon. Researchers have looked into the kinds of advertising that were used in the nineteenth century to lure people to the States: flyers that talked about gold lining the streets, posters claiming that farmers needed only to throw seeds at the ground, not even clearing it, and bumper crops of corn and wheat would emerge. Everyone was a millionaire, everyone owned his own business. Work was plentiful, land cheap and fertile, streets immaculate. It was a country without night pans, without offal, a nation of indoor plumbing and hot and cold running knockwurst. A place where every dream pursued was a dream realized. The researchers came up with the theory that America was settled by, therefore, and we are the descendants of, people disposed to believe the claims of advertising.

It was a two-way street for our father. For people to fall for something hook, line, and sinker you needed to offer them something they could believe in. Presentation was everything. You had to believe in the efficacy of what you were selling. Before you sold to anybody else, you had to sell it to, and believe it, yourself. Or at least believe that you believed. Our father had a phrase for that, too: word, line, and verse. You were swearing to the truth of what you were saying. *You don't believe me? God's honest truth. You could look it up, word, line, and verse.*

So it was with the stone soup. A part of us believed our father was cooking stone soup because a part of our father believed it, too. When we climbed down from the roof and came back inside along with everyone else, there it was, a pot of soup, and sitting on the counter was the stone, still steaming. We gaped.

"Just took it out," said our father. "Wash yourselves, we'll eat in a few minutes."

Our father served us. "A key ingredient of stone soup is the stone itself," he said. "You don't get this richness without the granite. Limestone is good, too. So's feldspar." He looked around the table at us. "God's honest truth. Word, line, and verse."

"Wally," said our mother. "Tell them."

Our father kept ladling. "In the Second World War there was a soldier who got separated from his company. He ended up in a small village ravaged by the fighting as it had gone back and forth, and he had no food. There wasn't much to be had in the village, either. He was hungry. Every door he knocked on he got the same answer: Sorry, no food. One woman gave him a big soup pot, however, and in the village square he built a fire and filled the pot with water. He washed off a chunk of rock that had been blasted from the village wall and put that in the pot. A woman came out to watch him. 'What are you making?' she asked. 'Stone soup,' said the soldier, stirring. 'It's a little thin, but a carrot might help.' 'I think I have a carrot,' said the woman and brought one back with her. An old man came by and asked, 'What are you making?' and the soldier said, 'Stone soup. So far I have the stone and a carrot, but some celery would be nice.' 'I think I know where I can find some celery,' said the old man. And so it went. One after another of the villagers came by, asking the soldier what he was cooking, and to each the soldier said, 'I'm making stone soup, and it's good, but you know what would make it just a little better?' and he would name another ingredient, and one by one the villagers, who could not feed the soldier or themselves, brought the necessary ingredients: flour, potatoes, tomatoes, salt, a chicken, onions, leeks, more carrots, garlic, pepper, a bit of bacon, a hunk of ham. To make room, the soldier took out the stone and kept adding ingredients, and the village and the soldier that night ate very, very well." Our father looked around the table, pausing to fix each of us with his gaze. He'd been drinking while we'd been out; his gaze was a little wobbly, his eyes glassy. "That's the way the story goes. Word, line, and verse. Now lately I've been hearing things about this family. Things about your sister. Things about my job. About my not having a job. Things I don't want people repeating. What gets said in this family stays here. Nobody in this family goes it alone. We are Czabeks. Never forget that. What are we?"

"Czabeks," we said.

"What was that name again? I don't think I heard you."

"Czabeks!" we said.

Our father went into the singsong of a drill instructor. "I can't *hear* you."

"*CZABEKS!!!*" we yelled.

"That's better," said our father. "Never forget that. We are Czabeks. Count on it. Believe it."

"Hook, line, and sinker," said Robert Aaron.

"Word, line, and verse," I echoed.

"I'll pretend I didn't hear that," said our father.

17. Odysseus in Later Life

THE DEMOCRACY OF FAILURE

I head down the field carrying a flashlight. I've drunk enough to have a buzz going, and I'm wondering if it's going to be the same old same old when I rejoin my siblings. It's already the same old same old with Dorie, but I'm not sure what to do about that.

In the lower part of the field, rising out of the scrub trees and marsh grass so pale it looks translucent, Ike's tepee eerily appears like a ghost from another century. It's the real thing, this tepee. Ike cut and trimmed the twenty-foot poles himself, cut and stitched the sailcloth, learned how to lash the poles, how to wrap the cloth so there's a smoke hole, and how to tie in a drip ring so the tepee stays dry even in a downpour. Deer ribs worked through slits in the overlap hold shut the entrance. Even though frost is settling, inside it's toasty. You can see the smoke rising from inside, hear the hum of the gas burner.

If there's a protocol for knocking on a tepee, no one's informed me what it is, so I just lift the flap and scoot inside.

"Speak of the devil," shouts Ernie. "Welcome aboard." He waggles his beer bottle. If he hurt himself falling off the roof, he's since self-medicated to where pain has no hold on him. "May you be in heaven half an hour before the devil knows you're dead."

I don't bother pointing out the contradiction. I sit down on a pile of woolen blankets. Underneath are straw and pine boughs. Ike says four couples could sleep here comfortably, though it's usually just him, Sam, and their children. Wally Jr. is sitting on "the couch"—two bales of straw covered by a tarp and a horse blanket. Meg and Ernie are next to me, Robert Aaron is across the way, sharing a bearskin rug with Ike. Between us a good-size fire blazes in a fire ring dug six inches deep and banked with granite rocks. Off to one side is the space heater, set on low. Everyone's face is a soft yellow-orange.

"Hail, hail, the gang's all here," sings out Ernie.

"No Cinderella," says Meg.

"No, no Cinderella," says Wally Jr. "We've established that. Next topic."

"I just hope it's going to be a nice day tomorrow," Ernie says, fishing in the cooler for another beer. "They'll cancel the balloon ride if the weather's not perfect, right?" He looks at me. I was the one who set up the balloon ride, contacting an outfit that would be willing to go up this early in the year, when the winds are unpredictable if not downright freakish.

"We're not going to decide anything tonight, are we?" I say. "I mean, if I just ask point-blank, 'What's going to happen with Mom and Dad the next couple of years?' nobody has an answer, right?"

Wally Jr. says, "Well, for starters, they could keel over tomorrow. I suppose then all our problems are solved."

Meg says, "Or they could live twenty more years, the last eighteen of them in Depends."

"Ish, man, I don't want to think about that."

"Who does, Ernie? But it's possible. And then what? Who's going to take care of Mom and Dad in their old age? You?"

"Maybe they've got a plan," Ernie says. "Maybe they've got it all worked out."

"This is Mom and Dad we're talking about," Meg says. "Their idea of a plan is a wish and a promise and a hope for the best."

"Dad believes in planning."

"Dad believes in miracles. And thinking about this stuff just makes Mom sad."

"It makes me sad, too," says Ernie.

"But that's not a reason not to think about it!" shouts Meg. "You want to wait till this problem comes up and bites you on the ass?"

"Whoa, whoa, what got into you?" Wally Jr. says. "Do we need to take some of Ernie's beer and shovel it down you?"

"No," Meg says very evenly, gritting her teeth, "we need to think about Mom and Dad. Because if *we* don't have anything worked out, and *they* don't have anything worked out, then we're going to have this same meeting in a few years, only with a much greater sense of urgency, and I will tell you all something now—I am not going to be the default and fallback position for all of you once you've decided Mom and Dad are too much to handle."

"Whoa, whoa, whoa," says Wally Jr. "Let's start at the beginning."

"The beginning?" Meg says. "What beginning? We're talking about an ending here."

And indeed we are. Which is why we are having trouble talking about it. Meg lays it out for us, what we are looking at, what anyone with parents in their declining years is looking at: independent living with some in-home care, be it in-home aides or visiting nurses, or something more along the line of assisted-living facilities, such as condominiums for the elderly, or group homes, or further down the road, nursing homes or hospices. Depending on our parents' health and finances, our finances, and what kind (if any) of estate planning our parents have done or are willing to do, we are looking at a whole host of possibilities and permutations.

"The real question here," Meg says, "is what kind of care would be best for them."

Everyone is silent. We know what kind of care would be best for them. We grew up with that kind of care. We grew up with Nomi. With Artu, too, though there was always the pretext that he kept up his own apartment. Our mother cared for Nomi until she died. And after Nomi died, Artu moved to his own apartment in a town five miles away and "dropped by" four or five nights a week until he, too, passed away. And when Grandma and Grandpa Cza-Cza's minds and bodies failed them, they, too, moved in with our parents. They'd never liked our mother, had worked actively against our father marrying that smoldering sexpot of a woman, but when dementia and heart attacks felled them, they were living with our parents, which is to say they were living with our mother since our father was away 80 percent of the time. Our mother, making sure they took their pills and got dressed in the morning and undressed at night. Making sure they bathed regularly, and when they couldn't manage that, bathing them herself. Combing their hair and shaving them. Feeding them, wiping their chins, changing their sheets, washing them up after their accidents, rolling them to one side of the bed and scrubbing the shit out of the mattress. "You don't know what it's like," our mother said to us, "lifting up an eighty-nine-year-old man's scrotum to clean beneath his testicles after he's soiled himself. And he's telling you not to touch him, he likes the smell of fresh bread in the morning."

"So," says Meg, looking from one of us to the next, pleased she's finally raised the Big Topic. "Who wants to volunteer? How shall we handle this? Who takes them first? Do we cast lots? Take turns—yearlong residencies with Mom and Dad—or do we pony up and pay one of us to take on sole responsibility? Or . . . or what, exactly?"

Ernie says, "I always kind of thought Mom and Dad would stay right here."

My thoughts exactly, but Meg is on to that like white on rice. "That's a lovely thought, Ernie, and I'd like to think so, too. But it still begs the question, who's going to look after them? Are you going to move here from Eau Claire? Is Emcee going to move here from Milwaukee? Robert Aaron from Racine?"

Wally Jr. says, "Claire and me live right up the hill."

"So you're volunteering?"

"No, I'm just saying Claire and me live right up the hill. We could look in on them."

"Lovely. And what happens when 'looking in on them' isn't enough? Are you ready to be the full-time caretaker? Do we hire a nurse? Move them to foster care? A nursing home? We're talking fifty, sixty thousand dollars a year for that. I checked. And the level of care—you know this, don't you?—varies from decent to despicable. You want round-the-clock care? Round-the-clock care my ass. In some of those places you're lucky if they turn you over every couple of hours so you don't get bedsores. 'Hey, Mom, how's it going?' 'Oh, fine, honey, no bedsores this week.' How's that for quality of life? Even a group home or assisted-living facility is going to cost twenty to forty thousand, depending on the situation. Heartland Home for the Elders—that's right here in town—runs thirty-eight thousand a pop. And who, exactly, is going to pay for that? What, we sell the farm? Chop up their assets, make them look poor? Then they'll qualify for Medicaid, and get warehoused with the rest of the dead and the dying?"

"Okay, okay," says Wally Jr. "We got a problem. Why are you getting so worked up about this? We'll figure something out."

"No," says Meg. "We won't 'figure something out.' That's not the way it works in this family and you know it. You boys are going to take a powder—just like Dad. You're going to complain about your jobs, the distance you'd have to travel, the lack of space in your houses, and it's all going to fall on me. I'll end up 'figuring something out,' and you'll all applaud me while your lives go on as before and mine goes right down the toilet!"

I have never heard Meg talk like this. The reason is simple: I was never around to hear her, and when I was around, I wasn't listening. None of us boys were. We had grown up in a male-centered family, inherited our perceptions of the world from our father. Men went off and did things. Our task, our responsibility, was to find new territory to strike off into. Even if we floundered, even if we failed, at least, by God, we'd gone off in new directions. And if it seemed too overwhelming to reinvent ourselves for the sake of that journey, if we were shaky in our manhood, well, there was always drink to give us courage. Maybe that's why we boys went bad all in a rush. We found alcohol, all in a rush.

The girls, we thought, had it easy. Freed from expectations of success and failure, they needed only to absorb, not flounder. We thought we understood Peg Leg Meg and Cinderella. No mystery there. We could ignore them freely. Slighted, they became slight. Insubstantial. Never mind that, as it was by our mother, the real burden of family was borne by them. Never mind that Meg was right and it was all going to fall on her. Our sisters, we liked to believe, were transparent. And perhaps our greatest act of hubris as boys was pretending we weren't.

So okay, the irony mobile has just pulled into our campsite. All those years we've agreed to disagree, and now that we need to pull together on something we find ourselves looking around at each other, wondering if it's possible. Ike feeds sticks to the fire. They crackle and burn, the smoke sucked up the lodgepoles and into the sky. Nobody says anything for a while.

Wally Jr., though, likes nothing better than beating a dead horse. "What about Cinderella?" he asks, and Ernie seconds it. "Yeah, what about Cinderella?"

I expect Meg to explode with exasperation again, but this time she's calm. "What about Cinderella? I don't know, what about her? You tell me."

The rebuke is so light it's crushing. The fact is, you cannot count on Cinderella. You can pray for Cinderella, you can feel bad for her, but you cannot count on her. She is our family's martyr, and martyrdom is a full-time occupation. No question, her travails are many and various, and many of them quite real—a long marriage to an abusive husband, ovarian cysts, a bout with breast cancer that required the removal of part of a breast—and as she was going through them we should have been kinder, more sympathetic. No doubt we would have felt sorrier for her had the word *martyr* not been tattooed on her forehead. At family get-togethers she spent her time sighing and making game little grins—yes, yes, I've been absolutely steamrollered by life, but aren't I brave for being one of life's bowling pins? It's hard empathizing with someone so enthusiastically long-suffering.

She was the first out of the nest, and desperate to prove she was happy. We wanted to believe she was. So did she. For a long time things took place under a cloak of silence and darkness, and neither she nor we were willing to lift the veil. And once it became obvious how awful it was, we were angry with her for allowing it to happen. She seemed to be cooperating in her own martyrdom, and for this we could not forgive her. At birthdays, at Christmas and Thanksgiving, she would show up in her habitual posture, pasty-faced, with pinched-in shoulders and an uncertain smile. Oh, woe is me. We couldn't stand it.

Here was something on which we could all agree—Cinderella had given up. We could put it in fairy-tale terms. Two minutes after midnight and she's sitting in a field on her ass, a smashed pumpkin and a litter of mice at her feet. And unlike the fairy tale, her prince is a shit and her fairy godmother a fraud. It wasn't only a kiss she gave the prince at midnight. The prince looks at the glass slipper as a memento of a memorable hump and pockets it. Later it falls off the mantel and breaks, and the prince shrugs. What was she doing with that ridiculous footwear in the first place? Those things made her walk funny. The remaining slipper Cinderella keeps wearing in the vain hope that the prince will notice the peasant with the obvious limp and take pity on her. But the prince's penis is happy elsewhere now, and what need has he of a limping, knocked-up strumpet? Oh, and did we forget to mention, he wasn't really a prince? He was the village goatherd, but the same idiot story that had her believing pumpkins were carriages and mice were horses and footmen transformed this dung-smelling, mead-swilling lout into a handsome prince. If you only closed your eyes and looked through the slits, and if the backlighting was just right, why . . .

Okay, so she didn't give up. She did something worse. She continued to believe. Kept limping around in that slipper until it broke and her foot got gashed and full of slivers. Then she wrapped the foot and kept limping around on the bloody bandage. How it played out is this: We were all at the Round 'Em Up (their name), the Drink Beer for Christ Festival (our name) that St. Genevieve's put on every summer to help retire the parish's debt. We were moseying through the craft tent, putting down chances for the raffle (first prize—a whole side of beef), trying our luck at the Ping-Pong ball throw, taking kids on the whirligig ride and the Ferris wheel, when we heard a shriek that sounded like an angel had been stabbed right in the middle of an orgasm.

You could hear it over the merry-go-round calliope, over the bark of the midway's hucksters, over the warbling of the beer tent's polka music, over the entire general din of the fairgrounds. It stopped everything. A single shriek that made your hair stand on end and your toes shrink inside your shoes. My God, what had happened? For a moment everyone paused. Then we all came running. We knew. Even as we ran, we knew. As Czabeks gathered from the far corners of the fairgrounds, from the hamburger stand and the pig rassle, from the carnival midway and the dyspeptic goldfish toss, we knew. We got the children off to one side so they wouldn't see. Cinderella's kids in particular. "What is it? What's happened to Mommy?" the youngest asked. The older ones knew. Even without knowing they knew. They wore on their faces their terrible knowledge. Their eyes had that preternatural look about them of animals who smell smoke in the forest even without knowing it's fire.

We got them away, we kept them from seeing, but they knew. The oldest, Okie II, broke away from the pack, and he saw what the rest of us, gathered in a loose semicircle in the beer tent, also saw. His father sitting on a wooden folding chair with a twenty-two-year-old woman on his lap. The woman bore him no relation though she might eventually bear his child. His eyes were closed and his knees were going up and down as though the music were still playing, as though he were keeping time to a beat only he could hear. Batta-bing, batta-bing went the melody. Batta-bing, batta-bing went Okie's stubby fingers on the woman's thighs.

The woman's name was Kathy Neesmer, and she was pretty if you liked big yellow hair and blue eye shadow and chipmunk cheeks and a slutty pout that years from now would make her look as dyspeptic and unhappy as the goldfish. Cinderella looked stricken. Her face had caved in after her scream, and she looked like her namesake at about midnight plus thirty seconds. So this was her prince? This beery galoot feeling up a coarse-skinned strumpet?

Okie II ran away crying. Cinderella's shoulders collapsed. She was shaking and crying into herself. Okie Sr. was nonchalant. "What?" he was saying. "Can't a man relax on a Saturday afternoon without somebody making a federal case out of it?"

"What is it, Okie honey? What's wrong?" Kathy Neesmer asked.

"My wife," replied Okie. "I guess we got her all bent out of shape."

Sarah let loose with another wave of caterwauling. Okie's fingers resumed their little drumbeat on Kathy Neesmer's thigh. "Well," he proclaimed to nobody in particular, "if she knows, she knows—that's the price of admission, right, babe?"

Wally Jr. stepped forward. He was responding to something Okie'd already said. "Bent?" Wally Jr. seethed, his fists rising. "I'll give you *bent,* you fucker."

"Wally, don't!" Cinderella wailed.

"What, are you going to punch me or something?"

"Or something," said Wally Jr., and his fist landed in the middle of Okie's face before Kathy Neesmer could get off his lap. You could hear the nose breaking even before the blood burst from it.

"Okie, Okie honey! Are you okay?" asked Kathy Neesmer, who'd spilled over backward with Okie and was now bent over him. Okie, her hero. Okie didn't try to get up. Wally Jr. was still standing over him, fists at the ready, daring him to. Tony Dederoff and his Dairyland Dreamers launched themselves into a fast polka, the musical equivalent of "Okay, everybody, show's over," and people went back to whirling away. It was a strange tableau. As a scene it lasted maybe two minutes, but as I stood there, it seemed to take on the arrested timelessness of a Brueghel painting: the dancers' nervous, sweaty smiles, the blotches of color, the laid-out Okie, the attendant Kathy, Cinderella standing close by, her arms crossed over her sunken chest, hollow-eyed and crying, waiting for her chance to give aid and comfort to the enemy. Had we not led her away, I believe she might have gone to him, too, and tried to elbow aside the woman who'd already replaced her. Oh, her fallen knight! He needed her!

That night we had a family powwow and decided to pursue that benighted Vietnam strategy of destroying the village in order to save it. If

Cinderella would agree to leave Okie, we'd each take one of her children while she put her life back together. If Cinderella couldn't do it, we would call Social Services and charge her and Okie with being unfit parents. We'd been in their house—no food, no hot water, a gas heater in the middle of the living room for heat. Okie had money for beer and women but nothing for his own family. Robert Aaron, a few years out of college, was the assistant director of social services for a county in central Wisconsin. He knew the ropes.

"You'd do that to me?" asked Cinderella.

"We'd do that to you to save the kids, yes," replied Robert Aaron. We couldn't tell if Cinderella was listening or not. Her face wore the shocked, vacant expression of someone whose interior regions are empty.

"Does it have to be this way?" asked our mother.

"Yes, it has to be this way," said Robert Aaron. "Otherwise, the county steps in and the kids will be placed in foster homes and we won't have any say in the matter at all."

"I don't believe you," said Cinderella.

"Try me," said Robert Aaron.

Our father just kept shaking his head. Our mother bit back tears. They were mortified. Had our parents really believed that in moving the family to the country they would be able to deliver us from evil? Yes.

They were wrong. But we understood. We had wanted to believe it ourselves.

Is it any wonder that later, when she was making her own late bid for happiness with Mel, we couldn't bend our minds around the thought that earlier our sister had relished her martyrdom? How dare she *not* be a victim now? Even though Mel is a relatively nice guy, seems genuinely to care for her, we call him the Prince, as though he had inherited the title worn by the dung-covered village goatherd. Cinderella is a failure in our family—a failure at being happy, a failure at being a victim. She became our sacrificial offering. We turned our backs on her, leaving her to her fate, then we intervened, landing on her like a pile of bricks. Did we do that because we believed that maybe then fate would, if not smile, at least be lenient with us?

Or did we beat up on her because she was like our father, and because we could?

———

Habitual action (whether it's martyrdom or sales)—is it method or madness? I wondered about our father, going to bed every night in a new place, waking up bewildered. Did things seem real if every room he slept in looked different from every other, yet vaguely familiar? Timbered north woods motel rooms or functional HoJos. Hotels with potted palms in the lobby, or drive-up rooms with railed balconies overlooking pine trees and dumpsters.

Maybe it didn't matter if he knew where or who he was. Maybe he evaporated, became a traveling factotum of his company, and therefore became something larger and more peaceful than he was with us. Maybe in his being on the road all those years, his strongest connection between himself and his steering wheel, the separation between wife and family became complete, and returning to what he nominally called home was a burden.

Odysseus spent all those years trying to get back to Penelope, but when he does, his story's over. While he's on the road, his story is still being written. It's still possible for anything to happen. We have no account of Odysseus in later life. Maybe he hated it. Maybe at home, steering cattle through a field with his sword beat into a plowshare, he longed for the sea the way he longed for home when he was away from it. That could certainly be said of our father. He loved the idea of home, of family, but he was uncomfortable in our presence.

So maybe the years of our father's travel became his cocoon against us, against the world. In the world but shielded from it. His car was his shield, bright and blazing in the sun. He identified with it, just as he identified with the company he worked for. It was a company car and he was a company man, and though we knew he loved us, his loyalty lay elsewhere. We failed to recognize that. When he came home, we were the unexpected, the unscheduled, the unplanned moil and roil of everyday life, most of which had been going on without him. His routine protected him from that. No wonder he took such care getting ready, packing his sample cases and testing kits, checking his weekly planner, selecting his shirts, his ties. He was packing for a war. In the back of the station wagon he kept two coolers, one for beer (and fish on ice) and one for foodstuffs—cheese, sausages, sardines, sliced ham and polenta, a jar of pickles, a loaf of bread, some Miracle Whip and mustard. Also riding in the back were five-gallon pails of sample product, plastic sample bags, sample jars, a sample briefcase, and a sample kit that he'd outfitted as a traveling bar with bottles of gin, vermouth, bourbon, and brandy.

This was our father, loaded for bear, off to the war.

His days had a routine to them, too. Drive all night, check into a motel, spruce up, be at the mill in time for midmorning meetings he'd set up two or even three weeks previously. If he was cold-calling, sweet-talk the secretary, meet the floor manager, the shop supervisor, try to set up a lunch. If it was an established account, or he was running a trial, be ready to ask about the kids, the wife, the fishing, the hunting, the high school football team, the Packers. Be ready with the mimeographed jokes, either to give or to receive. Have the belly laugh on hand. Have the patter down, then set up your trial, take your samples, do lunch, run the trial, take more samples, meet with the in-house biologists, the mill-wright, the shift foreman. Do meetings, conferences, presentations, dinner. Take the manager fishing. Be ready, all the time: patter, chatter, laugh. Big laugh. Booming laugh. Ha. Ha. Hahahahahahaha. Commiserate. *Sonsabitches.* Congratulate. *Attaboy.* Be quick with the quip, the smile, the grin, the nod, the wink, the tab. Always, always get the tab. After getting back to the motel, call Susan. The kids are already in bed. This is the check-in phone call. The "I miss you" phone call. Go over the day, stare at the light switch while you hear about the kids' and Susan's day. Feel the alcohol curling in behind your eyes. Squeeze them shut, feel the room gently sway. This is your life, *your life.* After you wish Susan a good night, after you tell her you love her, after you hang up, you make yourself a stiff one and settle in to do expense and lab reports. But the receipts for gas, lunch, and dinner can wait until you get home; you push those into an ever-growing pile. You'll get Emcee and Ike and Wally Jr. to write in the amounts on the blank receipts. You keep track—you know what you spend—and if the booze finds its way onto the dinner bill, well, that's part of the cost of doing business. You set up your field test in the petri dishes, measuring out the samples, putting them in the traveling incubator with the timer that won't bing when it's ready. You make another Rob Roy to help yourself concentrate. Measure, label, sip. You set the timer, wait for the results so you can do a count of how effective this new biocide is.

The weeks pass like this—on the road, selling, meeting, making presentations, drinking, schmoozing, taking a guy out after dinner to catch a few perch or walleye, writing up reports, doing lab work on the weekends and evenings, selling and schmoozing, tossing back shots and beers, selling and schmoozing, the drive from town to town, mill to mill. Paper mostly, a few paint plants—specialty chemicals, forest products division, Dinkwater Chemical, Dinkwater Park, New Jersey. Yeah, New Jersey. Naw, they got no paper mills in Jersey. But they got chemicals, they got plants, they got corn-fed midwestern scientists who know what they're doing. That's what you need—guys who know what they're doing. The guys on the floor at these mills—they know what they're doing. You can work with them. It's their managers and supervisors that you have to put on a different kind of act for. They're the ones you don't get sleep over, making that extra Rob Roy to see you through, your eyes swimming in their bloody sockets. You close your eyes, feel them buzzing in their sockets, your brain seeping into the back of your skull, yet there's this pressure, right above your eyebrows. Five minutes' rest will do you a world of good. Five minutes' peace from staring at the petri dishes with their little blotches of mold you have to count and measure—all that jazz. All that crap. Close your eyes, feel your brain gently buzzing, feel the electric light's glow as a sound, a fluttering by your earlobes, feel the changes in the room's temperature and air pressure through the soft fleshy lobes hanging beneath the ear cartilage. You're a bat, scooping up insects in the night outside just before they fly into the bug zapper. They smell something terrible when they hit the zapper's wires. It's as though their wings are made of petroleum. You dip, you swoop, you're catching them with your open mouth, sensing where they are through the minutest of wing flutters. You swoop out of the night. *Feed me, feed me.* Your brain is a single phrase of need, and your wife, your children are a long ways away.

Our father wakens to the smell of burning plastic. His trial is ruined, a melted blob. The smoke is terrible; the incubator stinks of burning bugs. He pulls it out; the petri dishes look like something that escaped from a Dalí painting. He has two choices: write up the numbers as he thinks they might have come out given what he knows about the products, and hope they don't ask to see the petri dishes, or run the petri dishes again and make arrangements to come back later in the week with the results. The problem is he's in Mosinee right now, in the middle of the state, and his next trial is scheduled for Wednesday and Thursday in Ashland, way up north. He can do it, but it means he'll be getting home Friday night close to midnight, and he'll be surly by the time he arrives, maybe on the downside of a buzz, and to counteract that he'll stop in Banana's or the Dog Out for a pick-me-up, lose track of time, and come home at 2:00 A.M. thoroughly shitfaced. And Susan will be waiting, furious and fuming. Then the kids will be up early, jumping on him, the little ones, anyway, and his head will be pounding, throbbing most likely, and Jesus Christ if it won't be like that all through Saturday and into Sunday, and maybe he'll get five minutes' peace and maybe not, and he can't wait already for next Sunday afternoon and evening to roll around, when he disappears from the family to get ready for the next week's trip, and here it is only early Tuesday morning of the previous week.

We had long suspected that for our father the motels and the bars were familiar, comforting places, with delights both expected and unexpected. He knew what he would find there, and anything out of the ordinary would be a pleasant diversion—the house special, a fellow Navy man at the bar, somebody who knew somebody who knew somebody. He knew how to act in places like these, whereas home was for him a frequently visited foreign country, a place where he knew how to get around but the locals seemed to be speaking another language, and their customs were so, well, *foreign*. Better to drink in your room than to have much to do with them.

Our mother, at times, felt the same way. We had broken her down. The strain of raising us virtually alone was too much for her. There was the financial strain—with so many kids, even if our father had been doing well it would have been tight—but there were the emotional costs, too. What is it like being alone all week, making all the decisions, and then having this man you love, this stranger, come home every weekend to upset the applecart with his flamboyance, his effervescing ideas, his schemes, his drinking? It probably would have been all right if our father had stayed on his high-flying clouds. She could have reasoned, "This is who I married. I knew what he was like from when he first wanted us to get married on TV." But could she keep saying it as our father's great ideas got shot down one by one and he sank into a different kind of abyss? As he kept changing companies, looking for that elusive thing he always wanted: respect.

It was not forthcoming. He had left Dinkwater-Adams because they did not value him enough to give him what he wanted, what they eventually gave to somebody else: territory in Wisconsin where he could buy a farm. At a church social a few years after moving, he ran into a Dinkwater-Adams rep from the northern suburbs of Chicago who now had the territory our father had coveted. He lived in the next town over from us. He had gotten the northeastern Wisconsin territory three months after our father quit the company.

It was the same way with Dinkwater Chemical. And Dewless Chemical and Drydell Chemical—all headquartered in Dinkwater Park, New Jersey. Our father was a company man, but he was not corporate. He loved the company; the company suffered him. Suffered him not because he didn't get results—our father could sell fire extinguishers to Satan—but because he didn't look the part. Or he looked the part from a previous decade. No tailored suit, no razor-cut hairstyle. Our father was fat, he was jowly, he wore Sansabelt trousers and clip-on ties. When we were little and wore clip-ons, this made perfect sense to us. Later they were an embarrassment. They were necessary for him, however, because when you are leaning over two living-room-size steel drums spinning at five thousand feet per second, if a tie end flops onto a drum's surface, you will be yanked into the machine and crushed into pulp in a matter of nanoseconds. With a clip-on tie all you lost was the tie. Over the years our father lost two ties that way, and he'd once seen a man disappear into the rollers, his viscera spurting from him like you'd squeezed a foil packet of ketchup. Even our television-sapped minds could understand that would not be as comical as in the cartoons, where animals were regularly pancaked under steamrollers and walked stiffly and two-dimensionally back to wherever they went to hatch their next scheme.

Still, it looked cheesy. When bolo ties briefly became the fashion, our father went from clip-ons to bolos and never went back. How bolos, with their bullet-weighted dangling strings, were an improvement on safety over the clip-ons was never explained to us. Perhaps he simply loved the look so much he was willing to risk the danger. Or maybe they stayed tucked inside his shirt better. Sartorially, he was clearly siding with the guys on the factory floor, and with the shift managers, most of whom started on the floor and who could make or break his trials for him, but it certainly wasn't the look the Dinks were promoting back in New York and Jersey.

Our father didn't have the right sound for the Dinks, either. He was loud. He laughed easily and often in a voice that could be heard from the shop floor to the shift manager's office. He did not like dirty jokes, and didn't tell them, but he could burst out with that crescendoing, booming laugh when they were told by someone else.

Our father played well in the Midwest. He was as at ease and as welcome on the shop floor as he was in the lab as he was in the manager's office. The managers—floor bosses booted upstairs along about the time their kids had college tuitions due—appreciated him. Our father knew where they liked to eat, and while he was treating them to ribs and beer he asked about their kids, groused with them about OSHA and Indian fishing rights, expressing his political views so that it always seemed he was agreeing with whatever was being said, whether the talk went conservative or libertarian or, occasionally, populist Democrat (but never, never liberal, not even in the early seventies, when conservatism momentarily dipped in popularity). He was one of them, as if on a given Monday they had woken up and decided to go into sales. He even looked like them, a collection of walking bulges, his shirts and pants sagging off him with all the accrued weight of what he'd stuffed into them, including a wallet so fat with business cards and membership cards and oil company credit cards that he had to keep it closed with a rubber band.

It irked the Dinks, I'm sure, that they were being represented by a lout in a bolo tie, and that they were paying him commissions he was sure to blow on fishing tackle and more of those goddamn string ties.

So they gave him shit territories, got him on straight commission while he was building up a territory, then when he had built it up, they cut the commission rate or raised his quota. Eventually they'd take that territory away from him, give it to some young buck straight out of college, and that kid would run it into the ground but look good doing it. So good they'd end up regional sales manager—the guy our father reported to. Our father hated those kids. They couldn't talk jackshit to the guys on the floor, and when it came to selling didn't know their asses from holes in the ground. Meanwhile our father would be given a new shit territory—probably a territory he'd built up earlier, had stripped from him just as it was starting to pay off, then run into the ground by some goon just out of college, and the cycle would repeat itself. It went on like this for years. When our father couldn't stand it any longer he'd quit, go to some other company—usually one that was shaky in its products and/or its distribution—and stay with them for a year, eighteen months, until either the company folded or our father's old boss called, worried about his hemorrhaging territory, and lured our father back with promises of base salary and 12 percent commissions he could only half-deliver on.

It was painful watching this happen. Even when we were too young to understand much, we understood our father was getting a raw deal, and it got worse as he got older, when the Dinks would really rather not have him around to pay him his retirement.

I could see the suits' side of things, too—how could they stomach this paradox? This fat, loud galoot who—damn it—knew how to sell things. It just wasn't right. Imagine, those barbarians taking a shine to this barbarian.

What our father most wanted, as his career wound down and he tired of the nine-hundred-mile, the eighteen-hundred-mile business trips, was to put an end to the grind of it. To keep working, but as an in-house consultant. To be recognized for his many years of loyal service and superior sales figures and to be honored—enshrined, really—in what might be considered the Peddlers' Hall of Fame. A consultancy, to teach the young bucks right out of college *how* to recognize their asses from holes in the ground. To ditch the suit and tie once they checked into their motel—save that for meetings with the Dinks in New Jersey—and to put on a sport shirt and some steel-toed wingtips with comfortable soles. Those three-hundred-dollar Italian numbers that look exquisite in Chicago don't look so hot when they've been soaking in debarking brine for a few hours and have dried wood pulp sticking to them. He'd instruct them to get a fishing license and to keep extra rods and reels in the trunk—or better, strung on special carriers inside the station wagon because you never know who wants to go fishing on his lunch break or after work. He'd tell them to lose the sedan and get a station wagon (or later, a truck or minivan or SUV), because even if you don't have family, it's smart to look like you do, and you need the space for hauling. To lose your East Coast affiliations for sports teams and start getting familiar with the rosters of the Packers, the Vikings, the Bears, and the Lions. And to be prepared to accept some good-natured ribbing on your lack of knowledge of the same.

He'd tell these guys where to stay, what to pack, who to talk to before you talked to "the guy in charge," and who to talk to after. He'd introduce them to the guys on the floor, give them anniversary dates and the wives' names and the kids' birth dates and years in school. What these guys liked to drink and where they liked to eat. He'd explain about CB lingo, how to be the back door for a lead semi, and why it was better to be the back door than the front door, or even to be sandwiched in between, and how it might be wise not to have a handle taken from Shakespeare. Pinhead and Gravy Train were good CB handles. Tybalt and Mercutio were not.

He would explain why the biggest highways were not necessarily the fastest, why 29 was a better bet than the wider, more heavily trafficked 10, with its deer herds that seemed to live by the highway, waiting for cars to leap out at. He would tell them to visit Hayward's Freshwater Fishing Hall of Fame, Rhinelander's Hodag Festival, Portage's Buffalo Chip Throwing Contest. They should enter wagers on ice-out contests, take up deer hunting (easier with a shotgun than with an auto), go to church festivals and tractor pulls. It went without saying to join the Legion if they were eligible, the Kiwanis, the Elk, the Moose.

"This is important," he would tell them. "Pay attention, you might learn something."

He would explain how being on the road was all about attitude. Mind over matter. If you don't mind, it don't matter. (Ba-dum-dum.) Attitude. How to handle the dark nights of the soul. How to roll into a town where you know absolutely nobody and make the town sing your tune.

The miles, the miles, how to fill the empty miles. All that green going past—woods, fields, marshes. White birch, yellow corn. The clover purple in its blooming. Blue lakes, blue skies. White clouds you notice only once in a while. It's a static picture you're driving into, and then it changes. Different formations, different clouds, not fields you're rushing past but trees. After a while you're not moving, the scenery is. The land itself is hurtling past. Astonishment on the faces of the villagers checking their mail once they realize the ground beneath their feet is moving at sixty-seven mph, with them on it, and the car zooming past is actually standing still. You tell the neophyte sales rep about the lazy streaker in Chicago who stood at a rail crossing minus his clothes and flashed the commuter trains that way. "It's all relative," says our father. He won't wait before adding, "Get it? Einstein? The theory of relativity?" The new kids roll their eyes. No doubt to them our father's routines sound old even if they are hearing them for the first time.

Which was part of our father's genius. His jokes, booming laugh, and hail-fellow-well-met schtick played well. The boys out East wanted panache, polish. The people our father called on wanted regularity, someone who looked like he was not from out of town. Our father was a known quantity, right down to his mimeographs of "What to Do in the Event of a Nuclear Explosion: 1. Spread Legs. 2. Place hands on ankles.

3. Bend over. And 4. Kiss your ass good-bye." He could tell the sales rep in training, "The boys in the lab like it if just before a trial you quote Einstein."

"Einstein?"

"Yeah, that one about God not playing dice with the universe. They may be scientists, but they go to church. You want to know a better one to lay on them? 'If we knew what it was we were doing, it would not be called research, would it?' That's Einstein, too. He was into six of one, half a dozen of another if you ask me. That's what relativity's all about—same difference."

"Say again?"

Our father would have a finger to his lips. "Shh. Loose lips sink ships." And drive on, his protégé taking notes, sometimes with question marks after the more inscrutable comments. *Loose lips sink ships? Look up ref.*

And our father would explain to the new guy the salesman's habit of talking to himself: "Sometimes you're just thinking, and it comes out your mouth. It's okay. You're not going crazy. You can only spend so long thinking about your wife and kids, and what you're going to say at the next mill and who you're going to see and where you're going to eat and after a while your mind goes blank." Our father would trail off then, the thought burning away like morning mist in sunlight, his brain a movie screen against which all the projected scenery clips past. He has entered that finite, scrolling universe of the Hamm's beer sign, and he sees the same thing over and over and over. Road, highway, river, sky. Rocks, clouds, fields, trees. Undulating blue, undulating green, undulating black-gray highway. Telephone poles whipping past. Cattails looking like cigars on sticks. Corn and trees a blur, the clouds changing but infrequently. It's like they're not moving and then they have. You blink, come back to yourself. What happened? You check mileage markers, the tenths ticking off, then come to the next whole number and it's been forty-some miles since you last knew where you were. Do the math—it's another seventy-eight miles to the Spotted Heron Motel on Highway 13, where you'll stay the night. Besides the Super 8, the Spotted Heron, the gas station/bait shop, the Dipsy Doodle Diner and Gift Shop, a campground and a couple lodges, the town's nothing. Good people, though. Margie behind the grill will recognize you, flirt with you over the pie, a flirting that won't go anywhere even though there are times you'd like it to. But Margie's stuck with her alcoholic husband just the same as Susan Marie is stuck with hers. Funny how you can see yourself as somebody's alkie husband once you see somebody else's alkie husband, and you find yourself wondering, What the hell is she doing with that loser? And then you think you're that loser, too, only you belong to somebody else, and generally you're able to maintain, and Margie is one of the reasons such a thing is possible. She'll call you Sugar, pour you coffee, and say things like "It's deader'n a doornail in here, sugar. What say we go out back for a quickie?" and you both know she's kidding. She'll go home to Mack, who fixes cars at the garage when he's not drinking under them, daring fate by smoking cherry cigars while he works, and you'll look over your reports in your room, and dull the illicit ache with a couple-three stiff Rob Roys until the room's orange carpet and green bedspread lose their focus and you find yourself wondering what Margie's last name is anyway, and where she might live, and could you find her if you just drove around for a while. You're jogging the keys in your hand when you realize you're being silly. What are the chances that you're going to find Margie at nine o'clock on a Tuesday night just driving around? Then you realize she might still be at the Dipsy Doodle and you could just drive by there, or check out Len's Hideaway. You could use the beer. You could use the fuck. And it's only when your brain utters that word that you realize your need, feel the fuel of the Rob Roys pushing you out the door, wondering what you'll say to her, wondering if your need is so obvious in your face every time you drive up here. Does she see that? Is that why she flirts? She sees your need plain upon your face and wants to do you a kindness? Hopes you'll recognize the need naked on her own face when she talks about a griddle quickie, disguising the obviousness of her intent with its obviousness? A chummy little fuck in a north woods town, two people ministering to each other's needs? She has needs, too, right? Mack with his gin fizzes and cherry cigars is no prize, right? Though what do you have to offer her that's better except maybe you shave, and your tongue isn't littered with bits of tobacco? That's a treat, right, your tongue in her mouth won't leave cigar detritus? And oh, sweet Christ, now you're imagining it plainly, picturing the two of you reclining here, in the Spotted Heron Motel, your home away from home, two whiskeys on the bedside table, the two of you cuddled up post-fuck (you don't even want to think about the lovemaking because you do, you *do* want to think about it), stroking each other's flanks, her skin pebbly as a basketball beneath your fingers, her nipples still erect from the air-conditioning.

And you can tell your protégé about how you deal with *that,* about how you walk away from *that* temptation, how you've been doing it for over twenty years now, denying yourself the simplest of illicit pleasures, the meaningless fuck, because you believed in the sanctity of your marriage, and knew the enormity of the stupidity you were tempted to commit before you attempted to commit it. Or maybe you don't say anything about that, ever, to anybody, because the traveling salesman jokes just assume you have, and denying it would simply confirm it for some people, but you carry it in your heart, how you almost fell, and there is shame enough in that. And a part of you is kicking yourself, too, because maybe she really wanted you to make a move, maybe that flirtatious invitation really was that, an invitation, no strings attached, and even in infidelity you are a failure. But no, no regrets. You walked away from that, and the only real regrets you'd have would be because you had pulled something stupid, like you are now, cruising back roads off Highways 13 and 77 outside Glidden in late twilight trying to find someone you're really hoping (not) to find. But still, you wanted to—want to, want to—and the wanting itself is a sin. Christ, don't you get any credit for saying no? For turning away? For driving around roads where you know you won't find her rather than going to Len's, where you most certainly will? And the next time you're in the Dipsy Doodle—tomorrow night, even—when the bells jingle over the door she'll greet you with "There's my lover" and a knowing, sad, necessary smile, and you'll both know what it was you passed on. And you'll instruct him, your young sidekick, who's never at a loss for bedside companions, on the finer points of fidelity and loneliness, and how, if you believe in the former, then the latter is necessary and unavoidable.

He could instruct them on it all, how to sell and how to live in the world—in short, how to act as though you believed the world was a better place than it was—but the suits had no interest in that. They never took him up on his offer, never gave him the one honor he thought they owed him, the single mark of respect he wanted accorded him in his old age—to be seen as a font of wisdom on the finer arts of selling. Not what they give you out of a book, but what you need to know if you're going to make it *out there*—out in the world.

They weren't interested, had no intention of honoring him like that.

And so it continued. His best accounts taken from him. His commission rate dropped. His quotas upped. His territory chopped or rearranged, parts of it given to others. When he got tired of it he went to a competitor, Dewless Chemical. Dewless was a family operation. Hands-on and homey. The employees like family. A problem: lots of the employees *were* family. So promises were made about advancement that were clearly not going to be kept when there was a son-in-law that our father was "taking under his wing." And as the company fell apart, they expected the company's nonfamily members to forgo, during this time of financial contingency—"just like family"—things like bonuses and paychecks. In fact, the nonfamily members of Dewless were seen as more familylike in this regard than the family itself. This was made plain to our father when the son-in-law, driving past Park Falls with him, had the temerity to open up a pay envelope, something our father had not seen for weeks, and do some math on the back of the envelope, referring as he did so to the uncashed check he held in his other hand.

"What's that?" said our father.

"My check and bonus," said the son-in-law. "Can you believe Pop's bonus checks for this quarter were only averaging thirteen percent?"

"Thirteen percent?" said our father.

"Yeah, and he expects me to swallow that. Can you fucking believe it?"

"No," said our father, "I can't."

By the time Dewless went Chapter 11, two of our father's paychecks had bounced. One was missing. "It's in the mail," a nervous Mr. Dewless promised over the phone. "And I will not come in your mouth!" our father shouted back. "Wally, the children!" said our mother. As though we didn't know who it was being screwed. He hadn't received a commission in six months. When they went belly-up, they still owed him six paychecks plus the commissions.

It was quite a hit. To get us through, Robert Aaron and I cashed in the money we'd been saving for college. The family's coffers remained unfilled. Our father blamed himself, as though he should have seen it coming. Perhaps he should have; perhaps he was blinded by almost, *sorta* being a consultant to that shit son-in-law, but when you got down to it, because Dewless *was* a family operation, our father's screwing was strictly small-time. To get really screwed, you needed a major corporation. Our father went back to Dinkwater Chemical for a spell—he was desperate—but he had feelers out, and one of his old friends, Benny Wilkerson from the Cicero Velvetones, was now a regional sales manager for Drydell Chemical, an outfit out of Dinkwater only slightly smaller than Dinkwater themselves. "But we're growing, and we need somebody in specialty chemicals in the Midwest, Wally. You could be that man." Our father was sold, sure he'd finally found a place that would treat him right. We were over the hump.

Too bad Drydell got grabbed soon after that—in the late seventies—by Perle Chemical, which in turn was snatched up by Lakeland Oil. Lakeland Oil didn't want to do paper, they wanted to do paint, so they sold off the paper unit to Dinkwater Chemical, and our father could either go back to the Dinks or switch to paint. He wouldn't have had any choice in the matter at all except Benny Wilkerson had been bumped up a couple levels in the moves, and while they were combining and downsizing—mostly salesmen our father's age—Benny was able to tell our father, "No promises, but if you're willing to learn paint we can keep you," which was as much of a display of loyalty as our father expected. In making that offer, however, Benny had stepped on the toes of the new paint manager and, sight unseen, had made an enemy for life. The paint manager wanted both Benny's and our father's heads on platters. And given that corporate communications during the merger had been placed in a blind trust operated by the Keystone Kops, he was able to get exactly that. Our father would talk to his regional sales supervisor, they would agree to something, "but just let me run it by the higher-ups," and by the time it went up and came back down the corporate pipeline, the person who'd agreed to whatever had been fired, left the company, or was to be found in a different department entirely, and the directive or agreement had been lost, forgotten, or changed beyond recognition. The new orders were accompanied by a memo welcoming a new regional supervisor to his tasks. No mention of what had happened to the previous manager. Our father joked that someone was killing the regional supervisors and distributing their body parts in industrial-size barrels of creosote and paint thinner. "It's how they got rid of Hoffa," he said. "Everyone thinks it was lead overshoes and a trip to the river, but I bet he's in a warehouse somewhere, his bones slowly dissolving until he's poured down the drain during a Superfund cleanup."

And so it went. Our father took to subscribing to the theory of prior arrangements. That it *was* a conspiracy. That everything—the whole goddamn world—was a conspiracy.

Conspiracies go better with drinking. The worst of it was when our father took absolute leave of his senses one evening and started screaming at the television set that Walter Cronkite was a Communist. I thought of Ahab. Twirling down, twirling down, twirling madly, madly down, a ballet of failure still tied to his obsession, a victim of the thing he most desired. Then I thought of failures less romantic. Not Ahab trailing like an afterthought behind the whale as it sank into the abyss, but Wally as Willy Loman. I knew how that ended up. I put the thought out of my mind. Besides, if Wally-Bear was Willy, that would make me Biff, and I didn't want to think about that much, either.

Our father was not one of those brutal drunks that ruins or blights lives. There was no hitting in our family, and although there was a lot of screaming, the verbal abuse was minimal. The anger was directed mostly inward. Broken green and bloody glass replaced our father's normal eyes as he slumped in his easy chair, lashing out at Walter Cronkite (a Communist!) and Hubert Humphrey (another goddamn pinko!) and teachers and unions and those who demonstrated against the Vietnam War or didn't vote for Ronald Reagan. Our father's days as a suburban Republican were over. There were enemies everywhere, they were in cahoots, and they were evil. He was now a nut, a crank, fodder for the extreme right's assault on the national consciousness in the years following Reagan's ascent to the throne. But these assaults on Walter Cronkite, we knew, were the outbursts of a deeply frustrated man, and in some ways I think our father was careful to pick remote targets that couldn't be held accountable.

He even forgave the companies he worked for. They were only doing what companies did when they were managed by the petty and the incompetent. It was not the company's fault; it was the fault of bad management within the company, and if our father could just get the higher-ups to recognize that, the scoundrels would be thrown out, an enlightened management would be installed, and all would be well in the land of the Dinks.

Our mother, for all her health problems, was a battler. She believed nothing would get better unless our father went to war against his own company, getting everything in writing, fighting for what was his, slugging it out with the higher-ups. Our father believed the higher-ups knew what they were doing. He would not fight. Instead he retreated into the belief that the very thing afflicting him would save him. Our father was good at this—clinging fast to opposing beliefs. Not giving credence to explanations that made sense.

He did not, for example, believe in the democracy of failure. That everyone had an equal chance at it, just like happiness. He thought only losers were punished with failure, and if he was failing, then it was his fault. He would rail against his company but then accept the wisdom of its arbitrary judgments. Elsewhere the world was full of conspiracies, but in his own life it all came down to him. He'd dropped it, the whole ball of wax. He deserved it, what happened to him. Failure was a meritocracy, and he was one of its minions.

He was helped in this belief by staying in touch with Louie Hwasko, his best friend, best man, and piano player for the Cicero Velvetones. Louie's life had not gone the way he had hoped either. His marriage to Helen Federstam had not lasted—Helen having decamped for California years ago—and his marriage to Shirley hadn't lasted either. They'd had a half dozen or dozen tumultuous years of too much drinking and too much cheating.

" 'Your Cheatin' Heart' should have been tattooed on her boobs," he told our father. "I couldn't keep up with her extracurriculars. When she was done with me for the evening, she sometimes went out and found somebody else."

We were at the Dog Out. Louie had come up for a visit. Shirley had left him. Our father indicated me sitting on the other side of him. I was old enough for a beer but made a point of drinking sodas when I was out with my father—my petty self-righteousness in action.

"Oh, sorry. Virgin ears, I forgot."

I let that remark pass.

"Anyway, she's going, she's gone. Took her suitcase and threw some things into it. Not everything, but I'm guessing when I get back the place will be pretty much cleared out. Too much drinkin', too much fuckin', that's what did us in."

"You should have just set her things out on the stoop when you first found out what she was like."

"What was she first like, Wally? When you first met up with her, what was she like? Was she like that all the time? She was plenty sweet to me,

I can tell you that. So when did she get this hankering for other men's dicks? Maybe I couldn't satisfy her, you know what I'm saying? That's what she always told me. 'Louie,' she'd say, 'I got a big heart and a bigger pussy, and you're just not doin' it for me like I thought you might.' "

"Don't talk like that." The way my father said it, I got the feeling it was something men didn't own up to even if it was true. It would be like betraying the brotherhood. Certain truths shouldn't be uttered. They might scare the horses.

"She changed, Wally. I don't know why but she changed. All of a sudden my being a dentist wasn't enough for her. Raising chinchillas and having the damn little things made into chinchilla fur coats for her—it wasn't enough either. She had such need, Wally, it was written right on her face. A big heart and a bigger pussy. I failed her, Wally."

"Don't talk like that," said our father.

Louie got up from the bar, plunked some quarters in the jukebox. Ray Charles's "Born to Lose" started playing, and Louie played along, his fingers finding the notes on the bar top.

"I gotta own up to something else, Wally. Shirley—she didn't just leave me."

"No?"

Louie shook his head. "She left me months ago. Some he-man seaman down at Great Lakes, some chief petty officer with a big dick. She moved in with him. This after I sent her all the money from the house. I lost my house, Wally. Sold it for a song. I couldn't stay there anyway. Too many bad memories."

"Where are you staying, Louie?"

"I'm a free man, Wally. I got me a trailer. I'm okay. I even get chicks to come back with me if I give them cab fare home."

"Cab fare," said our father.

"Plus a little something for their time."

"For their time," said our father.

"Hey," said Louie. "When you pay for the company you keep at least you know what you're getting, right?" He grabbed our father's forearm. "Am I right or am I right? Right?"

"Louie—" said our father, but Louie put his finger up to his lips and said, "Shh, shh." "I Can't Stop Loving You" came on the jukebox and they sang along with that, sotto voce at first and then louder. Then it was

Bobby Darin's "Mack the Knife." I thought of that Frank Sinatra movie that featured the song "One for My Baby (and One More for the Road)," and had that great sad moment in the bar where Frank says/sings, "So set 'em up, Joe. I got a little story you oughta know. . . ." I don't remember how that movie turns out, I just remember that sad romantic moment, the low lighting and the camaraderie of the bartender and Sinatra. It was like that now, only the bartender was taking a backseat to my father, who was singing about Sukie Tawdry and Lotte Lenya along with Louie. The desperate jocularity of the moment struck me, and I recalled a scene from another movie, one that featured Fred Astaire being all depressed and ended with Astaire dancing on the walls and ceiling. Amazing. I was hoping for something like that now. Louie was going to announce he was in love again; Shirley was all wrong for him, but he'd finally found some-body right, the sadder but wiser girl, as Robert Preston sang in *The Music Man,* and he was once again settling down. Those rebound girls—that was all behind him now.

And for a minute it looked like that was exactly the case. Louie said to our father, "I got options, Wally. This ain't the end of me. Not by a long shot. My woman leaves me, okay, fine. Who needs a wife, anyway? I got options. I got plans."

"Plans?" said our father.

"I'm applying to be recommissioned."

"With who?"

"The Navy."

"The reserves?"

"No, the reserves are for fat guys who want to relive their youth. No offense, Wally"—our father was still in the reserves—"but I'm talking about being where it means something. I'm joining the regular Navy again."

"Louie, you're forty-eight years old."

"They need my experience."

"They don't need that much experience."

"I'm a dentist. They have to take me. They need dentists."

Our father's voice got very quiet. Either this was urgent or he didn't want me listening. I listened anyway. "Why in Sam Hill do you want to be a Navy dentist, Louie?"

"Chicks," Louie breathed back to our father. "The chicks always dig a guy in uniform. I figure a guy like me could use the cachet to, you know, get him started. With the chicks, I mean. It worked on Shirley. Hell, it works on everybody."

"And what if they don't take you, Louie?"

Louie looked into his beer. "Then I'm going to blow my brains out, Wally. You wait and see."

Louie was as good as his word. I was in college when Louie received a letter stating that the United States Navy, with regrets, would not be recommissioning Lieutenant JG Louis John Hwasko. He had served his country admirably when called upon, but they no longer required his services. I was called home when our parents received the phone call informing them that their best man, our father's best friend, Louie Hwasko, was found in the trailer he'd lived in since Shirley left him, his brains blown across his kitchenette with his service revolver. He'd been scrambling eggs. The coroner said you'd be hard-pressed to tell what was eggs and what was brain.

"Why'd he do it, Dad?" asked Peg Leg Meg. If anyone had been handed a bum deal by life, it was Meg—born with one leg shorter than the other—but she couldn't understand how anybody could be a pessimist as long as you were still breathing on God's green earth.

"Because he was a failure," said our father. He kept saying it, too: "A failure, a failure." His voice was trembling. His shoulders shook. His gaze started to fall on us, but then he shifted it, out the window and over the fields for which he'd always had such grand plans.

18. We'll Put It on Your Bill

THAT'S THE WAY
THE COOKIE CRUMBLES

We're still bad-mouthing Cinderella when she arrives. Meg's saying, "She's not here, is she? Where is she? Why isn't she here? Tomorrow is the second most important day in our family's history and she's not here?" when Cinderella pokes her pale head inside the tepee and says, "Mom said you were down here."

"Oh, Sarah. We didn't hear you come down."

"I guess not."

"We were just talking about Mom and Dad."

"I heard." Cinderella's face still has that game, haunted look, as though she were apologizing for having intruded on our bad behavior. But there is an edge to her voice. We feel ashamed. It's also apparent she's been crying, but then she often looks like that.

"Mom says you shouldn't worry about things. She and Dad have it all figured out."

"They do?"

"Pretty much."

"Care to enlighten us?" I ask.

"She said to say you should hold your horses. They'll tell you tomorrow."

"They couldn't tell us now?"

"You couldn't have this discussion in front of them? Mom said, 'Everything in its own way, in its own time.' Besides, you're down here now and they're going to bed."

"Dad's awake?"

"He got up for a little while. Then he and Mom talked."

"How do you know all this?"

"I must've gotten home a little after you guys came down here. Mom was still up. She was crying." Nobody addresses the fact that Cinderella has evidently been crying, too.

Cinderella takes a deep breath to steady herself. "She seemed okay about it. Whatever you said to upset her—she said we shouldn't worry. That everything was taken care of."

"Taken care of how?"

"You know, it's the funniest thing. I asked Mom the same thing, and she got this curious smile on her face. 'We shall see what we shall see,' Mom said. Then she laughed and said, 'And that's the name of that tune.' "

"You're sure it was Mom who said that?"

"Dad had already gone back to sleep." Cinderella yawns. "I should, too. It's late."

She's about to leave, but Meg doesn't want her to go. "So, Cinders," she says. "Where were you tonight? We had things to talk about."

"Mel and I had some things to talk about, too."

"Oh?"

"You wouldn't want to know." She means all of us.

"Try us," I say.

"No, it'll make me seem like a victim, and I know how you hate that."

It's amazing how warm a tent can feel on a cold March night.

But Cinderella can't not tell us. She looks up at the tepee's crown, where the smoke escapes to the night sky. She takes another deep breath and sighs. "Mel's thinking of going back to his wife."

"Oh, honey," Robert Aaron says. "That's terrible."

"Bummer," says Ernie.

"Double bummer," says Wally Jr.

"Yeah, well—" She takes a step into the tepee, catches her foot, and staggers.

"Did he give a reason?" Ike asks.

Meg says, "I still want to know what Mom and Dad's plans are. How they think everything is taken care of." Her eyes narrow. "Did she tell you?"

Cinderella rights herself, then gets this sickly, sad, self-satisfied smile on her face. As though God had entrusted her with the secrets of the universe, whispered them into her ear, and she's dying to tell, but God has also whispered to her exactly what her punishment will be if she reveals them. She puts her finger to her mouth. "Shh!" she says, and you can tell she's answering both Meg's question and Ike's. "Loose lips sink ships."

Our father's life was saved by sex and cookies. Once Benny Wilkerson left Drydell and went to work for Dinkwater—which our father, right then, couldn't contemplate—our father's days at Drydell were numbered. A few months later he was given a pink slip; the paint division got reorganized, and his territory magically evaporated. Being unemployed again just about killed our father. Excluding the months when dying companies were promising him that pay and bonus checks were "on their way," our father was out of work nearly a year, and for several years running didn't pull in anything close to a regular income. What he did earn he spent on drink and fishing equipment. During that time the Arabs and Israelis had a war, Vietnam fell, Nixon resigned, there was an oil crisis, a recession, and a rise in worldwide Communism. African dictators rose and fell, South American ones murdered their own people, the dollar was shaky, prices and wages were frozen, and the Russian Bear was dancing. Closer to home, our father's best friend blew his brains out, and his oldest daughter was locked into a loveless marriage with an abusive husband.

The really horrible thing, though, was that our mother got a job.

A great many things sent our father to bars, taverns, saloons, and gin joints, but except for the news about Louie Hwasko, the most devastating news our father could receive was that our mother was employed outside the home. Robert Aaron and I had been working for some time already, our college funds had been zeroed out, but the idea that our father couldn't support our mother—no, no, that just couldn't be.

"Did it ever occur to you that I wanted to do it, Wally-Bear? Have a job, I mean."

"No woman wants a job unless she's one of them women's libbers burning their bras and waving the damn things in public at you."

"Lots of women have jobs, Wally, and they didn't burn their bras to get them."

"No wife of mine is going to have a job. You already have one. You're a wife and a mother. These kids are your job. I'm your job."

"You're my Job, Wally, not my job. Right now you're my not so little cross to bear. And 'these kids,' Wally? 'These kids' are nearly grown. Or hadn't you noticed? They're growing up and out, right under your nose, and they'd grow a whole lot faster if we had something in the house besides beer and tortilla chips to put inside their mouths!"

"Sure, that's right, rub it in. Rub my goddamn nose in it. Twist the knife in his guts, tell a man he can't provide for his family!" Our father was shouting. He'd been drinking since noon.

"I didn't say anything about you not providing for your wife and family. I'm simply saying I want to help out. There are a lot of us."

"And whose fault is that?"

"It's not anybody's fault, Wally. We wanted it like this, remember?"

Our father closed his eyes. At that moment it didn't seem he'd be able to recall anything without a great deal of difficulty. Finally he breathed, "I had you on a pedestal. A pedestal!"

Our mother sighed. "Well, it's not always fun being up on a pedestal, Wally. You get stiff. Sometimes we like to climb down and move around." She was rubbing his shoulders. "Maybe this is the best thing for us, you know?" We could see she was trying to make the best of a bad situation. It was why she had taken the checkout job at the same grocery store where I worked. She even appealed to the great mystery of their married life. "You know, Wally, maybe our 'you know' would be better if I got out of the house more. I'd feel friskier for having been out in the workaday world, and you'd feel friskier for having a more active wife."

You could tell from her voice's waver that she didn't believe what she was saying to him but that she desperately wanted to. It puzzled us why she'd want to. Our father was drunk and fat, and our mother was an attractive woman, though portly from childbearing and unhappiness. Frankly, we wondered how two round bodies managed to have sex at all.

We understood nothing of the intimacy of grooming, found in other primates, and we thought the excitement of body parts fitting together applied only to nubile bodies. We forgot, or never knew, that given the comic nature of genitalia, "you know" was a pleasure, a release, and a relief, the punch line to a private joke shared by our parents.

Even in times like this. Here they'd been arguing, our father angry and then despondent, everything—his dignity, his respect, his wife—slipping away from him, and now our mother was comforting him. Our father sat at the kitchen table, his head buried in our mother's belly, pitifully saying over and over in a weak little voice, "I want a job, a job. A job a job a job."

Our mother kissed our father's forehead and stroked his ears. "Why don't we put you to bed and . . . you know."

You know? Now? It was six o'clock on a Saturday evening. Had our parents no sense of decency? Decorum? They did and they did not. Our parents reminded us at that moment of Jackie Gleason and Audrey Meadows of *The Honeymooners*. When Ralph, after flying into one rage after another, and generally mucking things up royally, is finally forgiven and brought to rights by Alice, he is invariably flummoxed and perhaps mortified, but he is also thankful. "Alice, you're the greatest" was that show's tagline, and it didn't matter that Alice was a true beauty and Ralph a blustery buffoon. Something happened between them behind those closed doors that was good and healing and was worth staying together for. You didn't get that feeling with the Petries and their twin beds, or the Nelsons, whose bedroom you never saw. The singular magic of Ralph and Alice Kramden was that, babies or no, they had sex when that door closed at the end of the show. And they had it at Alice's discretion. For all Ralph's blustering, she held the reins of power in that relationship. And don't think Ralph didn't know it. It was part of what made him an impotent blowhard. He had to flex his muscles meaninglessly at least once an episode just to convince himself he was in charge even though he wasn't. And even as little kids we could see that about our parents as well. Ralph and Alice, Wally and Susan. "Alice, you're the greatest," indeed.

Our mother had a job, our father was despondent and emasculated, and our mother gave him her body to make him feel better. "I don't deserve you," said our father as our mother led him back to their bedroom, their fingers twined.

Said our mother, "No, Wally, you don't." And then right there in the hall she nibbled his ear. "We'll put it on your bill, Wally-Bear. We will put it on your bill."

"We'll put it on your bill, Wally-Bear"? Since when did our mother start speaking in our father's clichés? What did it mean, besides that our mother was going to keep her crummy little job as a cashier? It meant a great many things, chief among them that the balance of power was shifting in our family. Our mother, who never learned to drive and therefore was always along for the ride, was starting to feel as though maybe, for the sake of her family—no, for the sake of her sanity—she ought to be in the driver's seat more often.

Not long after this our father started selling cookies for Pewaukee Cookie and Biscuit. PCB was a tiny company trying to go head-to-head with Nabisco. Their headquarters were in a quasi-bucolic upscale exurb of Milwaukee. Their advertising made you think fat rural bakers of German extraction pulled their wares from stone ovens on long-handled wooden boards, but the factory itself was in an industrial neighborhood in Milwaukee, where skinny black guys hopped up on speed ran the ovens, and large black and Hispanic women ran the packaging lines and brought home as freebies corner-kinked boxes and cello-wrapped packages with ripped seals.

Our father did, too. We ate trial-size samples, broken remnants, and date-expired rejects, boxes of crackers and packages of cookies accidentally sliced open by a packing knife. By this time I'd had a summer job for several years replacing Nabisco cookie salesmen when they went on vacation, so I knew the routine. When you met one of your counterparts from Keebler or Archway or Milwaukee Biscuit, you exchanged goodies. A packing knife's slice rendered the package damaged, and that way you didn't have to bring home the same crap you sold all day. But our father never did that. He refused to take the other guy's stuff in trade. But why? I asked. "Because I work for PCB," said our father. Pride, belief—our father's gods did not die.

Even when he was selling cookies.

It might have saved him, having a job again, maybe even more than our mother leading him back to the marital bed. I can't vouch for that. But I knew there was something desperate about selling cookies for a living, and it required our father to summon up his courage to go out each morning. What our father didn't like was that it required no real selling. Everybody loves cookies, our father said, even the knockoff brands. There's nothing to it. So our father set himself the task of stealing six or eight inches of shelf space from that juggernaut Nabisco. Nabisco, being a juggernaut, commands the cookie aisle's center, and competing brands are shoved to the ends. Nabisco arranges their products using "bull's-eye" marketing, meaning their popular stuff—Oreos, Saltines, Ritz crackers—go in the bull's-eye center—and their own less popular sellers are out toward the fringes, further crowding their competitors' products to the aisle's ends. Our father wanted to change all that.

I "volunteered" to ride around on one of his sales trips. Given the precarious state he was in, our mother thought it "might be good" if one of us accompanied him, and I was the only one available. That summer I'd abandoned the white-collar world of Nabisco for the higher-paying drudgery of a canning factory, but it was closed because of a drowning in one of its cooling tanks. It wasn't likely to start up again soon—drought had delayed the corn season—and by the time it was, I'd be back at school. I've no idea what our mother said to him privately, but to me our father said he wouldn't mind the company. He even seemed pleased. Here was his chance to show how he could mentor a budding salesman. And his son to boot. For me this would be like a weeklong trip to the Office. The very idea thrilled and disgusted me.

We drove north up Highway 51. Our father chatted up the owners of Stop-N-Gos, Open Pantries, Bob's Gas and Grubs, Millie's and Izzie's Canteen Stand, Roy and Margaret's Bait and Grocery. We stopped at Indian souvenir stands with groceries attached, ditto bait shops and Quik Marts. Red Owls, Piggly Wigglys, and Sentrys, too. At the end of the day we crossed Highway 2 to Ashland, where we were booked into the Lorelei Motel. After dinner we walked down to the harbor and looked at the sailboats up from Chicago. "All that cocksucking money," said our father, "and they buy sailboats." Our father was a powerboat man, and this was the first time I'd ever heard him vent on the subject of money. He believed the rich deserved it, even when I pointed out that a lot of the wealth he saw was inherited. A grandfather in iron ore, a great-grandfather in timber. No matter. At some point somebody had done something to deserve it, by hook or by crook, and you could do worse than be born into a family of wealth.

"Al Capone had no children," our father told me as we walked along. "No legacy, no heirs. That was his one great mistake. That and he let the feds get him on income tax evasion. He had cabins and hideaways all through the great north woods. Did you know that?"

I knew.

The next day was hot and hazy, and clouds were building up in the west. That meant rain, and we hoped it meant a break from the heat. The company car's air conditioner was having a hard time keeping up with all our starts and stops. We'd visit a grocery store, write up a pitifully small order, then drive ten miles and do it again. Some of the towns we went through were paper mill towns. The muscles above our father's jowls worked furiously as we drove by his old stomping grounds, but he said nothing.

We knocked off earlier than expected in Spooner. We had a couple more stops to make, but at a little crossroads grocery named Mel's we ran into a young woman, a girl, really, running the counter. "Can we see Mel, honey?" said our father.

"Mel's gone," said the girl. She looked to be about seventeen. Pretty, the way girls in small towns are, a little stocky, her jeans tight, her pink T-shirt tighter, her black hair parted carelessly down the middle. She caught sight of me and grinned. I was new in town, and that meant I wasn't the same old same old. "Fishing," she added uncertainly. Then she smiled at me again.

"Mel's gone drinking," came a voice from the back. "No-account bastard."

"I'm here," the young woman said. She leaned forward and whispered, "I'm Celia."

At that the bead curtain behind the register parted to give way to a curlered behemoth in a housedress. This was a woman who looked like she wrestled pigs for a living. "Celia, get in the back," the woman ordered. She was holding a broom and smoking a cigarette.

"I was just talking to these gentlemen."

"These gentlemen ain't gentlemen. They're *salesmen*. And I'll handle 'em. Now get." She spat out "salesmen" as though we were vermin. Then I realized what was up. We were the punch line to too many jokes that had driven through town. This woman could just see it, a seventeen-year-old mother to be who couldn't remember the name of the "nice man" who'd knocked her up, then disappeared on down the highway. She was protecting her daughter from a horrible future. Better she got knocked up by some local boy she could keep her eye on and make do the right thing. Even if he turned out to be a bastard like Mel.

Our father cleared his throat. "Would you be able, in Mel's absence," he said, "to make decisions regarding the stocking of this store?" Our father's voice sounded unnaturally formal, and I wondered what had gotten into him.

"I make all the decisions about stocking this store, mister. Mel left that to me years ago when he decided the bottle he crawled inside was a better home than this one. And that was the last decision he ever made. And let me tell you something else, you slick city piece of shit, whatever you're selling, I ain't buying. Now get."

The first drops of rain, which had been threatening to come down all day, splattered on our windshield and on the trees outside. You could hear it sputter-tapping the tin roof awning over Mel's window. If we left right now, we could make the car before the deluge hit. But my father composed himself. He was not going to be driven out of a two-bit family grocery in a north woods town by a harridan with a chip on her shoulder. He refused. Instead he took out his order book and said, "I'll just make sure you've got enough stock for the shelves."

"I got all the stock I need. All the goddamn stock I'll ever need. Some of that stuff has been sitting on the shelf since last summer."

"Then I'll remove the postdated stock and get you new merchandise," said our father.

"I want the goddamn shelf empty!" the woman screamed. I had a hard time reconciling in my mind that this was Celia's mother until it occurred to me that once upon a time Celia's mom had probably been a lot like Celia, had married badly, and had paid for it ever since. Now she was just looking for excuses upon which she could unload all her grief and rage and unhappiness. It just so happened that today we were it. On another day it would be the water softener man, or the Coca-Cola salesman, or a representative from the Tri-County Bank, come to inform her that she had exhausted all her options vis-à-vis keeping this two-bit grocery afloat.

None of which comforted me when I saw the woman raise her broom and bring it down on my father's head.

"Mama, don't!" yelled Celia, who burst out of the back at the first crack of the broom.

"Ma'am, please!" My father threw up his arms to defend himself. "I'm trying to write an order here."

"I don't want a goddamn order here. I want you out of my fucking store." She was beating time on his shoulders and head with her broom; my father turned his back and hunched his shoulders. He had his order pad out, with the three carbons tucked between the sheets—one for him, one for the office, one for the driver, one for the customer. She was raining blows on his back, and her words and the rain outside, which was coming in gusts, seemed to beat time with her. "Do . . . I . . . make . . . myself . . . clear? . . . I . . . want . . . you . . . out . . . of . . . my . . . fucking . . . store!" The last three blows were delivered to the back of my father's skull. You could hear the broom's plastic frame cracking as it whacked bone.

"Dad! You're bleeding!" I cried as bright red blood burst into rivulets down the back of his head, spotting his yellow sport shirt crimson.

"Mama! Stop!" yelled Celia, but it was obvious the sight of my father's blood only infuriated the woman, spurred her on to greater fury. A lifetime of frustrations had broken through the dam of her bile-swallowing anger, and here! here! she had found an object upon which she could whale. She just kept hitting him and hitting him and hitting him. My father had sunk to his knees—no easy task for a big man—and he was covering his skull with his order book. *Whack! Whack!* went the broom on his order book. *Whack! Whack! Whack!*

"Dad!" I yelled. "Sound the retreat! Retreat!" But he couldn't seem to get to his feet, and when I tried reaching in to grab him, Celia's mother started swinging the broom at me. Bottles of salad oil and Karo syrup and Mrs. Butterworth's were knocked to the floor, crashing in time, it seemed, to the lightning flashes. I backed off. Celia's mother returned her attention to my father, who hadn't risen during his brief reprieve.

Celia had come up alongside me as this was going on, and her fingers reached for mine. We were holding hands, feeling the electricity of our entwined fingers, although we may have been feeling only the buzz from the electrical storm outside.

Meanwhile my father was getting the shit beat out of him.

"Make her stop," I said, and Celia squeezed my hand tighter and said, "I can't. She just gets like this sometimes, although usually she doesn't take it out on people."

Celia's mother was winding down. Perhaps her arms were getting tired. She paused for breath, perhaps to regroup before redoubling her assault on my father's cranium, and though it felt queerly strange and wonderful to have Celia holding my hand while my father was being beaten, I shook myself free and reached for my father, catching him under his arm. I half-pulled, half-dragged him to his feet. He slid in the Mrs. Butterworth's–Karo syrup goo for a couple feet before I could get him upright. "Dad!" I kept yelling. "Retreat! Retreat!" And once I got him on his feet, I pushed him toward the door. Then I lunged back under the deadly broom of Celia's mother to grab his sample case. She caught me a few times on my head and shoulders, slicing me open behind my ear before I was able to get out of there.

"Sorry!" Celia called as I sprang out the door, the bells above it tinkling in my wake.

Outside the wind beat furiously. The temperature had dropped, and cold rain and hail lashed down on us. It was like being attacked by ice cubes. "Shit and double shit!" yelled our father as he dropped his keys. We stood there while he fished for them in a large puddled pothole, then worked his way through the ring looking for the key. We were soaked and shivering by the time we got inside, and shivered more in the car's air-conditioned air. The AC, which had labored and failed us all day, was finally successful in chilling us to the bone. He shut it off and the windows fogged. With a handkerchief I started wiping blood off his head, trying to stanch the flow. The rain had helped clean the wounds, and although he had several lacerations on the back of his head and neck, he wasn't wounded too badly. He checked me for damage as well. The cut over my ear bled onto my shoulders. Our shirts were soaked with rain and blood, and our shoulders stung from the twin assaults of hail and Celia's mother. Our father was breathing heavily. "What say we knock off early today. Agreed?"

"Agreed," I said.

"Sorry about that back there. Usually if they don't like you they at least let you wait out the rain."

"You had no way of knowing," I said.

"Yeah," said our father, "that's the way the cookie crumbles." He took the handkerchief from me and pressed it against the back of his head. Then he put on the blower to clear the windshield. Just before he put the car in gear, he turned to me. "Thanks for getting me out of there."

I grinned, then said something that scared me. Was this how it started, the words simply coming out of your mouth? "I'll put it on your bill," I said, sounding just like our father.

That evening all I wanted was for us to have a good laugh over our adventure and maybe run into a remorseful Celia, who would want to make up for her mother's bad behavior with some bad behavior of her own. But over dinner—it was a supper club, but the rush hadn't come in yet, nor had the staff, so we were eating at the bar—our father started putting away Rob Roys at an alarming pace. I had often seen our father drunk or with a drink in his hand, but I had rarely seen him *drinking*. Even on our many expeditions to the Dog Out and Banana's Never Inn, expeditions that began with our father running out "to get a loaf of bread," his drinking seemed to occur while I was in the bathroom, or my mind was engaged by other things—the size of the barmaid's rack, for instance. Oh, sure, I'd seen him regularly sip his beer, even throw back a shot or three, but that evening our father wasn't giving the ice in his glass a chance to get soft.

"It wasn't always like this, Emcee," he told me, shaking his glass to get the barmaid's attention. The cubes, bereft of company, rattled hollowly. "God damn it, it wasn't always like this." The barmaid came and wiped the bar down, and my father slid his glass toward her. She nodded with a sad smile on her face like she knew just what he was thinking, and she was sorry there wasn't anything she could do about it.

Then I got to thinking that maybe there was. She was no great shakes in the looks department—chunky, with frizzy blond hair, a pasty face, and too much lipstick and blue eye shadow—but then my father was no great shakes in the looks department, either. She was not wearing flattering clothing—a green blouse that puckered at the shoulders and black tights that a woman with chunky thighs probably shouldn't be wearing—but we were a long way from home, and I was constantly checking the door myself, hoping to see a young woman walk in whose mother earlier that afternoon had tried to beat us to death. Loneliness and need make for strange partners, I thought. And our father had always, always, been a long way from home.

"It's a different culture, Emcee, selling like this. It's not even selling. What's to sell? Nabisco's got all the shelf space, and Keebler's got what they don't. And I can't get the margins low enough for the managers to give me their aisle ends. Nabisco got there first. Forty-five years ago they got there first. The fucking National Biscuit Company. And who do I sell for? Pewaukee Cookie and Biscuit. PCB. Christ. It sounds like one of them drugs you kids are always taking. Like the insides of my cookies are gonna send you into tizzies."

"Maybe you should use that as a selling point, Dad. Get marketing to rethink the demographics. PCB—cookies for stoners and hippies. You got the munchies? Don't want to lose your high? Buy PCBs, in the bright Day-Glo box."

Our father wasn't listening to me. He was thinking about customers, not consumers, and his were the store managers. That was who he was selling to—not the public but guys like himself, little guys trying to stay afloat between the devil and the deep blue sea.

"And who's there to sell to?" A rhetorical question. He wasn't expecting an answer. He was going to supply his own. "Nobody fishes after work in this business. Nobody goes out for dinner and drinks. It's not part of the culture. They work nights, or they beat it home to their wife and kiddies. Not that HQ gives me anything to seal a deal with anyway. I don't have that kind of expense account. And where are the premiums? *Here, take home a box of cookies?* Please." Our father rattled his glass again. "How am I supposed to sell when I've got no leverage?" His exasperation brought over the barmaid. She was bearing a fresh Rob Roy.

"You've had a tough day, huh, honey? Look, I feel for you, I really do, but you're scaring away the other customers." I looked down the bar. It was four o'clock in the afternoon. There weren't any other customers. She put my father's drink down, then leaned over her folded arms, her elbows on the bar. "Pretty soon, if you don't watch it," she said, "it's going to be just me and you." She held out her hand. My father took it. "Wally," he said. "Madeleine," she said. "People call me Maddy."

I cleared my throat.

"And Sonny makes three, eh?" Madeleine went to the sink and started dunking glasses. She hadn't introduced herself to me. I didn't like the way Dad was looking at her. I thought of Shirley, lo, those many years ago. Before she married Louie, what had happened between her and our father? Anything? How long had he kept that card in his wallet? Had he passed her on to Louie, damaged goods (though she seemed plenty damaged already when I met her at the Office), or had he settled for simply introducing her to someone who might appreciate her offers, knowing that nature would take its course, nature being the requisite coupling and uncoupling, with Shirley flying the coop eventually, as every woman did with Louie? I had no way of knowing, and my good thoughts to the contrary, it was something I wondered about, the nature of our father while he was on the road. I'd imagined him both good and fallen, noble and not so noble, and here was Temptation with a capital T, her boobs staring my father in the face.

I thought I knew something about that. I was dating someone right then that I was "practically engaged to," as people used to say. I'd gotten tired of waiting for Dorie Braun—she was long gone from Augsbury, had left even before I graduated high school. The last I'd heard she was living in either Milwaukee or Minneapolis, and one rumor was she was living off her rich boyfriend, and another rumor was she was living off her friendships with rich homosexuals (though in Augsbury nobody called them homosexuals). So I stopped hoping and fell in love with the first woman nice enough to sleep with me. Jane Brohm, one of my college classmates. Cute, curious, freckled, neurotic. That should have been fine, but it wasn't. The only thing we had in common was parents who drank too much. Where was Nomi to tell me I was making the same mistake as Cinderella? Maybe I was trying to tell myself that with Celia. It wouldn't have been the first time that summer that I'd been tempted to stray. There'd been a woman, too, in the canning factory where I was working—Rita Sabo. A few years older than I and a mom already a couple times over. I think we'd have hooked up, only she was pregnant. What was it with me and pregnant women? Patty Duckwa redux. Only here the temptation was not only real but possible. And if I was all but engaged to Jane Brohm, what was I doing lusting after Rita Sabo and Celia no-last-name? Was it like this for married people, too? Was it like this for our father? For our mother?

Our father seemed to suspect what I was thinking. "I have never cheated on your mother," he told me, lifting his glass to his lips. He often swore to this statement; either he suspected I was thinking it quite often or he had a guilty conscience.

"What about Mom? You think Mom cheats?" This was new territory. If we didn't want to believe it about our father, how could we possibly entertain the idea about our mother? Still—

"Your mother," our father said, swilling his drink again, "your mother wouldn't cheat if somebody stuck a dick in her mouth."

The sudden bitter, certain, and cold-blooded viciousness of our father's denial made me wonder—if I wasn't along, would he and Madeleine have shacked up? Would it have been one of those grief-and-guilt-stricken encounters, the imperative of need and ego overriding the imperative of fidelity? Or had he gotten over his scruples and squeamishness and for years had been hooking up with Margies and Jans and

Elsies and Karens? We didn't know. And the myth of the traveling sales-man is such that I expected, frankly, at any time to meet a doppelgänger family, all the children of ages roughly corresponding to our own—the dropped offspring of our father as he traveled from town to town while our mother was huge with each of us and our father, ostensibly, was in what he liked to refer to as "dry dock." Maybe Celia's mother was right to suspect and fear us. Maybe she knew far better than I what men on the road were capable of. After all, I was supposed to be in "dry dock," too, yet here I was, on the road all of two days and already imagining myself hooking up with Celia when I had a girlfriend already, a woman I would eventually marry. And hadn't I nearly hooked up with Rita Sabo, too?

And while our father might have been right about our mother—we didn't want to believe she was capable of cheating, either—we knew more about her, we thought, than he did. We had seen things he had not. A man deep in the throes of fucking up tends to be solipsistic. He has no idea what the consequences of his actions will be. They simply don't enter his field of vision.

Often, when our father came home stewed—particularly if he was working close to home, and they'd made an agreement that he would come right home from his rounds and he hadn't because he was busy buying rounds—our mother would ask one of us to drive her to a motel. "I am not spending another minute in this household!" she'd shriek, and although we knew this was directed at our always-absent father, we also knew it was at least partially directed at us. We were to blame—driving our mother away, driving our father to drink. Our mother would leave us, meet somebody, divorce our father, find happiness, and we would be orphaned or destitute. As she was putting on her gloves, waiting for Robert Aaron to finish heating his car, we would perform a ritual of hangdog glumness—lining up, touching our mother's hands, the hem of her blouse, the younger children whining and crying—and beg her to stay. Our mother would stand on the landing with her bag packed, heft-ing it, deciding. Sometimes she'd stay: "I'm doing this for you, and for the sake of our household, not for your father," she'd say. And sometimes she wouldn't. Which made us wonder. Did she? When she got to the Holiday Inn, did she park herself in the bar, as our father would have done, and talk to the first man who sat down beside her? Was her fury such that a man at the bar could entice her into a moral holiday, something she could say she had apart from our father? It didn't seem possible, but I realized then that everybody has secrets, and they stay secrets for a very good reason. And frankly, when our mother was this angry, when her eyes flashed green fire, she was capable of damn near anything.

Did they suspect of each other what we suspected of them? All that separation, all that time apart, all that grief and frustration and loneliness? Maybe they cut each other slack in this regard. Maybe they knew that about each other, or suspected it, but wouldn't go there, wouldn't ask or tell. Maybe they put the tab for that on each other's bill.

Certainly over the years our parents' marriage took a beating. When our father came home late or drunk, there was hell to pay the whole weekend, and our father couldn't wait to get out on the road again come Sunday evening. But when he managed to get home sober and on time, our mother was sweetness and light. They went out for Friday fish fries and came home giggling and playing grab-ass with each other. And even if our father was late, if he was at least trying—no unsteadiness to his gait, no broken glass in his eyes, an apology for traffic or a late lunch with a customer—our mother smiled, took his round head between her hands, kissed his balding pate, and said, "It's okay, Wally-Bear. We'll put it on your bill."

But as time went on, and our father seemed to be trying less, or trying more with poorer results, our mother said that less often. Hardly at all, really. And when our father tried to get back in her good graces, smiling his addled smile and saying, "We'll put this on my bill, right?" our mother only scowled, folded her arms, shook her head.

She refused to believe, though, at least in front of us, that anything extracurricular could be going on with our father.

"Your father is a good man," said our mother. "He would never be unfaithful, and Lord knows, he's had plenty of opportunity." And then she would tell us a story of when she was showing "out to there," and there was this other woman at the company Christmas party practically throwing herself at our father. "And your father didn't give that woman the time of day. He didn't even look at her." Yes, we wanted to say, but he was working for Dinkwater-Adams then, and was home every night. That was a long time ago. And did our mother know about Shirley writing her name with her fingernail in the unguent on our father's blistered neck? Of course she did. No matter. The company line was absolute, unbroken, unbreached and unbreachable fidelity. Which made us wonder—

did they conspire between the two of them to keep their dark secrets to themselves, and away from us? Or was the secret that there were no secrets, at least not the kind that could destroy a marriage once they were revealed?

Another mystery—and they were many and various—of our parents' marriage.

Something else we knew about our mother that our father didn't: Our mother's closest friends were lesbians. Linnie and Winnie. They'd bought the Bunkas place next door after Alfred Bunkas died, his mother placed in a home. Linnie and Winnie passed themselves off as sisters— Linda and Winifred Jones—who wanted to get away from Minneapolis on account of it being too hectic there. That was the story our father heard, anyway. But they came over often when our father was away, and over coffee with our mother they explained they were actually partners, married in a pledging ceremony, and Winnie had left her husband in Milwaukee, and she didn't want him to find her or their three kids. Our mother surprised us. "I know just how you feel," she said, and we were left to ponder which of Winnie's feelings our mother sympathized with in particular.

In fact, the only time our mother seemed anymore to be able to muster up any energy at all was when she wanted to see Winnie and Linnie. She would hobble across the field to see them and hobble home in the evenings before dinner or, if our father was gone, as he usually was, in time to see us to bed. What was she doing, spending all that time over there? We had no idea. Pouring her heart out, bonding, getting silly-ass drunk on port wine cheese and Beaujolais?

"Some things are best left private," said our mother, echoing Nomi, and that was as much of an explanation as we were going to get. It was, no doubt, as much as we deserved. Once, however, when I was on the roof mulling things over by myself and our mother was putting dinner together—I could hear her sing-humming off-key below me—distinct cries of "More! More!" wafted toward me from Winnie and Linnie's house. It was a midsummer day, and their windows were open. Huh, I thought. I wonder where they learned that?

"Penny for your thoughts," said our father, holding up his glass as though there were something written inside the bubbles, some pattern or message he was meant to see. Neither one of us had said anything since his crack about our mother, and the silence had gotten uncomfortable. I wasn't about to tell him what I'd actually been thinking—who does that, ever?—but I did have a question from earlier, before Madeleine started making eyes at our father.

"Why aren't you selling for Nabisco, Dad?" I asked, and he took a minute in answering. You could tell he was mulling over whether to tell me the truth or not. We had pauses like this before we were informed about Santa Claus, the Easter Bunny, and the fact that Molly was the main ingredient in our hamburgers.

Our father made Dizzy Gillespie cheeks and blew out all the air. He sighed, finished his drink. "They wouldn't have me," he said and shook his glass.

"Last one and then I'm shutting you off," said Madeleine. It wasn't seven o'clock yet. The place was filling up. She didn't want a drunk at the bar during the height of the rush.

"Nobody shuts me off," said our father. "I shut myself off."

Madeleine crossed her arms under her bosom. "Look, I don't want a scene. Somebody already whaled on you pretty good. My advice is leave now, then later we can treat each other with some tenderness. What do you say?"

"I say I'll leave when I'm goddamn ready."

The second bartender, a behemoth in a green T-shirt who'd just come on, walked over. "Problems, Maddy?"

"Naw, this sweet guy was just leaving."

"You got problems, holler."

"No problems, Kenny. Nada. Nothing at all." Madeleine smiled, and I wondered what it was about my father that caused certain kinds of women to believe they could take care of him. Was it that he resembled a fat puppy, the klutz of the litter? Madeleine whispered, "Get some sleep. Come back later. Leave sonny boy back at the motel."

"He's my son."

She straightened up. "Yeah, I know. I get off at eleven." She went back down the bar to take care of another customer.

"I have never cheated on your mother," our father repeated.

"It's okay, Dad."

"I'm a peddler, Emcee. A drummer. A detail man. A company crier. You can pretty it up and call me a commercial traveler, or a field representative or a field engineer, but what I do is sales. I'm a salesman. Now look at me. I take orders. I fill shelf space. I'm a goddamn traveling stock boy." He was close to crying. "Nobody knows what it's like out here. They just don't know." Soon tears were streaming down his corpulent face. He wiped them with a bar napkin.

"Are you okay, Dad?" The sight of my father blubbering had a profound effect on me. I was repelled; I was filled with love. I wanted to forgive him nothing; I wanted to forgive him everything. I got him down off his stool and helped him out of the bar. We left plenty to cover the tab and then some. Madeleine, shaking her head, scooped up the bills as we were leaving.

Between the alcohol and the beating he had taken, he was moving pretty slowly. Like he was learning how to walk again after surgery, little mincing steps accompanied by sharp intakes of breath and general unsureness. He winced as I got him into the car.

I drove us back to the motel, the Timberline Inn on the north side of Spooner. He was sawing lumber inside of fifteen minutes. I considered leaving him there, zipping out in the company car, and hitting all the area bars looking for Celia, or at least a younger version of Maddy, someone who might take a shine to me and wasn't fussy about my address in the morning. But I had the feeling that if I did, when I came back he'd either be gone or have company, and I was too small a person to risk finding out. So I stayed and watched *Charlie's Angels*. It was, I knew, the best I was going to do that evening.

I looked over at our father, a whale beached on his mattress, his snores riveting the air. Strangely, I understood now Maddy's interest in him. He gave off the aura of a good guy, affable and steady, just a little down on his luck, and with patience and nurturing, you knew he'd do right by you. This was somebody a woman down on her own luck, but still plugging away and hoping, could trust. Even if he sometimes did the wrong thing, even if he sometimes screwed up. You could still trust him. He was in this for the long haul. What woman, deep in her own heart, wouldn't want that?

Dorie, evidently. I want to tell Dorie that we can stay together, we can make it just as our parents made it, on the force of inertia alone, and the thing that scares me is she might feel the same way. Good grief, is that what we've come to? Still, it's something.

Had it always been like this and we just hadn't been paying attention?

I suddenly believed our father. He hadn't cheated on our mother. And if he had, who could blame him? Who could blame our mother, either? We are weak everywhere. We make mistakes, and other people—our loved ones—make accommodations. We hope the other party is willing to forgive us. We hope he or she is willing to put it on our bill. It scared me—to realize that one of our father's idiot clichés actually made sense.

The next day we had a lot of territory to cover. It was all red and white pine and blue spruce and green tamarack and blue sky and white birch and quaking aspen, their undersides silver and tremulous in the breeze. And the lakes and rivers glimpsed through the trees were like advertisements for God's vacation land, the water riffling, shimmering—I expected the Hamm's beer bear to come dancing out of the trees. On one stretch of highway the trees thinned and all of Lake Superior was open to us, with sailboats and clouds skimming the horizon, and it seemed as though the world was an open and new place. Not so for my father. We had lunch at the Dog 'N Suds in Minong, and I tried to entice him into riding the go-carts next door, but my father had on his thinking-drinking face—pensive, withdrawn, morose.

"C'mon, Dad, lighten up. It'll be fun."

Our father shook me off. I poked him in the belly, trying to get a rise out of him. "It's good exercise," I said. "Put the pedal to the metal."

"You think this is just fun and games up here, don't you?" our father said, suddenly angry. "You think it's just about going inside these stores and seeing what's on the shelf and ordering more of it, don't you?" I wasn't going to answer him, but yeah, that was pretty much the way I saw it. When I was working for Nabisco, there was the sweet-talking of the store managers to do, but cookies are not a product you need to hard-sell, especially in a resort area. They pretty much leap off the shelf. You're always wangling for display space, but that you're going to get some eventually is pretty much a given. You just want to tie it in to the big weekends—Memorial Day, Labor Day, the Fourth of July. But I wasn't seeing it the way he was, as a Nabisco competitor. As somebody who had to cajole, wheedle, beg, and finesse owners and store managers who, when he introduced himself, would say, "Pee-what-akee? Never heard of 'em." This was what our father was fighting against, and the ignominy of it infuriated him.

He was still going. "You think it's about taking orders and getting yourself some poontang, don't you? Like you're on leave, and you can schmooze up some nice girl at a bar and she's going to put out for you. Well, it doesn't work like that. You're dreaming if you think it is. It's nothing like that. It's—" Our father stopped. He was at a loss for what to say next. He wasn't selling. He wasn't doing anything he thought necessary to count himself part of the sacred, holy order of the peddler. He hadn't tried to sell anything to a soul all morning.

He shook his head, looked away. "Lunch is over," he said. "We've got more orders to take." I had never heard his voice so settled, so resigned. It continued in the afternoon. Our father went into the grocery stores and didn't seek out the managers or the owners. There was none of his usual patter, no exuberant greetings, no jokes. He didn't breathe a word to the people behind the counter in the smaller places unless they asked him what he thought he was doing. He got in, wrote his order, got out. We finished that day's route in record time.

That evening I managed to get him out fishing after supper, but he took no pleasure in it. He didn't say a word all evening, just quietly drank himself silly. I can't say I understood or empathized with him. I couldn't, twenty-one years old and hopped up with possibility, imagine the world being that foreclosed a place.

The best indication of how young and naïve I was is that I thought I was the wise one.

The next day we drove Highway 53, the car silent except for the hum of the tires, the occasional bursts of chatter on the CB, bursts of chatter our father left alone. We worked our way down to Highway 29 for the long drive home. Twenty-nine is dotted with towns all built on one side of now largely defunct railroad tracks, each town a tattered carbon of its neighbor and former self. Each has its pitiful grocery and gas station— some still sporting the green Sinclair dinosaur rather than the clean and corporate red-white-and-blue ARCO signs—and each has its feed mill and boarded up hotel and three taverns, which looked like additions to people's houses, as though drinking were a private pastime taken public, as though they were still in their living rooms, charging for beer and brandy shots. As we flew past we could see each bar had its two or three half-ton pickups parked out front. If I weren't along, this would have been the start of our father's long, slow pub-crawl home.

We were east of Chippewa Falls, and we'd not said three words since we'd started driving. We? Our father drove; he *always* drove. "It's a company car, Emcee, I can't have you driving it. The insurance risk is too great." I chose not to point out that after he'd tied one on after his skull was broken open by Celia's mother he was happy enough to have me drive, but maybe that was a stupor dispensation. The local road mix was red clay and granite, so the crumbling double-lane highway we were driving looked like a bit of ossified Georgia. Pine trees and open fields, the raised railbed on our right. We were zipping past fluffy white clouds shredded like cotton wadding. It was a beautiful day. Why couldn't we talk?

"You about ready for a potty stop?" asked my father, and I nearly burst out laughing. How is it that we never lose the language of childhood for certain fundamental pleasures and necessities? Potty stops and "you know." But it was frustrating, too. I'd been with him all week, and except for his drunken tirade we'd yet to have a conversation. I had been playing the role of our mother—the silent copilot, watching the scenery roll away and disappear behind us while our father silently drove on and on, lost in his own thoughts. It was a private place he went to when he drove, his talk saved for the truckers who'd "keep the front door open" or "watch his back door." Our father was selling to them, too, getting them to believe that in his company car he was one of them. I couldn't stand it, the ease of his camaraderie with them. The brotherhood of the road. At one point my father got all the guys on that stretch of highway on the same CB channel, the whole lot of them sawing away through Roger Miller's "King of the Road."

"What do you think, Dad, you think those guys make potty stops, too?"

"They do if they've got kids."

"Would they even know if they've got kids?"

"They know. Believe me, they know."

"And how would you know if they did?"

"It depends. Daytime nobody talks much, they're trying to make time. Where are the cops? What's the score of the Packers game? Nighttime, though . . ." He trailed off.

"What?"

"I don't know. I suppose it's everything that comes with night driving—itchy eyes, sore back, jittery bones. They're trying to stay awake.

I'm trying to stay awake. We talk. And with nobody else on the road, we talk regular, not CB lingo."

"About what?"

"Kids, family, wives. Where we live. What we're gonna do on the weekend. What we want out of life—you know, stuff like that."

It was as I feared. His relationship with these anonymous truckers was every bit as good as his relationship with us. Better, maybe. Founded on the same clichés during the day, but during the long nights he opened up to them, and they to him, so over time he probably knew some of those haulers better than he knew us. For us to get him to open up, he had to be half in the bag and ready to unload. It helped if he'd just had his head split open by an irate store owner, too. Though what you got then—what you always got, I suppose—was broken rage.

I tried again. Just straight out asked him: "And what do you think about when you're driving, Dad?" I wanted to know. I really did. I wanted him to tell me something, anything, that wasn't prepackaged, canned, a riff from his never-ending rap of taglines and clichés.

And he said, "What?"

"While you drive," I said. "What do you think about?"

"Oh, the usual things. Nothing much, really. The next day, the next customer. I think about your mom. You kids."

"Specifically, what do you think about?"

"Specifically?" He seemed distracted, like something on the road ahead of us really required his attention.

"Yeah, specifically. What do you think? About us, for example."

"Oh, I don't know. Things. The road sort of zips by me, Emcee, and I think about things. Nothing much, really. My thoughts just kind of wander." He nudged the car off the highway and into the gravel drive of Ed's Roadside Inn. "Let's stop in for a taste."

It was more than a taste. By the time we were coming down the long sweeping hills and climbing the rises east of Eau Claire, the sun was turning the telephone poles orange. We could almost hear those delicately curved wires singing. All that talk in the salmon-and-black wire, and I knew he'd never say it, what he thought about all those days behind the wheel. He hadn't offered up anything in the bar, and I knew whatever he was likely to say now would be the usual lines. "Your mom is gonna kill me. Well, you know what they do with horses, don't you?"

It was driving me crazy. I wanted to tell him I had doubts about my upcoming marriage. I wanted to ask him how did he know it was right with Mom. I wanted to ask if he thought Jane was a good match for me. But I couldn't get through to him.

Correction: I said nothing to him about any of it. Not a word of it. Still another indication that, for all my loathing of his reticence, I was learning silence at the feet of the Buddha of Repression myself.

So okay, another missed connection. We're going home now, and it'll be like always, another skirmish between our father's stewed indulgences and our mother's frayed nerves. Our father trying to sneak into the house—his home, his castle—like a lumbering bull, our mother pouring acid onto his flanks trying to keep him out, but then she drops the bucket, raises the drawbridge, and just starts wailing. And the seven of us will hear the fight, or pieces of it, and will pray for reconciliation, pray our mother will lower the bridge so we can all race across, into forgiveness, into family happiness. Or, in whispered conferences—more and more now—we will wonder why they don't just admit they are on separate shores and get a divorce.

Our father, when drunk, is remarkably prescient. Apropos of nothing—we haven't spoken a word to each other in miles—our father says to me, "We are family, Emcee. Never forget that."

I try not to think that this is what he says after each squabble, each fight, each family gathering that ends in screaming and slammed doors when it doesn't end in a fistfight proper.

We are a constellation, I want to say to our father. We are points fixed in space, given meaning only by an outside observer. We are defined by our relation to each other, by our distance, by the pattern we make, and we collide figuratively, which is good because generally it keeps the bloodshed down.

Rain stubbles the salmon-colored sky. I see it on the windshield. I see it falling on the fields. "What are you going to do, Dad?"

"About what?"

"About this job. It's like my summer job from last year, only worse."

"It pays the bills, Emcee."

"So you're going to keep doing it?"

"I'm a salesman, Emcee, it's what I do."

"This isn't selling, Dad. You know it, I know it. Quit kidding yourself."

"Never kid a kidder, kid."

If I'd been paying attention, I'd have heard something coming loose inside our father right then. His situation was bumping up against his own denial, and that wall of clichés he had always used for protection and privacy was falling down. In the battle of his psyche versus cold, hard reality, he was firing blanks.

"Could you just stop it, Dad? Stop with the clichés."

"This will reflect on your merit review." He was on autopilot now. It scared me.

"Enough, Dad."

"That's the way the cookie crumbles, Emcee."

"I mean it, Dad."

"Another county heard from."

"Jesus, Dad, will you just listen to yourself once?"

Our father was silent for a long time. Then he finally told me what he was going to do, and without his explaining, I knew it was going to be both better and worse than what he was doing now. Better because it beat having your head split open. Worse because this was going to be a far worse abasement. Worse because he was going to submit to it willingly.

"I'm going to call Benny Wilkerson," said our father. Then he looks out his window and says softly, "If you can't beat 'em, join 'em." And stares and stares and stares.

The car slides off to the shoulder right then, and I reach to steady the wheel. Dad, I say, we're drifting. The metaphorical aspects of this are obvious—years later I could have said it to Dorie—but right then I meant it literally. The car is drifting—a not uncommon occurrence, I'd noticed, in the late afternoon when our father got tired, but nobody drove the company car except our father, so you said something and jostled him awake.

Not this time, though. The highway is gleaming salmon in the angled sun behind us, and another failing town is shooting past, and the rolling countryside, like God's wrinkled brow, is growing dark in the twilight, and I'm going, Dad? Dad? as we weave into the oncoming traffic and weave back. My hand's on the wheel now, nudging us off the shoulder.

Dad? Dad? His head's nodding, his hands folded high on his immense stomach, the way he is after a large a meal when everyone's home. He means to visit with us, but the burden of the food and the wine is too great and he's asleep, his body doing the great work of digestion.

Would it be wrong to say I have imagined his death just like this? For years I have dreamed it. We are driving through a yellowy orange sunset, and the telephone wires above us and the road below have all gone salmon. And my father nods into sleep, a massive coronary, and I reach across, push his Sorel-booted foot off the accelerator with my right hand while my left keeps us from wobbling too much, then we're slowing and I've got the hazard lights on and I'm steering us back onto the shoulder and Dad's bulk is slumped sideways, his head tipped into his shoulder, his second chin making a third, and I'm shaking him now. Dad? Dad?

Slowing, slowing, slowing, until we come to the shoulder and stop. Whew, that's something, I say and turn, expecting him all the while to wake up.

Dad?

No response. And we'd all know it had to be like this, the Viking burial at sea, the old peddler on the highway.

Only it doesn't happen like that. His head slumps forward, and I'm angry but surprised, too, that something like this hadn't happened before. How many years has he been driving home half-baked, three sheets to the wind, shitfaced and drowsy, risking this, a sudden trip to the Land of Nod or a diabetic coma? How many years has our mother had to worry about this? So I'm screaming at him, "Wake up, Dad! Wake up!" and he can't hear me. When he's like this, there's no waking him.

Then his ear thumps the steering wheel and the horn blares and I know something is seriously wrong. I throw him back into his seat—no easy task—and try steering the car onto the shoulder. He falls sideways into me, and I shove him back against his window and try lifting his leg from the gas pedal while easing us onto the gravel. Only he bounces and falls back into the steering wheel again. The horn blares. His foot is fast on the gas. We pick up speed, sway off the shoulder and back into the lane of oncoming traffic. Car horns blare at us, other cars swerve off the road and back. The word *deadweight* suddenly hits me. I panic. I'm still screaming at him, "Dad, Dad, wake up!" as I smack him a good one on the thigh. Nothing. I lean back and kick his knee. Pop! and his knee bends at an odd angle. But his foot is free from the gas pedal finally, and I shove him sideways again. He slumps into his door, his fingers still locked over his immense chest. I get us back in our lane and then onto the shoulder. We coast like a freight car shunted onto a siding and left to gather its own inertia.

The suck of wind out the window is replaced by the crunch of gravel, but there is still a roaring in my ears, as though everything is rushing around and through me. And all that traffic is going by and still going by and still going by and still going by.

I get on the CB and start screaming, "Mayday! Mayday!" as though we are a ship lost at sea. A trucker ahead of us calms me down enough for me to give him our location. He says he'll relay it on channel 9, the emergency band, and to sit tight, somebody will be there shortly. Another trucker says he'll get to us in twenty minutes or so, and to sit tight, he knows CPR.

Sit tight, sit tight. Our father is dead! I want to yell into the microphone, what the hell good is CPR now? But I don't know a thing, really, about his condition. And I feel ashamed for panicking. I loosen his string tie, undo his shirt. He's breathing but unconscious. I'm shaking.

The trucker arrives, and a few minutes later an ambulance. We're closer to Wausau than Eau Claire, so they take him there.

Our father's heart attack didn't kill him. It nailed him pretty good, though. As I waited for our mother and my siblings, I was given a quick rundown of his condition. Right coronary artery—95 percent blocked. The other branches—blocked, blocked, and blocked. A surgeon drew a diagram and ticked them off the way mechanics inform you of the damage to your engine. This is going to cost him, the surgeon told me. He said the same thing to our mother when she arrived. "Yeah," she said, "but I'm the one who's paying."

"How is he?" Cinderella asked once our mother went in to see him. I'd say Cinderella looked stricken except she always looked stricken.

"Bad. He's Dad, only more so."

While we waited for our mother, I looked through the pamphlet given us by his surgeon: "Risk Factors for Coronary Artery Disease." It was just like those "How to Tell if He Still Loves You" questionnaires in *Cosmo*. Do you have high blood pressure? Do you eat a high fat, high cholesterol diet? "Do you think Dad's regular breakfast of eggs cooked in bacon and sausage grease counts?" I asked Cinderella. The doctor returned and explained that he was going to do an angioplasty once our father was stable. A balloon catheter would be shoved up the femoral artery in his groin and once it reached his heart it'd be inflated and either push the blockages out of the way or flatten them. He'd be in the hospital a few days and could recover at home after that. He would also need to take his heart and diabetes meds regularly and eat a more balanced diet. And there was the matter of the torn ligaments in his knee from when I kicked him.

Said our mother, "This should put the fear of God into him." Then she turned her face away so we couldn't see it crumple.

We stand around our father's bed as he's prepped for surgery. He's fussing, though, and the nurse is having a hard time with the IV. Our mother is scared and so angry at him for refusing to seek treatment or even a diagnosis until it's come to this that she explodes. "Look, Wally, if I can have all my insides taken out and not receive a word from you, comfort or otherwise, then the least you can do is sit still and let them make sure your heart keeps working, goddammit." That seems to work. The anesthetic cocktail he finally downed probably helped, too. In his hospital gown he has the hunted-and-caught look of a man recently castrated.

So how you feeling, Dad?

Oh, okay. You know this puts hair between your toes.

Our mother is calmer now. It's okay to be scared, Wally-Bear. I was scared. But I know, I just know, Wally-Bear, that you're going to come through this all right.

I hope so, honey.

So, Dad, you picked a hell of a way to find out if we loved you.

Not my choice, kitten. His head flops over toward our mother. Well, Suse, I never thought you'd be sitting under the apple tree with anyone else but me.

I wouldn't, Wally-Bear.

That's my Pumpkin. (Pause.) I love you, Susie-Q.

I love you, too, Wally-Bear.

I never told you this, Susie-Q, but I'm very happy you agreed to marry me.

You tell me all the time, silly.

But I mean it, Suse. I've had a great life. I wouldn't want anything to be different.

I know, Wally-Bear.

And, Suse?

We all lean in close. The nurses are checking their dials and things, tapping the bag that's dripping stuff into his arm. He's struggling to keep awake, to say this last thing before they wheel him away. Our mother finds his hand and squeezes.

Suse? he says. Sweetheart? I owe you.

Yes, says our mother with both more iron and more tenderness than I'd have thought possible. She's patting our father's hand; her eyes are filling with tears. Yes, Wally-Bear, you do.

19. Some Things Are Best Left Private

"Emmie, are you okay?" Our mother's face appears in the back bedroom window.

I'm on the deck. The deck railing, the furniture, the big clay plant pots—everything is covered with a fine rime of frost. The half-moon shines on the frosted ground, the stubble from the last cutting in the fall. You can see Cinderella's footprints coming and going, then the horde of us coming back up, after the frost had settled. Her appearance pretty much ended the evening—odd, since we were waiting for her to arrive. But her news about our mother and father having figured things out gave us an out—we didn't have to decide. Not yet we didn't. Unless, of course, Mom and Dad's plan is completely unworkable. So everyone went back to where they belonged except me, and I didn't want to go into the house yet.

I want to answer her, No, Mom, I am not okay. My bookstores are failing, my seems to have lost interest in me and my marriage is in trouble. But I can't tell her that. There's a kind of rule in our family: When you can't say what it is you are really thinking or feeling, ask about someone else. "Cinderella told us Mel's thinking of getting back with his wife."

"Yes, she told me that, too."

"I didn't even know he had a wife."

"Everyone has their secrets, Emmie."

"So, essentially, Mel's cheating on Cinderella with his own wife."

"I hadn't thought of putting it that way, but yes, I suppose he is."

"That's a pretty big secret."

"Yes," says our mother, "yes, it is."

"She had another one," I say. "Something she told Mel that maybe prompted him on the wife thing. Something she didn't tell us."

"Maybe she didn't want to tell you."

"Maybe. Is it something she wants you to tell us?" That's another informal rule in our family: if you want information conveyed to all the siblings, tell it to our mother. She's the family information dissemination officer. This comes in handy when you have something awful to disclose, like a divorce or a separation; the next time you see everyone, they all know what's up with you, and you haven't had to say a word.

Our mother sighs. It's not always clear whether she does the information dispersal thing because she likes it or because she feels she's helping protect her children. It's probably both. It must be lonely, being the icebreaker for the frozen seas in people's hearts. "I suppose you'll find out soon enough," she says. "They found another lump. In her breast. They want to remove everything this time, just to be sure."

"Jesus."

"It's going to be hard for her, and as a group you've not been particularly supportive." She's right, we haven't, but I don't say anything. Our mother says, "If there's one thing your father and I have always wanted, Emmie, it's for you children to pull together. To work together as a family."

"I know, Mom, I know."

"You know, Emmie, you can pay lip service to something and then go do the exact opposite. Or want to do the right thing and find yourself doing something else entirely."

"Is that how you explained Dad's behavior over the years?"

"Don't bad-mouth your father, Emmie. He's a good man, and he tries hard—"

"I know, Mom, I know."

"It's just sometimes he—"

"Mom, you don't have to explain it to me."

"I wasn't going to, Emmie. There are things that happen in a marriage that you can't explain to anyone, even to yourself."

"You got that right."

"What's bothering you, Emmie? You've looked distracted ever since you got here."

"I don't know, Mom. I don't know that I want to talk about it."

Up in her bedroom window, speaking from behind her screen, our mother is in her role as priest confessor. This has always been a comfort for us: you can tell her things and she listens without judgment. But because what is happening between Dorie and me is just a feeling I have, not an announcement I want to make, I don't want her knowing about it. Every once in a while our mother confuses her roles as confessor and publicist.

"That's okay, Emmie," she says. If this weren't a screened window she'd reach out and cup my chin. "It's late, Emmie. You should get some sleep. Me, too. Tomorrow is a big day. For all of us."

"Cinderella told us you have things worked out, you and Dad. For after tomorrow, I mean. What have you and Dad figured out?"

"Your father and I—" Our mother starts, then stops. She has this kindly look on her face, like she knows I'm trying to cajole information out of her when I wouldn't share mine with her. She smiles. "Everyone has their secrets, Emmie. You of all people should know that."

After the light went out in our mother's room, I was still at loose ends. I still didn't want to go inside and lie down next to my wife. I'd have gone back to the tepee, but Ike was there, so I went back on the roof. The rungs of the aerial were ice cold, but it felt good climbing up. In our haste to get down earlier, we'd left the cooler. I counted this as good fortune. I grabbed a beer and sat near the roof's peak, my back against the chimney. I'm here, I know, for the same reason we so often went to the rooftop in our teens: escape from ourselves. When the clutter and the craziness seemed too much for us to handle, when we needed to get away, when we needed to gather, we climbed the aerial to the roof, where we could talk, be ourselves. We could be anybody else we chose to be as well. And when our mother got tired of being the trouper and she was laying into our father, it was where we went to argue about whether it wouldn't be best if they just called it a night on their marriage.

"Don't be crazy," said Peg Leg Meg. "They love each other."

"Well," said Wally Jr., "they got a piss-poor way of showing it."

The one thing we would do up there that most bonded us, though, was what we called Rooftop Cinema. How many times in our youth, via *Saturday Night at the Movies,* did we see *Jason and the Argonauts* or *Hercules,* Steve Reeves battling monsters and armed skeletons, or *Casablanca,* or *The Maltese Falcon,* or *Rear Window,* or *Hatari!* with Red Buttons and John Wayne, or *McLintock!* with John Wayne and Maureen O'Hara (our father's favorite), or *Seven Brides for Seven Brothers* (our mother's favorite— she loved Howard Keel), or *Captain Blood* or *Robin Hood* or *They Were Expendable* or *The Longest Day* or *Harvey* or *It's a Wonderful Life* or *Command Decision* or *It Happened One Night* or *The Road to Morocco* or *The Secret Life of Walter Mitty* or *The African Queen* or *Birdman of Alcatraz* or *Gone With the Wind* or *The Magnificent Seven* or any of a thousand other films that filled our heads on Saturday nights and gave us our notions of how the world was and how it should be?

Up on the roof we re-created them. We had help in this. Borowski.

Borowski had a first name, but nobody knew what it was. It didn't matter. Borowski was Borowski. What he was doing hanging out with us I've no idea. Our mother loved him. He said "Please" and "Yes, ma'am," so she was willing to overlook the fact that he drank too much, got into fights, and had a grade point average in the low one-point-somethings. "He's just a little misguided," said our mother, who was willing to tolerate in others what would drive her crazy in us. It was rumored Borowski had parents, but nobody had ever seen them, and when you asked him, he simply said they'd divorced and he never wanted to see them again. He worked for Tony Dederoff and lived there, more or less. We, too, worked for Tony Dederoff from time to time, which was how we knew him.

His other connection to us was that he, too, loved the movies. He was even willing to act them out for us. We'd climb to the roof as though it were the balcony, and Borowski, down below, would put on a matinee. Sometimes we'd jump into the landscape of our dreams to help out. "No, no, no, you've got it all wrong," we'd say. "When the rhino impales Red Buttons in *Hatari!* it's like this—" And then we'd demonstrate, bent over, two-by-fours pressed to our foreheads as we ran at each other, trying to gouge, trying to maim.

We rarely did complete movies. Usually it was just scenes. The beach landing scene and the parachute scene from *The Longest Day,* fistfights from westerns, sword fights from all those Errol Flynn movies, send-ups of the great kissing scenes. "Frankly, my dear, I don't give a rat's ass," said Borowski, holding Peg Leg Meg in a clinch, and Meg would fly into hysterics. "That's not how it goes!" she'd protest, and Borowski would promptly drop her. "You want to get kissed or not?" She'd scramble to her feet and they'd try it again. She had a terrible crush on him, and God bless Borowski, who'd screw anything that moved (back in high school he'd slept with Dorie a few times, if the rumors were true), he did not take advantage of it. Meanwhile we'd hoot and holler and call out for the grapefruit scene from *The Public Enemy,* or re-create the rooftop scenes from *To Catch a Thief* and *Where Eagles Dare.*

Our ebullience sometimes roused our parents, who came outside to see what we were up to. "What in God's name is going on out here?" our father would ask. They'd stand in what, in a theater, might be the orchestra pit but which was actually our alfalfa field, and by turning their heads this way and that they could take in our antics both on the ground and on the roof. "Oh," said our mother. "It's just the normal noises, Wally. Leave them be." And they'd go back inside, either to wrangle away some more or to make up. Given that we'd been driven outside by their fighting, we counted it a victory if later, sitting above their bedroom window, sipping beers, winding down, moonlight washing over the fields, we heard the sounds of two large bodies administering love to each other, and our mother's "More! More!" echoing into the night air.

No such noises, normal or otherwise, tonight. Our farm is laid out before me in the moonlight—the fields, the woods, Ike's tepee nestled in down by the marsh. A fine layer of frost over everything. Below me in the drive is our gift for our father. Tony Dederoff must have driven it over while we were in the tepee. He'd have known our father was already in bed, and he knew what a charge it would be if, in the morning, when everyone awoke, there it'd be, gleaming.

The next thing I know I'm in the driveway dropping its tailgate. Tony left the keys in the ignition. The tailgate gives beneath me, and I think about time and its passing, and what our mother said about secrets. Maybe the two are related. Maybe this is the beer talking, but I don't think so. Consider how time accelerates as we age. As my siblings and I grew away from each other, away from home, the years passed, quick and then quicker. I tried explaining this once to our kids. How when you are little time seems to go so slowly—the clock hands barely budge—but when you're older whole months simply fly by. The device they use in old movies to indicate time passing, calendar pages falling like leaves— it's true. And here's the reason: when you're four, say, a year of your life is a full quarter of your life. When you are eight, it's an eighth. Still a sizable amount. When you're twenty, though, it's a twentieth, when you're thirty, a thirtieth, and so on. Each year is a smaller fraction of your life. So time itself seems to speed up.

When things don't seem to be happening in your life, when you seem to be waiting for the next thing to come along, then time slows down again. When I left home for school, for example, the family to me seemed to remain constant. I was the one who was meteoring across time. No doubt if I were listening to Ernie's and Peg Leg Meg's stories of that time, though, I would realize that there was a lot going on while I was absent. Things that happened to them while I was gone that I will never know. And vice versa. Maybe that explains some of the distance between me and my siblings. Maybe not.

There's also this: in the great wash of time, things take place without our seeing them. They don't show up on our radar screens, and when they finally do register, we are reminded of how quickly time moves, and how different things are. It throws us for a loop.

In families—in marriages—people experience time at different rates. They pay attention to different things. This is what gets families and marriages in trouble.

Take, for still another example, Nancy. Harold's Nancy. Harold, our cousin who dared suggest to our father that marrying Nancy might be a reason for not going into the military, and his fiancée, who in Evergreen Park that night had been poked and prodded by our relatives—as we did with Meg's Greg, and Cinderella's Mel, and anyone else who dared enter our closed circle. How she'd good-naturedly put up with it, though that evening must have crawled by agonizingly slowly for her, as evenings did for us when our father went out of control. Had time speeded up for her once the party was over and she and Harold escaped into the cool evening air? Had they found someplace—the backseat of a car, maybe— and had a good laugh over what they'd been put through? Did they experience a little calm pocket of time right then, a moment when they understood each other completely? And then had time speeded up as they locked on each other's eyes and started fumbling with each other's clothes—the opening of Harold's belt and zipper, the hiking of Nancy's skirt, her underwear scrunched down her hips, then peeled down her shins and over her ankles, and then, joy, joy, all that frenetic, frenzied, rapturous joy? Which slowed down eventually, their heartbeats slowing, their breathing slowing, time slowing. I can imagine Harold sighing, and Nancy, underneath him, sighing, and time coming almost to a standstill when she breathes to him, "Will you love me forever?" And Harold, exquisitely sated with his new knowledge, breathing back, "Oh, baby, absolutely."

And then what? The old story: they got married, had kids, Harold was sent to Vietnam. When he came home there was a huge party at his parents' place. It must have been ninety-seven degrees that day, and Harold was sitting in a lawn chair wearing a T-shirt, a sport shirt, and a wool sweater. I couldn't believe it. An argyle cardigan sweater. And a blanket draped over his lap. And he kept saying, "I'm cold, Ma. I just feel really, really cold." What had happened to Harold? Nobody knew. Our father, maybe, but all our father said was "He'll snap out of it. He just needs to unwind." Unwind from what? Nobody was saying. But he was going to be all right, wasn't he? His time there had just been this hunk ripped out of his life, right, but he was still the same Harold, wasn't he? But why did he feel so cold?

Nancy was there, wearing a sexy dress that was too tight given that she'd had two babies, but she seemed upset, haggard, wrung out, as though having him back was as great a strain as dealing with his absence had been. I hadn't seen her since Harold's bon voyage party prior to boot camp, but for some reason I expected her to be unchanged. Harold was supposed to be unchanged as well. But they'd both changed. A lot. Harold looked like someone who was kicked and was waiting for someone to kick him again, and Nancy was flustered and impatient, the way our mother was when we got on her nerves and our father once again was AWOL.

A few years after that welcome home party, Harold comes home early one day from his Borden milk route and finds Nancy in bed with his son's third-grade teacher. In all recountings of family lore, that is the point at which Nancy ceases to exist. Naked, legs open, caught by her husband in an adulterous embrace with another man, and then she vanishes. I don't mean there was any foul play; there were court hearings, custody arrangements, things of that nature, but as a part of our family's history, Nancy was erased, eradicated the way Lenin's and Stalin's associates kept disappearing from official photographs. And here is what I found myself wondering as I leaned on the chimney and nursed my beer, our parents' farm spread out beneath the moon and flickering with hoarfrost, and what I think of now as I sit on the tailgate—what was it like for Nancy in between the time she asked that question of Harold in the backseat of a nearly new Dodge Dart and his homecoming? Or between his homecoming and her affair with her son's teacher? I imagine the two of them stuck in the shudderings of time. For a while time stops for Nancy, it's held in suspension. Her man is away, she is waiting for his return, she is a new mother, she is holding down the fort, she is a trouper. But she is also lonely, and the entire country seems to be one big love-in, and she is plodding along, not even a woman anymore, just somebody's wife, somebody's mother. Then at a PTA meeting someone says hello with what seems like more than casual interest, and you are amazed to find that spark alive in you again, the spark that says someone notices you as a human being, and time once again begins its acceleration until all you can imagine is when you will see him again, see him next. You don't even know how things had unfolded; they simply had. And now you have secrets, secrets you have to keep from your husband.

And your husband? He had been frozen in time while he was away, no? Stuck in that terrible place. And when he came back he was a different person, unrecognizable except for his features. Someone or something else was inhabiting the body that you lay down next to at night. It made your skin crawl. You know you should not feel like this, you know your husband needs you to lead him back from wherever it is he's been, but you are so caught up in your secret life that you cannot see the forest for the trees. There is only the next rendezvous, the next time *he* leaves for work, and you know it can't go on like this, the keeping of secrets and the disorienting passage of time. Something's got to give. You start taking chances, have your lover over later in the afternoon, almost daring yourself to get caught. Perhaps you want to, perhaps that's the way to end this, get things out in the open, so that the disassociations of time can rectify themselves, so you're no longer stuck in two kinds of time, the dead time of being with your husband and the electrified, alive time of being with your lover.

And then you are caught. Are things better now? What then? What happens then?

It's funny, but I haven't imagined what it must have been like for Harold. I can't go there—nothing like that ever happened to me—but he must have experienced even wilder, more violent dissociations. The agonizing slowness of battle in contrast to his heart's clamorings, the drizzling away of days on the base, one by one by one, knowing his kids were zooming through their childhoods without him. The one thing that would keep him from going bonkers was knowing there was a constant in the world, his wife, Nancy. Sure, he had his own secrets, things that had happened to him and things he'd done that he couldn't tell anybody, not a soul, but that was par for the course, wasn't it? You walled up those things inside you, came home, and picked up where you'd left off. That was the way it was supposed to happen, wasn't it? And then to come back and discover that everything had changed! He'd stayed the same—at least that was what he kept telling himself—yet everything back home had changed.

How do you reconcile these changes? How? You close your eyes and hope for the best. And then it turns out that isn't enough.

Which brings us to Dorie and me. She had been alone for a long time before we got married, she said, and she wanted to be alone now. She started lining up bike trips one after another—a trip across Iowa followed by a trip from Madison to Duluth. For weeks I wouldn't see her. She checked in by phone every once in a while, but it was as though she were living one life and the kids and I were living the one she'd left. And each time she came back, she seemed a little more distracted, a little more disengaged. When I asked her if she was having an affair, she replied, "Don't be silly," which wasn't, technically, an answer to my question.

Things came to a head on New Year's Eve. We were at a friend's party. At midnight it felt as though I was holding an alien being in my arms. Like you're on one of those dates where she kisses you to get rid of you. On the way home I asked her, "Do you still love me?" It had been a while since I'd heard her say it.

"Don't be silly. Of course I love you."

Then I asked, "Are you still in love with me?" There was an uncomfortably long pause.

She sighed. "I still love you, Em. It's just I'm not 'in love' with you anymore." She paused. "What I'm trying to say, I guess, is that it's not that I love you any less, I just don't love you the same way I used to. You understand that, don't you?" She looked at me. We'd come to a stop sign. I was staring at the roadway in front of us. "Oh, Christ, you don't. You don't understand, do you? Oh, shit, I shouldn't have said anything."

Little micalike flakes of snow were drifting down. An inch had already fallen. Tree limbs were etched white, the snowbanks, gray earlier in the evening, were pristine again, amber under the streetlights, softly blue in the shadows. In another life, it would have looked pretty. A car behind us honked. "Em, honey? You need to drive now."

But I couldn't. I couldn't make the car go. My hands rested on the Villager's steering wheel, but I couldn't move them and I couldn't move my feet. The car behind us swerved to get by, laying on its horn all the way. Still I didn't move. A couple more cars drove around us before I could make my body work. I drove us home, slowly. We crept along, but in my mind we were flying, the car fishtailing, the new snow acting like sawdust on a freshly waxed floor. We were clipping the sides of cars. Dorie was screaming, "Em, stop!" I hit the accelerator hard. I cut cars off, swerving around them. Horns blared, a cacophony of blaring. Everything except what was right in front of me was a blur. "Em, stop it, you're scaring me!" I didn't stop. Ahead of us a traffic light went yellow, then red. I accelerated. I aimed for the heart of the intersection, where an SUV was waiting to make a left turn. *"Emmiieeeeee!"*

I managed to put the car in park at the curb. Dorie opened her door. "You coming?"

"In a while. I just want to sit here a spell."

"Em, I'm sorry. I shouldn't have said anything. Are you okay?"

"Well," I managed to say, "at least now I know."

"I feel awful, Em. I didn't mean to make you feel devastated. I thought you knew."

"I'll be in in a little while," I said.

Sometime later a police officer tapped on my window. I rolled it down. "Hey, buddy. I've cruised this neighborhood three times the last two hours and you've been here the whole time. What's your problem?"

"My wife's not in love with me anymore."

"She in love with somebody else?"

"Not that I'm aware of."

"She messing with somebody else?"

"Not that I'm aware of."

"Then what you have, my friend, is not a problem. It's a marriage. Look, if you're trying to kill yourself, you're doing it wrong. You gotta be in an enclosed space for that to work." I just looked at him. He shook his head. "I'm kidding, okay? You kill yourself and I'll have to arrest you. And the paperwork for that is a pain in the ass."

He gestured with his chin over the roof of our car. "That your house?"

I nodded.

"Get in it. Chances are your wife is in bed waiting for you."

She was, but I slept in the guest room that night, and things between us have gone downhill from there.

There are many family tales I could tell, tales of wonder and woe, the everyday tragedies that made us who we are, each in his or her own life—the beaten martyr, the social worker, the bookstore owner, the Indian cook, the pissed-off cripple, the drunk accountant, the tentative human resource manager. I've given only a fraction of them here. And I know I have done a disservice to my siblings by not telling their stories here, or by not allowing them to tell their own stories, or at least their versions of the stories I have told. No doubt their versions would be different from mine. That is perhaps a task or an enjoyment for another time—after all, there will be funerals to attend to soon enough, and we will be gathering again, in grief rather than in celebration, and in those drunken nights of attempted reconciliation and consolation there will be time enough for those stories.

Who knows, by then we may all be married to different people. But once again I am speaking for myself.

Besides, this is our parents' story, not ours, though no doubt the reason I've told it is ultimately selfish. I have tried to save my own life with the truest story I could tell, even if I had to imagine or make up most of it. So be it. There is so little we can ever know of someone else's life. Even if they are your parents. Even if she is your wife.

For now there's merely the collective us and the collective them, and the mystery for us is this: how did they manage for so long to remain a couple? And can Dorie and I manage it, too?

Dorie's beautiful blond head peeks around the side window. "You want company?"

"It's a free country."

"Not the welcome I was expecting."

I scoot over for her. "This is like old times," she says, "climbing roofs, sitting on a tailgate. In high school I used to climb the water tower for rendezvous up there. Or somebody always had a van or a pickup and we'd find some deserted road. Not too hard back then."

"That wouldn't have been with me."

"You never asked."

"You wouldn't have even if I had asked."

She fishes a beer for herself and one for me from the cooler, which I'd brought down from the roof with me. "Coulda, shoulda, woulda, Ace. Why didn't you ask me now?"

"I thought you were sleeping."

"You didn't check, though, did you? How long have you been out here?"

"Coupla hours."

She feels my hands. "Brr, they're like ice. See if I let you touch me with those things."

"I'm sure you could find somebody else. If you haven't already."

"What is with you, Ace? Do you want to talk or just throw accusations around? Because I don't need this."

"You don't seem to need much of anything."

"What's that supposed to mean?"

"It means you're never around. It means that even when you are around, you're someplace else. I don't know about you, but when your partner's distracted and disengaged while you're making love to her, it sort of makes you wonder where her interest and engagement are."

Dorie laughs. "Isn't distracted sex better than no sex?"

"I don't know, is it?"

Dorie sighs. "You're right, Em. I have been focusing on other things."

"Look," I say. "I know all these trips and the workouts and whatnot have to do with your being happy and at home inside your body, especially after the kids, but I'm wondering if someone else isn't being at home and happy inside your body as well."

"You're kidding, right?"

"All I know is you've been putting a lot of distance between us. I just figured there was someone else. Isn't that what it usually means—a moving away is a moving towards?"

"I was moving towards myself, Em." Dorie inhales and sighs. "You know what your problem is, Ace? You have a hard time imagining me wanting to do things completely on my own. Okay, I got involved in myself. I'm sorry if I got distracted and overcompensated—"

"Overcompensated? Overcompensated? Oh, that's rich. That's lovely—"

"But that does not mean I'm screwing somebody else! What is with you?" Dorie exhales hard. "Christ, I wish I still smoked. How did we get on this subject anyway? I just came out here to make nice. Look, honey, will it make you feel any better if I tell you I'm not seeing anyone? If that's what you're worried about, don't be."

She says this so calmly, so reasonably that I want to be calm and reasonable myself. But I can't do it. I open up my mouth to speak, and it comes pouring out of me—the rage, the fear, the jealousy, the despair. "Not seeing anyone? Not seeing anyone! You kick me in the balls, and then you think you'll make me feel better by telling me you're not seeing anyone?"

"When did I kick you in the balls?"

" 'I'm not in love with you anymore, Em. I love you, but I'm not in love with you.' What's that? A postcard from the house of happiness?"

"So that's what's making you so angry? Look, I said I was sorry I ever said that. I'm sorry I burst your bubble. If I'd known you were going to feel destroyed by that, I never would have said anything. Lots of people in marriages aren't in love with their partners anymore. That doesn't mean they don't have good marriages."

"Is that why you told me you weren't in love with me? To demonstrate the strength of our marriage?"

"Look, Ace, do you want to call it quits? Is that what you want?"

"Not so loud. You'll wake up our parents."

"Like they haven't been in conversations just like this."

"That doesn't mean they have to hear ours."

"Fine. You have the keys? Put this thing in drive and let's go."

We do. The Nomad has a floor shift, and it's rather delightful working a clutch again. In a few minutes we're shooting over hills, driving out to where the land flattens by the river north of St. Genevieve's. It's marshy here, a mix of scrub trees and waterlogged fields. Half-mile gaps between houses—it'll be a while before they get around to putting in subdivisions here. Finally, on a long stretch of empty road, I pull over. There's a house tucked into a clump of woods on the other side of the river and an abandoned bridge that no longer connects this road to the access road on the other side. We haven't said anything for a while. The sky is absolutely clear above us. I drop my hands to my lap. "What's happening to us, Dorie? What in God's name is happening?"

"I don't know, Em. Some things you can't explain."

She puts her hand over mine, but I don't grasp it. "I thought we had a good marriage. I mean, if anybody had a decent marriage, it was us, right? So how could this happen?" I'm someplace between crying and laughing. "Why did you say you weren't in love with me?"

"Because I wasn't, Em. It comes and goes. Haven't there been times when you weren't in love with me?"

Like right now? I want to say, but I remember Nomi's words: Some things are best left private. So I say instead, "But I would never say so, and you know why? Because it would hurt you. So why did you tell me? Because you wanted to be honest? Please. It's why I keeping thinking you had an affair. I want a *reason* for all this unhappiness, something I can point to and go *'j'accuse!'* or however the French do their finger-pointing. But it's more elusive than that. You probably don't even know yourself why you said it, but you did, you can't unsay it, and I go around with this kicked-in-the-balls feeling of incredulity: how has this happened to us?"

Dorie looks at the sky and sighs again. "Christ, you're even more sentimental than your father." She lifts her beer from between her legs and sips. "Okay, truth. In the past year, year and a half, I have spent time rethinking the marriage. I have thought of getting out. No doubt that was why I said what I said. I wanted to hear what it sounded like. But haven't you noticed, Em, that lately I've been *trying* to make nice? I don't want to call it quits. I've got too much invested in this marriage. Besides, you're a nice guy and the world is full of creeps. You're not a creep. Who else would make love to a pregnant woman when her breasts were big and sore and she felt like a balloon?"

"I don't know if I want to be known simply as the noncreep in your life."

"Well, there isn't anybody else I'm auditioning for the part. C'mon." She squeezes my hand, gets out of the Nomad. Once I'm out, too, she hugs me from behind, kisses me behind my ear. This is the closest we've been in years to a "moment." "Look, Em, you're my husband. That isn't going to change, okay?"

"You're still not in love with me, are you?"

She squeezes my belly, a marital Heimlich maneuver. "Give it time, Em. I'm trying. And it's not easy. You've been distant, too." Another squeeze. "You know what I think we need, Ace? Enthusiastic marriage repair." She snuggles up to me. "It's too bad I was pregnant with Henry when you first brought me home to tell your folks we were getting married. Remember that? We were so desperate to find a place to make out, we were like a couple of teenagers—"

"We're not teenagers now."

"We weren't then, either."

I know what she wants to do here—buy my silence with her body—but we haven't talked out things that have gone too long not being talked about at all. She *is* trying, and I'm being a petulant bastard, but I can't stop myself. The event to which she's referring—Dorie and I parked in front of Wally Jr.'s shed, which we thought was out of the way, and we were half-naked in the backseat when he came home from working a swing shift. He wanted to put his truck away. So he slid into the front seat of our car, announced, as we were scrambling to cover ourselves, "I didn't see nuthin'," moved our car ten feet, parked his truck where he wanted it, and went into his house. Never said a word about it again to either of us. And we were horny enough not to let that stop us from finishing.

Dorie shakes her head. "Christ, whatever happened to Wally Jr.?" She shakes her head again. "Your family," she says. "It's even more fucked up than mine was."

"That's a definition of family, isn't it? I mean, look at us—two brothers in AA, one who ought to be, the whole lot of us with dispositions in that direction, we've got four divorces among us, not including you and me if it comes to that—"

"It's not going to come to that, Em—"

"Things break down, Dorie. They do. You don't mean for them to, but they do. You start off in one place and you think you're heading towards Y and you end up in X. And you have no idea how you got there, how you ended up in this other place." I think about how Cinderella's marriage ended, after we caught Okie cheating on her, and it was clear, too, he was beating her up. Each of us took one of her kids; Dorie and I got Okie II, her oldest. Skinny kid, haunted eyes, always crying about something. We thought we were saving him. We thought we were saving everybody. Cinderella had broken from Okie, and it was just a matter of time before her kids were returned to her. Then Okie Jr. started stealing from us, and we said, Well, he's going through the lurchings of adolescence. He was a sensitive kid, Okie Sr. had really whaled on him, he was bound to act out. The other kids were going through their own lurchings as well. Only this permanent smirk seemed to take up residence in Okie Jr.'s mouth and nothing we said seemed to get through to him and we ended up shipping him off to Mom and Dad. And he stole from them, too, and as soon as he could leave he left and hasn't been back. The last I heard he was in California laying carpet alongside former dot-com moguls. Supposedly he's got a wife and two kids now himself. And our mom, the original "you will always have a home to come home to" lady, has two—two!—great-grandkids she's never seen, never met, never held. And she isn't likely to, because Okie Jr. is so damn much like his father it's not funny.

I sigh, my chest filled with disappointment. "Remember what happened with Okie Jr., Dorie? And you remember what happened when Cinderella's Amy got pregnant and wasn't intending to marry the father? Mom said, 'She didn't do anything anyone else in this family didn't do, she just got caught at it.' "

"And this has what to do with us, Em? What are you saying?"

I'm somewhere else now. I'm not even trying to answer her. "I mean, think about it. Our parents together fifty years, yet more than half their kids manage to marry so badly they get divorced. And you and I—after what, a decade and a half?—we're on the outs, too—"

"You could be in if you wanted to be, Ace."

"—Or how about this: our parents move us out of the burbs because they aren't safe, and you and I plunk our kids down in the middle of a city, in what's politely known as a 'transitional' neighborhood. You think about it, in our family we're either reversing trends or taking them to their logical extremes."

"Em, are you okay?"

"You know what the problem is? All those stories that try to end themselves with a wedding. They kiss, fade out, and that's that. They want us to believe that time itself stops right then: And they lived happily ever after. As though there was nothing more to be written, as though nothing else could happen."

"So stuff happens, Em. What's your point?"

I want to say something to her about how people experience a marriage at different rates, and the secret is not getting caught up in any one moment and thinking that moment is the whole. How that probably explains why my first marriage didn't last: we couldn't imagine the unhappy times ever ending. We were twenty, twenty-two. Time spread out before us like a galaxy. Spend all of it with one person? What on earth were we thinking? And yet that's exactly what I want to do with Dorie. I want to tell her how it's tearing me up inside that maybe she doesn't. That maybe she's bored with me, tired of the whole thing, and she's having tryouts on the road to stave off the ennui of being with me. I try telling her that, but I end up babbling, "I can't help it. I still feel like I'm losing you." And there it is, the nub, the very heart of it.

"Honey, you want to fool around? I'm getting leg jitters, look." We're sitting on the tailgate, our legs doing lazy pendulum swings. I look down and she's right. Her legs do this sometimes, a little dance of their own, and they can't stop. It's like she's had too much coffee. "The only thing that distracts me enough to get it to stop," she says, "is good sex."

"So what happens when you get jittery legs on your bike trips?"

She shucks off her jacket, peels off her pullover. She shivers, and her breasts rise from the cups of her bra. She pushes me down into the Nomad's bed. "What, you think I find a hunk and fuck his brains out? What do you think, Ace? I suffer. Alone. In a school gym, or in a tent, or in a B and B. Biking is like a chastity belt. You should watch people try to sit down. It's comical. Except for the young marrieds who mistakenly think it'll be romantic, everyone's groin is on fire at the end of the day. And it's not lust. A & D ointment is *not* an aphrodisiac. My labia are too sore for fucking, trust me."

"But not now," I say, running my hands from her hips to her breasts and back again.

"No, not now. Right now it feels very, very good." She has her eyes closed.

"This isn't going to be a pity fuck, is it?"

"You're going to drive me away, Ace, you really are. You know that, don't you?"

"You wouldn't tell me if you had fucked somebody, though, would you?"

"No, if you must know, I probably wouldn't. But I don't see how that matters, seeing as how I haven't."

"I found the diaphragm, Dorie. And the nightie you pack in your saddlebag."

She sits back. "Christ."

"You want to tell me again you weren't fucking anybody?"

"I didn't use them, Em. Not once. Not ever."

"You're going to tell me you took them along, neatly sealed in a plastic ziplock by accident?"

"I just wanted to feel like a free agent again, Em. It doesn't mean anything. Like your dad—he's probably had the same condom in his wallet since Korea. I packed that stuff because I wanted to feel as though something *were* possible. I mean, I wasn't interested in that, not really. But I took it along anyway. Just to feel as though there might *be* a 'just in case.' Now," she says, undoing her bra and pulling her arms free, "we can either make use of this fine evening or we can call it a night. What do you want?"

In the moonlight and the cold, Dorie's breasts are magnificent—pendulous, full, the nipples smilingly erect. Patty Duckwa's breasts had nothing on Dorie Keillor's, and I am calling to mind an idealized pair of breasts last seen a third of a century ago.

Dorie's body has a geometry that invites contemplation. I contemplate it for some time, running my fingers over her upraised nipples, over the gooseflesh of her arms and legs and belly. Her body glistens. You can almost see a light steam rising from it into the cold night air. I'm not sure that an act of love in the back of a station wagon is necessarily the best thing for our marriage right at this moment, but I am ready to vote in favor of it, too.

But just as she mounts me and we grunt-groan the success of her landing, I say, "Was there?" and she says, "Was there what?" and I say, "With the diaphragm and the nightie—was there a 'just in case'?" And she says, "Em, do you really want to know the answer to that?"

"Knowing is better than not knowing," I say, and she says, "You think so, huh? What if I told you I slipped? I didn't, but what if I told you that? That early on, when all this started, I made a stupid mistake, something I couldn't undo, and that you could either forgive and forget about it or let it eat away at our marriage until there's nothing left? What would you say to that, Em? Is that something you'd really want to know?" She searches my eyes hard right then, as though she's looking for something in there she really needs to find. "Em," she says, "you just need to have a little faith." And then she rises up on me and drops down, then does it again, and soon, despite my doubts, we're both in a place beyond speech, beyond language, where we both know everything and understand nothing.

Later we lay side by side, spent, heat rising out of our bodies. "That was lovely, Ace, but now I'm freezing." She sits up, pulls on her sweatshirt and jacket. "Besides, we should get some sleep. Sun's going to be up in a couple of hours." We get up. "Will you look at that," she says, stepping into her underwear. "That's sort of amazing, isn't it?"

The skinny black trees, the leaves, every brown blade of marsh grass is filigreed with hoarfrost. The bridge glistens, the trees seem blanketed in a fog of their own frost. Everything is both soft-focus and sharply delineated, white and gray and black, as though etched by both fog and razor blade. Dorie kisses me and gets the rest of her clothes on.

"It is amazing."

Dorie opens her car door. "You coming?"

"In a minute."

I watch her beautiful blond head duck inside the Nomad. She turns the ignition, starts the heater. I still have a few swallows of beer left. The sky is getting that grayish light to it that means morning isn't far away. It was on a night—a morning—like this one a long time ago that Robert Aaron told me Audrey was pregnant. At the time he felt like he had his balls nailed to the wall. Yet he and Audrey have managed, and come this fall their oldest is herself getting married. I think about our parents earlier this evening, our mother ready to send our father's croquet ball into the outer reaches of the stratosphere, but she gave him a break instead.

I'm not sure who gave who a break tonight. Whatever happened with Dorie while she was not in love with me, whatever she did or wanted to but didn't do, I will have to let it go. Some things are best left private, Nomi always said, and Dorie, too, is operating under that credo.

What keeps people married? I wonder, my deflated but still happy penis providing, perhaps, the most elemental of answers. Still, there are other reasons. How had our parents managed, particularly once the "you know" cooled between them? It was a mystery to me. Most things are. I walk out to the end of that broken bridge, the concrete greasy with frost. A part of me wants to get back into the Nomad with Dorie and drive all night. Another part of me wants to drive off the bridge.

Could it be as maddeningly simple and complex as this: that love and anger will keep you beside each other, night after night, till the end of your days, provided you're both willing to keep your mouths shut and to suffer your fate, which is to be alone in unaloneness? I don't know. It doesn't seem fair to either party, does it? But then, who said anything about life being fair to anybody?

The sky now is that yellowy gray of early morning. Back at the car I finish my beer and nestle it with a friendly clink against its brothers in the cooler. I hoist it into the wayback just as Dorie calls over the backseat, "C'mon, Em, your wife is cold and sleepy." Reason enough, I suppose, to go back home.

20. The Balloon, the Roof, and the Kitchen Sink

WILLY-NILLY IS A PATTERN, TOO

Everyone is still alive.

There is more than a little relief in writing that sentence, though its truth, I know, is temporary. The closest we have come in our family—our mother falling down the stairs, our father's heart attack, Wally Jr.'s accident that left him a cripple—has left us feeling like lightbulbs in a hailstorm. It is that last event, however—or the sequence of events that followed it—that sent our father around the bend.

Wally Jr. was in the shed, working on Mikey Spillsbeth's exhaust system, the two of them under Mikey's most recent taxi—a midnight blue Bonneville with a harvest gold right front quarter panel. Mikey never married, and his last date might well have been with Cinderella when both were still in high school a quarter century ago. At forty-two he was still the Augsbury Taxi, still ferrying kids around town, still helping his parents with their half-assed orchard, still suspected by parents of "being up to no good" with their kids, and still more than a little creepy, though nobody had ever heard of him doing anything to anybody. He was also still sweet on Cinderella, oddly enough, and part of us thought that would be an okay match and part of us wanted to laugh. Certainly he would do her no harm, and after Okie that in itself seemed like a recommendation.

But he never got the chance. The Bonneville had flunked the emissions test once already, and the thought of the taxi being grounded was too much for Mikey to bear. He practically begged Wally Jr. to help him get the exhaust system up to snuff. So it was that Wally Jr. was welding and Mikey was holding the pipe in place when the double-jack system holding the car up gave way and came crashing down on the two of them. Wally Jr., no stranger to the undersides of cars, heard the first creak of the jack slipping on the concrete floor, that deadly metallic scrape, and heaved himself out from under on the dolly.

There were only two problems: one was that a dolly, with its tiny little wheels, doesn't move as fast horizontally as a three-quarter-ton Bonneville that's dropping only nine inches does vertically; the other was that there was only one dolly. The Bonnie caught Wally Jr. right above the kneecaps and severed or smashed pretty much everything connecting his thighs to his calves.

It also landed on Mikey Spillsbeth's chest and face.

You have no doubt heard of feats of superhuman strength performed by people in desperate circumstances. Car doors ripped open, heavy objects pushed aside, whole cars lifted. The adrenaline rush reigns supreme. Well, those people had leverage, and they didn't have crushed skulls. Grunting in absolute agony, before the shock completely froze him, Wally Jr. managed to lift the chassis sitting on his legs just enough to see that Mikey's face was a flattened mess. Then he screamed, dropped the Bonneville on himself, and passed out.

A neighbor, Howard Zipfel, putting in a load of hay, heard the scream and drove over. Entering the shed, he encountered a curious sight: it appeared as though Wally Jr. had managed to triple the length of his legs. His kneecaps were just barely under the Bonneville, and coming out the other side were his feet. It looked funny for just a second, like a magician's trick, and then Howard realized what had happened. Fortunately there was a block and tackle in the shed, and Howard was able to get the chain around the engine block and hoist the Bonnie up high enough to slide both bodies out. Looking at all the blood, he thought they were both dead.

He was half right.

We were deep into the family diaspora by then, scattered not so much geographically—though at various times you were as likely to find a Czabek in California or New York as in the Midwest—as spiritually. We did not seem to have much truck with each other. All those years of being told "We're a family, a family, goddammit!" You hear that often enough, and after a while you say, "So what?"

But you also internalize the epithet. We *were* a family, for good or ill. It's like that corny growing-up story everyone tells. How you spent your childhood beating up or picking on or getting beaten up by or getting picked on by your brother or sister (or both—in our family it was always two picking on one), but just let some outside offer come in to do the picking on or the beating up for you, and whoa, Nellie, Katy, bar the door, the Czabeks have closed ranks.

So it was when we got word that Wally Jr. was going to lose a leg, and that our parents were being sued by Angus and Marcie Spillsbeth. We gathered around Wally Jr., who told us he'd felt worse, his fingers absently playing with where his one knee had been, and we told him to "buck up," and "hang in there, bro," and other inanities. We felt like idiots.

"It coulda been worse," Wally Jr. said. "What about that guy over in Neenah who got his back broke? You hear about that? He was messing around with somebody's wife. She's twenty-one, they're estranged"— Wally Jr. pronounced this "ex-stranged"—"not boinking, if you get my drift, and she turns up pregnant. So the ex-stranged husband goes over to this guy's house, finds him in the garage, and smashes him in the back with the blunt end of an ax. Neighbor says it sounded like pencils being crushed with a ball-peen hammer."

That was meant to lighten us up.

Our father had as little clue how to deal with a invalid son as we did an invalid brother. What was he—what were we—going to say? "You know what they do with horses?" Our father's clichés, almost never adequate to the situations for which they were deployed, were particularly inadequate now. Coming into Wally Jr.'s room, our father would mutter and shrug and try not to notice his namesake. He was preoccupied with something else entirely. He could not reason his way around getting sued. He had moved us out of Elmhurst years ago to be among real people, honest people, the kind of people who did not get divorced, who did not sue over slips on the ice, falls from the swing set, the kind of people whose kids did not get pregnant, whose kids did not use drugs, whose kids did not die or lose their legs. The kind of people who did not suffer from diabetic impotency, or blindness, whose wives did not hang out with lesbian couples who lived in the neighboring farmhouse, nor, for that matter, did lesbians live in the neighboring farmhouse. The kind of people whose sons did not drink excessively and whose daughters did not marry men who beat them or cheated on them or who abused their kids. In short, he wanted to live in a place where no one ever got hurt, or acted badly, let alone drowned, died, or had his legs crushed. Where a man could come off a long, frustrating week on the road and find everything exactly as he had left it, the people and the place he left behind preserved in amber, perfectly, absolutely unchanged. His position in the universe fixed, safe, secure. He believed in this, as much as he believed that a man was the head of his family and his wife was his devoted helper and his children were adoring and silent and conveniently semi-invisible, which would allow him to ignore them with a clean conscience. These mythical children: they never grew up, never had problems, and then they, too, were magically and safely adults, with perfect wives and husbands and children of their own. The Great Chain of Being, extending outward in every direction, holding us all firm and secure within its links. The Great Chain of Being, as he envisioned it, extended even into his professional life. He believed the company would honor him in his old age, bestowing upon him prestige and respect, and if he had an inkling that this was all a crock of shit, he gave no indication that he knew. You could almost forgive him his inability to understand that the world did not, would not, conform to the picture of it he had in his head. Oh, oh, that it did!

Where was this place, where people were unfailingly kind, and generous, and decent, and good? We had no idea. All around us, certainly, there were plenty of good, generous, decent people. But there were also louts, fools, knaves, idiots, jerks, dunderheads, and a large quantity of what our mother called "no-goodniks." And then there were lots and lots and lots of people like us. People in the middle, muddling along, stuck in ruts, people blundering into one fool situation after another, buffeted about here and there, hither and yon, willy and nilly, and always, always, always hoping for the best. The win somes, lose somes. The galoots.

That we could be sued by such people—by people like us—our father could not fathom.

"People are different nowadays, Wally-Bear," said our mother. "People will sue at the drop of a hat." She was looking at the papers the family's attorneys had mailed over.

Our father glanced through them as well, then went back to making a refill of his Bloody Mary in a tumbler the size of a 7-Eleven Big Gulp.

"They oughta be shot," he said.

"Oh, Wally-Bear, don't be saying that," said our mother, as though he were joking, but you could tell by the adamant look on our father's face and the speed at which our mother was trying to shush him with jocularity that he wasn't.

"They don't deserve to live," said our father.

"Wally-Bear, shush now," said our mother.

"Vermin. It's like the goddamn Trilateral Commission and the fucking World Bank."

"Wally, the children."

We looked at each other. Children? Meg was twenty-five. And it wasn't as though we hadn't heard this before. Impotent rage had been our father's strong suit for years. What he had a harder time with was understanding that the world was not a conspiracy. That everything did not fit together malevolently like some humongous, universe-size, patchwork quilt.

He brought up Ben Keillor, our neighbor just up the road. Ben Keillor had drunk himself silly years ago, and then, when he was dying of cancer, he took it into his head that he could grow, using different crops, the image of a bottle in a forty-acre field for a whiskey distillery. The distiller was going to pay Mr. Keillor a huge fee for this. They would take photographs and use it in their advertising. His own wife thought he was being taken for a ride, but Ben insisted, told anyone who was willing to listen (and quite a few people who weren't), no, no, this was on the level. This was the real deal. They'd pay him to grow the bottle in timothy and wheat and corn and alfalfa, and they'd fly over and take a picture, and if they used it they were going to pay him a king's ransom for his trouble.

"If?" asked the skeptics, his wife among them.

"They will," Ben insisted.

"And what are they paying us if they don't use it?" his wife, Matty, asked.

"They will," Ben insisted. Matty didn't argue. He was dying of lung cancer. His insides were all torn up from the chemo. She was going to let him win this one. The bigger losses, she told our mother, were coming down the road anyway, and they were driving a Mack truck. If her husband didn't want to get out of the way, well, that was his business. He'd suffered enough. Better, she thought, if his dreams killed him rather than something else.

Our father, of course, had a great affinity for Ben's harebrained scheme. Why not wheat and timothy, corn and alfalfa? He liked the marriage, too, of old-time hand planting with modern technology: after everything was growing, the liquor company would check Ben's work and take photographs from an airplane. Aerial photography and farming—our father loved that. Never mind that they weren't connected. In his brain they were—as though the next great thing since crop dusting was farming from an airplane. He could see it coming. When he had a spare minute he'd go over and check out how Ben's bottle was coming along. He'd stand there and make conversation about free enterprise and Niels Bohr and the green revolution and punctuate his speech with slugs from a glass mug filled with a Bloody Mary that he carried around with him as though the mug was growing out of his stomach.

Ben suffered him because our father also kept a hip flask in his overall pocket, and whenever Ben took a break our father would offer him a snort. If you gazed out the window at them, it almost looked as though our father was supervising him: the two men in the field, one on his knees, plucking and planting, the other standing over him, gesturing with what looked to be a beer mug flashing white in the sun. No doubt our father came to see himself in that role as well. Or if not in a supervisory capacity, then as a partner in the dream.

By God, they were going to make that bottle fly!

So when it all came to naught, when the distillery announced they "had decided to go in another direction" (they ended up doing it all on computers), and they sent a check for Ben Keillor's time and trouble, a check for a ridiculously tiny amount compared to what they'd promised had they actually used the photographs they'd taken, our father was perhaps more crushed than Ben Keillor was.

Or maybe not crushed. Not despondent like Ben Keillor was. No, our father was outraged. The Great Chain of Conspiracy had raised its ugly head. Something evil was afoot.

I had never figured this out, how our father could put all his trust in a company like Dinkwater-Adams or Drydell Chemical or the Dinkwater Corporation, and then, when the company turned its back on him, he blamed not the company for doing what companies did but something larger, darker, more evil, something "out there" that had sucked the company in to do its bidding. A distillery hadn't exercised its kill-fee clause; rather, the Trilateral Commission, the World Bank, the one-world movement, and nameless enemies of capitalism—including but certainly not limited to Communism and the liberal media—had banded together to put the kibosh on Ben Keillor's whiskey bottle grown in a field. The last great dream of Ben Keillor done in by a conspiracy. The reach—the insidious reach—of that conspiracy! It was something.

So we were sued by Angus and Marcie Spillsbeth, neighbors if not friends, and our parents, who'd almost paid off the farm, had to start from scratch again on their mortgage. The settlement was in the neighborhood of the low six figures, and the insurance on the shed covered only part of it. The settlement would have been worse except Wally Jr. in a wheelchair, with his little stub legs, made a hell of a witness during the pretrial depositions. Credit Wally Jr. When his attorney said he could get the whole farm if he sued our parents, too—all that suffering and mental anguish stuff—Wally Jr. said, "Fuck you, we're family! We're goddamn Czabeks!" and pushed his wheelchair out of the office. The attorney for the plaintiffs, perhaps realizing that in a still nominally rural area— where accidents happened and were taken as a matter of course—he'd have a hard time rounding up a jury sympathetic to the idea of willful or intentional malfeasance, offered to settle. Angus and Marcie, despite their lawsuit and the dollar signs dancing in their eyes after years of eking out a living with the orchard, probably didn't have the heart for a long trial, either. Anyway, it was quietly over, and people settled in for their grieving.

Except for our father. Although the settlement was not crushingly onerous, it was plenty bad, and that he'd been sued at all set something off in him. After the settlement our father went a little squirrelly. This went beyond his old assertion that Walter Cronkite was a Communist. Now they all were: Rather, Chung, Morley Safer, Andy Rooney—that whole *60 Minutes* crowd—Peter Jennings, sure, him too—he spent all that time overseas, didn't he? In *London*!

"Dad, he's Canadian. He was a London correspondent."

"What's he doing on an *American* broadcast then?"

This culminated in our father wanting to blow up the Smithsonian. To commemorate the fiftieth anniversary of the bombings that ended World War II, the Smithsonian Institution planned an exhibition that would look at the event from various perspectives. In addition to tracing the history of the bomb, and how the four-and-a-half-ton Little Boy came to be loaded into the belly of the B-29 bomber *Enola Gay* (and a similar bomb, code-named Fat Man, came to be loaded in the belly of the bomber *Bocks Car*), the exhibition also would examine the aftermath of that bombing run: how the cities of Hiroshima and Nagasaki essentially ceased to exist, 115,000 people blown into oblivion outright, another 100,000 dying later of burns and radiation sickness. Veterans' groups, particularly the American Legion, were incensed that the focus wasn't entirely on how the bombs ended the war and saved American lives. One of those lives being our father's. The Smithsonian tried to explain they wanted the exhibition to look at the larger picture, from a less nationalistic perspective, but the firestorm of criticism was tremendous.

Eventually the Smithsonian scrapped the idea for an exhibition altogether. That didn't sit well with a lot of people, either. *Nothing* to commemorate the bombs that ended the war? What were they thinking?

What our father was thinking was that the Smithsonian should get a taste of its own medicine.

"Somebody should drop a Little Man or a Fat Boy on the fucking Smithsonian," said our father. He got his "I have a dream" gleam. "I . . . *I* should drop a bomb on the fucking Smithsonian. *I* should. Yeah, I should, goddammit."

"Wally-Bear, stop being ridiculous," said our mother.

"Ridiculous? Who's being ridiculous? I was one of the Americans whose lives were saved by those bombs. Goddamn Communists."

"Wally, you're being silly."

"Silly? Is it silly to love your country? Is it silly to lay down your life for your country? Is it silly to be proud of your country? I'll show you silly. I'll blow up the fucking Smithsonian. That'll be silly. That'll be real silly. People will be laughing their asses off over that one."

We shouldn't have been worried, but we were. Our father was adamant. Bombing the Smithsonian—it was a patriotic act. Reagan was right. Government *was* the problem. The Smithsonian's planned exhibition only confirmed his low opinion of any institution run by the federal government. He'd visited the Smithsonian once when he was near Washington for his ship's reunion. They were doing Gettysburg and all the usual D.C. sights. What he came away with from the Smithsonian was how ill-kempt and dirty it was. Nobody wiped the dust off anything.

Didn't these people have any pride? Evidently not. So between the dust and the *Enola Gay* exhibition, our father wanted to blow up the Smithsonian.

He wanted to shoot the homeless, too, and nuke Baghdad, but the homeless were scattered all over the country, and he had no control over our country's military arsenal. But the Smithsonian—that was another story. Of late our father had been expressing admiration for the militias. We were worried. Was this where his impotent rage would find its outlet?

"Concord and Lexington," our father said. "Who was it fired 'the shot heard round the world'? A militiaman, that's who. Maybe they don't tell you that anymore in your history books, but I know what I know. The country's going to hell in a handbasket. Maybe it's time for a different kind of shot."

"Wally"—our mother was staring right at our father, her eyes blazing green fire—"you will do no such thing."

"We shall see what we shall see," said our father.

Though he stammered and hawed in front of our mother, when she wasn't around, he muttered about it constantly. He could bluster his way through a whole afternoon of talk and television, clicking from *American Sportsman* to *Fishing with Charlie Giles* while detailing exactly how a small group of trained men could infiltrate the outer defenses of the Smithsonian—the perimeter, our father called it—and once inside, slip undetected (the preferred method of handling a covert operation) or, if necessary, blast their way to the building's very center and there leave enough high explosives—nitroglycerin, plastique, and dynamite—to take out the diseased cultural heart and sick soul of a morally drifting America. We tried to picture it. Six, seven retirees, with Humpty Dumpty–like bodies, their bellies straining and then overwhelming the waistbands of their Sansabelt trousers. There they go, sidling down the hallways of the Smithsonian. Their noses rounds of cauliflower, their cheeks broken masses of river veins. Balding, golf-shirted, bearing Uzis and sensible shoes. Their watches can give you the correct time in three time zones, and walkie-talkies dangle off rings on their fishing vests. They are registered members of the AARP, the American Legion, the Loyal Order of Moose, the Shriners, the National Rifle Association, AAA, and the Sacred Heart of Jesus. They are grandfathers, Rotarians, members of the retired reserves.

They are also terrorists.

In those pre–9/11 days, blowing things up and being an antigovernment terrorist were still things to which our father (and talk radio) could aspire. Not anymore, of course. But for a while there, in the mid-Reagan years, magazines of dubious distinction began appearing in our parents' living room, mixed in with the mountain of paper on the dining room table, the stacks by their armchairs. We had always gotten catalogs of hunting equipment, camouflage, camping equipment—the whole panoply of outdoor living—which our father perused from his armchair. But now they were getting magazines touting the dangers of Vatican II, the need for a return to the Latin Mass, magazines warning of the Second Coming, magazines and flyers explaining how the economy would collapse and why the coming social, economic, and political apocalypse would be good for prepared, red-blooded, God-fearing Americans.

Our father, of course, would never call himself a radical. He was a patriot, a reservist, an American. And Americans knew their duty. Our father's duty was to make phone calls. All those years in the Legion and the Navy Reserves and the Coast Guard Auxiliary—he had an address book thick with names and numbers. Late into the evening he would make phone calls. Cold calling. The old pitch. The cajole. He found it harder selling an idea, though, than he ever did trying to move pharmaceuticals or chemicals or cookies. Even among the disgruntled, he found few takers. Hearts and minds—it was a tough sell. He would explain, he would nod, he would become impassioned, get irate. Shout, scream, plead.

"My country, right or wrong!" our father shouted into the phone most evenings.

You could almost hear the person on the other end saying, "Exactly, Wally. That's why blowing up the Smithsonian isn't such a hot idea."

"Extremism in the defense of liberty is no vice," countered our father.

"Blowing up the Smithsonian is," said his friends and acquaintances. "In fact, Wally, it's a crime. You can't go around blowing up buildings, Wally. People are liable to get hurt."

"You can't make an omelet without breaking a few eggs," said our father.

"People aren't eggs, Wally. Would you listen to yourself?"

"All that's needed for evil to triumph is for good men to do nothing," said our father.

"The evil, Wally, is thinking the Smithsonian is the enemy. Cut 'em some slack. The Smithsonian is an American institution. They made a mistake."

"We have to blow up the Smithsonian in order to save it," said our father.

But his entreaties fell on deaf ears. In the end, not one of his friends agreed to join him, and quite a few suggested he get counseling or seek medical attention.

Our father remained a conspiracy of one.

In his defense, he didn't try to contact the people most likely to take up his cause, people who might actually have been persuaded to take up his harebrained scheme as their own. He made no calls to the Freemen, to the Michigan Militia, to the Posse Comitatus, to the militias in Oregon and Montana and Colorado.

"*Those* people are nuts," our father declared.

"As opposed to what?" asked our mother.

"Don't start," said our father.

"Don't *you* start," said our mother. She had gotten more feisty since he'd retired, less likely to say, "*Wally . . .*" in that pleading voice of hers that let us all know she was going to lament yet tolerate his excesses. No more. Now she put the hammer down, snorted at his wilder ideas, and when he got started with one of us present, would roll her eyes and say, "Wally, don't. Just don't."

Rebuffed by wife and friends, our father was reduced to muttering that it wasn't all that great a museum. He'd been to the Smithsonian. Its exhibits were dusty.

Is this how families end? Not with a bang but a mutter? Our father chafed against the out-of-court settlement. He chafed against the houses going in all around us. He chafed against the kinds of people who were filling those houses, people who drove their snowmobiles and ATVs willy-nilly across our fields and through our woods. People who picked our asparagus and wildflowers and hunted our land without asking. The privilege of trespass drove him crazy. And his oldest daughter had gone on welfare, had worked for Mel while still getting government checks, which made her a welfare cheat, and now her kids—his grandkids!— were having kids. Half the kids at the school didn't know who their father was, or had some guy who was their mom's boyfriend serving as their father, or were getting raised by their grandparents, which was what our mother was doing with most of Cinderella's kids. Cinderella, beaten down for years by Oswald Grunner, had found love, or something close to it, later in life, and wanted to be the belle of the ball again. She had no time for her own kids. So the younger ones hung out at our parents' house until, like the older ones, they found friends to hang out with, and they all quickly learned how to apply that hardened polish that allows naïve kids who aren't being raised by anybody except themselves to fend off both that which hurts and that which helps. Did this make them any different from Ollie Cicerelli, lost soul from our youth? And if they weren't different—if we weren't any different—what had our father protected us from? Or was it just a delaying tactic, an attempt to get us to adulthood before the whole house of cards collapsed?

"What's up with Dad?" we'd ask each other when we got together for holidays, gathering on the roof or in Ike's tepee. We'd drink beer, smoke cigars, and discover that we had no answers. Or too many. But clearly, something had been taken out of our father. He looked terrible. For most of our lives he'd had the body of an onion wearing size fifty-two boxer shorts. Now his boxers, bunched at the waist, protruding from his multipocketed shorts, sagged to his knees, and his rumpled nose and broken-veined face were the color and texture of a pomegranate.

"What's up with Dad? What's up with Dad?"

"Nothing a Rob Roy or a Bloody Mary won't cure," said our father when we asked him. He held up his glass. "V8, garlic salt, pickled peppers, and peppered pickles—that's the secret to a long life," he'd insist, and it was true: his drinks, except for the alcohol, resembled vegetable markets. Pearl onions, pickled asparagus, celery stalks—you name it, it sprouted from his drinks. Our mother kept trying to get him to see a doctor, but he didn't believe in doctors. "They only give you bad news," he said, and for him it seemed to be true. Then again, he went to see a doctor only when something bad had already happened—cataracts, for which he needed surgery, a touch of glaucoma, ongoing heart problems. His treadmill numbers were abysmal.

But that was only the beginning. After Christmas dinner he dropped like a stunned cow in the middle of the living room. Another heart attack? No, a stroke. In the hospital they discovered he'd had a series of ministrokes before that. That might explain, the doctor said, some of his wilder pronouncements. The brain, the doctor said, is a funny organ.

"You'll notice, Doctor," said our mother, "that none of us is laughing."

The stroke was not crippling. "No biggie, as strokes go," said the doctor—another comment that was met with an icy stare from our mother. This doctor looked like he went Rollerblading between shifts at the hospital. He exuded the confidence of the healthy. "Just what I need," said our mother, "a decathlete telling me my husband is dying."

But he wasn't dying. He was collapsing, his body giving way beneath him the way sand castles dissolve at a beach. The high blood pressure, the stratospheric cholesterol numbers, the hardened, then weakened, arteries—everything they'd warned him about for years was now accumulating in his body as though prizes were being given for having one of everything. In the scavenger hunt for preventable maladies, our father took first prize. His infrastructure was breaking down. His skin had acquired the papery look of the aged. His fingers had started to curl, as though the tendons had decided that it was too much work to stretch out fully. He shuffled along on shitty ankles, moving the bulk of his body about our living room like a barge nudging a much bigger ship into harbor.

It didn't help that he "watched" his diet, his drinking, and took his medicines on a schedule so random that it was charitable to call it a schedule. This had been going on for years.

Finally, though, one January a county cop pulled him over for weaving erratically on Highway 45. He was returning from the Dog Out. The cop thought he had a live one.

"I've only had a few beers, Officer," said our father.

"I'm sure," said the officer. "Could you close your eyes and touch your nose, please?"

Our father could.

"Could you walk this line?" Our father could. He had shitty ankles but decent balance. Or maybe decent ballast. The cop was perplexed. He was sure he had a DWI. Still, there was something about the way our father stared at him. The cracked veins, the watery, unfocused eyes. He waved a finger in front of our father's face. It was clear that one of our father's eyes wasn't tracking the officer's finger. If this guy wasn't drunk, what was he? He gave our father a Breathalyzer test. There. That was what he wanted to see.

"I'm sorry, sir, but I'm placing you under arrest."

"For what?" Our father's speech was slightly slurred.

"Driving while intoxicated. Your blood sugar's way above what it should be."

Said our father, "I'm not intoxicated."

"No? Then what are you?"

"Diabetic." Our father shook his head. "I haven't been a good boy about taking my medicine."

"No, my guess is that you've been a good boy at taking a different medicine. Why don't we go to the station house and see exactly what kind of medicine you've been taking?"

Our father collapsed again at the station house. An ambulance was called. Our father came to in the hospital with an insulin drip in his arm and a medical alert bracelet identifying him as a diabetic on his wrist.

"I don't want to wear this," our father said.

"You do if you ever want to drive again," said our mother.

"Doctor's orders?"

"No, the police officer's. You're lucky he has a diabetic brother-in-law. He said he'd drop the DWI to a 'driving while impaired' if you'd agree to see a doctor regularly and wear a bracelet."

Our father scoffed. "What does he know?"

"He knows, Wally-Bear, that you're blind as a bat in your right eye."

It was true. His collapse at the station house had been another ministroke. The blood vessels at the back of his eyeball had burst, filling his eye with blood. The fact was he needed to quit drinking or risk a coma while he was driving. A diabetic coma while he was on the road: that scared him. He also had a cataract developing in his good eye. It was a miracle, the doctor said, he could even see the road, much less weave on it.

This news sobered our father. Even though he wasn't selling anymore, the idea of having his driving privileges taken away—it was too awful to think about.

"I guess you can let things slide for only so long," said our father.

"No shit, Sherlock," said the doctor.

"And I'll be better if I do like you say?"

"Well, you won't be any worse. But let's face it, Wally. You've done a number on your body, and medical science can do only so much. But let's at least give it a fair shot, shall we?"

Strangely enough, our father agreed. He had cataract surgery and another angioplasty. He wore a black patch over the exploded veins in his eye. He finally started taking his diabetes medicine, his blood thinners, his beta-blockers. He semi-quit drinking, he semi-watched his diet. Or rather our mother watched his diet for him. Now, at Thanksgiving and Christmas, just like us when we were children, he's the one who receives the one-third glass of champagne and has to sneak the other two-thirds. And when it's time for the toast, he holds up his puddle of bubbly and gets this elfin grin on his face like he knows he's getting away with something.

We smile, too, relieved he's alive. But we're a little scared, too. He's not gotten away with everything he thinks he has. It's now been a good decade since those strokes, since he wanted to blow up the Smithsonian, but his body and his mind's slow collapse is exactly why we gathered last night to talk over what we should do about our parents.

His flesh sags in ways it never did when he was a hundred pounds heavier. He's still a big man, but it's like watching a fat, juicy sausage being reduced to a hard biscuit before your eyes. You want to say he looks good, but he doesn't. Partly that's your fault. You had gotten used to his obesity. Now it's a shock to see him shrunken and sunken like this.

I think of all the things he missed out on: first steps, first words, first stitches, First Communions, first arguments, first dates, first plays, first graduations, first this, first that. But why limit it to firsts? What about the thousands upon thousands of quotidian events that made up who we were and who we are? Why skip over those? He wouldn't. We only think he would because he did miss them. And even as adults we believe that if he missed them, then he wanted to miss them. We weren't listening to the stories he told us, and he wasn't telling us everything anyway. His fascination with his time in the service, his selfishness, his self-absorption—it was a way of coping with long absence. And in his own mind, everything he did he did for us—the move to Elmhurst, the move to the farm, the long, long hours traveling, the sacrifice of family time for the slightly bigger commission, the kahuna commission waiting out there in the deep of both plumbed and virgin Territory.

The Territory, the Territory. Our father rocking along to the rhythm of the steam train pistons in the opening number of Meredith Willson's *Music Man,* crying along with the other peddlers on the train, "But he doesn't know the Territory!" Yet being enamored of Robert Preston—Professor Harold Hill—who doesn't know the Territory and doesn't care to, who plays by his own rules, who digs deep into his bag of tricks, and pulls one out of his ass. Our father believing the world worked that way, some alchemy of the two. He was with the peddlers on the playing-by-the-rules thing, yet he cheered Robert Preston every time he fooled the townspeople who wanted to see his credentials.

Our father played by the rules. He inhaled them. He became them. He hated them. But he continued to believe in them. And he took all of us—wife and kids—along for the ride.

Like most couples starting out after the war, our parents were young and scared and hopeful. They either didn't know or didn't want to believe that what was coming down the turnpike was aimed straight at them.

Drugs, Divorce, Depression, Death—the Four Riders of the Suburban-Exurban Apocalypse—you couldn't stop any of it. Bad things happen. Bad things happen to everybody. Our parents wanted to believe differently. Everybody did. Everybody was the exception. Everybody was the rule.

Our father thought he could beat the rules by playing by them. The odds were stacked against him, but in excess there was possibility. In excess there was hope. They had seven of us trying to beat the odds, trying to get ahead of the curve. Our father threw himself into our mother again and again in the sheer exuberance and exhilaration of beating the odds.

It is a curiously American belief. But then, our dad is America. Our parents are America. His bald head, his piebald arms. We are safe now from his schemes. Or are we? And why did we rebel and reject and scoff in the first place? Because his was a generation that dared to believe in dreams? Because ours was one that didn't? Or was it simply that their dreams, being more modest, also seemed attainable, and while we were dreaming big—world peace, the brotherhood of man—we couldn't bear to see somebody else striving for something more modest, something that seemed to be so easily, impossibly within our reach?

We are up on the roof, all of us. Even Wally Jr., whom we again haul up with ropes, then block the wheels on his chair so he won't go rolling off the gutters. We packed our parents off earlier, drove them to a field, watched them board a balloon, watched the launch, followed them for a little while, then hightailed it back here and scrambled up on the rooftop so we could watch them come in over our heads. We can hardly believe it. We are waiting for our parents' arrival, and they are arriving by balloon. We also got everyone from their wedding party who is still alive to witness this. They are going to come over the hill from Otis Kempke's farm, over Wally Jr. and Claire's double-wide, over our heads, and they are going to sit that balloon down in the lower part of the field, where we've painted a bright red X on the shorn alfalfa. And we are going to climb down, those of us on the roof, and get in cars and trucks and drive or run down our field to greet them, to drink champagne—more champagne! we've been drinking it all day—to toast them, to wish them another fifty years together. They have survived—my God!—and we are stunned and taken aback and grateful.

We have spent the day talking about our parents. There is a nursing home on the horizon now, yes, regardless of what other remedies—elder home, assisted care facility—we try before that, but we're not going to talk about that now. Partly because it shames us that none of us is willing to look out for our parents 24-7, the way they devoted their lives to looking out for us and their own parents, and partly because we are celebrating their expansive past, not their limited future.

"Our parents are America," I tell my siblings, and they scoff, tell me I'm cockeyed. It's getting near dusk. I've been drinking champagne since breakfast. The sky is pink and pale blue and gray, the color of a mollusk, and the fields still have that look of winter about them. The wind is raw even though it's barely blowing. We had to pay extra to get the balloon company to take our parents up on a day like this; their season usually starts in late April or early May. "But it's for our parents," we explain, "their fiftieth wedding anniversary," and for a couple hundred extra dollars the operator agrees to do us a favor.

Perhaps I am cockeyed. "I have always thought of our father as an immense man living a small life," I say, and I try to explain. I tell them that, like most of us, he did not live his life to its fullest margins. Or rather, having glimpsed, when a young man, just how wide those margins were, he decided to take on instead something he thought he could manage.

"He ain't dead yet, Emcee," says Wally Jr. "Stop eulogizing him."

But I can't stop. Our mother, I continue to tell them, got an even smaller glimpse of what the wide world had in store for her, but she was in love with our father, and she acceded to what he wanted, and it was a long time down the road before she realized she had settled for less than what she wanted—Wally-Bear was plenty, I think she reasoned—and by then it was too late.

"Modest hopes, modest dreams," I tell my siblings. Waiting for our parents to ride over our heads in a balloon, I find I am suddenly sentimental, forgiving. I think back to those photos taken of our parents before they were married. That photo of the skinny young man in the alley with his hat flying away behind him, and the one of the young woman in the velvet dress, sitting on a tricycle with a lot of juicy thigh showing. A borrowed car, a trike, and a certain devil-may-care cheeriness and willingness to face the world and all it had to offer—that's what our parents had to start with. And from that our father hoped to deliver us into a land of milk and honey. And to create for himself an impregnable castle to come home to after he was done with his weekly fight with the world.

Our mother wanted even less. Companionship, someone to drive her around, an enclosed circle of safety within the borders of our house. She didn't expect such safety out in the larger world, where she knew, things happened. In fact, out there she expected them to happen—disappointments in love and sex, unfulfilling jobs, backstabbing co-workers, incompetent supervisors, bad marriages, cretinous lovers. "But you will always have a home to come home to," she told us, meaning her home, our first home. And when we would call home from far away, she would entertain us by reciting a litany of catastrophe shocking in its plainness—deaths, dismemberments, divorces, suicides. As though if she recited this litany she could pretend, could convince herself, that we would never find a place within it.

If our parents had bigger dreams, if they wanted more, they didn't tell us.

In the last years of the twentieth century, our parents gave up any hope of their family surviving intact into happiness. For our father, this was something to rail against, bitterly. For our mother, the most she seemed to hope was for us to survive into contentment. To weather whatever came with a certain grace and dignity, and when that failed, to shrug and keep our opinions to ourselves.

We learned to rail. We learned to shrug.

Our parents weren't ahead of the curve so much as they *were* the curve. Or rather, once upon a time they were the curve, when they left Chicago with all those other post-Korea hopefuls. Then they were ahead of the curve, when they decamped the suburbs for the country. Then they were behind it again, holding out as the farms disappeared and the subdivisions mushroomed. Finally, as their taxes skyrocketed, they wondered if they should rejoin the curve, sell it all off, the farm our father had always dreamed of, and take the very tidy nest egg that resulted and move to Montrose, Colorado—the last great dream of our father, as it turns out.

They sprang that on us at the end of brunch. Before the wedding party and all the friends and relatives arrived for the public party, before the balloon launch, we got together, just the family. Wally Jr. in his wheelchair, Cinderella minus Mel, whom she would never marry, Robert Aaron and Audrey and their brood, Ike and his wife, Sam, and their blended families, me and mine, Ernie and the pregnant Cindy, Peg Leg Meg and her beau, Greg. Here we all were, gathered on the day of our parents' fiftieth wedding anniversary, giddy as kids on Christmas morning.

Things had gotten better. After Wally Jr.'s accident and our father's breakdown, things did get better. He had been chastised, we had been scared; it seemed like things were heading toward normal. Even some of his financial schemes have turned out okay. A dozen and a half of the black walnuts did make it to maturity, and some high-end cabinetry company will pay our parents fifty thousand a tree. And the land itself? Let's just say our parents' wants will be well-funded. We've turned out okay, too. I married Dorie Keillor, the world's unlikeliest girl next door. Things remain rocky between us, but we are still married. Ike, too, had remarried. Granted, it wasn't a church wedding, but it was a ceremony. He and Sam pledged their troth beneath a scrub oak on some hillock in western Montana. They showed us pictures. Lots of sky, a cabin, the humans insignificant. There are seven people in the photographs: Sam, Ike, Sam's three kids from a previous marriage, Ike's two from his. The bride is wearing jeans and a Russian peasant blouse, the groom fringed buckskins and turquoise. His hair is plaited, and the braids rest on his chest like matching pull cords. The children stand like sentinels in a feral *American Gothic,* holding spears instead of pitchforks. They are their own tribe. Somewhere in Tennessee, Ike's two other children live with their mother. They will never know him. We will never know them. But the rest of their kids are here, and Robert Aaron and Audrey, not tired of love, adopted Janie and Joe, then had Jake, a late surprise they cherish simply for his existence. Peg Leg Meg got married and divorced—a first marriage as short and disastrous as my own—and she seems happy enough with Greg. Even Cinderella's children have fared better in some instances, and certainly no worse, than other children of divorce. Perhaps the best indication, though, that the offspring of Cinderella and Oswald Grunner are going to be all right is that, except for Okie II, they all want their mother's maiden name back. They want to be Czabeks.

So there were our parents, surrounded by fecundity, thirty-eight fecundities in all, the sprawl of progeny, our father's philosophy of excess made flesh. And what does our father do? He drops the big one on us.

"We're selling the farm," he says. "And moving to Colorado."

"Wally-Bear, don't exaggerate. We're *thinking* of selling the farm. We're *thinking* of moving to Colorado." We look at them, dumbfounded. First, because we don't believe they would do it. Don't believe they could do it. We don't care if their prospective new home is in a happy valley, a place where the temperatures are mild, even in winter. Where the sun shines always and the winds are temperate and a man and a woman can look forward to their remaining years together with other empty-nesters in retirement condos and ranch houses, well-serviced and well-fed, in green fields, beneath a mountain's majesty and a canyon's red and yellow walls and God's unending and azure sky. They would be moving away from their children and grandchildren. They want to move away from all this? Away from *us*? What are they thinking?

"Mom," I ask, "is this what you meant last night when you told Cinderella that you and Wally-Bear have everything taken care of?"

"Not completely," says our mother enigmatically.

Not completely?

"We have other contingencies," says our mother, and it's clear she's not going to offer up anything more. We are ready to write this off as another of our father's scatterbrained ideas until he zizzes the rubber band off the rolled-up plans he's had drawn up by a developer. We decide to humor them.

"Who?" asks Ernie.

"Don't worry," says our father. "Someone reputable."

"A reputable developer," says Ernie. "That's a contradiction in terms, ainna?"

We drink, we toast, we cheer. Our parents' guests will be here soon, and then we need to drive our parents over to Chetaqua and get them in their balloon so they can make their grand arrival midparty. But first our father wants to show us his plans. He rolls them out across the chip dip and the artichoke hearts, across the mayonnaise and the mustard, across the rye bread and the dill pickles, across the salami and the sliced ham.

And there it is. The very thing our father had fled thirty-five years previous—a subdivision on top of our farm. Everything lotted out, sweeping roadways leading back to one cul-de-sac after another, irregular pie slices and puzzle pieces carving up God's green acres. The woods—gone. The marsh—a pond now with "lake access" or "lake frontage" lettered into the lots that face it. The fields subdivided into curved lots that look like aerial views of 1950s furniture, dotted lines marching across our farm like schematics of how to carve up a side of beef.

"What gives, Dad?"

"Yeah, what gives?"

"All my life," says our father, "all my life I've wanted to live out West." This is a lie. He's never said any such thing to any of us, ever. He's had plenty of dreams, but living in Colorado was never one of them. He had been driven mostly by the curious but common belief that someplace else was better than where he was. Safer, greener, less corruptible, less corrupting. Virgin soil. A place where a man's dream, like his seed, could take root and flourish. Our father believed in it, in the Holy Grail of open space. Many years ago it had been the open prairie of Elmhurst, the last stop on the trolley line out of Chicago. A decade later it was the seemingly unbounded space of ninety-nine acres three and a half miles from the nearest town. Now it was a valley in a state he had visited only once.

We are stunned. What this means is that for our father, no one place mattered. For all his talk about rootedness and family and home, place is replaceable. It is simply the variable x that finds its way into our father's equation for happiness. In his heart, our father is the Ancient Mariner. He is Odysseus, he is Arthur, he is Magellan, searching, searching, always searching. Which makes our mother Penelope and Guinevere and whatever poor woman Magellan had taken for a wife. I wasn't crazy about how any of those stories turned out. I wasn't crazy about how this one was turning out, either.

"But I thought—I thought you liked it here," I said. I was perplexed and angry, and I didn't know why. Or maybe I did, and I didn't want to admit that. It had to do with Dorie, and with the realization that what you thought was stable could turn into sand beneath your feet. My wife, my father. Was I the only person in this family who did not like surprises, who wanted, after all, even more than my father, for things to remain the same? Have I become my father, or who I thought my father always was, the one person I could never imagine myself becoming?

But then a voice wiser than mine—it was Wally's, it was Meg's, it was Ike's, it was Robert Aaron's, it was everyone's—said, "Let it go, Emcee, let it go. It's what he wants."

"But how does he know what he wants if it keeps changing?" I cried. I could not believe this was happening.

Said our mother, "Wally-Bear, why don't you tell them the real reason?"

A giddy light enters our father's eyes. "Your mother and I don't have to go anywhere," he says. He starts pointing out things we hadn't seen right off: the circles that indicate fire hydrants, the circles for light poles. "It's like Elmhurst when we first started. We'll lay out everything. We'll do everything ourselves. It'll have everything but the kitchen sink— improved lots are a lot more valuable, you know. Why have the developer pocket everything when we can develop it ourselves? We can form our own corporation—Czabek's, Incorporated. Ernie can handle the financing, Wally Jr. and Ike the bulldozing, Emcee writes the brochures, Robert Aaron and I will do the selling, Cinderella and Meg and your mother will run the office. We'll be a family business. We'll keep our house right in the center, here"—our father points—"and then we'll buy up other farms and do everything all over again. And that's when your mother and I will retire, and you'll all be together. Everyone will be together, like a family, like—"

Our father caught our faces. He stopped. What he was proposing was impossible if not ridiculous. Quit our jobs, move home to the family farm, then work in tandem to eradicate its existence and live on the rump estate that was left? What was he thinking? Of all the harebrained, ill-conceived, idiotic—

We bit our tongues. What could we say to him? What could we possibly say?

"Is this what you meant by contingencies, Mom? That we'd all live here, helping out, both with the development and with you and Dad?"

"Your father was just thinking this was something that we might all agree on. He didn't really think—"

"You're right, Susan," said our father, his voice trembling. "I didn't really think. I just . . . I just thought . . . Christ, I don't know what I thought." His fingers traced the curb lines of his dream development. It was only then that we noticed the names of the streets: Lucinda's Lane, Aaron's Court, Emil's Drive, Eisenhower's Circle, Wally's Way, Ernest's Place, Megan's Terrace. "I was meaning this as a kind of legacy for . . . you know . . . you kids. And your kids. And your kids' kids. I guess I've always—I've always—" He couldn't finish. His head had dropped to his chest, and it was bobbing up and down and his shoulders were shaking.

If this were a comedy, I would try to find, I suppose, some way to end this with a marriage. As though marriage ends all problems. And if it were a tragedy, I suppose I'd find some way of ending it with a death. Our father's, I suppose. I could have him driving out to Colorado, his new promised land, and dying over the wheel of his car, slumped and fading, the car coasting to the side of the highway, not unlike the way he suffered his first heart attack.

But then his heart was always under attack.

If I were poetic, I would make the night of his death be one of those nights when the aurora borealis is draping the sky with rivers and canyons of light—yellow, green, purple, red, and white—dancing and weaving, shimmering and wheeling. Our mother would have that to look out on; she would have more than one thing to gape at with awe.

As I write this, though, everyone is still alive. It's not going to last, no. But it is.

Marriages don't end things. Death neither. Things continue. They go on. It's what's in the middle, the before and after, that matters. Marriage and death are just station markers. In between and in between—that's life.

And near the end of his life, our father didn't want to end anything. He wanted to start over. God bless him. Like everything else in his life, his ideas had no rhyme, little reason.

Willy-nilly, Artu would say.

Willy-nilly is a pattern, too, our father would say.

"It's okay, Wally," said our mother. "There are other possibilities."

Our parents excused themselves. They had a balloon to catch.

———

You don't catch a balloon like you catch a taxi. We drove our parents over to Chetaqua, a sleepy little village of one and a half streets twenty years ago that's now one of the biggest bedroom exurban communities in the valley. They've grown because when they incorporated, they gobbled up as much surrounding farmland as they could, miles and miles of it, and claimed it all as part of their tax base. In the southwest corner of the township is a huge open field, mostly mowed marshland, that's destined to become Chetaqua's business park–golf resort in another couple years. For now, though, it's where American Antiquities and Romance launches its balloons.

Flo and Eddie Brumfeld, the proprietors of American Antiquities and Romance (in addition to the balloon rides, they own a B & B and an antiques store in Neenah), greet our parents and us and introduce themselves. Flo snatches a cigarette out of her mouth and says, "Flo and Eddie, the Turtles, yeah, yeah, we're so happy together," even before I can ask.

Flo is the businesswoman. She's nervous and quick, despite being a tad on the heavy side, and she smokes unfiltered Camels just as fast as she is able. You get the feeling the balloon rides and the B & B were her husband's ideas, ways of diversifying the business, and she's gone along, but mostly to keep an eye on him, so he's not floating over half the countryside, giving free balloon rides to whoever asks.

Eddie is the balloon operator, a man with an orange-gray walrus mustache, a beer gut, and a comb-over. Their balloon is red and blue, tethered to steel stakes driven into the ground with a mallet. Up close, it looks like a malignant mushroom.

"Welcome, welcome, is this the happy couple?" he says. "Fifty years? I don't believe it. You look like you just eloped," he says. Sotto voce he adds, "Do your parents know about this?"

"Their parents are dead," Flo hisses. "And we're not getting any younger ourselves."

Eddie breaks into his pitch. How fast they're going to drift, given the wind, how high up they'll go, again depending on wind conditions, how it's going to be marvelous, marvelous, marvelous. "You'll see your friends' and neighbors' houses like you've never seen them before," he says. "We'll be sneaking up on deer, on cranes, on geese. Keep your eyes peeled for the deer herds. My favorite thing is how they don't know we're there until our shadow crosses over them. For some reason that spooks them. Somehow they can tell we're not just another cloud. Maybe it's something they teach in deer elementary school—"

Flo, meanwhile, is handing out business cards to all of us, and a sheet of paper detailing prices for both the B & B and the various merchandise they sell from the back of their pickup truck—glassware and coffee mugs featuring balloons, ballooning T-shirts, scarves, sweatshirts, baseball caps, and the matching purple Polartec fleece jackets Flo and Eddie are wearing, which sport a bright red balloon and their company logo across the breast pocket.

"They'll scatter every which way," Eddie's saying. "It's something to see."

"So why don't you get aloft and see it?" says Flo, taking a stepladder out of the truck. She puts that up against the balloon's woven basket and stands there waiting, her hair blunt and unkempt, her face pinched. She wants to get this show on the road. You wonder if maybe a certain bitterness hasn't come to her on account of it appears that Eddie gets to do the cloud hopping while she's stuck on earth, driving the support truck.

We head over to the balloon, form a loose semicircle around it. Flo and Eddie help our parents aboard. It's tricky with our father. He's big and bulky and unsteady on his feet. Our mother's no spring chicken, either, but with a boost from Eddie she steps into the basket. Our father needs to be propelled in by Flo and Eddie, and even then it appears he's in danger of tipping backward. Robert Aaron and Ike and I rush forward, and it looks a little like the flag raising on Mount Suribachi, the last couple of us straining but not really helping.

"Remember," says Eddie once they're all in the basket, "I'm the captain of this ship. If you want to get married while we're airborne, I can do that."

"And if you want to get divorced," Flo mutters just loud enough for me to hear, "see me."

"You kids can follow your folks in your cars, or you can drive ahead. I know where your place is, and I'll be aiming for that X you painted in your field. I don't think I'll be able to miss that, though with a balloon you can never tell. You catch the wrong current, and the next thing you know you're drifting towards Canada and points west."

"I should be so lucky," Flo mutters. I have half a mind to tell Flo she's in the wrong business, but it's a nice afternoon and I don't feel like getting my head bit off.

Eddie says, "Sometimes I do that just so's I can get out of the house for a spell, right, dear?"

"Ha-ha," Flo says. She's smoking a cigarette, waiting to cast off the lines. She gestures to Robert Aaron and Ike and me to help her. Eddie turns to our parents. "You folks have any last words before you start the ride of your life?"

Our mother takes our father's hand and says, "I believe I've already been on the ride of my life, thank you." Our father chuckles. "But there is something I want to say to my children." Our mother takes in a deep breath. She's collecting herself. "I never told you kids this, at least I don't think I ever did, but when Nomi died, the last words that came out of her mouth were 'More! More!' That seemed so much like Nomi. And I've always wondered—was she calling out for something specific? Did she want more light, more warmth, more water, more coffee, what? When I asked, she couldn't tell me—she was answering to God right then, not me." Our mother pauses, her face trembles, she wipes her eyes. Her voice quavering, she continues. "But I think what she was really doing was calling out for more of everything. I understand that. You kids don't know this, but I called out 'More! More!' every time we made one of you. And I'm glad you got us that station wagon. You don't know this, either, but most of you were conceived in the back of one. Exuberant excess is not a bad thing. And that's what I want to say to you kids. I—your father and I—we're not ready yet for things to be over. We still want more of everything. You may find that hard to believe, but we do." She pauses again. Then she says, "I want to leave you with Nomi's blessing. She used to say it at weddings and anniversaries, and since she's not here to say it, I suppose it should be me: 'May your progeny be as the sands upon the sea, and may they be as good to thee as ye have been to me.' "

"Is that a threat or a promise, Mom?"

Our mother smiles through her tears. "Which do you think?"

"What about you, sir?" says Eddie. "You want to say anything?"

We're waiting for the litany of clichés to come pouring forth, but our father shakes his head. "No," he says, "I believe their mother has said everything there is to say."

"Well then," says Eddie, checking around the basket and the gauges on the propane tank. Satisfied, he says, "You ready, ma'am?" Our mother nods assent. "Ready, Wally?" Our father gives us the thumbs-up. "Ready, Flo?" Flo flaps her hand at him, as though she's saying, "Leave, already."

Eddie adjusts a nozzle just beneath the canopy, and a jet of flame shoots blue and yellow into the canopy's neck. Flo yells at us to cast off the lines, and the balloon jerks up a few feet, then lifts and sways and rises as Eddie opens what seems like the throttle. Our mother whoops, our father starts to fall backward, then steadies himself with his hands. They look over the side, at the ground and at all of us gathered on it. To them, we are shrinking rapidly.

"Bye! Bye-bye!" we call. We're waving like mad. Our mother waves, our father gives the thumbs-up again. We get into our cars and follow them, caravan-fashion, for a dozen miles. It's a matter of making the necessary turns on the back roads and keeping them in sight. Flo gestures us ahead. We're to speed up, shoot ahead, and greet them when they touch down.

Borowski is on the lawn with the other guests. We've arrived and climbed on the roof—we want this show to go on right over our heads. But something is keeping our parents—did the wind die down for a while? Did they have problems with the balloon? It's getting dark enough for the yard lights to have gone on. To pass the time, Borowski performs backyard theater, comically reenacting dramatic scenes from movies under the yard lights below us. His rendition of Steve McQueen at the end of *The Great Escape* is magnificent. It's hard to fake a motorcycle leap, but he does it, launching himself onto an invisible fence. Also magnificent is his "Frankly, my dear, I don't give a damn" scene from *Gone With the Wind*, which he performs solo this time, holding himself in his arms, half bent over while delivering Clark Gable's line. Everyone claps and cheers and calls out for their favorite scene. Borowski's honoring as many requests as he can—he is our crowned fool—when Peg Leg Meg cries out, "I see them! They're coming!" and we cross around to the other side of the roof, the other side of the house, to watch them drift in.

The balloon was red and blue when we launched it, but in the gathering darkness it is magenta and midnight. It's coming in low, so low we wonder if they are going to clear the house. Our father, even reduced in his old age, is still quite a load. We see our mother waving. Her eyes in the twilight are glistening. She's crying, she's so happy. Our father is talking to Eddie. You can tell they're getting along. Eddie even lets our father work the propane fire that heats the air inside the balloon. We are waving and calling out, "Do you like it? Do you like it? What do you see?"

"Everything!" calls out our mother, like the voice of God. "I see everything!"

They are almost on top of us now. They are so close we can touch the basket. Our fingers graze the weaving, our fingers are reaching up to touch our mother's, our father's hands. We have to step out of the basket's way or they are going to knock the lot of us, even Wally Jr., off the roof. Dorie catches my hand. It feels good holding it. "Steady, Ace," she says. "I don't want to lose you."

"Ready?" calls out our father, and our mother cries out, "Ready!" And we are not sure if it is our father or Eddie who does this, but there is the sudden hiss and *whoomph!* of flame shooting up, and then the balloon itself lurches and starts to rise.

"Good-bye, good-bye," cries our mother, waving, and we are puzzled, but we keep waving. Their friends, their family—all of us waving, crying out. The balloon, with our parents in it, continues to rise. They are moving quickly. "I love you, I love you all," cries our mother. "And that's the name of that tune!" echoes our father. No doubt he is saying other things as well—that'll put hair between your toes, no guts, no glory, we shall see what we shall see, et cetera, et cetera—but we can't make out any of it. Their voices are growing faint. The hill drops away beneath them, they pass over the big red X done in spray paint on the alfalfa, and still they rise. The balloon gains altitude to clear the trees, to clear the pines on the back hill, to clear the hill itself, and still they rise, their position marked by the burst of flame from underneath the canopy.

It is growing dark. Venus has come out. The Big Dipper, too. Soon other stars will be visible as well. But not our parents. They have risen and disappeared. Except for the light of the stars, the great vault of the sky is empty.

Below us in the drive, gleaming beneath the yard light, sits our father's '55 Chevy Nomad, abandoned. Our father, I realize, did not want to drive at all. He wanted to fly.

Standing on the roof, my hand arrested midwave, I remember something from this morning. Folding a last load of laundry for our parents prior to the day's festivities, I came upon a pair of our father's boxer shorts. Saggy, loose, rent, droopy—they were a lot like our father himself. I held them up and realized that he had not, because of the diabetes and the drinking and the heart medication, had an erection in many years. "I know you know we know you know," I said to that empty pair of boxers, and it's what I say to the empty vault of the sky now. It's up to somebody else now. Other people. It didn't start with them, and it won't end with them, either.

But our mother is still our mother, our father still our father. And if the word is to have any meaning at all, then it is to be found in embracing a sagging, balding, red-faced man who seemingly has no future, with love.

Of course before our mother and father left for this grand adventure, we hugged them. Of course we gathered around. And as we stare into the spot of sky, now vacant, where they last were, we are each of us coming to the same knowledge. That we are not going to sell this plot of earth. Not now, not ever. It will fill in around us. And our children and grandchildren will grow up surrounded, much as we did, all our lives. Not protected from a goddamn thing, but happy.

Sweet Christ, happy!

Acknowledgments

This book couldn't have existed without the help of my friends and family. So many, many thanks to A. Manette Ansay, to Robert Boswell, to Ehud Havazelet, to Kevin "Mac" McIlvoy, to Jim Marten, to Toni Nelson, to Rick Ryan, to Steven Schwartz, to Carol Sklenicka, to Ellen Bryant Voigt, and to all the faculty and numerous students at the Warren Wilson College MFA Program for Writers, with whom I learned so much. For duty above and beyond the call: Charles Baxter. Sainthood for Rick Russo and Pete Turchi, for the love, advice, suggestions, and support throughout their readings of the manuscript. Special thanks and gratitude to Nat Sobel, for continuing to believe, and for his many suggestions that improved the book; to Judith Weber, for her help; and to Jon Karp, for his patience and his careful editing of the manuscript. It would not be the book it is without all of their insight and advice. I would also like to thank all the folks at Random House who worked on this novel: Susan M.S. Brown, for her careful copyediting; Evan Camfield, for all his work; Jonathan Jao and Jillian Quint, for all theirs, particularly the hand-holding; and to Gene Mydlowski and Beck Stvan and the rest of the design team for helping make this a beautiful book. Thanks, too, to Marquette University, for the time and financial assistance in getting this novel written; to the Guggenheim Foundation, for their generous support; to Krystyna Kornilowicz, for her support over the years; and to Lisa Zongolowicz and Ben Percy, for their help in preparing the manuscript. I am also deeply indebted to my children, Tosh, Roman, and Hania, from whom I learned how to resee the world.

Portions of this novel originally appeared, in slightly different form, in *Witness* and in the *Sycamore Review*. Portions of "Our Mother, the Trouper" appeared in *Townships,* edited by Michael Martone. Two chapters, "Loose Lips Sink Ships" and "And That's the Name of That Tune," appeared in different form in the collection *The Clouds in Memphis.*

Thanks to Ernie Garven for writing the Hamm's beer jingle.

The

COMPANY CAR

C. J. Hribal

A READER'S GUIDE

A Conversation with C. J. Hribal

Caroline Goyette, a writer for the Milwaukee *Shepherd Express,* speaks with C. J. Hribal, author of *The Company Car.*

Caroline Goyette: You describe *The Company Car* as an epic for "the little people." What do you mean by this and why do you think it's important that this story be told?

C. J. Hribal: There was really a whole generation of people—they call it the Greatest Generation—who had survived not one war but two, plus they'd come of age as kids during the Great Depression. They'd had things happen to them in war, and what they wanted more than anything was to re-enter American life and get back to normal. What that meant for waves and waves of them was getting married and pumping out babies [laughs] and becoming company men. In the fifties and sixties, there was this idea of just going along with stuff because that's what was expected of you. These people are parts of the backbone on which this country's built—that great wash of humanity just wanting to fit in and not having things necessarily go quite the way they wanted them to. I focused on one particular family and the way in which the Great American Dream plays out for them over fifty years.

CG: You worked on the novel over a period of seven years. Could you talk more about the process of working on the novel, especially how the characters or the plot evolved over time, or how the finished product may have turned out differently from the idea you began with?

CH: I wanted to tell the story of fifty years in America through one family, or fifty years in one family and that would sort of be what America went through. It was a common pattern—still is, really—starting in a city and then moving to the suburbs, and then to the exurbs or, in the case of this family, they skip over the exurbs and go to a farm, which of course ends up filling in all around them. So you've got that kind of arc going on.

Initially I was going to start with the parents getting married on TV and end with their fiftieth wedding anniversary. I wrote it straight through like that, and the draft was about 800 pages long. It took me about four years to write it, two years to get the first 600 pages done, and then about a year and a half, two years to get the last 200 pages done. My agent showed it around, and a lot of people liked it but they all essentially said the same thing: it's too long, it's 800 pages. Jonathan Karp at Random House said he really liked it and if I could get the book down to 600 pages, he'd be interested in it. My agent Nat Sobel and a bunch of friends who'd read it gave me some great suggestions on how to tighten it up and, since it was so long, some ways to put a little more pressure on it. What I ended up deciding to do was to take the ending event, the fiftieth wedding anniversary, and open with that, with the kids gathering for it, so now there's pressure at the beginning, a frame that squeezes the narrative on both ends and that you keep coming back to throughout. The other thing I added to it as I was revising was the narrator's own marriage unraveling while they're celebrating his parents' fiftieth wedding anniversary. It's got this kind of bittersweet thing going on. The kids themselves are deciding what to do with their folks because they're getting to an age—again, this is happening all across this country, has been for a while—where you have to ask yourself what do you do with your folks when they get too old to take care of themselves, or they're getting close to it and you have to make decisions. So there's a celebration and a bittersweet quality. It's funny, I think I ended up adding more plot lines that way, but it ended up being a shorter book.

CG: Eight hundred pages down to 400. That sounds like agony—

CH: And it was.

CG: In retrospect, was it necessary in some way to write those 800 pages to get the 400?

CH: Oh, no question. I think this is true for a lot of writers: you end up writing a lot more pages than you end up using. There are all the things that you need to discover, that you have to get on the page, that the reader may not need. So often your first draft or your second draft is really more of a record of your process of discovering things, it's not necessarily the story people are going to read. Were there things I really liked that got chopped? Oh, you betcha. What it really did, though, was force me to go in and tighten things up as much as I could. I cut out some things I liked but they were probably just digressive, ultimately. There's a part of me that says, well, I'll hold that and it'll be in another book sometime. There was a whole plot line with a lot of the kids' lives in it that was in the original that I ended up taking out because the book became focused on the parents' marriage. And I'd like to use that some other time. In terms of this book, it's still pretty expansive but it's more controlled.

It really only took me about six months to do the cutting and revising, but it took me about a year, a year and a half, to steel myself to actually doing it. First, you're kind of monkeying around the edges of it, saying, "Well, if I do a little of this, oh, if I do a little of that," but in fact you've got to hit a point where you just say, "You know what, it doesn't need to be here; it's got to go." I should say, too, I didn't cut it to 400 pages. The final draft was 500 manuscript pages, but that's 400 in print.

CG: Augsbury has been the setting for several of your works. What makes you return to it?

CH: A small town in a rural community on the edge of a burgeoning area, like the Fox River Valley of Wisconsin, which is a bunch of communities that are all exploding in population—that allows me to really think a lot about the changing nature of America and the Midwest. For me, Augsbury is a place that I don't have to reimagine every single time, which allows me to focus more on the characters, and yet at the same time, the setting and the landscape are a very real part of what I'm working on.

CG: Wally's clichés are a barrier to communication with the family and at the same time, they become a kind of family language—other family members find themselves using them. I'm curious about how the idea for them developed.

CH: I borrowed from my own family. Some are family clichés, but in fact when I started telling people about them, people were really willing to offer their own to me. You'd find them in all sorts of places, those kinds of statements that parents say, that you say you will never say to your own kids, which you then find yourself saying to your own kids. Because they're clichés, they don't carry that much meaning, but at the same time, they're freighted with all the events around them when they were uttered, and so they do become meaningful within a family. I think it does actually help bind this family together and make them feel part of each other, in a way, even though at the same time, within that family, it causes barriers to communication. I'm reminded of that great Vietnam cliché: "We had to destroy the village in order to save it."

CG: The parallels between Emmie and his parents—both the ones he explicitly acknowledges and the ones we observe through his narrative—were these a surprise to you as the writer?

CH: I suppose there's the sense in which we all become our parents, in one way or another, for good or for ill. I didn't set out with that, but as the story evolved, I realized that there were in fact parallels. One of the stronger ones for me came out later in the book, when Emmie realizes things are swirling around him and he has no control. He's always had a troubled relationship with his dad in terms of trying to understand where his father was coming from. But when the ground under his own feet changes in dramatic ways, he starts to understand—and I don't think he's conscious of how much it is like his father—that in fact, he doesn't want things to change. The ironic thing is that his father changed fairly regularly. One of the basic misapprehensions Emmie had was that his father was a kind of stick-in-the-mud. As he becomes a more staid person himself, he appreciates his dad. Ironically, his dad is getting ready to make the next move. In other words, there are parallels in terms of the ways they approach both change and stability.

CG: Emmie seems to be telling this story both to claim it for himself and his children, and, in light of his own troubled marriage, to discern how people manage to stay together for fifty years. Does telling the story bring him closer to answering the question or just to a more complex understanding of the problem?

CH: He's mystified by it going in; that's terribly troubling to him and he's very anxious about it. Over the course of examining his parents' relationship and telling about his own, he comes to understand that it's always going to be a mystery, you're not going to come up with the definitive answer because there isn't one. And in a weird way, that ends up being comforting.

CG: Do you see this as Emmie's story, in the end? Or is it bigger than he is?

CH: One of the family nicknames for him is Emcee. I see Emmie as the ringmaster, introducing these family stories, these whirling dervishes of stories, of which his is one. So he is very much a part of it, but he's trying to tell a larger story here, and although it's very much the story of his parents, it's also the story of all those strivers, the "greatest generation," the silent majority.

CG: Wally thinks he can protect his family by moving them to the country, and of course this isn't the case—people die in the country, people get hurt in the country, people get pregnant out of wedlock in the country. There's a moment at the end of the novel where Emmie counters his father's belief with his own hope for the children and grandchildren of the family, to be "not protected, but happy." Does protection preclude happiness?

CH: There's this idea that you can keep everybody in a bubble and the outside world can't touch them. It really is a truly noble idea. But it can't happen. The outside world intrudes anyway, in all sorts of ways. I think it's also very much an American belief, this idea that you can move to a safe place. That's sort of what's generated America's migrations for much of the last part of this century, to the suburbs, the exurbs, the small towns. It's not as though the world doesn't follow you, or you're not going to find the world there, too. It's like being inside one of those hourglass timers and trying to keep the sand from coming down on you; it's going to come down anyway. And I think ultimately you can be happy in spite of the fact that that's going to happen, and that's what Emmie comes to understand.

CG: Many of the episodes in the novel are told from Emmie's childhood perspective, or from Emmie remembering his childhood perspective. The things he sees, to whatever extent he understands them, emphasize further the difficulty of shielding your children from the world. How did you go about putting yourself into that mindset, and did it help that you have children yourself?

CH: Oh, there's no question having children helps. I say in the book, thanks to my kids for teaching me how to resee the world. You get a different perspective just because you're on a different level, and you're a different height—you're always looking up when you're younger, and the whole world is a mystery. In the book, Emmie's parents' marriage is a mystery; his own marriage is a mystery. Once you have kids you're confronted by the biggest mystery, or challenge, of all. Their coming to engage the world causes you to remember when the whole world was a mystery for you, too. As a kid, you puzzle over the mystery of the adult world. Having kids who constantly ask the "why" questions or the "how come" questions, reminds you of what you felt as a child—it's not like you don't have that perspective within you, it's just that as you get older, you shut it off. To turn it on again or to remember how I used to see the world when I was a kid, I adopted a voice. I was very conscious about this, of writing in a voice of someone who's older, but who could, in talking about the past, find himself sliding into that child's perspective; it's called double-focus narration or retrospective narration. It's not just the adult looking back, but the adult re-feeling those events, so that the reader feels it as Emmie felt it as a kid, while also being aware that it's an adult telling the story with an adult sensibility; that way you can cross the gap between the way things were perceived and the way things actually were, presenting them both.

CG: Like the narrator, you grew up in the Chicago suburbs and moved to the country; you worked as a cookie salesman. I wondered if you could talk a little bit about the process of beginning with literally what you know, and moving beyond that to create something that transcends personal experience, something that's fictional, that's art.

CH: That's always a tough question. Things happen to you, things happen to your friends, things happen to your family, you hear about things that happen to people you don't know, you imagine things that have never happened, and it all becomes this amalgamation. When I first wrote the novel, I designed it so that each chapter had a big event, and there was lots of exposition in between. What I ended up doing in my revision was cutting out a lot of that exposition. The exposition tended to be stuff I remembered happening, and the big events were completely made up. What ended up in the novel was much more of the things that I made up. Those were the things I found myself giggling over because they were more outlandish. I think what happens with a lot of writers is you start with a kernel of something that might have really happened and you transform it into something that feels as real as if it had happened, even though it never did.

CG: Did growing up on a farm help you to develop the work ethic necessary to write?

CH: Being Catholic doesn't hurt, either. Guilt, guilt, guilt, guilt, guilt [laughs]. Growing up on a farm, there's just lots of things that have to get done. We were always told, before you get fed and go off to school, the animals get fed, because you can't *not* feed them—you just always knew there were things you had to do, whether you wanted to or not. There was that sense of responsibility. All the way through, my parents encouraged us to have jobs and to earn our own money. And I think that's actually a great gift parents can give their kids, to teach them that they've got to work for stuff. So I had a series of terrible jobs, and that really made me appreciate the people who did jobs like that. I was also very conscious that these were not the jobs I was going to do my whole life. It made me a little more appreciative of what I had been given.

I worked in a canning factory—just brutal, exhausting work. Your vocabulary drops over the course of a summer to essentially twelve words, half of which are expletives, and you come out of that and you go, "Whew, life is okay." If you don't have to do that, you appreciate how much work that really is. These people aren't "losers," which is what our culture often tells us they are. They're doing hard work, necessary work.

CG: Will we hear more from the Czabecks?

CH: There's a part of me that wants to tell the kids' stories. There were whole narratives (about the relationships between the kids) that wound up on the editing room floor, and I'd like to conclude those. I think Emmie's going to show up again as a minor character in another novel down the road. That's happened often with me: somebody who's a major character here shows up in the background of somebody else's story; somebody who's a minor character in this story gets their own story later. I sort of like that idea, like a small town you can walk through and see people and imagine what their story might be. Everybody's the main character in their own story.

Questions and Topics for Discussion

1. In what ways is Emmie like his father and in what ways is he like his mother? Where do you see these similarities most strongly in the novel?

2. How do Emmie's similarities to his parents illuminate your understanding of Emmie's relationship with his wife? What parallels exist between the two couples?

3. How did you respond to the character of Dorie, Emmie's wife? Did you like her? Did you find her sympathetic? To what extent did Emmie's portrayal of his mother as the primary caretaker of the family—alone with seven children while her husband is on the road or drinking—affect your view of his wife's resistance to assuming that role, her desire for independence and escape? To what extent did Emmie's sympathy for his mother extend to his wife?

4. How does the Zbigniew Herbert epigraph, "It's good what happened / it's good what's going to happen / even what's happening right now / it's okay," encapsulate the novel's themes?

5. Despite their struggles, what are the qualities that make Wally and Susan Marie's marriage work? Does the marriage hold together be-

cause of social mores about divorce, or out of habit or momentum, or something more?

6. In the chapter "Loose Lips Sink Ships," the author uses retrospective narration to allow the reader to experience Emmie's childhood. Was this effective for you? Do you prefer one type of point of view in general? Are there other literary techniques used in the novel that you found particularly effective?

7. How is change and/or the passage of time treated in the novel? How do the various characters deal with change? Wally? Emmie? Dorie? Susan Marie?

8. What is Emmie's attitude toward his family story? Is he nostalgic? Reverential? Critical? Matter-of-fact? What does the way in which he tells us the story reveal about his character? Do you have a family story? How has it affected who you are today?

9. Trace the situations in which the issue of fidelity emerges in the novel. How do questions of marital fidelity or infidelity connect with themes of loyalty, independence and personal identity in the novel?

10. What series of events bring the Czabecks to leave the suburbs? What major events and/or details stand out from their years on the farm? What similarities exist between the two locations?

11. In the first chapter of the novel, photographs of Wally and Susan Marie as young people are described in great detail. How do these descriptions prepare us for the stories and characters that are to come? How are they connected to the novel's themes? Did you find these descriptions helpful?

12. Did you feel this novel was Emmie's story primarily, or was it a bigger story?

C. J. HRIBAL is the author of *The Clouds in Memphis,
Matty's Heart,* and *American Beauty*. Hribal was born in
Chicago and grew up on a farm in Wisconsin. He
received his B.A. from St. Norbert College in De Pere,
WI and his M.A. in creative writing from Syracuse
University. A professor of English at Marquette
University and a member of the fiction faculty at the
Warren Wilson College M.F.A. Program for Writers,
he lives with his three children in Milwaukee.

Visit the author online at www.cjhribal.com

ABOUT THE TYPE

This book was set in Bembo, a typeface based on an old-style Roman face that was used for Cardinal Bembo's tract *De Aetna* in 1495. Bembo was cut by Francisco Griffo in the early sixteenth century. The Lanston Monotype Machine Company of Philadelphia brought the well-proportioned letter forms of Bembo to the United States in the 1930s.